Taken for Revenge

When only seduction will settle the score!

Three supersexy, contemporary romances from
three favourite Mills & Boon authors!

In September 2009 Mills & Boon
bring you two classic collections, each
featuring three favourite romances
by our bestselling authors

TAKEN FOR REVENGE

Bedded for Revenge by Sharon Kendrick
Bought by a Billionaire by Kay Thorpe
The Bejewelled Bride by Lee Wilkinson

PURCHASED FOR PASSION

Shackled by Diamonds by Julia James
A Mistress for the Taking by Annie West
His Bought Mistress by Emma Darcy

Taken for Revenge

SHARON KENDRICK
KAY THORPE
LEE WILKINSON

MILLS & BOON

First published in Great Britain 2009
Harlequin Mills & Boon Limited,
Eton House, 18-24 Paradise Road, Richmond, Surrey TW9 1SR

TAKEN FOR REVENGE © by Harlequin Enterprises II B.V./S.à.r.l 2009

Bedded for Revenge, Bought by a Billionaire and *The Bejewelled Bride* were first published in Great Britain by Harlequin Mills & Boon Limited in separate, single volumes.

Bedded for Revenge © Sharon Kendrick 2006
Bought by a Billionaire © Kay Thorpe 2005
The Bejewelled Bride © Lee Wilkinson 2006

ISBN: 978 0 263 87138 8

05-0909

Printed and bound in Spain
by Litografia Rosés S.A., Barcelona

BEDDED
FOR REVENGE

BY
SHARON KENDRICK

Sharon Kendrick started story-telling at the age of eleven and has never really stopped. She likes to write fast-paced, feel-good romances with heroes who are so sexy they'll make your toes curl!

Born in west London, she now lives in the beautiful city of Winchester – where she can see the cathedral from her window (but only if she stands on tip-toe). She has two children, Celia and Patrick, and her passions include music, books, cooking and eating – and drifting off into wonderful daydreams while she works out new plots!

Don't miss Sharon Kendrick's exciting new novel,
***The Italian Billionaire's Secretary Mistress*,**
available in October 2009 from
Mills & Boon® Modern™.

To Michèle et Claude Bertrand,
for their wonderful hospitality and for showing
me a different side of glorious Paris.

CHAPTER ONE

CESARE DI ARCANGELO'S eyes narrowed as he watched the woman begin to walk down the aisle, looking as though butter wouldn't melt in her beautiful mouth, and he found he wanted to crush it, lick it, bite it, eat it.

Yet he felt the flicker of a pulse at his temple and was aware of the faint wash of disappointment—for he had wanted to feel nothing, to remain as coolly indifferent as women always accused him of being. But as she approached, in a cloud of silk-satin and lace, that hope shattered within him. He felt anger rise like poison in his blood, but something else too. Something more powerful still—which it seemed that all the years could not diminish. Something which had kept the human race going since the beginning of time.

Lust.

And maybe that was better—because if lust was a problem then it had a pretty simple solution.

The sound of the organ music was building up to a crescendo, and the heavy scent of the flowers was intoxicating, but all Cesare could see from his seat near the back was Sorcha, smiling, her bouquet held in front of a waist which was as sensuously narrow as it had been when she was just eighteen.

What a gorgeously sexy bridesmaid she was…

Feeling the hard, heavy tug of an erection straining against the exquisitely tailored trousers of his morning suit, Cesare briefly clenched and then flexed his hands, willing the hard throb of desire to disappear.

He had slid into his seat at the back of the church at the very last minute. It had been a low-key but deliberate lateness—for the sight of Cesare di Arcangelo tended to create interest and excitement wherever he went.

Mega-rich, sexy Italians seemed to be on the top of everybody's wish list. It was why the hottest hostesses in all the major cities in the world pursued him with the fervour of astronomers who had just discovered a brandnew planet.

He scanned the congregation for Sorcha's mother. Yes. There she was—in a hat as big as the Sydney Opera House—and even from this distance it was easy to read the cat-got-the-cream satisfaction of her body language. She must be very pleased—for a rich son-in-law spelt hope for a family firm beset with problems. Would Emma's new husband be willing to pour the necessary funds into the family business to keep creditors at bay?

Cesare doubted it. Money only worked up until a certain point—after that, you might as well hold it up to the winds and let it scatter. Problems had to be fixed; they couldn't be patched up. His mouth twisted. All problems.

The bride and groom were now passing, but he barely gave them a glance. Nor the parade of chubby little bridesmaids, or the scowling pageboys clad in satin romper suits which they would never forgive their mothers for forcing them to wear.

No, it was the only adult bridesmaid, with the bright, strawberry blonde hair woven with tiny rosebuds, who commanded his total, undivided attention. She was his problem—the unfinished business which he needed to put to bed. Beautiful Sorcha Whittaker, with the green eyes, and the bright hair like a waterfall, and a body as supple as an eel.

He had her trained in his sights, like a hunter with his prey fixed—for he wanted to see her reaction when their eyes met for the first time in… How long was it now? A pulse began to beat at his temple. Seven years? A minute? An eternity?

He saw her knuckles tense and her footsteps falter so much that for a second she almost came to a halt. Time froze as he stared into eyes as green as a rainwashed woodland and saw the confusion and consternation which flew into them as she stared straight back.

Cesare watched her face blanch and her lips tremble and felt a fleeting moment of utter triumph—swiftly followed by frustration that he could not just take her there and then.

If only this were not a crowded place of worship.

How much easier if they were alone and he could swiftly remove all the underwear hidden beneath the canopy of that monstrous dress—could swiftly obliterate desire and frustration with sweet release.

And then just walk away.

For a moment he was powerless—as once she had made him powerless all those years ago. But soon she would have fulfilled her role as bridesmaid, and then he would take the power back with relish.

'Bride or groom?' asked the delicious-looking brunette in banana-coloured silk who was standing beside him.

Cesare swallowed, for his erotic thoughts had inevitably made him ache. He flicked his eyes over the brunette, who widened hers so provocatively that she might just as well have had *Yes, please!* tattooed on her forehead. 'Groom,' he answered drily. 'And you?'

'Mmm. Me, too. He said there were going to be some gorgeous men here, and by heck—he wasn't lying!' The brunette batted her eyelashes quite outrageously. 'Any chance I could cadge a lift to the reception?'

Cesare's mouth hardened into a smile. 'Why not?'

Outside the church, Sorcha was standing in the wedding group while it seemed as if a thousand photos were being taken. But her smile felt as if someone had slashed it across her face with a razor.

Her eyes flickered over to the tiny church and she saw a tall, broad-shouldered figure emerging, having to bend his head to avoid bumping it on the low door, and her heart felt as if someone had ripped open her chest and squeezed it with a bare fist.

Cesare!

Here!

'Sorcha! This way! Look at the camera!'

With an effort she tore her eyes away from him and a flashbulb exploded in her face, temporarily blinding her. When it cleared he had gone. But there was her brother, Rupert, standing in a group, and she hurried over to him, completely ignoring the appreciative comments which came from his fellow ushers. Her mouth was dry and her heart was beating like a drum. And it hurt. It shouldn't do, but it hurt.

'Who in their right mind invited Cesare di Arcangelo today?' she managed, though her specially perfected chief bridesmaid smile didn't waver.

'Oh, he's here, is he?' Rupert looked around and an odd expression came into his eyes. 'Good.'

'Good?' Sorcha tried to squash all the instinctive fears which came scurrying to the forefront of her mind. Because none of them might be true, and it was her sister's wedding day, after all.

It was supposed to be a happy occasion, a joyous day—like all weddings should be. And it had been—right up until the moment when she had seen Cesare's dangerously handsome face and had felt her heart clench as if it was making up its mind whether to beat again.

Just the sight of his brilliant black eyes had taken her

back to another time and another place—and mocked her with the lesson she had been learning ever since. That no other man could ever match up to him. And one look at him had reminded her exactly why.

Her mouth was dry and her breath was rapid, but she sucked in a deep breath and tried to stay calm. 'Rupert, did you know he was going to be here?'

There was a pause. 'Er…kind of.'

'*Kind* of? And so did Emma, presumably—since she's the bride?'

'Yeah. Ralph's family does a lot of business with di Arcangelo. You know that, Sorcha.'

Yes, she knew that—but it was one of those things you knew and kept pushed to the back of your mind. The same way that you knew natural disasters occurred, but you just didn't spend your time thinking about them until you had to. 'And it didn't occur to any of you to have the decency to tell me he'd been invited, in view of our…our *history?*'

Rupert looked vaguely bored. 'You went out with him a few years ago—what's the big deal? And any-way—he asked me not say anything. He wanted it to be a surprise.'

She wanted to yelp—*What do you mean, he asked you not to? I am your sister, and as such I take prece-dence over Cesare di Arcangelo—in spite of his afflu-ence and influence.*

'Oh, it's certainly a surprise,' said Sorcha lightly—but if she said any more then Rupert would think she cared. And she didn't. Not any more. She had to get things into perspective. Cesare was simply part of her past who would soon be gone, if not forgotten.

But why was he here? What possible reason could there be for re-establishing a family connection which had fizzled out years ago? Loyalty to her brother? Had they really been that close? Or was it just what it seemed—he was attending the wedding of a son of a business colleague?

It was like being caught in a trap which no one apart from Sorcha could see. Even though the sun was shining, and the church was picture-postcard perfect, and the bells were pealing out, inside she felt a bleak pang of regret. Time healed, that was what everyone said—and now it seemed that the rest of the world had been colluding in a great big conspiracy of lies.

But she played her part to the maximum and flashed a series of bright, happy smiles for the cameras until they wanted just couple shots of the bride and groom and she could escape.

She just wasn't sure where.

With an odd kind of sixth sense, Sorcha suddenly became aware of being watched as surely as if eyes were burning into her back, branding her pale skin through the delicate silk-satin of her bridesmaid dress. And—try as she might—she couldn't stop herself from turning round to see, even though she knew exactly who it was.

This was the true meaning of the word *irresistible,* she thought as she tried uselessly to pull against the power he exerted. As if she were a snake and he some charmer, summoning her against her will. And she looked round to find herself dazzled by the ebony gaze of Cesare di Arcangelo.

Stay away, Sorcha prayed silently—but her prayer went unanswered. Sunlight bouncing off his gleaming blue-black hair, he walked across the church path towards her, tall and dark and supremely confident— leaving a sulky-looking woman in a bright yellow dress glaring at his retreating back.

Sorcha felt a lump in her throat—as if someone had rammed in a pebble large enough to block her wind-pipe—and she briefly closed her eyes, imagining— almost praying—that she would pass out. What a merciful release that would be. To faint and discover when she opened her eyes again that Cesare had gone— as if he had never set foot here in the first place. Almost as if she had dreamt it all up.

But she did not faint, and there was no mercy. Or dream. Instead, the air came flowing back into her lungs as she stared back at him—and just the sight of him was the visual equivalent of a punch in the solar plexus.

'Cesare,' she said, and it came out as a whisper.

He was wearing a pale, formal suit in grey, made from some expensive fabric which hung and hugged his muscular body in all the right places. Whoever had designed it must have decided that hinting at a man's raw sexuality was the way to go—or maybe it just had something to do with the man who was wearing it.

The grey contrasted with jet-dark hair which was thick and silky-straight—just like the outrageously thick black eyelashes which shielded eyes as rich as dark chocolate. He looked more like an international sex symbol than the millionaire entrepreneur he really was—who had taken the long-established wealth of the di Arcangelo family, transformed it into super-riches and made himself into a bit of a legend in the process.

Everything about him was perfect—even that slightly restless expression on his face, and the cold and quizzical eyes that hinted at an intellectual depth which lay beneath the charismatic exterior. She had once thought that it wasn't possible for a man to be as gorgeous as Cesare, but somehow he had defied the improbable— and seven years had only added to his striking physical impact.

Somehow she managed to pull herself together—even though there was still some remnant of the lovestruck girl inside her who wanted to wrap her arms around his neck and pull his gorgeous face down to kiss her, wriggle her untutored body restlessly against the hard perfection of his.

Her heart was hammering, but somehow she inclined her head politely—so that to the casual observer it would look as though the chief bridesmaid were greeting just another guest.

'Well,' she said coolly. 'This is a surprise.'

'Don't you like surprises?' he murmured.

'What do you think?'

He smiled as he sensed the tension in her. 'Ah, Sorcha,'

nurmured, his gaze travelling with slow insolence over the body of the only woman who had ever rejected him. '*Bene, bene, bene*—but how you've grown, *cara.*'

She wanted to tell him not to look at her like that—but that wasn't entirely true, and she didn't want to be branded a hypocrite. Because even while she despised that blatantly sexual scrutiny, wasn't there some traitorous part of her body which responded to it?

She could feel it in the soft throbbing of her pulses and in the uncomfortable prickle as her breasts thrust against the lace brassière she wore—as if her nipples were screaming out to be touched. And Cesare would have noticed that. Of course he would. Once, in that protective way he'd had with her, he would have defused the sexual tension. But not any more. Now he was just taking his time and enjoying it.

And the time for social niceties was past. She had to protect herself. She had to know the truth.

'What the hell are you doing here?' she demanded.

Black brows were arched. 'What an appalling way to speak to an invited guest, *cara,*' he answered silkily. Because now was not the time to tell her. *Non ora.* He was going to savour the timing of this, to maximise the impact when he dropped his bombshell straight into her beautiful lap. 'Didn't you know I was coming?' he questioned innocently.

'You know very well I didn't—since my brother says you left instructions for it to be kept all hush-hush!' Sorcha fixed him with a questioning look, reminding herself that this was *her* territory and that he was definitely trespassing. 'So why all the cloak and dagger stuff? Do you want to be a spy when you grow up, Cesare?'

He gave a soft, appreciative laugh—for opposition always heightened the senses. He thought how much more spirited she had become with the passing of the years, and oh, but he was going to enjoy subduing that fire. 'Why? Do you think I'd make a good one?'

'No. You'd never blend into a crowd,' she retorted, before realising that although it was the right thing—it was also the wrong thing to say. It might have sounded like a compliment, and that was the last thing she wanted. 'Why didn't you warn me?'

'Maybe I knew how much you would have opposed my being here,' he observed.

'You were right.'

'And maybe I wanted to see your face when you did. To see your first genuine reaction. Do you remember the last time we saw one another, my *love?*'

In spite of the sarcasm which dripped from it, the word made her heart clench. Until she reminded herself that it was a redundant word as far as they were concerned—as unreal as everything else about their relationship. The engagement that never was, the happy-ever-after which never happened. How could something which had never really existed, have hurt so much?

She gave him a blank look. 'I don't believe I do.'

'Liar,' he said huskily, black eyes sliding over the tight aquamarine silk bodice and the exuberant thrust of her pert breasts. His gaze lingered long against the tiny tips of her nipples, which looked so startlingly sharp against the shining material, and he wished that he could take his tongue to them. 'Do you remember how it felt to be in my arms and to have my tongue inside your mouth? Are you regretting now that we didn't ever get around to having full sex?'

She flinched as if he had hit her. As if he had led her down a predictable path and she had failed to see where it was heading—except that Cesare had never been explicit like that with her before.

Yet she was letting his words wound her, and she was in danger of making a fool of herself. People were already starting to turn round to look at them—as if the almost tangible tension between them was setting them apart. Murmured questions were buzzing around the high-society guests, and Sorcha's gaze darted around to meet frankly curious stares.

His black eyes followed hers. 'Do you suppose they're thinking what an attractive couple we make?' he murmured. 'Do you suppose that they are imagining the contrast of your pale skin being pinned down by the darkness of mine? Are you imagining it too, *cara mia,* just as I am? Do you think that they would be disappointed if they knew the reality of our lovemaking?'

Her pulse rocketed. 'Cesare—stop it. Just *go*. Please! Why are you doing this?'

This was better, much better. Her lips parting in breathless appeal, her eyes darkening at his erotic taunt.

With a cruel pleasure which excited him, Cesare continued to play with her as a cat would a helpless mouse.
'What a way to greet the man you once claimed to adore.'

Sorcha felt the blood rushing to her ears so that they
were filled with a roaring sound, like the ocean. 'I was
young and stupid then,' she said hoarsely.

'And now?'

'Now I'm old enough to realise the lucky escape I had.'

'Well, then, we are agreed on something at least,' he
answered evenly.

Sorcha hesitated. Maybe she had got him all wrong.
Maybe he wanted to make peace. Maybe... She peered
over his shoulder to where the brunette in the biliously
coloured outfit was still standing staring at him and her
heart pounded. 'Is that your...girlfriend?'

He heard the acid tone in her voice even though she
did her best to disguise it, and turned his head to glance
over at the woman, who wiggled her fingers at him in a
wave. 'Sindy?' He gave a slow smile. 'Jealous, Sorcha?'

'Not at all.' But she was lying, and Sorcha wondered
if Cesare realised that. She found herself wanting to lash
out like a little cat—to say that the woman's skin was
sallow, that she was wearing the wrong colour, that she
was not fit to be his girlfriend. But that was all wrong—
she shouldn't be feeling this way. Not now.

'Have you spoken to my mother?'

'Not yet. I'll catch up with her at the reception.'

Sorcha froze. 'You're coming to the reception?' she
whispered.

Cesare smiled. This was better than he could ever have anticipated! 'You think I have flown all the way from Rome to hear a couple repeat a set of vows which will probably be broken before the year is out?' he questioned cynically. 'I may not be a big fan of weddings, but nobody can deny that they offer an opportunity to indulge in some of the more pleasurable aspects of life. And I shall look forward to being back in your house.'

The black eyes glittered in a way which took her right back to forbidden territory—more emotional than erotic, and all the more dangerous for that.

'Shall we dance together later, Sorcha?' he finished. 'Perhaps even go for a swim, just like the old days—*si?*'

But the old days were gone—long gone. She wanted to convince herself that the person she was then had been markedly different—so that if the younger Sorcha had walked up and said hello she wouldn't be able to recognise her. And yet while in many ways she *was* different—in others she felt exactly the same. Why else would there be such a dull ache in her heart when she looked at the man she had believed herself to be in love with?

'I would tell you to go to hell,' she said slowly, 'if I didn't think you'd already taken up a permanent berth there!'

'Why? Do you want to come and lie in it with me?'

His soft mocking laughter was still ringing in her ears as Sorcha pushed her way through the crowds to where a dark limousine was waiting to whisk the bridesmaids and pageboys back to the reception. Four young faces pressed anxiously against the glass as Sorcha gathered up armfuls of tulle and silk and levered herself in next to them.

The bridegroom's niece scrambled onto her lap and planted a chubby finger right in the middle of her cheek.

'Why are you cryin', Sorcha?'

Sorcha sniffed. 'I'm not crying. I just got a speck of dust in my eyes.' She dabbed a tissue at her eye and then beamed the worried child the widest smile in her repertoire. 'See? All gone!'

'All gone!' they chorused obediently.

Sorcha bit her lip and turned it into another smile. How simple it was to be a child in a world where things vanished just because an adult told you they had. The monster under the bed had gone away because Mummy said so.

But memories were like those childhood monsters—always lurking in dark places, waiting to capture you if you weren't careful. And some memories burned as strongly as if they had happened yesterday.

CHAPTER TWO

SORCHA had met Cesare di Arcangelo the summer she'd turned eighteen, the hottest summer for decades. It had been the year she'd left school and the year most of her classmates had finally rid themselves of the burden of their virginity—but Sorcha had not been among them. Her friends had laughed and called her old-fashioned, but she'd been holding out for someone special.

But that summer she had felt as ripe and ready as some rich fruit ready for picking—and hormones had bubbled like cauldrons in her veins.

She'd arrived home from a final school trip to France on a baking hot day with a sky of blinding brightness. There had been no one to meet her at the station, and no reply when she'd phoned the house, but it hadn't particularly bothered her. She'd had little luggage, and because it was beautiful and so green, and so *English* after the little mountain village of *Plan-du-Var,* she had decided to walk.

The air had been unnaturally still and the lane dusty,

but the sky had been the clearest blue imaginable—with birds singing their little hearts out—and suddenly Sorcha had felt glad to be home, even if she was slightly apprehensive about the future.

Up until that moment everything had been safely mapped out for her—but with the freedom which came from leaving school came uncertainty too. Still, she had worked hard, and she'd been offered a place at one of the best universities in the country if her exam results were as good as had been predicted.

She'd approached the house by the long drive—the honey-coloured mansion where Whittakers had lived since her great-great-grandfather had first got the bright idea of marketing his wife's delicious home-made sauce. From humble terraced house beginnings, her great-great-grandma's unique recipe had become a national institution, and soon enough money had poured in to enable him to satisfy his land-owning longings and buy himself a real-life stately home.

But of course that had been in the days before a croissant or a bowl of muesli had become staple breakfast fare—in the days when a full fry-up with Whittaker Sauce had been the only way to start the day. The slow, gradual decline in the family fortunes had soon begun, but it had been so slow that you didn't really notice it, and it was much easier to ignore something if it just crept up on you.

Sorcha had given a small sigh of satisfaction as she'd looked towards the house, because in that moment it hadn't looked stately, it had just looked like home. From this far away you didn't really notice that the walls were crumbling and the roof needed replacing, and of course in the summer months it really came into its own.

Come winter and there would be so much frost on the inside of the windows you could write your initials in it and see the steam of your breath as it rushed out against the cold air. Anyone else might have capitalised on the house's assets and sold it, but not Sorcha's mother, who was hanging on to it with grim determination.

'It's a huge asset,' Mrs Whittaker always pronounced, and no one could argue with that. Rural it might look— but a few miles beyond its expansive grounds lay a road which took you straight into London in less than an hour.

Pushing open the oak front door, Sorcha had gone inside to an echoing silence, where dust motes had danced in the beams of sunlight which flooded in through the stained glass. She'd seen a man's cashmere sweater lying on one of the chairs—beautiful and soft in palest grey—and raised her eyebrows. A bit classy for Rupert! Her brother must have given himself a pay rise.

The house had been empty—so she'd gone up to her bedroom, with its schoolgirl echoes of prizes—rosettes won at horseriding and shiny silver cups for swimming.

From there she could see the pool, and to her astonishment she'd seen that it had been cleared—instead of turgid green water with leaves floating on it like dead lilies it was a perfectly clear rectangle of inviting aquamarine.

Pulling open a drawer, she'd found a swimsuit and

squeezed herself into it—she must have grown a lot since last year. Overnight, she'd seemed to go from being a beanpole of an adolescent to having the curvy shape of a real woman. She was going to have to go shopping.

The water had felt completely delicious as she'd dived in and begun to swim, length after length of slicing crawl, each stroke taking her further and further into a daydream. She'd been so wrapped up in her thoughts that she hadn't noticed the man who was standing there until she had come up for breath, exhausted, sucking in the warm summer air as the water streamed down her hair in rivulets.

Sorcha had started. For a moment all she'd registered was jet-dark hair and silken olive skin, but as she'd blinked the water out of her eyes she'd seen that it was a stranger—and a disturbingly handsome stranger, to boot.

In a pair of faded jeans and an old black T-shirt, he'd looked like one of the gardeners her mother employed to try and make a dent in the overgrowth at the beginning of every season. Unfortunately, he'd also had the arrogant and mocking air of a man who was supremely sexy and who knew it. His black eyes had gleamed and suddenly Sorcha had felt unaccountably shy.

'Who…are you?' she questioned.

She rose out of the water like a nymph and Cesare froze, his mouth drying as he saw the firm flesh, green eyes and the lush, perfect curve of her breasts. *Madre di Dio*—but she was exquisite.

'My name is Cesare di Arcangelo,' he murmured, in a velvety-soft accent which matched his exotic looks.

'You're Italian?'

'I am.'

'And… Well…' She didn't want to be rude, but really he could be anyone. And he was so dangerously gorgeous that she felt…*peculiar.* 'What are you doing here?'

'Take a guess, *signorina.*'

'You've come to clean the pool?'

He had never been mistaken for a worker before! Cesare's mouth curved into a smile.

He guessed who *she* must be. Her hair was too wet to see its real colour, but her eyes were green with flecks of gold—a bigger, wider version of her brother's. He knew deep down that there was a long-established rule that you treated your friends' sisters as if they were ice-queens, but it was a rule he found himself suddenly wanting to break.

'Do you want me to?' he drawled. 'Looks pretty clean to me. Anyway, I don't want to interrupt your swim.'

Sorcha shook her wet hair, but something about his hard, lean body was making her pulse race. 'No, that's fine. Don't worry—I've finished now.'

There was a long pause while they stared at one another, and the teasing became something else, while something unknown shimmered on the air.

'So, why don't you get out?'

Did he guess that she was scared to? Because she could feel the tight tingle of desire which was rucking her swimsuit across her breasts and making the tips feel so hard that they hurt?

'I will in a minute.'

'Do you mind if I get in and join you?' He put his hand to the first button on his jeans and shot her a questioning look, but the sight of her dark-eyed confusion made him relent just as Rupert came round the corner.

'Cesare! There you are! Oh, I see you've met Sorcha. Hello, little sister—how are you?'

'Very well,' she said, biting her lip and dipping down into the water in the hope that its coolness might get rid of her embarrassed flush. 'Considering that no one came to meet me at the station.' But she was angry with herself, and with the black-eyed Italian for having made her feel…what?

Desire?

Longing?

She frosted him a look—which wasn't easy on a boiling hot day when your hair was plastered to your head and your heart was racing so much that it felt as if it was going to leap out of your chest. 'Cesare?' she questioned acidly, wondering why the name sounded familiar.

'Cesare di Arcangelo,' he said. 'Rupert and I were at school together.'

'Remember I told you about the Italian who bowled women down like ninepins?' laughed Rupert. 'Owns banks and department stores all over Italy?'

'No,' answered Sorcha in a voice of icy repression. 'I don't believe I do. Rupert, would you mind handing me my towel?'

'Please, allow me.' Cesare had picked up the rather

worn beachtowel and was handing it towards her, holding her gaze with his black eyes. Her coolness intrigued him, for he had never experienced it from a woman before, and her lack of eagerness hinted at a pride and self-possession which was all too rare.

'Forgive me,' he murmured as he held the towel out. 'But I couldn't resist teasing you.' Yet his mockery had been deliberately sensual, and it had been wrong. He had noted her reluctant, embarrassed response—and now he could have kicked himself for subjecting a beautiful young woman to such an onslaught.

He sighed. Her mouth looked as if it were composed of two folded fragrant rose petals which he would have travelled the world to kiss. And he had behaved like some *impacciato* idiot.

And she is the sister of your friend—she is out of bounds.

'*Will* you forgive me?' he persisted.

He sounded as if it mattered, and Sorcha found she couldn't hold out against what seemed to be genuine contrition in his eyes.

'I might,' she said tartly. 'But you'll have to make it up to me.'

He gave a low laugh. 'And how will I go about doing that? Any ideas?' he questioned innocently, and something passed between them at that moment which he had never felt before. The rocket. The thunderbolt. *Colpo di fulmine.* Some random and overwhelming outside force—a kind of unspoken understanding—

which took the universe into the palm of a gigantic hand and began to spin it out of control.

'I'll…I'll think of something,' said Sorcha breathlessly.

'Anything,' he murmured, and at that moment he meant it. 'And it's yours.'

There was an odd kind of silence and then Sorcha hauled herself out of the pool in one fluid movement, water streaming down her long legs. Never had she been so conscious of her body as in the presence of this Italian.

'Cesare's come to cast his expert eye over the Robinsons' latest business plan,' said Rupert. 'I'm hoping I might be able to persuade him to look at ours!'

The Robinsons were their nearest neighbours—fabulously rich, with four eligible sons—one of whom their sister Emma had been dating since *her* schooldays.

'Does that mean I have to be nice to him?' Sorcha asked.

Black eyes now mocked her. 'Very.'

But as she draped the towel over her shoulders Cesare averted his eyes from the body which gleamed like a seal in the tight, wet swimsuit. And wasn't it strange how the smallest courtesy could make you feel safe with a man who was danger personified?

'Do you ride?' she asked suddenly.

Cesare smiled. '*Do* I?'

That was how it started. He'd set off for the Robinsons first thing and return about lunchtime, and Sorcha would be waiting for him in the stables. He would saddle up and they would gallop out together over the lush fields.

And the way her face lit up when she saw him would stab at his heart in a strange and painful way.

'Bet Italy is never as green as this,' she said one afternoon, when they had dismounted and their horses were grazing and she and Cesare were sitting—sweating slightly—beneath the shade of a big oka tree.

'Umbria is very green,' he said.

'Is that where you live?'

'It is where I consider home,' he said, trying and failing not to be rapt by the distracting vision of her breasts thrusting against the fine silk of her riding shirt, her slim legs in jodhpurs and those long, sexy leather boots. He stifled a groan and shifted uncomfortably as she lay on her back, looking up at the leaves.

The air was different today. It felt thick and heavy— as if you could cut through it with a knife—and in the distance was the low murmur of approaching thunder. It reminded him of the storms back home, and the warmth of the soil and the pleasures of the flesh. Cesare could feel a rivulet of sweat trickle down his back, and suddenly he longed to feel her tongue tracing its meandering salty path.

'Really?' she questioned.

He blinked. Really, what? Oh, yes. The weather in Umbria—*just* what he wanted to talk about! 'We have many storms close to Panicale, where I live—but that is why we have such fertile soil.' Fertile. Now, why the hell was he thinking about *that?*

'Have you always lived in Umbria?' Sorcha persisted, because she wanted to know every single thing about him—what he liked for breakfast and what music he listened to, and where was the most beautiful place he'd ever been— 'Umbria, naturally,' he had replied gravely.

'No,' he sighed, 'I grew up in Rome.'

'Tell me,' she whispered.

What was it about women that made them want to tear your soul apart with their questions? And what was it about Sorcha that made him tell her? But he was spare with his facts—a houseful of servants and ever-changing nannies while his parents lived out their jet-set existence. A childhood he did not care to relive in his memory.

And suddenly he could bear it no longer. 'You know that I am having difficulty behaving as a house-guest should behave?' he questioned unsteadily.

Dreamily, Sorcha watched the shimmering canopy of leaves. 'Oh?'

'I want to kiss you.'

She sat up, oblivious to the creamy spill of her cleavage, or the effect it was having on him. On her face was an expression of a tight and bursting excitement— like a child who had just been given a big pile of presents to open.

'Then kiss me. Please.'

He knew in that instant that she was innocent— though he had guessed at it before—and in a way it added to the intolerable weight of his desire, and his position here in the house.

'You know what will happen if I do?' he groaned.

'Yes,' she teased, in an effort to hide her longing, and her nervousness that she would somehow disappoint him—that somehow she wouldn't know what to do. 'Your lips will touch my lips and then— Oh! Oh, *Cesare!*'

'*Si!*' he murmured, as he caught her against him. 'All those things and more. Many more.' He pushed her to the ground and brushed his lips against hers, making a little sound of pleasure in the back of his throat as he coaxed hers into opening.

The kiss went on and on. He had never thought it was possible for a kiss to last so long—he felt he was drowning in it, submerging himself in its sweet potency. The blood pooled and hardened at his groin and he groaned again—only this time the sound was tinged with a sense of urgency.

'Cesare!' she breathed again, as his thumb circled against the tight, damp material which strained over her breast. 'Oh, oh, *oh!*'

He sat up abruptly. This was wrong. Wrong. He sprang to his feet and held out his hand to her. 'Let us move away from here!' he ordered. 'And where in the name of *cielo* is your mother?'

'She's up at the house—why?'

'She is happy for you to ride with me alone every day?' he demanded.

'I think so.'

Did she not know of Cesare di Arcangelo's reputation? he wondered. Did she not realise that women offered themselves to him every day of the week? And would she not be outraged if her daughter were to become just one more in a long line of conquests?

He looked at her, his eyes softening as he saw the bewilderment in hers. For Sorcha was not like the others. She was sweet and innocent.

'Cesare?' Sorcha questioned tentatively.

'It is all right, *cara mia.* Do not frown—for you make lines on that beautiful face.' He kissed the tip of her nose. 'Let's go and swim, and cool off.'

'But Rupert's down by the pool!'

'Exactly,' Cesare said grimly.

But once Cesare kissed Sorcha it was like discovering an addiction which had lain dormant in his body since puberty. It was the first time in his life that he had ever used restraint, but he quickly discovered that sexual frustration was a small price to pay for the slow and erotic discovery of her body. And that delayed sexual gratification was the biggest aphrodisiac in the world.

Sometimes he took pains to make sure that they *weren't* alone together. And he quizzed her on her views so that sometimes Sorcha felt as if he was examining her and ticking off the answers as he went along.

He knew she had a place at university, and he knew that the experience would change her. And—*maledizione!*—was it not human nature for him not to want that?

The long, glorious summer stretched out like an elastic band, and they lived most of it outside. There were parties and dinners and a celebration for Sorcha's exam results, which were even better than predicted, but soon the faint tang of autumn could be felt in the early morning air, and Cesare knew that he could not avoid the real world for ever.

'I have to think about going back,' he said heavily.

She clung to him. 'Why?'

'Because I must. I have stayed longer than I intended.'

'Because of me?' She slanted him a smile, but inside her heart was aching.

'That is one of the reasons,' he agreed evenly, pushing away the memory of the blonde who had told him she was pregnant. It had caused outrage when Cesare had demanded a paternity test, but his certainty that he was not the father had been proven.

He thought how easy it was with Sorcha—and how restful it had been to have a summer free of being hounded by predatory women on the make. He was twenty-six, and he knew that sooner or later he was going to have to settle down—but for the first time in his life he could actually see that it might have some advantages.

He was confused.

He wanted her, and yet to take her virginity would be too huge a responsibility, would abuse his position as guest.

He wanted her, but still he hesitated—because he wanted to savour the near-torture of abstinence, recognising that the wait had been so long and so exquisitely painful that nothing would ever feel this acute again.

He wanted her, and yet in his heart he knew that he could have her only at a huge price.

'Oh, Sorcha,' he groaned, and knew that he could not go on like this. *'Siete cosi donna bella.'*

He pulled her into his arms and began to kiss her, softly at first, and then seekingly—so that her lips opened like a shell, with her tongue the wet, precious pearl within.

With a savage groan he cupped her breast, feeling its lush, pert weight resting in the palm of his hand. He flicked his thumb against the hardening nipple and knew that with much more of this he would suckle her in full daylight. And what else?

'We can't stay here,' he said grimly.

'Let's go inside,' she begged.

He had held out for so long, until he was stretched to breaking point, and silently he took her hand and led her into the house, to the darkened study, whose windows were shuttered against the blinding sunlight.

They kissed frantically—hard and desperately—and suddenly Cesare's hands were all over her in a way he'd never allowed them to be before. He pushed her down onto a leather couch. His hand was rucking up her dress, feeling her thighs part, and as he inched his thumb upwards she writhed in silent invitation.

He had just scraped aside her damp panties and pushed a finger into her sweet, sticky warmth when they heard the sound of a door slamming at the far end of the house. Sorcha sat bolt upright and stared at him with wide, frightened eyes. He pulled his hand away from her.

'*Merda!*' he swore softly. 'Who is it?'

'It must be my mother!'

'Are you sure?'

'Who else could it be?'

Hurriedly he smoothed his hands down over her ruffled hair and silently left the room, disappearing for the rest of the afternoon until just before pre-dinner drinks were served when he went to find her alone, sitting on the terrace, her face unhappy.

He knew that the timing was wrong—but he also knew that this must be said now. He felt as you sometimes did when you walked through the sticky mud of a ploughed field after a rainstorm. It was the price he knew must be paid for his body's desire, and yet he was too het up to question whether it was too high.

'Sorcha, will you be my wife?'

She stared at him. '*What did you say?*' she whispered.

'Will you marry me?'

Rocked and reeling with pure astonishment that such a question should have come out of the blue, Sorcha heard only the reluctance in his voice, and saw the strained expression on his face.

'Why?' She fed him the question like a stage stooge setting up the punchline, but he failed to deliver it.

'Need you ask? You are accomplished and very beautiful, and you are intelligent and make me laugh. And as well as your many obvious attributes you are a virgin, and that is a rare prize in the world in which we live.'

'A *rare prize?*' she joked. 'That matters to you?'

'Of course it matters to me!' His black eyes narrowed and his macho heritage came to the fore. 'I want to possess you totally, utterly, Sorcha—in a way that no other man ever has nor ever will. And I think we have what it takes to make a successful marriage.'

He was talking about her as if she was something he could own or take over—like swallowing up a smaller company.

And it was the most damning answer he could have given. Sorcha was not yet nineteen and she hadn't even begun to live. She was at an age where love was far more important than talking cold-bloodedly about a marriage's chance of success. Yes, she had fallen in love with Cesare—but he had said nothing about loving her back. And how could she possibly marry him and give the rest of her life to him in those circumstances? And throw her hard-fought-for university education away into the bargain.

He would get over it—and so would she. Yes, it would hurt—but just imagine the pain of an inevitable failed marriage with a man who didn't love her? That damning phrase came back to echo round in her head.

A rare prize.

She looked at him, masking her terrible hurt with an expression of pride.

'No, Cesare,' she said quietly. 'I can't marry you.'

CHAPTER THREE

THE bridesmaids' limousine pulled up in front of Whittaker House, and Sorcha helped the little ones clamber down, forcing herself to concentrate on the present in the hope that it might take her mind away from that last painful night with Cesare and its aftermath.

She remembered the way he had looked at her after she had turned down his proposal of marriage—with bitterness in his brilliant black eyes. She had tried to explain that she wanted to do her university course and get some kind of career under her belt, and that had seemed to make him angrier still.

And she would never forget the things he had said to her. The things he had accused her of. That she was a tease and that some men would not have acted with his restraint—and that he should have taken her when she had offered herself to him so freely.

How could deep affection so quickly have been transmuted into something so dark and angry?

That day they had crossed the line from almost-lovers into a place where there could never be anything but mutual distrust and hatred on his part.

And on hers?

Well, she had vowed to forget him, and to a certain extent she had succeeded—but her recovery had been by no means total. For her, seeing him today was like someone who suffered from a dreadful craving being given a hit of their particular drug. And even though she could see contempt in his eyes, hear the silken scorn in his voice, that wasn't enough to eradicate the hunger she still felt for him.

But she could not afford the self-indulgence of allowing herself to wallow in the past because it was the present that mattered. And it was only a day—when she had an important role to fulfil and surely the necessary strength of character to withstand the presence here of the man she had once loved.

Pinning a smile to her mouth, she swallowed down the dryness in her throat and looked around the grounds.

There was certainly a lot to take in. The gravel had been raked, the lawn had been mowed into perfect emerald stripes, and not a single weed peeped from any of the flowerbeds. She had never seen her home look so magnificent, but then for once cash had been no object.

Emma had been going out with Ralph Robinson since for ever, and her new husband was sweet and charming—but most of all he was rich. In fact, he was rolling in money, and he had splashed lots of it about in an effort to ensure that he and Emma had the kind of wedding which would be talked about in years to come. And Whittaker House might be crumbling at the seams, but no one could deny it looked good in photographs.

The youngest of the bridesmaids tugged Sorcha's dress.

'Can I have ice-cream, please, Sorcha?' she pleaded. 'Mummy said if I was a good girl in church I could have ice-cream.'

'And you shall—but you must eat your dinner up first,' said Sorcha. 'Just stay with me until we're in the marquee, so we don't get lost—because we're all sitting at a big, special table with the bride and groom.'

'Bride and *gloom,* Daddy always says,' offered the more precocious of the pageboys.

'Very funny, Alex,' said Sorcha, but the smile on her face died as she saw Cesare climbing out of a low silver sports car, then opening the door for the brunette.

Sorcha stared at her in disgust—the woman's dress had ridden so far up her thighs that, as she swung her legs out of the car—she was practically showing her underwear. Didn't she know that there were graceful ways to get out of a car without showing the world what you'd had for breakfast?

And why should you care?

But if she didn't care—which she didn't—then why did Sorcha find it impossible to tear her eyes away from him? Because Cesare could have been hers, and now she would never know what it would have been like—was that it? Somehow it didn't matter how many times you told yourself that you had made the right choice—you couldn't stop the occasional regret. And regret was a terrible emotion to live with.

The brunette was laughing up at him, her fleshy lips gleaming provocatively—with sensual promise written on every atom of her being.

'Come along, children,' Sorcha said quickly, before he caught her studying him like some sort of crazed stalker.

But Cesare saw Sorcha bend and tie a bow in a little cherub's curls and giggle at something the little one said and his mouth twisted. He knew that women sometimes used children as a prop when men were watching them—a silent demonstration of what wonderful mothers they would eventually make. Was that pretty little tableau all for *his* benefit, he thought sourly, to show him what he'd missed? Oh, but he was going to enjoy her reaction when she discovered what was coming to her! Abruptly, he turned away to toss his car keys to a valet.

Sorcha led the clutch of children around to the marquee, feeling a bit like the Pied Piper of Hamelin, but the presence of Cesare was like a dark spectre lurking in the background.

How the hell was she going to react to him for the rest of the afternoon and evening, if the mere sight of him unsettled her enough to set her pulse racing and set off all kinds of feelings churning around inside her?

She walked into the marquee, which looked as if it was competing for inclusion in the Chelsea Flower

Show, and for a moment her dark mood evaporated. She forgot all about Cesare and all worries about the business and just enjoyed the spectacle of her sister's wedding reception instead.

There were blooms everywhere—tumbling and filling and falling over in tall urns dotted around the sides of the tented room—and ivy wreathed around the pillars. Roses were crammed into copper pots on each table, reflected back in the gleaming crystal and golden cutlery, so that the whole room looked a mass of glorious, vibrant colour.

Maybe they could hire the house out as a wedding venue on a professional basis? she found herself thinking. Wouldn't that help the current cashflow situation?

She reunited her young charges with their parents until the meal began, showed an elderly aunt to her seat, and then dashed to the loo to reapply her lipstick. But when eventually she couldn't put it off any longer, she began to walk towards the top table—and her heart sank with a dull dread when she saw who was dominating it, perfectly at ease, with the lazy kind of grace which seemed to come to him as naturally as breathing.

She could see her mother at the far end in her huge hat, shrugging her shoulders in a *don't-ask-me* kind of way. But even more annoying was that Cesare appeared to have captured the attention of the entire room—and it was supposed to be the bride's day!

His ruggedly handsome and impeccably dressed figure was exciting jealous glances from men as well as greedy ones from women, and as she grew closer Sorcha could hear people on the adjoining tables.

'Who is he?'

'A rich Italian, apparently!'

'Available?

'Let's hope so!'

But Cesare wasn't reacting to the interest buzzing around him—his black eyes were trained on only her, so that by the time she reached him Sorcha felt as jittery as if she had just walked the plank and was about to jump.

She stared at the thick black hair which once she had had the freedom to run her hands through, and those slanting, aristocratic cheekbones along which she had wonderingly traced a trembling fingertip as if unable to believe that he was real and in her arms. 'You,' she said, and was appalled to hear her voice tremble.

'Me,' he agreed, his eyes glittering with satisfaction as he saw the look of consternation on her face.

She gripped the back of her seat. 'Is this some kind of bad joke?'

'If it is then I must have missed the punchline,' he answered silkily. 'Am I making you feel weak at the knees, *cara?* You seem a little unsteady on your feet. Why don't you sit down?'

He pulled the chair out for her and she sank into it, too shaky to defy his commanding manner and wondering if she had imagined the feather-light touch of his hand across her bare shoulder. 'How have you managed to get yourself seated on the top table? And next to *me?* Did you change the *placement?*' she questioned suspiciously.

He thought how she had grown in confidence over the ensuing years, how the shy young girl had gone for ever, and his blood heated. Oh, yes, this time he would enjoy her without compunction.

'No, I did not change the *placement,*' he said softly. 'Perhaps they felt sorry for you, being on your own. I take it you *are* on your own, Sorcha?'

Oh, how she wished that she had managed to sustain some of those random dates she'd had into something approaching a proper relationship. How she would have loved to rub Cesare di Arcangelo's smug and arrogant face in it if she could have airily produced some unbelievably gorgeous and eligible hunk and said, in that way that women did, I'm-not-trying-to-be-smug-or-anything-but-this-is-my-*boyfriend!*

But how could she have done, even if such a figure had really existed? Whoever she lined up—however rich and however eligible—would fade into humdrum insignificance beside the luminous sex appeal of Cesare.

'Yes, I am on my own,' she said coolly, because she had learnt that being defensive about it only made people probe even more. 'I don't need a man to define me.'

'Well, that's lucky, isn't it?' he mocked.

'Why are you bothering to sit next to me if all you want to do is insult me?' she hissed.

'Oh, but that isn't *all* I want to do, *cara mia.*' The black eyes roamed over her with breathtaking arrogance, lingering on the lush swell of her breasts, and very deliberately he ran the tip of his tongue around the inside of his mouth. 'There are plenty of other things I'd like to do to you which are far more appealing.'

Sorcha turned her head, desperately hoping that someone might come to her rescue, swoop down on her and whisk her away from him. But no one came, and no one was likely to interrupt them—since the *don't disturb us* vibes which were shimmering off Cesare's powerful frame were almost tangible.

Maybe they needed to have this conversation. She hadn't seen him since that day when he'd packed his bags and managed—she'd never been quite sure how— to get a helicopter with a stunning woman pilot to land on the front lawn and whisk him away.

And after today she wasn't likely to see him again. So maybe this really would help her to move on—to eliminate his legacy of being the man whom no other could possibly live up to. Maybe she needed to accept that by settling for someone who didn't have his dynamism and sex appeal she would actually be happier in the long run.

'Just say whatever it is you want to say, Cesare.'

It occurred to him that she might be shocked if he gave her a graphic rundown of just what he would like to be doing to her right then, and he ran one long olive finger around the rim of his wine glass.

'What are you doing these days?' he questioned.

Sorcha blinked at him suspiciously, like a person

emerging from the darkness into light. 'You want to hear about my life?' she asked warily.

He smiled up at the waitress who was heaping smoked salmon onto his plate and shrugged. 'We have two choices, Sorcha,' he said softly. 'We can talk about the past and our unfulfilled sexual history, which might make us a little…how is it that you say…? Ah, yes. Hot under the collar.' His gaze drifted to her bare neck. 'Not that you're wearing a collar, of course,' he murmured. 'And it would be a pity to taint that magnificent chest with unsightly blotches, don't you think?'

Sorcha lifted her hands to her cheeks as they began to burn. 'Stop it,' she begged, and cursed the debilitating effect of desire which had turned her voice into a whisper.

'You see? It's happening already. And it's all your fault for being so damned sexy,' he chided, but he realised he had made himself a victim of his own teasing, and that his erection was pushing hard against his thigh. He shifted uncomfortably. Only this time the brakes were off. She wasn't eighteen any more, but a woman—and he was no longer morally obliged to handle her with kid gloves.

'The alternative is that we make polite conversation like every other guest in the room. Safer by far, don't you think?'

Sorcha swallowed as she felt the blood-rush slowly drain from her face. Safer? Today he looked about as safe as a killer shark! Had she been blind to his almost tangible sex appeal before—or just naïve enough to think that he would protect her from it?

And he had, hadn't he? He had treated her like a piece of delicate porcelain.

Sorcha bit her lip—because what was the point in re-membering that? She didn't want to feel soft and warm about him—not when his eyes were gleaming dark and intimidating fire at her. But she wasn't going to let him intimidate her, was she? All she had to do was get through this ordeal without showing any further sign of weakness, then it would be over and Cesare would be gone—and with him all the bittersweet memories he evoked.

She watched the bubbles in her champagne glass fizzing their way to the surface. 'So what do you want to know?'

'Where are you living these days?'

'I'm…' She hesitated. *At home* made her sound as if she were five years old. 'Living at the house.'

'Really? Isn't that a little—' he shrugged his shoulders '—repressive?'

Now, why did she feel stung into defence? 'It's an enormous house—and anyway, I've only just moved back. I've been living and working in London. I've bought a flat up there, actually—but I'm renting it out at the moment.'

'Really?' he mocked, and his mouth hardened. 'And what about your *career*?'

There was something in his tone which she didn't like or recognise. Almost as if he were going through the me-chanics of asking her questions to which he already knew the answers. Or was she just being paranoid, crediting him with powers he didn't have simply because his attempts at 'conversation' sounded like an interrogation?

But she was proud of her work—and why shouldn't he damned well know it? 'I got a job straight after university for one of the best firms in the city and I worked for them until recently. They offered me promotion to stay, but I...' What was it about his manner which made her reluctant to tell him? 'I decided to work for the family firm instead. So here I am.'

He raised his dark brows. 'Ah! That explains it.'

'Explains what?' Sorcha frowned. 'I don't have a clue what you're talking about.'

'You don't? Forgive me, *cara*—I should have said nothing.' He lifted the palms of his hands upwards in an apologetic gesture, although his face didn't look in the least bit apologetic.

'No,' said Sorcha coldly. 'You can't dangle a carrot like that and then snatch it away.'

'I can do any damned thing I please,' he retorted. 'But I will take pity on you.' He shrugged his broad shoulders, enjoying seeing the convulsive little swallow in her long throat at his deliberate use of the word *pity*. 'It's just that rumours in the business world...well, you know what they can be like.'

'I never listen to rumours,' she said fiercely. 'Whittakers has had a few problems, it's true—but we're undergoing an upturn and things are looking good!'

'*Good?*' Cesare smiled, but it was a hard smile

edged with scorn. 'What a hopeless little liar you are,' he said softly. 'Whittakers is going down the pan fast— and if you don't know that then you aren't fit to be employed by them.'

If she had been anywhere else but sitting at the top table at her sister's wedding, wearing enough aquamarine silk-satin to curtain the entire staterooms of a large cruise-liner, then Sorcha would have stood up and left the table. But apart from the obvious logistics of rapid movement in such a voluminous garment—she had a duty to fulfil. She knew that, and he knew it, too.

'Every company goes through a rough patch from time to time,' she defended.

'Some do. It's just that Whittakers seems to be enjoying a permanent rough patch,' he drawled.

And suddenly Sorcha wondered why on earth she was tolerating this egotistical man giving her the benefit of his opinion. She hadn't asked for it, and she didn't particularly want it.

She glanced across the room as if he hadn't spoken, to where the brunette was sitting with an untouched plate of food and an empty wine glass, staring at him like a hungry dog.

Sorcha gave him a cool smile. 'Did you really come here today to discuss the fortunes of Whittakers?' she questioned lightly. 'I'm sure you could find more interesting things to do than snipe on about profit and loss!'

He followed the direction of her gaze and smiled.

'I'm sure I could,' he murmured. 'But I'm not looking for a one-night-stand—at least not tonight, and not with her. I'm going to enjoy getting to know my new colleagues instead.'

There was triumph gleaming from his black eyes, and the smile of pure elation which curved his mouth sent Sorcha's pulse skittering. But this time it was not desire which was making her feel almost dizzy, but fear—a nebulous, unformed fear which was solidifying by the minute.

'Colleagues? What colleagues?'

He savoured the moment, knowing that in years to come he'd remember this as the moment when his obsession with her had finally lifted.

'You and I are going to be working together,' he murmured.

'What are you talking about?'

'Rupert has brought me into the company as troubleshooter.'

The chatter of the guests receded and then came roaring back again, so loud that Sorcha wanted to clamp her hands over her ears and stare at Cesare in disbelief.

'I don't believe you. He wouldn't do that.' Her shocked words sounded as though she was speaking under water.

He shrugged his broad shoulders. 'Why wouldn't he?'

'Because…because…' *Because he knows the history between us.* But that was the trouble. Rupert didn't. No one did. Not really. They had kept it pretty much hidden, and afterwards she certainly hadn't confided that there had been a proposal of marriage. She suspected that they would have looked at her as if she was crazy to turn a man like Cesare down.

So she had locked it away, thinking that the less said, the sooner it would be mended. And in theory it should have worked. A summer squall of a love affair should have just blown over—but Cesare's legacy had been to leave an unerasable memory of him stubbornly lurking in her mind.

'Rupert wouldn't have done something like that without asking me first.'

'Are you sure, *cara*?' he questioned cynically. 'I suggest you ask your brother.'

Sorcha's throat dried, because there was something in his eyes which told her that he was telling the truth. And she knew then that her instincts had been right after all. He hadn't just shown up at the wedding to join in the celebrations, hand over an exquisite present and say hi to all his adoring fans. 'No,' she whispered.

'Yes,' he said grimly.

'But why?'

'Is that a serious question?' he demanded. 'Surely you must know that if something is not done soon, then Whittakers will cease to exist.'

Sorcha shook her head. 'That's not what I mean, and you know it. I don't believe you're operating out of the goodness of your heart. This can't just be because you've seen an ailing company and you want to increase its profitability.'

'Why else could it be?'

'Because…' She thought of the way he'd been looking at her, the things he'd been saying to her, the sense of something dark and sensual and unfinished between them. 'Because I think you want to sleep with me.'

He laughed softly. 'Oh, Sorcha,' he murmured. 'Of course I do. And how refreshing of you to acknowledge it so early on. I've heard of performance-related bonuses, but this puts a whole new slant on the subject!' He started laughing. 'Tell me, *cara*—are you offering me what in business terms is known as a *golden hello*?'

Her fingers were itching. She would have liked to rake them down his rugged olive cheek or to curl them around a glass of sticky liqueur and hurl it all over his pristine white shirt.

He glanced down at them. 'Don't even think of it,' he warned quietly. 'We don't want a scene at your sister's wedding, do we? Or do you want to grapple with me in order to get me to kiss you?'

He rose to his feet and looked down at her with eyes which had suddenly grown hard as jet, and Sorcha stared at him, realising that beneath all the civilised veneer there was nothing but coldness in his face.

'You're going?' she questioned, her heart pounding painfully in her chest.

'I'm expecting a call.'

'Don't you know it isn't done to just disappear from a wedding breakfast before the toasts?'

'Thanks for the etiquette lesson,' he said softly. 'But

I've squared it with Rupert. Just make sure you're in the office tomorrow morning first thing. Eight o'clock. I like to start early, so don't be late.'

Sorcha wanted to say something cutting and brilliant—to tell him that he had no right to order her around as if she was his subordinate. But he was right—they didn't want a scene at her sister's wedding. She was forced to endure the sight of him leaving, while the brunette in yellow made an unseemly scramble to her feet and followed him out of the marquee.

CHAPTER FOUR

'WHAT do you mean you *had no alternative*?' demanded Sorcha, raking her fingers distractedly through her hair, which was already rumpled.

She turned to face Rupert, the morning sun bright on his face as it flooded into the boardroom which was lined with framed posters advertising the famous Whittaker Sauce. Each one featured an apple-cheeked old lady stirring a steaming pot, a look of satisfaction on her face, and the splash line was: JUST LIKE GRANDMA USED TO MAKE!

Sorcha's green eyes sparked accusatory fire at her brother, but inside she was hurting. 'You mean that someone was holding a gun to your head and telling you that you had no alternative but to hire Cesare di Arcangelo to save the company?'

'No, of course not—'

'Well, *why*, then?'

'You've seen for yourself how bad things are, Sorcha. And Cesare has a reputation for turning things around—

look what he did for the Robinsons. Their profits went through the stratosphere! I gave him a call, not really thinking that he'd have the time available, and when he offered to come over straight away I couldn't believe it.'

'Couldn't you?' Sorcha shook her head. How naïve Rupert sounded—but then he just saw Cesare for what he thought he was, without understanding the complexity of the man's nature or the deviousness of his mind. 'But *I'm* here, now, Rupes. I came back here specially, to be Marketing Director. Shouldn't you at least have discussed it with me first?'

There was a silence.

'But, Sorcha, you've only just started with the company,' said Rupert gently. 'What with the wedding and all—I simply haven't had the chance to tell you before now, that's all. And there's nothing really *to* discuss, is there? You know that Cesare's reputation is legendary. So who in their right mind would throw up an opportunity to have him work for them?'

Who indeed? Women who'd had their hearts broken didn't count—or rather, their feelings weren't up for consideration in the big, brash world of finance.

She had been caught on the back foot—feeling not only cheated but shocked by her near-lover's reappearance. But even if she'd *known* that Cesare was about to dramatically reappear in her life would it have actually changed anything, other than allowing her time to prepare her response to him?

And would that response have been any different?

Could it have been? Even if she had been the greatest actress in the world and pinned the brightest smile to her lips that wouldn't have changed the uncomfortable cocktail of emotions he had stirred up, would it?

Rupert sighed. 'I'm sorry, Sorcha—but, whatever your private opinion of Cesare, nobody can deny the man's reputation as a sharpshooter.'

'Don't you mean an egotistical control freak who can't keep it in his trousers?' she questioned bitterly.

'Rule one of business,' drawled a velvety voice from behind her, and Sorcha whirled round to see Cesare walking into the room, a briefcase under his arm and a glint in his black eyes. 'Never badmouth your colleagues within earshot. Didn't they teach you that at business school, Sorcha?' He put the briefcase down on the vast desk. 'What else is it that you English say? Walls have ears? *Ciao,* Rupert.'

Sorcha wanted to scream—feeling as if she'd just been given a walk-on part in someone else's life. That this couldn't really be happening. There was nowhere to look but at Cesare, but even if there had been she wondered if she'd be able to keep her eyes off him.

He was dressed to look as if he meant business, which meant a suit—but something in the way he wore it transformed it from the mere everyday garment which other men wore to work.

It looked cool enough to be linen and fine enough to be silk, exquisitely cut in the Italian style—loose-fitting and utterly modern, yet hinting at the pure, hard muscle beneath. She found herself searching his face for dark shadows, wondering if he had gone home with the brunette last night, and it bothered her that she should even think about it—that it could make her heart contract with jealousy.

'You underhand swine!' she accused.

'Sorcha!' choked her brother.

There wasn't a flicker of reaction on Cesare's face. 'Rupert—would you mind going on ahead to the factory?' he said evenly. 'I'll join you just as soon as I can.'

'Sure thing,' said Rupert, who seemed glad of the escape route.

'Oh, and Rupert?'

'Mmm?'

'I may be a little time,' Cesare murmured, his black eyes fixed unwavering on Sorcha.

'Yeah.'

There was a pin-drop silence while Rupert left the room and closed the door behind him, and Cesare put his hands on his narrow hips and looked at her.

Way back he had vetoed mixing business with pleasure, and he wouldn't usually have been turned on by a woman wearing severely cut office clothes, but in Sorcha's case it was different. He felt a nerve flicker in his cheek.

Two top buttons of her plain silk shirt were unbuttoned, showing a sliver of a gold chain with a pearl attached which dipped invitingly towards the shadow of her cleavage. A classic pencil skirt clung to the pert line of her bottom and skated down over her thighs. Cesare

wondered how he could have forgotten the slender curve
of her hips, or how long and rangy her legs were—
especially in those high heels.

She was like a very classy racehorse—all athletic
power and stamina sheathed by sheer elegance. A
woman in peak and very beautiful condition. Why the
hell hadn't he just had her when he'd had the opportunity, guaranteeing her nothing but a postscript in the catalogue of his sexual experience?

'I think that you and I need to have a little talk, don't
you, *cara*?' he questioned silkily.

Sorcha's heart was pounding. Yesterday at the wedding, when he had told her that he had been brought
in, it had been nothing more than a theoretical nightmare. Today, however, it was harsh reality, with him
standing beside the shiny table her father had used to
sit at as if he were born to stand there—arrogantly
wielding all the power. But she was *not* going to let him
intimidate her.

'You've come up with a magic solution to all our
problems, have you, Cesare?'

'*Soluzione magica?*' he mocked. 'Aren't you a little
old to believe in fairytales? No. But I have a few ideas.'

I'll bet you do. Sorcha stared at him stonily as he
pulled out a sheaf of papers from his briefcase and
flicked through them until he found the ones he was
looking for. Then he leaned forward and spread them
out on the table like a card-dealer, looking up at her with
a question in his glittering ebony eyes. 'You have

studied all these figures which highlight the company's decline with heartbreaking accuracy?'

'Of course I have.'

'Really?' His eyes burned into her, his lips curving around his cold, judgemental words. 'And what course of action do you propose we take to halt the downturn?'

He was enjoying this, Sorcha realised furiously. In the same way that a policeman might enjoy interrogating a guilty suspect or a sadist might enjoy pulling the wings off a butterfly. And he would enjoy it even more if she allowed him to see that he was getting to her. So she wouldn't.

It was easier said than done. She moved her shoulders edgily. 'I'm looking into sales movements, distribution patterns, rises and falls in trading—you know. The usual thing.'

'Yes. Precisely. Hashing over the past. *The usual thing,*' he agreed, leaping on her phrase and repeating it with icy sarcasm. 'But innovation is everything in business—you must know that, Sorcha. Working for the family firm doesn't mean you have to undergo a common sense bypass.'

'You think you're very clever, don't you, Cesare?'

'I think that's a given,' he retorted softly. 'But this has nothing to do with ego or brains, and everything to do with achievement!'

His eyes were blazing now, and even though he was revelling in the mutinous expression on her lovely face it was by no means what motivated him. Because—no matter what unfinished business there was between him and Sorcha Whittaker—this was all about pride, and a very different kind of pride from the one she had wounded by her refusal to marry him.

He had taken on this task and it was a challenge— and Cesare was a man who always rose to a challenge and conquered it.

The Whittaker scheme interested him only in the way in which an overfed cat might be mildly interested in a small mouse which had foolishly strayed into its path. But the venture afforded him the delicious opportunity to seduce the only woman he'd ever asked to marry. Turning around the ailing company was a purely secondary consideration, and he knew that he could easily afford to fail. In fact, lesser men might have got some perverse kind of pleasure from seeing her made broke.

But even if he hadn't been loyal to Rupert, Cesare's nature and his need to succeed were such that he would not tolerate failure—of any kind—and didn't his relationship with Sorcha represent just that? Surely the ultimate satisfaction would be to bed her, win the praise of her family by reviving their fortunes, and make a packet for himself into the bargain? Put her for ever in his debt before walking away—this time for good, giving her the rest of her life to reflect on what she could have had. Yes. A perfect plan.

Prendere due piccioni con una fava.

To kill two birds with one stone…

He sighed. *Si.*

His raised his eyes, enjoying the frustration which she was failing to hide. 'Rupert has been trying to drum up more trade—but you've got a brain in your head, Sorcha. Didn't it occur to you to put it to use to try and work out why the products aren't selling?'

'You think it's that easy?'

He shook his dark head. 'Not easy, no. Simple, yes. Sit down.'

She hesitated, and then perched on the edge of the boardroom table instead of pulling out one of the chairs which stood around it. His eyes mocked her.

'Demonstrating your equality?' he murmured.

'You wouldn't know equality if it reached out and bit you!'

Laughing softly, he sat down in one of the soft leather chairs and leaned back to look at her, wondering if she would have chosen such a highly visible vantage point if she had realised the view it gave him of her derrière. Or that the material of her skirt was stretched so tightly over her bottom that he could see the faint outline of a thong.

His resulting erection made him wince. *Serves you right,* he thought, as he reached down into his briefcase. 'I've been going back through the Whittakers advertising budget over the past year—'

'It would be madness to cut the budget,' she interjected quickly.

'I'm not suggesting we do—please don't put words in my mouth,' he snapped. *Put your breast in my mouth instead.* His erection grew even harder as he pulled out a copy of a popular women's magazine. 'Take a look at this.'

She did as he asked, glad to have the opportunity to look away from that hard and fascinating face and concentrate on something other than the soft, warm coil of desire which was slowly unfurling in the pit of her stomach.

Why couldn't she just be impartial to him—good looks or no good looks? She'd met men who were almost as hunky as Cesare—though it was true that they didn't seem to have his inbuilt arrogance, or the ability to be in charge of a situation wherever he happened to be at the time.

She didn't want to *feel* anything other than maybe a vaguely grown-up sensation of *There's the man I thought I was in love with—the man who asked me to marry him.* She wanted to feel that thing you were supposed to feel when you looked at someone from a past which seemed very dim and distant—that she was looking at a complete stranger. So why didn't she?

Trying to quell the tremble in her fingers, she flicked through the magazine he had given her. There was a big spread on a former weathergirl's latest attempt to conquer her weight problem, with a few tantalising insights as to why she was attracted to violent men, there were gossip items and recipes, a problem page and a fashion shoot, and—amongst the other advertisements—an ad for Whittakers.

Sorcha had grown up seeing bottles of the family sauce plastered over various publications since the year dot, so it was no big deal—but she always felt a little glow of satisfaction when she saw one of their full-colour promotions.

'You mean this?' She looked up at him. 'It's good, isn't it?'

'It's good for what it is,' he answered carefully.

'Why are you talking in riddles, Cesare—am I supposed to be looking for anything in particular?'

He studied her lips and thought how he would like to wipe that nonchalant expression off her beautiful face with a long, hard kiss. 'Does anything about it strike you as different?'

'Not really.'

'Not really,' he echoed, biting back his irritation. He leaned back further in his chair. 'It's the same advert you've been using for years.'

'So what? It's a good advert!'

'I will tell you *so what, cara,*' he said softly. 'If companies do not change—then they die—that is a rule of life which applies to everything and everyone. And it shows a certain arrogance towards the general public if you treat them with contempt, not even wanting to bother to *try* and change.'

She stiffened. '*You* have the nerve to talk about arrogance?'

Cesare drew in a deep breath. He would have liked nothing better than to talk about arrogance, since it was the kind of subject which soon had women railing and then pouting and then sending out messages

which would result in a silent little tussle, and then…
then… But he couldn't risk making love to her. Not
yet.

'We are going to be changing the campaign.'

'Shouldn't that be a question rather than a statement? Or have you been given *carte blanche* to do
exactly what you want without running it past me first?'
she demanded.

He didn't bother answering that, and the fact that she
didn't pick up on it meant that she was perceptive
enough to realise that maybe she wouldn't like the
answer. 'Granny cooking up home recipes on the
kitchen table no longer strikes a chord,' he said slowly.

'But people relate to that! They think it really *is* great-
granny! The whole family business thing is what defines
us! It's what makes us different to all the other brands!'

'I know that.' He paused. 'And that is why we're
planning to upgrade the company with a brand-new
image—spearheaded by one of its very own family
members. A new generation to front the Whittaker
campaign. Imagine the publicity.'

'And just which member of the family did you have
in mind to front this new advertising campaign?' The
question sounded mechanical, because even as she was
asking it she knew that there was just her, her mother
and Rupert. Unless Cesare meant *Emma,* and she was
away on her honeymoon.

He gave the ghost of a smile. 'Oh, come on, Sorcha,'
he said softly. 'You may not have impressed me with

your business acumen so far, but there is only one person who can do it. You know that and I know that.' His black eyes glittered. 'And that person is you, *bella donna*.'

CHAPTER FIVE

SORCHA froze as she looked into Cesare's dark, mocking face. 'No.'

'No?' he echoed.

She clenched her fists. 'If you want someone to front your new advertising campaign, you'll have to look somewhere else.'

'But we've already decided that it has to be a family member—your mother is the wrong age, your sister is the wrong marital status, and your brother is the wrong sex.' His lips curved into a smile. 'We want to reach out and capture the single person who is living on their own—to introduce a whole new market to a very traditional product.'

'No, Cesare.'

'Why not?'

'Because I'm not a model!'

'Ah, but that is the whole point—we don't want a professional model,' he murmured silkily, and he bent down to pick up a large black cardboard envelope from which he pulled a thick sheet of cartridge paper in the manner of a magician withdrawing a rabbit from a hat. He handed it to her.

Inside was a mock-up of an advertisement featuring a girl with bright strawberry blonde hair—drawn to look just like her, she realised with a sinking feeling. On the table in front of her were all the delicious ingredients of a sandwich in the making, with a bottle of Whittakers Hot n' Spicy in the foreground.

The girl was sucking her finger, her eyes gazing wide and coquettish at the camera, and just one word was splashed across the top of the page. SAUCY!

'Simple, but effective,' said Cesare, and he felt weak with desire just imagining Sorcha sucking on *his* finger, and on…

'Just imagine the publicity,' he said huskily. 'This could be big, Sorcha. Really big.'

'And if demand increases—just how are you planning to meet it? Are you just going to magic up X amount of sauce from nowhere, Cesare?'

He gave her a narrow-eyed look of admiration. 'Leave that to me.'

He spoke in a tone of voice which told her that nothing was going to be a problem—and, infuriatingly, she believed him. But he hadn't taken into account the unpredictability of human nature had he? Or of women in particular? 'You've thought of everything, haven't you?' she breathed.

His smile was satisfied as he waited for the plaudits to come his way. 'I've tried,' he murmured.

'Well, you should have consulted *me,* shouldn't you?' she questioned crisply. 'Because I can't do this.'

His smile vanished. 'Why not?'

'The rest of the family would never agree to me taking centre-stage.'

'They already have.'

They already have.

'Emma thinks it would be good for you.'

Emma thinks it would be good for you.

'And your mother—'

'Stop it!' she screeched. 'I don't want to hear!'

It had taken a moment or two for her to register what had been niggling at her all along, but his words helped it to snap into crystal-clear focus.

Not only had he been brought in behind her back and then demanded that she be kept in the dark until it was too late to do anything to change it. But now—just as if they were engaged in some old-fashioned spy story— he had been briefing against her. It appeared that he had been masterminding a whole great scheme involving her—only she was the last person to know!

Sorcha glanced at the beautifully executed mock-up. This wasn't something which he had just had an artist scribble up in a few minutes—this had all been carefully planned. She had been excluded, and the rest of the family had colluded with him. It felt like a betrayal in the most complete sense of the word.

'You must have been working behind my back for weeks,' she said in a stunned voice.

'I thought it preferable if we presented it to you as a *fait accompli*.'

She looked at him, stunned. 'You bastard,' she said softly.

Cesare's blood heated with an inevitable sense of triumph—because, in a way, wasn't this exactly what he had wanted all along? For the precarious veneer of civility which had existed between them to be smashed by a simple word of contempt—leaving him free to give in to what he had wanted to do from the moment he'd first laid eyes on her again. And everyone knew that conflict made the best aphrodisiac in the world.

'Is that what I am?' he questioned as he walked towards her. Her eyes were filled with fury—and something else, too—or were they just mirroring what was in his? An unbearable hunger he had only just realised had been building away inside him all these years.

'Then maybe I'd better start behaving like one.' And with one unequivocal gesture he pulled her to her feet and into his arms.

She saw it coming—of course she did—but the pressure of his arms and the heat of his body drove everything from her mind—other than how much she had dreamed about this over the years, despite all her best efforts to suppress it. Sometimes in the middle of the cruel and indiscriminate night she had awoken to relive the achingly unfulfilled pleasure of his kiss—as someone stranded in the desert might remember how a glass of cool water tasted.

'Bastard!' she said again, but it came out on a shuddering breath of pleasure as he splayed his fingers possessively over her back. And this time something had changed. She was no longer eighteen years old, with a watchful mother lurking around in the house and a man who almost didn't trust himself to touch her for fear that he would lose control. He was certainly trusting himself to touch her now.

She felt her knees weakening, so that instead of wrenching herself away from him she sank inexorably against him. It felt as if every taut muscle and sinew was imprinted against her. A body like rock and skin like silk—when had she learned to find that particular combination so utterly irresistible?

'Damn you,' she managed indistinctly. 'Oh, damn you, Cesare di Arcangelo!'

'But you don't want to damn me,' he taunted.

'Yes, I do,' she returned, and wondered how her voice could sound so reedy.

His gaze raked over her face and read the stark hunger in the emerald brilliance of her eyes. 'You want this,' he grated harshly. 'We both want this.'

She told herself she would have denied it—but she would never know. Because the answer she had begun falteringly to frame was obliterated by the heady power of his kiss as he drove his mouth down hard on hers. And was this so very wrong? To give in to something it had nearly killed them to deny themselves in the past?

Hard and punishingly, he plundered her lips—and never had a kiss so overwhelmed him, leaving him weak and dizzy, like a man who had dragged himself out of the water after swimming too long.

Was that groan his? And that sigh—was that his too?

But even while his big body shuddered with unstoppable desire his response angered him. Which buttons did she always press which so weakened him—he, a man who neither needed nor wanted anyone? His anger transmuted itself into a desire to show her exactly that. To give her a coldly efficient demonstration of his sexual powers.

He dragged his mouth away from hers and brushed it over her neck. Her head tipped back as he did so, and the ponytail of her fiery hair dangled behind her. He wrapped it around his wrist like a bright, silken rope. His other hand reached for her breast, splaying possessively over the silk-covered curve and feeling the nipple peak and harden beneath his questing fingers.

'Cesare!' she cried.

'What is it, *cara*? Is that good?'

'It's… It's… Oh, Cesare.' She wanted to call him darling—her darling—her sweet and wonderful and beautiful darling—Cesare. But he wasn't her darling, was he? Not any more. He was just a proud and angry man who was setting her on fire with the mastery of his touch.

'I should have done this years ago,' he ground out,

and pushed her back against the table, brushing aside all the papers and sliding her bottom onto the cleared space, scarcely aware of what he was doing, only that he was being driven on by a power greater than himself. 'And then I could have rid myself of your face. Rid myself of your pale, beautiful body. Taken the memory of you and screwed it up into a tiny ball and tossed it onto the fire.'

That didn't sound like affection—it sounded like the very opposite. Almost as if he despised her. Resented her. It should have killed her desire stone-dead—so why was it only escalating? 'Maybe you should—'

'Should what?'

'Stop what you're doing,' she breathed.

'But you don't want me to stop, do you?'

'Cesare—'

'*Do* you? You would kill me if I stopped, wouldn't you, my haunting green-eyed witch? You would rake those talons down over my bare back and draw blood, and then you would suck it off, like a vampire.'

'Yes! No!' No—no, of course she didn't want him to stop, and the visual imagery of his words almost made her faint. He was right. She had wanted this to happen since for ever, and even before that. 'Do it,' she whispered. 'Do it and get it over with. And then leave *me* with the peace that you so obviously crave, too.'

'Oh, don't worry,' he vowed furiously 'I intend to.'

The skirt was tricky, but there wasn a skirt in the world which would have defeated Cesare di Arcangelo.

Never had his experienced hands trembled so much. He rucked it up over her knees, and then further still, to reveal hold-up stockings clinging to pale thighs, and he sucked in a ragged breath, his resolve almost leaving him, but not quite.

Now he could see the fine triangle of lace which hinted at the soft red-gold tangle of hair beneath, and he touched her there with ruthless precision—lightly grazing his finger against her moist heat so that she cried out.

'Shut up!' he bit out. 'We don't want any of the secretaries coming in. There is only going to be one woman coming, and it is going to be you, my beauty.'

'Oh, Cesare,' she whispered helplessly.

He skated his fingers over the cool silk of her inner thigh and she writhed restlessly, impatiently—Cesare knew then that he had her completely in his power, but that he must use that power wisely.

For once he gave her the orgasm her body was so badly craving might she not just turn around and tell him to go to hell?

His fingers stilled and she groaned.

Or would it make her more compliant if he satisfied her now?

He needed her co-operation just as badly as he wanted to have sex with her if his scheme were to succeed. Wouldn't leaving her wanting him more make her much more acquiescent to his wishes? For hunger was one of life's great motivators, and sexual hunger the most powerful of all…

He thought of all the times he had pulled back from the brink that long, hot summer, and it gave him the strength to resist pulling her panties right off and plunging into her there and then.

But she writhed her hips again, giving a little whimpering sound of something fast approaching pain, and Cesare knew that she was past the point of no return. His smile was cruel and triumphant as he acted quickly, swiftly disentangling from her to stride across the room and lock the door. And then he came back and began to unbutton her blouse, and suddenly his triumph became a kind of submission.

'Oh, *cara,*' he groaned as he peeled away the silk to reveal the twin thrust of her lush breasts encased in pure white lace. Like a virgin, he thought helplessly, and bent his head to suckle her through the lace, feeling her buck wildly beneath him.

Blindly, he felt for her again, his hand sliding up her skirt and finding her damp warmth, and suddenly he wanted to taste it. Taste her. He tugged at her panties and she lifted her bottom as he edged them down, over her knees and past her ankles, until they dropped to the floor.

She was positioned perfectly, he realised as he began to trace the tip of his tongue up over her stockings to where lace became skin and then beyond, where the skin was softest of all and exquisitely sensitive. And then the folds themselves—moist, warm, secret entrances to her most honeyed treasure. He felt the tip with a touch so light it was almost a whisper, and he felt her little shudder of disbelief. He moved his tongue, curling the very edge of it around her in a rapid little circular movement which had her groping wildly for his shoulders, tangling her fingers frantically in his hair and crying his name out until he shushed her.

Even before he felt a rush of sweet moistness against his lips he could sense her release, and he held her hips while she began to shudder against his mouth. And then he moved away to take her in his arms, pressing his fingers hard against her while she convulsed around them, and he kissed away her wild cry until—to his astonishment—the cry became real. And tears, great shimmering tears, began to roll down her cheeks. He felt them mingling with their merged mouths—so many different flavours of her—and heard the choking little noises she made as she tried to recover herself.

He drew back from her, his black eyes hooded—for he never trusted women's tears. They turned them on and off at will, as weapons of manipulation, that was all. As a deterrent they could not have come at a better time, though, for they stilled his own sexual hunger so that he was able to rein it in—a feat of self-control which few other men would have been able to manage under the circumstances.

'You cry?' he demanded. 'I do not please you?'

It was an absurd question to ask—for surely he must have known that he had? Sorcha felt hopeless—helpless, shaky and insecure, and completely out of her depth—as if he had scraped away the top layer of skin and left her raw and vulnerable, unsure what to do next. She shook her head.

He smoothed her hair away from her damp face and frowned. 'What is it?'

'That… That…'

She looked almost *shy,* he realised. *Shy?*

'What?'

She felt the blush wash upwards from her neck and she opened her eyes, biting her lip. 'It was just… Oh! With your tongue… Well, I mean, I've never…'

He held her still. Were his ears deceiving him. *'Never?'* he demanded shakily.

She shook her head.

For a moment Cesare stilled, and then he buried his face in her hair, closing his eyes. It was like music to his ears, though he scarcely dared to believe it. Had she hungered for him so badly over all these years that there had been no other man for her?

He slid his arms around her waist and levered her back up, smoothing her hair and looking into her eyes. 'You're trying to tell me you're a virgin?'

There was a split-second silence, and Sorcha was so tempted to lie. To tell him what he really wanted to hear—and wouldn't that make it much easier to bear? Then the way that she'd reacted might have been a bit more understandable—if she'd loved and wanted and waited all that time for him to make love to her then who could blame her for what she had just allowed to happen?

But she couldn't lie. Not to Cesare. And certainly not

about something as important as that. She knew how highly he rated purity—wasn't it the main reason he had asked her to marry him?

'No, I'm not a virgin,' she said quietly.

Now she had made him into a fool! Or had he only himself to blame for the sudden leap of hope he had felt? As if she wouldn't have had a long line of lovers…not when he knew how instantly she reacted to a man's touch.

His mouth curved. 'Your lovers must not have been good lovers,' he drawled. 'If they did not know how much a woman likes to be eaten.'

'You are disgusting!' she breathed.

'You weren't saying that a minute ago.'

Distractedly, she tugged at her skirt and straightened her blouse over her swollen breasts. It was like waking up from a dream when she hadn't even realised she'd been asleep.

What the hell would he think of her now?

Yet *he* had started it—set the ball rolling with that almost punishing kiss. *And you let him. Egged him on. Incited him in a way which was almost wanton.* Was it any excuse to say that she hadn't been able to stop herself? That once she had felt Cesare's lips on hers it had been like falling down a well straight into paradise?

She ran her tongue over her parched lips. 'That should never have happened,' she said hoarsely.

'Shouldn't it?'

Briefly, she closed her eyes. 'Not at the office!'

Cesare bit back a little murmur of satisfaction. The location had only added to its allure—but it was neither the time nor the place to tell her that her sudden capitulation to his kiss and its subsequent repercussions had been among the most erotic things to happen to him in a lifetime of erotic situations. That piece of knowledge would make her a little too powerful, and *he* liked to be the one with all the power.

And what was it about her that she should weave such magic over him even now? Because his desire for her had eaten away at him over the years? Or because she was so unexpectedly responsive? He swallowed down the bitter taste of jealousy—for that would not further his cause. He wanted her, and he intended to have her, and angry accusations about the men before him would not help his cause. And why should he feel jealousy over a woman for whom he felt nothing?

'And what about you?' she whispered, suddenly aware of how selfish she must seem—as if her own pleasure was the only thing which counted. This might not be a love affair made in heaven, but Cesare must be going out of his mind with frustration. 'Don't you…? Don't you…want…?'

'Sorcha—do not look so fraught. Let us acknowledge what we have—the chemistry between us is *incredibile,*' he murmured. 'Of course I want you—but I do not want our first time to be marred by a lack of time. By wondering if the phone will ring or one of the secretaries will knock on the door. Yes?' He lifted her onto the ground, enjoying the scarlet flush to her cheeks. He lifted her chin with his finger. 'Yes?' he said again.

His words only reinforced how *stupidly* she had behaved—without even a thought of what this could do to her career. This was the career she had sacrificed so much for, was it? She could afford to throw it away—along with her self-respect—just because sexy Cesare di Arcangelo had touched her?

She pushed his arm away. 'This is crazy,' she whispered.

'Crazy?' He gave a slow smile. 'That is not the definition I would have used, *mia bella.* It was *stupore*—amazing. And it is going to be amazing again. In fact, it's going to happen in my hotel room tonight. You know it is.'

He silenced her protest with a finger placed over the soft cushion of her lips, and she could smell her own raw scent on him and her eyes closed helplessly.

And when he took the finger away, she did not argue with him.

CHAPTER SIX

SORCHA'S mobile began to ring, and her green eyes narrowed as she looked at the unknown number. Cesare. She would bet money on it.

Cesare.

After he had gone off to meet Rupert, she had been completely distracted by what had taken place in the boardroom. Had that been his intention? To show off his sexual wizardry and rub in exactly what she'd been missing out on? Hoping perhaps to reduce her to a shivering jelly—as she lived out that erotic encounter, moment by moment? Was he also hoping that she would be unable to work properly so he could tell her that she was no longer required by the company? Perhaps his bizarre idea about having her front the Whittakers advertising campaign was nothing more than a double bluff?

No. Cesare might be underhand and devious—but she doubted whether even he would stoop so low as that.

But she had to claw back some of her self-control—to show him that she wasn't just some malleable female he could twist and pull like one of those rubber cartoon characters she'd used to play with as a child. She pulled the sheet of figures she'd been working on towards her, so that at least she was properly armed with a few facts in case he tried to interrogate her about how she'd spent her day.

She cleared her throat and clicked the button. 'Sorcha Whittaker.'

'Hello, Sorcha Whittaker,' purred the rich Italian accent down the tinny line of the mobile. 'What are you doing?'

Had he guessed she'd been thinking about him—or was this just par for the course with a man like Cesare? She swallowed, closing her eyes, trying to rid her mind of the image of his dark, mocking face—the feel of his mouth against hers and his hands brushing against her skin.

How had this happened when it had never happened to her before? That a man could start making love to you and suddenly you couldn't stop thinking about him.

In the intervening hours he had obsessed her. It was as if he pervaded her every thought and action—as if nothing she could look at in her immediate surroundings would not remind her of Cesare.

'I've been working,' she said.

'How very disappointing. I thought you'd be thinking about what I was doing to you a few hours ago,' he said softly. 'I know that I have.'

'Cesare—don't.'

He leaned against the wall of the Whittakers factory, alone now that the last of the staff had just trooped off home for the day. 'But it should be interesting to see what you've come up with. I'll pick you up at seven. We are having dinner tonight, remember?'

He had said nothing about dinner—he had merely intimated sex in his apartment. Sorcha shivered. With distance between them it suddenly seemed easier to say no.

'I don't know if it's such a good idea,' she said quietly.

There was a pause. 'You haven't changed, have you, Sorcha? You still like to tease men until they're going out of their mind. Promising, and then failing to deliver.'

The accusation hit her like a poison dart—but didn't some of what he'd said ring true? She could not take what she wanted from him like a greedy child and then back away, scared that she was going to get hurt. But if she didn't want to get hurt then she was going to have to protect herself—and that meant ruthlessly eradicating the side of her that wanted to beg him to be sweet to her, to pretend that he really cared for her. Because if there was no pretence, then she wouldn't start building up any foolish hopes, only to have them shattered by the harsh hammer of reality.

'Actually, I wasn't attempting to tease you at all,' she said coolly. 'I was speaking the truth, if you must know—I really *don't* think it's such a good idea. But that doesn't mean I'm not going to come.'

His relief that she wasn't backing off was only heightened by her cool response, and Cesare closed his eyes and bit back a sensual retort, recognising that he was skating on very thin ice—and that she was unpredictable. But if she thought that adopting an air of faint resignation meant that he might relent and call the whole thing off then she had underestimated him very badly indeed. She owed him—in more ways than one.

'I will pick you up at seven,' he said.

'Make it seven-thirty.'

He was left staring at the phone after she had severed the connection, and it occurred to him that he simply wasn't used to being left hanging on. Goodbyes to women he was intimate with were invariably protracted, with Cesare usually coming up with the let-out clause: *I have to go. Someone's trying to get through to me.* And then he would receive a breathless apology or a pouting little protest on the lines of *Oh, Cesare—you're always so busy!*

But he was only busy when he chose to be. He had reached a position of power and authority when it was always possible to delegate. These days he cherry-picked his jobs with the same ruthlessness which had taken him to the very top of the tree.

He had inherited much from his overambitious mother and father—including a need to make it in his own line of business, despite the vast amount of wealth he had inherited after their deaths.

His eyes narrowed suddenly as he glanced around the empty car park and the concrete jungle beyond, inexplicably comparing the scene with his orchards back home in Italy, and suddenly he felt a great pang of homesickness.

He drew out a set of keys from his pocket and looked up at the sky. By travelling the world he was missing all the seasons, he realised—the natural pace of the world was passing him by.

He thought about the August crop of damsons which grew in the gardens of his villa. About how they became so plump and ripe that they tumbled from the trees— glowing on the grass like purple jewels with succulent golden flesh inside. They would be out soon, he realised.

How long since he had bitten into their sweetness and let their juice run over his lips? How long since he had given himself time to gather in the harvest?

And why had this place suddenly made him start thinking about home? Cesare frowned as he thought about the rural retreat he'd bought as an antidote to the cold splendour of the Roman mansion in which he had spent a lonely childhood.

I need sex, he thought, as he loosened his tie and headed towards his car. Just sex.

And tonight you are going to get it, he thought with a slow smile of satisfaction as he climbed in behind the steering wheel of his sports car.

Sorcha stared out of the window to the front lawn, where a peacock was strutting and fanning its deep shiny turquoise feathers, squealing like a newborn baby.

Her hand fluttered to her throat to play with the pearl which hung from a fine golden chain, and she could feel a pulse beating at the base of her neck. It was almost as if she needed to touch herself to check that she was real—for she felt curiously detached, as though this evening was happening to someone who wasn't really Sorcha Whittaker, someone who had taken over her body for a while.

Because the real Sorcha Whittaker didn't have gasping orgasms across the boardroom table from a man she was certain despised her. Nor would the real Sorcha Whittaker have changed her outfit four times this evening until she was sure she had struck just the right balance.

Except that she still wasn't sure she had made the right choice, and there was no opportunity to try another because the long silver bonnet of Cesare's car was nosing its way up the long gravel drive.

The bell rang, and she ran downstairs and opened the door to see Cesare standing there, his head slightly to one side. He had taken his tie off, but otherwise he looked the same as he had done at work—save for a hint of dark shadow at his jaw.

With the evening sun behind him his olive skin looked almost luminous, and his thick hair was as darkly glossy as one of the ravens which sometimes strutted across the lawn before being chased away by the peacocks.

'Hello,' she said, and suddenly she felt confused. This felt like a date, and yet she was damned sure it wasn't a date. It was nothing more than a sexual liaison—a settling of old scores. But she felt as shy as a woman might feel on a first date—and that was even more peculiar—because how could any woman in her right mind feel shy after what had happened between them today?

Maybe because she *wasn't* in her right mind.

Cesare's eyes flickered over her. She was wearing some floaty dress in layers of green, with tiny little gold discs sewn into the fabric, her hair was loose down her back and she wore gold strappy sandals to flatter her bare brown legs. 'Pretty dress,' he murmured.

'Thank you.'

'You're ready?' He could see the wary expression in her eyes as she followed him out to the car and he told himself that it was inappropriate to ravish her on the doorstep—particularly since her mother and her brother might be around. Of course they might not be—but if he asked, then it would make him sound…

As if he was abusing the hospitality they had offered yesterday—just as they had offered all those years ago?

But it was actually more complex than that—because Cesare realised that he hadn't taken memories into account. He hadn't realised that they were such a powerful trigger into feeling things you didn't want to feel—until you reminded yourself that memories were always distorted by time. They had to be. They weren't constant—because no two people's memories were ever the same, were they?

Yet being with Sorcha like this mimicked a time when life had felt so simple and sweet—when he had felt unencumbered by anything other than the long, hot summer and the slow awakening of his senses.

But there was that distortion again—because that hadn't been part of Sorcha's agenda, had it? While he had been handling her with kid gloves she had been leading him on—playing with him with the clumsy confidence of a child who had mistaken a tiger-cub for a kitten. And she was just about to discover what it was really like in the jungle…

'Music?' he questioned, once they had strapped themselves into the car.

Sorcha sank into the soft leather of the seat. 'If you like.'

He slid a CD into the player as the car pulled away in a spray of gravel, but Sorcha almost wished she could tell him to turn it off again as the most heart-breakingly beautiful music swelled up and resonated through the air, so that you could hear nothing else but the voice and the song.

It was a man, singing in Italian, and she couldn't understand a word of it—but maybe she didn't need to. All she knew was that it was the most beautiful and sad song she had ever heard. It made her think of love and loss—and pain and happiness—and the man beside her. Sorcha closed her eyes.

She had to pull herself together—because it was pointless to feel things which would only be thrown back in her face, to want things which could never be hers.

Cesare glanced down at the hands which were

clasped in the lap of her dress—at the way her fingers interlocked, the way they gripped when the music reached a crescendo—and he bit down on his mouth, hard, in an effort to dispel his own frustration.

Because unless he stopped imagining himself pulling over into a lay-by and slipping his fingers between her legs, this was going to be a very long and uncomfortable drive.

The car drew up outside the only hotel in the village—the Urlin Arms, which was run by a slightly dotty ex-admiral who rated eccentricity over efficiency. It was his old family home, which had been converted, and the fact that the place had 'character' compensated in a small way for the constant stream of junior staff who were always flouncing out in a huff and leaving the Admiral in the lurch.

'You know this place?' asked Cesare as he opened the car door for her.

She clambered out of the low car and stood beside him, looking up at it. 'Yes. Of course. I remember when it was first converted.'

'Do you like it?'

'I love it. It's just…'

'Surprising that I've chosen to stay here?' he observed wryly.

'A bit.'

His black eyes mocked her. 'You thought I would have rented a glass and chrome extravaganza in London, did you?'

'Why, Cesare—are you a mind-reader?'

'No, I'm just good at reading body language,' he murmured. 'Especially yours.'

But Sorcha's poise was in danger of slipping as she followed him inside—where the Admiral was having his customary gin and tonic and regaling a tyre salesman from Humberside with the problems in the modern Navy.

'Evening, Admiral,' said Sorcha, forcing a smile and hoping that he was as man-of-the-world as he always claimed and wouldn't mention to her mother or Rupert that she'd been caught sneaking up to a hotel bedroom with Cesare di Arcangelo.

Why?

Because it felt wrong?

Because he was her boss?

They went upstairs to where he had obviously rented the best room. There were some fine pieces of furniture—a grandfather clock with a sonorous chime, a beautiful sandalwood chest, and faded silk rugs sprawled on polished floorboards.

Sorcha walked in and felt frozen to the spot, not sure what she was expected to do or say as Cesare pushed the door shut and leaned on it, studying her. And then his eyes narrowed and he turned and began walking towards a wooden drinks cabinet. 'Drink?' he called over his shoulder.

'Drink?' she echoed blankly.

He reappeared at the door. 'Wine? Or did you think

I was going to leap on you as soon as you set foot inside the door?'

Sorcha swallowed. 'How would I know? I've never been in this kind of situation before.'

Their eyes clashed. 'Me neither,' he said softly.

Some of the tension eased out of her. 'Wine, please.' She walked around the room, picking things up without really looking at them, trying not to look nervous when inside her stomach was tied up in knots.

Cesare came over and handed her a glass of red wine.

'Thanks.' She sipped it, and then took a bigger mouthful. 'Gosh—it's delicious. The Admiral must have better taste than I thought!'

He smiled. 'Actually, it's mine. My wine, that is. It is made from grapes which are grown in my own vineyard. The vines will be growing heavy now—with great clusters of grapes growing darker under the sun.'

His voice was dreamy enough to hurt, and suddenly Sorcha couldn't bear it. If she had married him she would have been mistress of those vineyards, too—as proud of their yield as he was—while instead she was standing awkwardly in a slightly scruffy hotel room, making small-talk while the real agenda simmered away unspoken. The elephant in the sitting room.

She put her glass down with a hand which she was suddenly afraid was going to start shaking. And he must not sense her reservations or her nervousness—because that would surely tell a man as clever as Cesare that she was vulnerable. If he thought that this was simply about a powerful sexual attraction which had never been properly explored then wouldn't she be safe? Maybe she would. For when they had taken their fill of one another perhaps they would discover that nothing remained.

She curved him a smile—a deliberately provocative smile she had no memory of ever smiling before. Where did a smile like that come from? Did you learn it from watching films? she wondered. Or was there just a moment in life when you met the only man for whom it was appropriate?

Cesare put his glass down beside hers, and for a moment he just savoured the anticipation of what was about to happen. At last. At *last*.

And then he beckoned to her. '*Venuta,*' he said softly, and held his arms out. '*Venuta, cara mia.*'

She did as he told her, went into them and felt them tighten round her. His breath was expelled from him in a hiss—like air being released from a pressure cooker.

'Cesare,' she breathed, on a note which sounded broken.

And that was when he began to kiss her. Her arms fastened around his neck as hungrily she pressed her body closer to his—and as he kissed her he began pushing up the filmy dress. Up over her bare thighs, his fingers luxuriating as they kneaded the soft flesh, as if they were reacquainting themselves with an old friend.

And Sorcha realised that she could not play passive. Not this time. This was the command performance—for one night only! Remember that, she urged herself. Don't be lulled by sweet sensation and unrealistic wishes just because his lips are soft and his kiss passionate enough to make you start indulging in make-believe.

She slid her hand between his legs and he groaned. Gently, she rubbed her palm down over the hard heat of his arousal and the pressure of his kiss increased—until he drew his head away, his black eyes looking as opaque and distant as a man in the midst of a fever.

'You think I am going to do it to you here?' he questioned unsteadily. 'Is that what you want? You are one of those women who like it any place except in bed?'

One of those women. He might as well have slapped her. Sorcha shook her head. 'No,' she breathed.

He scooped her up without warning and carried her through into the bedroom, laid her down on the bed—and perhaps he sensed that his words had been clumsy, for he started to stroke her and soothe her, and anoint her skin with feather-light kisses, and speak to her in words of soft Italian.

He worked her up into such a pitch of longing that Sorcha was barely aware of the gauzy drapes which fell in soft folds over the imposing four-poster bed. Quite honestly it could have been a bare mattress on the floor of a downtown apartment she wanted him so much—and suddenly she was tearing at his shirt, pulling at it in a frenzy.

He started laughing as a button went bouncing across the floorboards, but he lifted a shoulder to help her shrug him out of it, and when his chest was bare she touched it wonderingly, curling her fingers in the dark whorls of hair which grew there.

'You are hungry? Like a tiger?' he murmured.

But his laugh grew slightly unsteady as she unzipped him, pulling off his trousers as best she could and murmuring as she skated her fingertips over the dark silk of his boxers.

His eyes snapped open. 'Don't,' he warned.

'Or what?' she questioned breathlessly.

'Or this.' It was time to take back control—before he was fooled into mistaking this unique situation for something else. With a fluent efficiency born out of years of practice he peeled her dress off and tossed it aside, then unclipped her bra and sent it across the room in a lazy arcing movement. And then, with a hard smile of enjoyment, he caught the fabric of her mint-green panties between his hands and ripped them apart.

Sorcha's mouth dried and her eyes widened. 'Cesare—'

'Do you know how many times I've fantasised about doing that?' he grated as he pulled her down onto the bed, peeling off his boxers as he bent over to straddle her. 'And this?' he whispered, as he cradled his erection and pushed it close to her.

He paused only to reach for a condom, which it seemed he had conveniently placed ready beforehand, and Sorcha began to get a terrible feeling of panic. This wasn't how it was supposed to be. Oh, she had known exactly what was going to happen, and her body was crying out for him, but it all seemed so…so…*mechanical.*

All those dreams she had cherished were about to be dealt a fatal blow. But maybe that was best—it was only forbidden and impossibly perfect dreams which made it impossible to move on. Reality was a much safer beast.

He felt her tension and kissed her with slow deliberation until he felt all her apprehensiveness dissolve—even though the effort it took nearly killed him. 'I want you,' he ground out. 'And I want you now.'

'You've…you've got me.'

He entered her slick tightness and he was lost—as if he had found himself in the middle of the sea and a mist had come down so that he couldn't see any more, could only feel.

And—*Madre di Dio*—could he feel her! For a moment he felt shaken by the power of each perfect thrust.

Was she doing okay? she wondered as feverishly she kissed his shoulder. Was it acceptable for her to float away on this sensual bubble? Because it had never felt like this before—never, never, never.

Like an adult who had just got back on a horse after years of abstinence, Sorcha tried to remember the moves which pleased most, and she wrapped her ankles around his back and writhed her hips.

For a moment he froze. He looked down at her and his eyes were black, almost…hostile.

'What? What is it, Cesare?'

'Oh, but you are…good, *cara*,' he said unevenly. 'Very good. I thought you would be.'

So why did it sound like an insult? And why did something alter from that moment? The pitch and intensity of his movements changed, and he drove into her like a man who had been starved of sex all his life. You and me both, she thought. And—even though she tried to fight it—she felt herself swept away by the longest and most powerful orgasm of her life.

She was still crying out helplessly against his shoulder when Cesare followed, with one final deep thrust which sent him spinning off into a place of unbearable sweetness. It seemed to take him a long time to return to earth.

After it was over he lay back against the bed, staring upwards at the ceiling of a bedroom that wasn't his, oddly shaken by what had just happened. But that was because he had waited so long, he told himself—and now that the wait was over the hunger and the passion would die a natural death.

He turned to look at Sorcha. Her bright hair was tumbled across his pillow and her skin was rose-pink. But her eyes were closed.

'Are you sleeping?' he questioned softly.

Behind the sanctuary of her closed lids, Sorcha composed herself before opening them. Act like you don't care, she told herself.

'No.'

His eyes narrowed as he searched her face, but it was blank, like an unpainted canvas—as if she felt nothing.

Yet how could that be? Even if she no longer had any great affection for him, he was experienced enough to know that her orgasm had been of the bone-melting variety. Cesare prided himself on giving a woman pleasure—indeed, it often inspired an almost slavish devotion in his lovers. Compliments were his due, and always effusive. Always. But not, it seemed, from Sorcha. He traced a finger along her shoulder and she shivered. 'You liked that, *cara?*'

Keep it real, she told herself. Protect yourself. He must know how good he is. 'It was…' Sorcha shrugged. 'It was okay.'

For a moment his face darkened. 'You mean you were *faking it?*' he demanded in disbelief.

Sorcha started laughing. 'I'm not *that* good an actress.'

He relaxed. 'Ah, I see—you are teasing me?'

'Aren't you used to being teased, then, Cesare?'

He pulled her closer. 'Not,' he said silkily, 'at moments like these.' Women tended to idolise him. His ego was vast, but it was not self-delusion which made him sometimes feel like a trophy—not when he knew that women sometimes boasted of having been his lover. Lately he had found the very obvious conquests a bore. He looked down at Sorcha's bright hair. Yet she had been the easiest conquest of all. Or had she? He felt a twist of inexplicable pain.

'You have had many other lovers?' he demanded.

She turned her face towards him and her green eyes were serious. 'Do you ask every woman that?'

'Of course I do not. But it is different with you.'

'Why?' she whispered.

Because I wish I'd been the first. Because I cannot bear the thought of another man doing to you what I have just done. 'Just curiosity.'

'But it's none of your business, is it?' she asked sweetly. 'I haven't asked you how many women *you've* had.'

Cesare felt wrong-footed. 'That is different,' he said stubbornly.

'*Another* thing that's different? My, my, Cesare— where were you when women got the vote?'

He could feel a mixture of exasperation and frustration, because she still hadn't answered his question. 'You were right,' he said suddenly. 'We could never have been married. For I could never have tolerated a woman with strong opinions such as yours, which often do not coincide with my own.'

'Then everything has turned out for the best, hasn't it? Of course if we'd married my opinions would have been different,' she said. 'Because you would have helped form them.'

'And you think that would have been such a terrible thing?' he demanded, even though deep-down he admired her independence of thought.

There was a pause. She knew that there was an easy answer to give—but what would be the point? This— whatever it was they had between them—was not destined to last, so why not be honest at least? 'Well, yes—I do. Because then all I would have been was an extension of you—with no intellectual freedom of my own.'

It was one of the things he now found so exhilarating about her company—this feisty and challenging mind she had developed. But surely to admit that—even to himself—would represent a loss of face? 'And that is why you will never find a husband!' he stormed.

Sorcha stared at him, and then started laughing. 'I can't believe that a sophisticated man of the world just came out with something as crass as that!' But her laughter died when she saw the sudden dark look of intent on his face.

'In the bedroom a man is just a man, *cara mia*—and his response is rather more...*primitive*. And that is the double-edged sword—because the kind of man who turns you on is precisely the kind of man who will not tolerate your need for independence and freedom.'

'Cesare...' She wanted to say *Don't*. But she couldn't, because her body was craving his once more. And maybe he was right—maybe she *was* doomed to want what she could never have. An alpha-man who could never accept the woman she really was.

'Nothing to say, *cara?*' Luxuriously, he splayed his hands over the silken globes of her bottom and bent his mouth to her ear. 'Then let me say it for you... In the end, all the things you claim to want count for nothing, because you cannot resist the demands of your body. And though the spirit is willing, the flesh is very weak.

If I had asked you objectively whether you wished to find yourself in my bed, you would have answered no—and yet here you are. It must distress you sometimes to acknowledge that your sexual drive is so strong.'

She stared up at him, the hurt shimmering in her eyes. 'You think I react like this with every man? That I let anyone do what you did to me in the office this afternoon?'

A slow smile of satisfaction spread over his face. 'You mean it is just me?' he murmured.

Sorcha felt as if she'd walked into a silken trap and he had nearly tricked her into giving him the answer he wanted.

Suddenly she wanted to hurt him back—to lash out at him the way he'd been doing ever since he'd come back into her life.

'You want to slot me in as yet another of your damned stereotypes, don't you?' she stormed. 'Where once I was your precious virgin, now I'm a loose woman. But how loose? That is the question. How many men will you decide I've slept with, Cesare? Ten? Twenty? A hundred?'

'Stop it, Sorcha,' he said suddenly, as the mental pictures her angry words conjured up became unbearable.

'Then stop judging me by your archaic standards! Do you want to know how many?'

'No.'

'You don't?'

His eyes glittered. 'I just want to know if any of them were as good as me.'

She stared at him. 'You are unbelievable.'

'So I'm told. I'll take that as a no.' He kissed her and then lifted his head, an arrogant thrill curving his lips as he stared down at her rumpled, rosy beauty. 'I want to see you smile. Ah, *that* is better.' He stroked his hand down over her waist and felt her shiver. 'Now I'm going to make love to you. And then…'

Sorcha swallowed as he traced his tongue along the curve of her jaw. He was tormenting her, teasing her, and yet she didn't want him to stop it, because his soft cajoling was more enticing than anything else. 'Then?' she whispered.

Cesare touched the tip of his tongue to her ear. 'I think we must discuss the campaign.'

Sorcha stared at him.

'I've made an appointment for you to see an old friend of mine,' he murmured. 'He has an exhibition starting in London.' His eyes glinted. 'He used to be one of the world's most famous photographers until he gave it up. But he's agreed to do this job as a favour. It is,' he finished with satisfaction, 'a very great honour.'

For a moment he might as well have been speaking in his native Italian. Sorcha jerked her head away and blinked at him.

'What are you talking about?'

'The new face of Whittakers. You.' He nodded to himself.

She sat upright in bed, bright hair streaming down over her bare breasts, suddenly finding that rage was a far easier emotion to live with than willing surrender. 'Excuse me, but I don't actually remember *agreeing* to do it.'

'Really?' He slid his hand between her legs. 'I thought you just had.'

Sorcha covered his hand with hers and halted its sensuous progress. 'Let's make one thing clear, Cesare,' she said. 'The sex is separate. I'm with you now because I want to be. Not because I'm allowing myself to be seduced into agreeing to have my photo taken.'

His eyes narrowed. 'You mean you're refusing to do the job?'

She gave him a demure smile. Oh, but she was enjoying this. Why didn't some enterprising person write a book on how empowering it was to defy a man who thought it his right to issue commands and have them instantly obeyed?

'That's not what I'm saying at all, Cesare,' she said patiently. 'I'll do it because I can see the sense in it. And if it works I'll be the first to pat you on the back—since that is so clearly what you like. But my decision has absolutely nothing to with your skill as a lover.' She saw the incredulous look in his black eyes and resisted a smile of triumph. 'And now—if you don't mind—I'd like you to drive me home.' She slid her legs over the side of the bed in a graceful movement which he followed with a kind of helpless hunger.

'Home?' he repeated, in a voice of strained disbelief.

'Please.'

'Do you mind telling me why?' he demanded.

Hearing the outrage in his voice, Sorcha lifted her head and steeled herself to meet the hot and sensual challenge which sizzled from his black eyes, reminding herself that sex appeal as powerful as Cesare's was a very dangerous thing. It made you want to mould yourself against his silken olive skin and be made love to until the stars faded from the sky. But that would be a disaster—and a recipe for tip-tilting her emotions so much that she wouldn't be able to think straight. And wasn't it bad enough already?

She recognised that she was still vulnerable around him. That just because she had had mind-blowing sex with him it didn't mean her heart had been granted some sort of special immunity from his spell. 'We'll have to be careful,' she said.

Cesare's eyes narrowed. 'Careful?'

Sorcha bit her lip. Did he think she was talking about contraception? Was that the only level his mind operated on? 'I want to keep this secret,' she elaborated. 'I don't want anyone finding out, and I assume that you don't either.'

'Oh, do you?' he questioned dangerously.

She had thought that this would please him. But the glitter in his eyes did not look like pleasure, and the steely note underpinning his stern voice did not sound like pleasure. 'Surely you agree with me, Cesare? For one thing it's highly unprofessional for two people working together to be...' She struggled to think of a suitable description, but the only one which came to mind wasn't even true. 'Intimate.'

There was a pause as he weighed up her words. 'But that's not the real reason you want to keep it secret, is it, Sorcha?' he asked softly. Yet inside Cesare was reeling. *He* was the one who usually laid down conditions within a relationship. Never before had a woman dared to impose her rules on him, and he wasn't sure he liked it.

For a moment there was another silence. 'No.'

He raised his dark brows. 'So, are you going to enlighten me, *cara?*'

And—despite all her intentions—Sorcha suddenly found that it took a lot of courage to articulate her fears, to face up to the truth, no matter how bitter the reality.

'Well, your position here is only temporary, and therefore if we embark on an affair it isn't destined to last—it's just a short-lived pleasure. We don't want anyone building it up into something it isn't.' She shrugged. 'And we don't want other people projecting emotions on us when it finishes. If they don't know about it—they can't.'

'You really have this all worked out, don't you?' he said admiringly.

'Kind of.' What choice did she have? What other way to protect herself against certain heartbreak?

She bent over to pick up her discarded bra and Cesare quickly shut his eyes in erotic agony. Was she deliberately tormenting him? Sliding the filmy lace garment over her breasts with all the sensual show of a stripper?

With a simmering fury he climbed out of bed, feeling as if she had wrong-footed him yet again.

'So really,' he said slowly, 'this strategy of yours is designed to thwart any hurt pride?'

Sorcha nodded, turning away from the temptation of his magnificent naked body. 'Surely you can understand that, Cesare?'

Pride? Oh, yes—he could understand that. He knew the pain and the comfort it could bring. If pride were a degree course at college, then Cesare would have picked up a first in it.

CHAPTER SEVEN

'OKAY, Sorcha—if you could stand just over *there.*'

Sorcha stood on the chalk cross the assistant was indicating while they held light meters up close to her face and wobbled sheets of white paper around the place. She had only been there half an hour, and already she was bored out of her mind. How did professional models manage it? she wondered, devoting yet more silent sympathy towards that breed of overpaid beanpoles, because at least it stopped her thinking about…

Wriggling her shoulders, she smiled at the assistant. She was *not* going to think about Cesare and the way he had assumed he could seduce her into doing any damned thing he pleased.

Still, at least in some things she had shown him that she had a mind of her own. Every time he had made love to her she had insisted on going home to sleep in her own bed, even though he had tried his best to make her stay. Even though he was…was…

She shivered and closed her eyes. Why remember the

way his lips had trailed a slow path from neck to belly and beyond? The way he had made her cry out in surrender, her back arching helplessly as he gave a low laugh of triumph?

Why think about that *now,* when she was trying to be strong as she prepared to have her photo taken, trying not to melt when she thought about his dark, irresistible face?

That was why her need to sleep apart from him was so urgent—so necessary—for who could predict what would happen in those strange, unreal hours before dawn, when you were lying so close to a man who had been part of your heart for so long? How difficult she might have found it not to cradle him in her arms and tenderly stroke his thick black hair—to tell him that he made her feel whole again.

And was it her fierce resolve which made Cesare seek to demonstrate *his* power over her in different ways? That if he could not have her at night, then he would avail himself of every other opportunity which came his way? Did he take more than erotic delight in seducing her again and again at the office, despite her breathless protestations that it felt wrong?

'It does not feel wrong to *me, cara,*' he had murmured as he'd pushed her back against the boardroom door and rucked her skirt up, and thrust into her long and hard and slow. 'It feels oh…so…right.'

And Sorcha had sobbed softly into his shoulder as he brought her to another shuddering orgasm, telling herself that she had only herself to blame for this surreptitiousness. That *she* was the one who had demanded it be kept secret.

That morning he had picked her up from the house to drive her to the photo-shoot, and during the drive she'd seemed to be aware of him in a way she never had been before.

As if even the strip of hair-roughened wrist which showed beneath the crisp, starched shirt-cuff with its gleaming golden cufflink was of endless fascination to her. As though she could have studied his skin for hours and never tired of it.

Was that because his collecting her was about as close as they had come to replicating a date?

But there had been no kiss to greet her, just an atmosphere of simmering tension in the car, which Sorcha had tolerated until she'd been able to bear it no longer.

'Is something wrong, Cesare?'

'Wrong?' He gave a short laugh. 'I want you so much that I can barely drive in a straight line—what could possibly be wrong?'

'I thought you would have worn yourself out yesterday,' she said tartly.

He shot her a glance. 'So did I,' he observed drily.

And in spite of everything, Sorcha's heart leapt with longing. 'Why don't you stop the car and kiss me?' she said softly.

'Because we're stuck on the M25, you're about to be photographed by a genius—and time is money,' he snapped frustratedly.

'Well, you're the one who booked it!'

'Please don't remind me!'

Sorcha stared at the jammed road ahead, and sighed. 'Why don't you tell me how you know the photographer?' she said.

'Are you trying to change the subject?'

'What do you think?'

There was a silence.

'Well?' she prompted.

It was hardly a state secret, was it? 'Maceo and I have known each other since we were kids,' he said.

'Schoolfriends, you mean?'

Cesare's mouth twisted. 'Not exactly.'

'Not exactly…what? Neighbours?'

'No. We met at judo lessons.'

'And you've been friends ever since?'

'Men don't look at friendship in the same way as women,' he answered slowly. 'But, yes, we're friends. Look, we're here,' he murmured, unable to hide his relief as they drew up outside the studio. 'You go inside. I'll see you in a while.'

Sorcha turned to look at him. 'Lucky me,' she said, and his eyes glittered in response.

'That's exactly what you said last night,' he murmured. 'Twice, I recall.'

'Only twice?' she retorted, and he laughed.

The assistant's voice broke into her erotic thoughts. 'Don't bite your lip, Sorcha—there's a good girl!'

'Sorry,' said Sorcha automatically. *Good girl?* How did models *stand* it?

The studio was situated in the heart of London, in a large, nondescript basement which seemed to be buzzing with life and people. As well as the assistant, there was a stylist and *her* assistant, plus two representatives from the ad agency which represented the Whittakers account.

Everyone in the place was wearing some kind of denim—apart from Sorcha, who had been given a ghastly gingham apron to wear to promote the sauce and had *not* been expecting an audience.

'Can someone push that piece of tomato out of the way? Can you lift your head a fraction higher, Sorcha? No—a bit to the left!'

Sorcha's smile didn't falter, because she was determined to give it her best—even though she could very easily play the role of victim and claim that she had been forced into doing the shoot. Indeed, she could do it with such bad grace that she would be pronounced hopeless—and then the whole scheme would have to be rethought. *Then* there would be egg all over his gorgeous face.

As a way of getting back at Cesare it would be a masterly move. But getting back at him for *what?* For being autocratic? Because that was *him*—he was right— it was part of what attracted her to him as well as what ultimately made them incompatible.

She couldn't punish the man just because he was

making her feel stuff she didn't want to feel. You couldn't hold someone else responsible for *your* mood—because in the end that was all down to you.

There was a bustle and a buzz, and Sorcha looked round to see what all the fuss was about just as a man dressed entirely in black walked into the studio with Cesare directly behind him.

'Is that the photographer?' Sorcha whispered.

'You don't know?' The assistant looked at her as if she had just been beamed down from another planet. 'That's Maceo di Ciccio,' she said. 'And that's Cesare di Arcangelo with him—oh, but you know *him*, don't you? Didn't he bring you here?'

'He certainly did,' said Sorcha pleasantly.

Cesare gave her a cool look, and she sent him an equally cool one back, which made his eyes narrow in mocking response. But Sorcha knew that she was playing with fire. That the feelings she had had for him all those years ago hadn't just faded away into nothing. He still amused her and he still stimulated her, on far more than just a physical level—and that was where the danger lay.

Men were good at keeping things purely sexual, and women were notoriously bad at it. Even worse, sex brought out an emotional response in women which had the capacity to make them weak as kittens.

Well, that's not going to be *me*, she thought fiercely.

She watched as the photographer was greeted with reverence by all his acolytes, and Sorcha couldn't help thinking that Maceo di Ciccio was on the wrong side of the camera.

He was wearing black jeans and a fine cashmere sweater. His face was rugged—with harsh angles and slanting black eyes—but although his mouth was soft and sensual, there was an almost cruel curve at the edge of his lips. With his ruffled black hair, he looked a little like a buccaneer—the kind of man who would just go all out to get what it was he wanted. And, looking like that, she didn't imagine he had to try very hard.

Cesare watched while an assistant held a light meter under Sorcha's chin, and he wondered where his expected feeling of triumph had gone. He had got his way, because she was here—even though she didn't look as if she particularly wanted to be—and he had been enjoying some mind-blowing and no-strings sex with her into the bargain!

So what was the cause of the black mood which had enveloped him since he'd got out of bed that morning? Alone, after she'd damned well made him drive her home at some godforsaken hour. As usual.

And that was the irony—because he *liked* to sleep alone. He liked to wake up when he wanted, rather than have some female slipping out from beneath him, disturbing him while she went into the bathroom to clean her teeth and brush her hair in order to achieve that just-got-out-of-bed look.

Sometimes in the cold, cruel light of day it wasn't easy to make conversation, and the easy talk of the night before became stilted and formal. At night you had the cloak of darkness and the comfort of wine to take the edge off uncomfortable silences.

She had tied him up in knots yet again, and he damned well resented it!

'But she is beautiful,' Maceo suddenly murmured in Italian at his side. 'You told me she was a witch.'

Cesare looked at her, and a sudden unease prickled at his skin. 'Witches can be beautiful,' he drawled. Ignoring his friend's assessing expression, he leaned back against the wall to watch as Maceo walked across the studio towards her.

'*Ciao, bella,*' said Maceo softly, and Sorcha got the sudden intimation of being in the presence of a creative genius. Pulling off the cashmere sweater to reveal a black T-shirt beneath, he handed it to a waiting assistant and narrowed his eyes. 'So you are Sorcha, *si?*'

'Yes, that's me.' Sorcha smiled nervously. 'Um, you *do* know I'm not a professional model? In fact, I've never done anything but family snapshots in my life.'

'I can tell—but that is perfect,' he murmured. 'Just as *you* are perfect. I am not looking for the professional model, with her face just *so,* who tosses her head back—*so*…!'

He gave an exaggerated flick of his dark head and Sorcha giggled.

'That is good,' he said softly. 'I want you to laugh, for you must be….how do you say? *Saucy! Si,* for that is what Cesare wishes. For the sauce!'

All the assistants laughed sycophantically.

Across the other side of the studio, Cesare felt his face turning to stone. Since when had Maceo decided to ham up his Italian side—and *why*? Especially when Maceo's English was as good as his own. But he answered his own question when he saw Sorcha responding as if he was God's gift to women. Couldn't she see through all that hand-waving stuff?

Apparently not. Because now she was nodding her head energetically at something that the photographer was saying to her. Usually the two men formed a strong mutual admiration society, but suddenly Cesare felt like withdrawing his membership.

He had known Maceo since they were both five— when their two very different worlds had collided at a weekly judo class. Maceo had won a scholarship to study it, and it had been one of Cesare's many after-school activities, designed to keep him out of the house.

Maceo had risen from the slums and had had to claw his way up from the very bottom—perhaps that was what had helped give him his unique talent for seeing behind the masks that people presented. He had photographed models and princesses, queens and criminals— and then grown bored with it.

With the money he had earned, Maceo had bought an ailing fashion magazine and discovered that he had a talent for breathing new life into media ventures. These days he owned a TV station, several more magazines, and was proprietor of one of Italy's top-selling newspapers. He rarely took photos—only when the fancy took him. This favour to Cesare had amused him and been gladly given—so why the hell was Cesare now wishing that he had gone the more conventional route and employed someone that the ad agency had recommended?

And why was he feeling jealous of Maceo when Sorcha was a woman he was merely having sex with in order to finally get her out of his system?

Maceo smiled at her. 'You are ready, *bellezza?*'

Sorcha nodded—even though her heart was racing with nerves—feeling like a lamb headed for the slaughterhouse as she stood in front of the charismatic photographer. 'Ready as I'll ever be,' she gulped.

'Then come over here. Just here—you see? Just ignore the stylist—she paints the tomato with oil to make it look shiny. Relax, Sorcha. Just relax. *Si,* that is better. Now, put your finger in your mouth. Yes. That is perfect. Ah, *si!* You are perfect. *Bellezza!*'

A nerve flickered in Cesare's cheek.

He knew that in order to get the very best out of a subject Maceo was photographing it was necessary for the subject to relax. So why shouldn't Maceo call Sorcha beautiful, when that was nothing but the truth?

And why the hell was it eating him up?

Sorcha could feel her heart hammering. This was a *nightmare*—especially with Cesare standing in the shadows of the room, his silhouette looking so darkly forbidding. All she could see was the glitter of his eyes, but she could sense his disapproval as surely as if it were radiating in waves from his hard, lean body. And *who* was the one who had set this whole thing up?

Defiantly, she licked her lips and pouted.

'Now, look at me as you would look at your lover,' demanded Maceo.

This was harder, and stupidly Sorcha blushed. Was that because her lover was standing on the other side of the room, glowering at her? She heard a door slam, and when Sorcha looked up Cesare had gone.

'No, *cara,*' Maceo urged, as he followed the direction of her gaze. 'Not that look. Not the shy in-love smile, but the grown-up foxy smile. The look of a confident woman. Comfortable in her own skin—knowing that she gives pleasure as well as receives it.'

In a way it was better that Cesare *had* gone, because at least now Sorcha felt more able to deliver—if only to prove to herself and to Maceo that his assessment had been completely wrong. It had not been a shy in-love smile at all. Not at all. Because she wasn't in love with anyone.

She put her finger into her mouth, widened her eyes at the camera, and thought of Cesare, naked and luminous.

'*Perfetto!*' applauded Maceo.

She tilted her head coquettishly, looking as if she had just been told a delicious secret as she remembered the things he had whispered last night as he had thrust long and hard and deep inside her.

'*Meravigliosa!*' murmured Maceo.

Sorcha really started getting into it—tossing her head like a filly and meeting Maceo's enigmatic black eyes.

'Now you see why the models toss their heads…*so?*' he observed wryly.

He shot roll after roll of film, and by the time he'd finished Sorcha felt exhausted. She picked up her bag and jacket. Maybe modelling wasn't quite as easy as it appeared on the surface.

'Ah, there is Cesare,' murmured Maceo sardonically as they walked out into the reception area. 'With the sunny smile.'

Cesare was pacing the floor like a dark, caged tiger. He barely flicked her a glance, but directed his attention to Maceo.

'What the hell was *that* all about?' he questioned in Italian.

'Could you be a little more specific?' answered Maceo, in the same language.

'I asked you to take her photograph—not to try it on!'

'If I *had* been trying it on, then she'd be leaving with me,' boasted Maceo. 'If you can't hang on to your women, di Arcangelo—then don't take it out on me.'

The two men stood glaring at one another, and Sorcha had had quite enough. She marched out of the foyer and left them to it. Let Cesare travel back on his own—*she* would get the train!

She was halfway down Marylebone High Street when she heard a distinctive voice calling out her name and the sound of footsteps behind her. When she turned round, there was Cesare—his dark face a picture of barely repressed rage.

'Where do you think you're going?' he demanded.

'To the station! I wasn't going to hang around while you and Maceo had your Italian conversation class—I'd already had an exhausting morning.'

His mouth twisted. 'Yes, I could see that.'

The undertone of accusation in his voice was unmistakable. 'And what's that supposed to mean?'

'Do you think I am blind, Sorcha?' he asked hotly. 'I saw what was going on between you and Maceo.'

'*Going on?*' she choked. 'You mean the flirting, which I assume he does as automatically as breathing with every woman he photographs?'

'I know what kind of a man he is!' he declared. 'And the reputation he has with women. He does not know that there is anything between us, so why wouldn't he make a pass at you?'

'But there *is* nothing between us!' she flared. And didn't part of her just long for him to reject that assumption?

But Cesare didn't seem remotely interested in defining relationships—he was not letting up on the subject which interested him far more. 'You are saying that you didn't find him attractive?'

Sorcha sighed. This was difficult—but keeping her own emotions in check to lessen the risk of getting hurt did not mean that she couldn't be in some way honest about the way she felt.

'Under different circumstances, I suppose I might have done,' she said carefully.

His eyes narrowed. 'What kind of circumstances?'

If she had been a child, she would have stamped her foot. 'Oh, you can be so dense, Cesare! I thought I'd made it clear to you that just because I wasn't a virgin when I slept with you it doesn't necessarily follow that no man is safe from my advances! I don't deal with a multitude of partners at the same time.' She stared at him. 'Do you?'

'No.' There was a long silence while he stared at her, and suddenly some of the tension left him. Some, but not all. 'Am I going crazy?' he questioned softly.

'I don't know—are you?'

'Yes,' he groaned as he pulled her into his arms. He wanted to tell her that it wasn't supposed to be like this— he had thought he was going along in a straight line, yet he was encountering twists and turns all along the way.

'I find myself wanting to kiss green-eyed women in the middle of a busy street,' he murmured.

'Cesare—you can't.'

'Can't I?'

'Think of your reputation.'

'What about yours?'

Sorcha couldn't remember the last time she had been kissed in public. It didn't last long, and it wasn't one of those awful kisses which made other people feel sick— with the couple looking as if they were enjoying a three-course meal.

No, it was brief and hard and intense—in effect, it was a powerful stamp and a demonstration of Cesare's mastery, and when she drew back from it she was breathless, oblivious to the red double-decker bus which trundled by and the people who were turning to look at them.

'Now what?' she questioned.

'Let's find a hotel,' he said unsteadily.

CHAPTER EIGHT

SUNLIGHT streamed in through the windows and Sorcha sleepily opened her eyes and yawned. She had often wondered what kind of people spent the afternoon in bed in a hotel, and now she had discovered the answer.

People like her.

She glanced at the figure in the bed beside her. Cesare was sleeping, his magnificent body stretched out like an artist's model, the olive skin glowing against the rumpled tangle of white sheets. But while his muscular body was hard and lean, his face in repose had a curious softness about it. Thick black lashes formed two shadowy arcs, and the luscious mouth was curved into a sensual little pout.

How many beds had he lain in like this? she wondered. Had he spent anonymous afternoons in luxury hotels in all the major cities around the world? For this was a very different venue from the Urlin Arms, with its faded carpets and temperamental staff. Here the drapes were pure lined silk, the chandelier French, and the writing desk antique.

How many women? Did they all blur into one eager and giving body? In a year's time would he have to frown to remember just where it was he had stayed with her?

There was a glint from between his half-closed eyes, and a hand reached out to rest with easy familiarity on her thigh. How well sex could mock real intimacy, thought Sorcha with a pang.

'You look lost in thought,' he murmured.

'I was.'

'Are you going to share it?'

What an emotive word *share* could be—did he know that? Did women leap on it like hungry little puppies because it hinted at something beyond the communion of bodies which had just taken place?

'You won't want to hear.'

'Try me,' he murmured, stretching his legs and making no attempt to hide his renewed stirring of desire.

'I was wondering if you made a habit of this.'

'This?'

There he was—already playing for time! 'Having sex with women in anonymous hotel rooms.'

He studied her thoughtfully. 'What do you think? That every time I visit a city I pick up a beautiful woman and take her to bed?'

'Do you?'

He laughed. 'Once—a long time ago—I went through a stage of doing exactly that.' It had been when he had left her, when he had been hurting—not expecting to hurt, nor wanting to, as if he had a divine right to somehow be immune from the pain of relationships.

There had always been willing women—and at that time it had seemed that the supply of them was endless. It was almost as if his icy indifference had turned them on, providing them with the challenge that they might be the one to break through that cold heart to find the warmth of the man beneath. They never had, of course—and Cesare had turned away more than he had slept with. He had felt like a gorged child who had been given permission to spend the night in a sweetshop.

'It sounds like every man's idea of heaven,' said Sorcha, hoping that her voice didn't sound sour—because how he lived his life was his business, not hers.

'It wasn't,' he said flatly. 'Predictability is boring, and when something is so easy to get, it doesn't have the same value.'

Sorcha went very still. 'You didn't have to fight very hard to get *me* into bed,' she said in a small voice.

His voice was cool and mocking. 'You don't think so? This seduction actually started *seven* years ago—and, using those sums, I'd say that you were actually the hardest of all.' Black eyes hardened, became watchful. 'And what about you, Sorcha, since this seems to be true confession time?'

'What do you want to know? Actual numbers, like in that film—where I go through my conquests one by one and make you laugh?'

Laugh? He winced, knowing that the fierce stab of jealousy which shot through him was unreasonable— but then, he had never been accused of being a reasonable man.

'No,' he grated, and, unfolding his big, lean body, he got out of bed. 'Let's have a drink.'

Had he suggested that to distance himself? Because the conversation had taken a distinctly confessional turn? She watched while he went to the fridge and pulled out a bottle of champagne, efficiently disposing of foil and cork before handing her a fizzing glassful.

Sorcha sat up in bed, sipping at the cool champagne while Cesare climbed back in beside her, thinking that she really ought to be enjoying this moment. Imagine if she wrote about it in a postcard home. In bed, overlooking Regent's Park. Fabulous sex. Fabulous man. Fabulous wine.

So why was there this terrible ache of emptiness inside her?

'It wouldn't take very long,' she said.

Cesare frowned as he took a long draught—he who never drank in the middle of the day, but who suddenly wanted something to take the edge off his heightened senses. 'What wouldn't?'

'To list my lovers.'

'I don't want to hear about them, Sorcha,' he clipped out.

'Him.'

His eyes narrowed. 'What?'

'Him, not them. Singular, not plural. Just one. Before you, that is.' She wondered why she was bothering to defend herself—because that was really what it amounted to. Why his opinion should be so important to her. Was it just that she needed him to know that she had acted in an extraordinary way with him—or rather *re*acted? And didn't she run the risk of looking rather pathetic—like someone who was setting out her stall, saying, *Look how relatively untouched I am?*

'One?' he repeated incredulously.

'That surprises you?'

'Of course it does. It isn't many for a woman your age.'

'I didn't realise I was defying some kind of national average.'

'Why did you tell me?' he demanded suddenly.

'Why do you think?' She clutched her glass in two hands in case she spilled wine all over the bed. 'I couldn't bear it if you imagined that I did...well, what I did with you...with lots of men.'

There was a pause, and he knew that in light of her honesty he had to be honest in return. 'I didn't think that, Sorcha,' he said slowly. 'There was such a...' He shrugged. 'That kind of combustive sexual chemistry is rare, believe me—I know.'

He put his glass down, took hers from her hands and placed it beside his, and then drew her into his arms and down onto the bed.

His mouth was cool and tasted of wine, and his body was warm, and Sorcha felt a sudden and overwhelming wave of real yearning which transcended mere sexual desire. She kissed him back, long and deep, and then she rolled out from beneath him, kneeling beside him as she bent her tongue to his nipple.

'Sorcha,' he groaned. 'What do you do to me?'

She let her tongue slide all the way down his belly, along the thin line of hair which arrowed towards where he was hard, and she licked him tentatively, so that he groaned again.

His hands tangled in the silk of her hair as she took him into her mouth, and never had he felt more helpless and vulnerable as she rocked her head up and down. He could feel his climax building and building, and part of him wanted to stop her, to take control away from her and to thrust all that pent-up desire deep into her body.

But it was too late.

She felt the shudder which began to convulse the powerful body, heard an expression of disbelief torn from his lips and closed her eyes as she tasted him. Afterwards he pulled her back up the bed and cradled her in his arms—and that *did* feel like real intimacy.

But she mustn't *do* that—perhaps that was where she went wrong? Thinking that it was more than it was—as if some fantastic orgasm would suddenly give him a complete personality change and he'd start opening his heart to her. But it was in her nature to try, and she wanted him to let her share more than just his body.

She pulled at his shoulder, knowing that it was the wrong thing to do but unable to stop herself. As if she needed to have it written in giant letters for her to finally get the message that he wasn't interested in anything deeper than this.

'Cesare?'

He sighed, knowing just from the tone of her voice what was coming. 'What?'

'Why did you come back?' She met his eyes as he turned back to face her. 'Oh, I know that you're friends with Rupert, and you wanted to do him a favour, and you'll probably make lots of money—but why was it so important for you to seduce me?'

There was silence for a moment.

'Because you were the best sex I never had.' He smiled, but it was a cold and thoughtful smile. 'For years the thought of what I had missed out on ate away at me like a disease, so I wanted to do this—no, I *needed* to— just to lay the ghost of what has haunted me ever since.'

There was a pause. 'I see.' Sorcha let her eyelids close so that he would not detect the wavering hurt which was making her eyes shimmer with tears. 'And now you have.'

But that was the trouble. Cesare narrowed his eyes. He hadn't.

'We'd better get dressed,' he said abrasively. 'I have a flight to catch.'

'A flight?' she echoed blankly.

'I'm meeting Rupert—we're flying up to the North. The new factory is about to go into production. Remember?'

'Yes, of course.' What an idiot he must think her—they had talked of nothing else for weeks. Yet business couldn't have been further from her mind—all her thoughts were full of *him,* and it was time she pulled herself together. One day soon Cesare would be gone, and she did not need her career to be left in tatters as a consequence of his going.

She stared up at the ceiling. 'It's such a gamble,' she moaned. 'Starting production before you know whether the new campaign will be a success. What if we manufacture loads of extra bottles of sauce and nobody buys them?'

'Life is a gamble, Sorcha—and sometimes you just have to go out on a limb and take a risk.' He stroked his finger over her face. 'I'll only be gone a few days. Will you miss me?'

Sorcha began to get dressed without answering—because what did he expect? Adoring compliments or declarations of affection? How egotistical was that? Especially as he had been so brutally honest about what she meant to *him.*

She bit her lip.

It wasn't the most glowing testament in the world, was it?

She was the best sex he'd never had.

CHAPTER NINE

'THERE'S a journalist outside,' said Rupert. 'And he says he wants to speak to Sorcha.'

All eyes around the table looked at her. The board-room was packed with accountants, operations managers and sales reps, but all Sorcha was aware of was the piercing black gaze which seemed to be stripping her bare—or was that simply wishful thinking on her part? Oh, but she had missed him.

Cesare had been away for weeks. He'd flown straight from the new factory over to the States, and then back to Italy for the centenary celebrations of one of the di Arcangelo department stores. He'd been in regular contact—but you never really knew what was going on behind the scenes when you dealt in phone calls and e-mails.

He had arrived back to discover that a lot of the press interest seemed to be focussed more on the fiery-haired model than on the product—which was every marketing man's idea of a nightmare. He had only calmed down when he had seen the sales figures, which had gone through the roof.

Across the boardroom he met Sorcha's green eyes with soft fire—because even the supremely confident Cesare had been unprepared for the ripple effect of his original idea.

Nobody could have predicted the outrageous success of his revamped advertising campaign. As Rupert had said, products hadn't just been flying off the shelves— they had been leaving them in whole squadrons!

'So, are you going to talk to this journalist, Sorcha?' Cesare questioned, his voice underpinned with silken sarcasm. 'Or perhaps we should think about hiring a PR person especially for you, who could cope with all the interview requests!'

'There's no need to make it sound like something *I've* done, when this whole campaign idea was *your* sugges- tion,' she retorted. 'If you start rubbishing it now, then it doesn't really reflect well on *your* judgement, does it, Cesare?'

They glared at each other across the room. Had he thought that his absence might bring him immunity from desire? He wanted her, he realised. He still wanted her. He had missed her like crazy. Crazy. His scowl deepened. 'So, are you going to talk to him?'

She looked around the table. 'I'm happy to take advice on it.'

Rupert shrugged. 'Well, you know what they say— there's no such thing as bad publicity.'

'It's certainly been good for Maceo!' piped up one of the secretaries, who had been completely smitten by the Italian photographer.

The campaign had given Maceo's retrospective exhibition an extra boost of publicity. The photos he had taken of Sorcha were absolutely brilliant, causing one of the broadsheet newspapers to wonder why he had given up taking photos professionally.

'I don't know what all the fuss is about,' said Sorcha, wishing that some of it might die down.

'Are you being disingenuous?' Cesare's voice was withering as his gaze flickered over the giant poster of Sorcha sucking on a digit. 'It looks like soft porn!'

'Thanks!' she snapped. 'I can't believe you just said that. *You* approved the original concept—remember?'

'I was not expecting it to look like…like…!' But that was not strictly true. He had known exactly what it would look like. He had underestimated the interest it would provoke, true—and he had also failed to take into account the fact that he would still be feeling this frustrating and pointless jealousy. Because none of this was working out as he had wanted.

He had planned to have cast her aside by now—instead of which, he had flown back hungry for more of her. And—damn it—he didn't *want* to want her—not any more! Looking for something to focus his rage on, he looked again at the poster. 'What was Maceo thinking of?'

'Sales, presumably,' she said sarcastically.

Now they faced one another.

'The journalist is waiting, Sorcha,' Rupert reminded her quietly.

Part of her wanted to go out and do an interview just to rile Cesare. But she knew that wouldn't be the act of a mature person, and so she shook her head. 'Well, I don't want to talk to anyone. Rupes, would you mind referring them to our PR people? Say that my contribution to the campaign was a one-off and that I shan't be doing any more photo-shoots?'

Rupert pulled a face. 'Crikey—are you sure, sis? Don't you want to capitalise on this?'

'There's nothing *to* capitalise on.' Sorcha met the mockery in Cesare's eyes and hesitated. She wanted to say how much she had given up to go to college—but wouldn't that be a revelation too far, especially now, here, in front of all these people? And especially in front of *him*. But there were other ways of saying that her education had been both important and necessary to her.

'I didn't work hard at university to see my entire career culminating in being the face on the front of a sauce bottle.'

Black eyes burned into her.

'Yeah,' said Rupert, nodding. 'And we kept that other photo for over fifty years—so there's probably no need!'

'Rupert!' said Sorcha indignantly. 'That wasn't why I said it! It's a bit much to have my magnanimous gesture thrown back in my face!'

But to her astonishment everyone started clapping,

and even Cesare was giving a grim kind of smile—and, oh, *why* should that feel like a far greater achievement than quadrupling sales?

Because she had missed him like mad, in spite of all the things he'd said to her in bed that afternoon in the hotel? Because she couldn't sleep at nights for thinking about him and he was still obsessing her waking hours, no matter how much she tried?

Had she thought that he might come in here this morning and brush her lips with his when there was a quiet moment, murmur that he'd like to see her alone in his office? And what would she have said? Well, yes, obviously.

But she couldn't have been more wrong.

He hadn't made a single indication that he still wanted her. Not one. No accidental brushing against her arm. No manoeuvring to get them alone together. Nothing. Had he decided while he'd been away that it was better if the affair ended?

'Well, I think that's everything,' Cesare was saying. 'Enjoy Berlin, Rupert.' He looked up as Sorcha stood up. 'Would you mind staying behind for a moment, Sorcha?'

Her heart slammed against her ribcage and a wave of dizziness swept over her. 'Of course.' She waited until everyone had trooped out of the room and looked at him expectantly, wondering if her face hid her terrible fear that it was all over. 'What is it?'

'No ideas about what might be on my mind?'

She was about to say, *I'm not really in the mood for*

riddles, when something in his eyes stopped her. 'This is a…well, it's a bizarre situation, isn't it? You coming back after everything that's—'

He cut across her words with a ruthless statement. 'You still want me.'

It was not a question.

There was a pause as she looked at him.

'Yes.'

'And yet you do not take the initiative?' He walked over to the window and leaned against it, his legs slightly apart, hands resting on his narrow hips. 'You do not ring me while I am away, or send me a text. Or even come into work early this morning, knowing that I am back.' *Waiting for you.*

His lips curved into a mocking smile. 'What's the matter, Sorcha? For all your professed love of equality and independence are you really one of those little-girl lovers who have to be seduced? Perhaps to absolve them from any guilt that they might feel?' His black eyes glittered. 'So that if a man starts to kiss them and touch them they feign a little resistance—and when they can resist no more and give in… Well.' He shrugged his shoulders. 'Then they have no one to blame but the man.'

'Who's talking about blame?' Sorcha shifted uncomfortably. 'Not me.'

'So how long are we going to keep up this ridiculous charade of pretending that we don't want something when we're dying to give in to it? You want me, Sorcha.

So why the hell don't you come over here and have me, before time runs out?'

'Before time runs out?' she echoed. 'What do you mean?'

He laughed. 'Are you crazy? Do you think that I'm going to carry on staying at that…*hotel*, keeping an eye on your little company, when I have plenty of my own to run? Do you think I'm here for keeps—to be your lover whenever the whim takes you?'

Sorcha winced. It was funny the games that your mind could play on you. She had always known he would go, and yet some part of her had imagined him staying here, frozen in some kind of time warp, until some kind of resolution had been made. Except that there wasn't going to be a resolution. They were just two very different people who happened to be overwhelmingly attracted to each other.

The best sex he'd never had.

For Sorcha it was different, because she had grown to realise that Cesare meant more to her than that. He always had done. The love she had felt at eighteen had been real enough, but as fragile and as tender as her age. He had frightened her then, with his lack of emotion, and that was why she had hit out blindly and rejected him. Deep-down she had known that it had been the right thing to do—but hadn't she always regretted that it had ended the way it had?

She knew that she had wounded his pride, and maybe he would never forgive her for that, and yet she wanted to get closer to him and didn't know if that was possible. No one was saying they could go back—but couldn't they build on the huge and obvious attraction between them? Didn't men relax their guard when they had sex with a woman? Even a man as formidable as Cesare?

And now he had told her that his time here was limited—it was down to that old thing of choice again. Should she live for the moment and remain his lover? Or should she opt for her own kind of pride and withdraw gracefully while she still had the opportunity to do so?

She turned her back on him and Cesare felt the sharp tang of disappointment. But he would get over it. There was no way he was going to beg. Until he saw her walk over to the door and lock it, and then come back towards him, unbuttoning her blouse as she did so.

His eyes narrowed in question. 'Sorcha?' He swallowed with difficulty.

'What?' The final button freed, she took the blouse off and hung it carefully over the back of a chair. 'Can't have it creased for my meeting this afternoon, now, can I?' she questioned innocently.

'Sorcha—'

He made to move, but she stayed him exactly where he was with an imperious gesture. Her hand reached round to unclip her skirt and then to slide the zip down. She stepped out of it, folded it, and hung it next to the blouse.

She turned to face him wearing nothing but a lacy bra, panties, silk stockings and a suspender belt. And high heels. Cesare swallowed. Oh, those heels! Briefly, he closed his eyes.

'Have you missed me?' she questioned.

'Yes.'

'Then come away from the window,' she told him, 'and show me how much.'

For a moment he honestly wasn't sure whether he could move, but somehow he managed it. Loosening his tie, he began walking towards her, and something in his eyes made hers widen.

'Cesare?' she questioned uncertainly.

He gave a low laugh. 'What's the matter, Sorcha?' he murmured as he stood in front of her. 'Bitten off more than you can *chew*?' And he took her unprotesting hand and ran it along the hard ridge of his erection, shuddering as he did so.

'Feel in my back pocket,' he suggested silkily.

She did, kneading his buttock as she extracted a condom. 'Do you always come prepared?' she questioned unsteadily.

'I don't always come,' he murmured, wryly remembering their first rather one-sided encounter on the boardroom table.

'Then I'd better make sure you do today,' she whispered.

'Oh, Sorcha.'

The way he said her name made her want to dissolve. She wanted to kiss him—tiny, tender kisses on every centimetre of his silky olive skin—but she suspected that kissing wasn't part of this erotic scene they seemed to be making up as they went along. And kissing made her weak—whereas seduction was giving her power.

She undid his belt and unzipped him, carefully freed him—easing him out into the palm of her hand—and he moaned.

'Shhh. I don't want anyone to know what we're doing.'

He found the fact that she had told him to be quiet unbearably erotic—almost as erotic as her kicking off her own tiny panties, pushing him down to the floor and then straddling him.

'How's *that?*' she questioned disingenuously as she lowered herself down to sheath his silken steel column.

He shook his head, unable to speak, unable to do anything except helplessly lie there while she rode him. Oh, sweet heaven…

He began to cry out as sweet release seized him, and she lowered her head to capture his mouth, her lace-covered breasts covering him with their warm curves as she kissed him. And still she thrust her hips towards him, so that as his pleasure began to fade out her own orgasm swept her away, and she arched her body like a bow.

He caught her bottom and anchored himself to it, watching as she threw her head back and moaned—silky hair tumbling all the way down her back.

When it was over, they stayed exactly where they were—controlling their unsteady breathing, staring at one another in quiet disbelief.

'What's Italian for "wow!"?' mumbled Sorcha.

'It's the same.' He stroked his hand over her waist reflectively, and then lifted his arm to glance at his watch. 'Better move, baby,' he murmured, with the lightest of smacks on her bottom. 'I have a phone call to make.'

'Sure.' Somehow Sorcha kept her face composed, even if his words made her feel like a discarded hooker.

But you shouldn't start a no-strings office affair unless you could accept it for what it was.

Sex.

CHAPTER TEN

'How about some coffee?'

Cesare looked up from the paperwork he'd been working his way through at his desk, and his eyes narrowed as they focussed on Sorcha.

'What?' he questioned, and rubbed at his temples.

'Coffee,' said Sorcha, wondering why she couldn't get rid of the feeling that she just wanted to shake this whole situation to make it the same as it had been before he'd left for his long trip to the new factory, the States and Italy. But she couldn't. And it wasn't.

In the bittersweet days since he'd returned Sorcha thought he'd been distancing himself from her—despite the red-hot satisfaction of their sex-life. Was it just a kind of preparation for his eventual departure? Or was it just her paranoia?

Cesare stifled a yawn. He had worked late last night, after everyone else had gone home, and then done a conference call with LA. And since he'd arrived that morning he'd been ploughing through a pile of papers with Sorcha on the other side of the table until she had disappeared into the private cloakroom a few minutes ago.

Now she had reappeared, and it seemed that she had taken off her shoes and stockings. Cesare saw the glint in her shimmering green eyes and guessed from their hungry expression and from the way she was walking that her panties must have come off too.

She wasn't just offering him coffee, that was for sure.

'I'd love some,' he replied blandly.

Sorcha frowned. 'Coffee?'

He leaned back in his chair and studied her, rubbing his eyes. 'That *was* what you were offering me, *cara*— unless my ears were mistaken.'

Giving him a slightly unsure smile, Sorcha dropped her shoes onto the carpet and walked over to the coffee machine, where she fiddled around and poured two espressos, then put them both on his desk.

'Here you are.'

'Thanks.'

She watched him pick his up and sip it, and frowned. She had thought that he might have telephoned her last night when he'd finished working. She had been willing to slip over to the hotel to see him—but he hadn't phoned.

And she had deliberately arrived at the office early this morning—but he had sauntered in after Rupert, and there had been back-to-back meetings all day. All she'd been able to do was look at him with a kind of helpless longing and growing frustration.

She felt as if she was doing a balancing act the

whole time—trying to appear cool and not look as if she was some desperado whose world was going to cave in after he'd gone.

But even she had her limits—and surely, as his lover, a few rights, too? She drew a deep breath. 'So, are you going to tell me what's wrong?'

'Wrong?' Cesare put his cup down, and now Sorcha could see the shadows beneath his eyes and a pang of guilt suddenly hit her. 'Why should anything be wrong?'

'I just thought…' Her words tailed off as she read something in his eyes she didn't recognise.

He stood up and came towards her.

'What?' he demanded. 'You thought that something might be wrong because for once I didn't leap up and start tearing at your clothes when you snapped your pretty little fingers?'

'But I thought that's what you like to do!' Sorcha stared at him. 'You've never complained before.'

'Of course I haven't!' he said, in a voice of dangerous silk. 'Because what man in his right mind would complain when a woman is constantly demanding mind-blowing, erotic, no-strings sex and demanding that *he* keep it secret?'

'Presumably you have your reasons,' she said coolly.

Cesare stared at her in frustration. It was the fantasy that most men dreamed of—and he was fulfilling every sweet, sensational second of it.

He had tried telling Maceo about it over dinner in Rome last week, and the photographer had told him that

if he was really complaining he needed to see a psychi-
atrist, because no-strings relationships were the only
ones which worked—and did he think Sorcha might be
interested in doing more modelling? Cesare had swallowed a mouthful of wine and told his friend to go to hell.

Cesare studied Sorcha thoughtfully. 'We never
spend the whole night together—never sleep together,'
he observed.

'That might be a bit of a giveaway, don't you think?'
she asked. 'Some bright spark like my mother or my
brother might put two and two together and very
cleverly come up with the answer of four!'

Cesare knitted his dark brows together. *Maledica la
donna!* 'And we never eat together,' he observed.

'That's not true,' she protested. 'We often have a
working lunch.'

Sure they did. Tongue sandwiches in a deserted lay-by.

'*And* we had dinner with my family on Sunday—you
know we did!'

'Yes, I know that,' he agreed dangerously. 'And when
we weren't being forced to endure a hundred damned
wedding photos which all looked the same—you spent
the whole time studiously avoiding looking at me except
when was absolutely necessary. I will tell you something, Sorcha—if anything is designed to alert them to
the fact we're having an affair, then that certainly is!'

'Since when did you become such an expert in
human behaviour?' she demanded.

He stared at her. 'Since I started dating— *Dating?*'

He gave a hollow laugh. 'Let me rephrase that—since I started having sex with a woman who thinks no further than the nearest erogenous zone!'

She rushed at him with her clenched hand raised to pummel him in the chest, but he caught her easily by the wrist and brought her up close to him.

He could see her eyes dilating so that the green was almost completely obscured by ebony saucers of desire. And he could feel her breath warm against his skin— her lips so close that he could almost taste their sweetness. And how easy it would be. How ridiculously easy.

'Oh, yes,' he taunted. 'You want me now, don't you, Sorcha? You want me right now.'

'You know I always want you,' she answered in confusion. 'Did you…did you start the row deliberately to….?' But she saw the expression of contempt in his eyes and knew that her assessment had gone horribly, horribly wrong.

'You think I wanted to inject a frisson of imaginary *conflict* into our relationship?' he demanded incredulously, and he let her hand fall from his as if it was something contaminated. 'Dear God!'

He walked away from her—away from her sweet allure and her dangerous kind of magic. He looked out of the window at the summer clouds blowing across the sky.

'My wild little Sorcha, who is always up for sexual adventure,' he murmured. 'Anyway, anywhere and anyhow. God forbid that we should just go home to bed at the end of the evening, like any other couple!'

Incredulously, she stared at the formidable set of his back. 'Is that what you want?'

He turned again and his face was expressionless. 'It is too late for that, Sorcha—don't you understand?'

She shook her head, as if trying to dispel the confusion. 'No, I don't understand!'

He shrugged. 'We have forged the pattern of our relationship. It is what it is. We work and we have sex—and now that the work is coming to an end…well, it follows that the sex will, too.'

There was silence.

'Is that all it's been?' she questioned painfully. 'Sex?'

'How would you describe it, then?' he challenged softly.

And suddenly she realised what he was doing. 'Why are you turning this around on me?' she demanded, acknowledging how clever he was. Emotionally, he had pushed her away and sought refuge in sex, and now he was accusing *her* of compartmentalising! She couldn't win, she thought—or rather Cesare didn't want her to. There would be only one winner in this scenario, and he was going to make sure it was him.

'You're the man who runs a million miles away from feelings!' she stormed. 'If I've acted this way, it's only because that's the way you intimated I *should* act. What's the matter, Cesare—are you angry because I've actually gone along with it?'

'That is *enough*!' he gritted.

'No, it isn't! We never talk about the things which are going on inside, do we? Like we never talk about when you asked me to marry you—'

'I don't want to discuss it, Sorcha!' His voice cracked out like a whip.

'Well, I do! You wouldn't listen to me when I tried to explain myself, to tell you that you were frightening me with your list of suitable qualities you desired in a wife. I was eighteen years old, for God's sake, Cesare, and I really loved you. All I wanted was some love and affection in return—and you couldn't give it to me.'

She waited, wanting some reaction, some denial, or even a furious justification—but there was nothing. His face was like ice, his expression frozen, and Sorcha let out a shuddering breath. Nothing had changed, not really. Back then he hadn't been listening, and he wasn't listening now.

'I'm sorry,' she whispered, because she saw now that she had been wasting her time in ever thinking that they could build something new on the rocky foundations of the past.

'Sorry?' He was angry. How dared she do this to him? Why *should* he subject himself to unnecessary emotional pain, when it was easier just to lose himself in the silken-soft sweetness of her body? And, oh, when he was far away from England he would find himself another woman—one who wouldn't torture him like Sorcha did with all this *stuff*.

He gave a cool smile—which concealed the decision

being made—and he felt a familiar sense of liberation from having made it.

'Cesare?' she whispered tentatively.

'Lock the door,' he ordered.

Sorcha did as he asked, but something was different—or rather, *he* was different. He drew down the blinds and shut the world out so that the light in the office was muted and it was as if they had created their own private world.

And then he took complete control—as if he was giving her a masterclass in seduction. The Latin lover personified, he skimmed his fingertips over her skin, lowering his head to graze his lips over her neck, carrying her over to the leather couch at the far end of the room and laying her down on it.

Her bright hair was tumbled all over her flushed face and he reached down to brush a wayward lock away. Sorcha's eyes suddenly shot open, for something had *changed* and she couldn't work out what it was.

'Cesare?' she whispered again

'Shhh.'

He kissed the tip of her nose, then her eyelids, and then her lips, and it was easy to let her misgivings melt away beneath the expert skill of his touch. She shut her eyes tight as he stroked her and murmured soft words in his native tongue into her ear, and she had to bite back her own desire to tell him how much she—

Her eyes snapped open as he entered her, and he stilled.

'What is it?'

Sorcha swallowed. 'Nothing,' she whispered. She tangled her fingers in his thick dark hair as he moved again, and the sweetness of the act was enough to push crazy and stupid thoughts out of her head.

I don't love you, she thought brokenly. *I don't want to love you.*

Afterwards, they lay there, with Sorcha struggling to get her thoughts back on some kind of normal track, but she felt as if she were trying to wade through treacle as she battled to tell the difference between what was real and what was fantasy.

You don't love him.

He lifted her off him and began pulling on his clothes again. 'I'm catching a flight to Rome this evening,' he said.

'But you've only been back a few days!'

'I need to have one last look at those figures. And get a few things straight in my mind.' He gave a brisk, slightly efficient smile—she had seen him use it with the secretaries, but never with her. *Never with her.*

'The company is doing just fine,' he continued. 'The new factory is up and running—in fact, the relaunch has succeeded beyond my wildest dreams.'

He spoke in the gentle tone of a doctor who was delivering a horrendous prognosis to a patient—a mixture of kindness and resignation. She wanted to grab hold of his broad, strong shoulders and yell, *I don't care about the company—what about us?*

But something in his eyes stopped her. Was it a warning? That they could do this in one of two ways—

and if they chose the dignified way to end it, then they needed the assistance of their old friend.

Pride.

'You're leaving, aren't you, Cesare?' she questioned, using every effort of will to prevent her voice from breaking.

'You knew I had to leave some time.'

Of course she had. 'And…what will you do?'

'I'll go home to Panicale. I don't want to miss the harvest this year.'

Something in the way he said it made her heart heavy. Her lips framed the question she hardly dared ask, and yet some masochistic urge compelled her to. 'You sound like a man who has a yearning to settle down.'

'Well, of course I do, Sorcha—doesn't everyone? One day I want a family of my own, as I imagine you do, too.'

She saw a glimpse of his future and saw that she had no place in it. So this really was the end. Sorcha swallowed down an impending sense of terrible loss.

She thought about the tips Maceo had given her when he'd been taking her photo. That if you pretended you felt something hard enough, then it would look real to the outside world. And if that was what Cesare really thought of her, then railing against it wasn't going to change his mind.

'What time's your flight?' she asked.

Cesare's face did not betray one flicker of reaction, and indeed he convinced himself that the brief twist of his heart was merely surprise at her response. Why, he should applaud her poise and her cool control. How many times had he told a lover that he was leaving only to have her sobbing and begging and pleading with him not to go, or to take her with him?

His mouth curved into a mocking smile. For once, he had met his match—and the irony was that what made them so alike was the very thing which would ensure they had no future together.

'At eight.' He lifted his arm to glance at his watch. 'I want to go and say goodbye to the staff at the factory.'

'Do you…?' She gave him a tentative smile, but she wasn't going to put him in the awkward position of having to reject her. She injected her question with just the right amount of levity. 'Do you want me to come and do the waving hankie thing?'

It occurred to Cesare that Sorcha Whittaker really must be his nemesis if she could make such a flippant comment when he was walking out of her life for good. Did he really mean so little to her that her beautiful mouth could curve into that cool and unfeeling smile? Damn her…*damn* her!

He hadn't intended this, but he knew that he had to do it one last time. Reaching for her, he snaked his arm round her waist and very deliberately brought her up close, so that she could feel the hot, hard heat of his new erection, and he saw her pupils dilate with surprise and pleasure.

'No need for that,' he murmured. He unzipped himself and sheathed himself in protection for one last time. 'Because when I remember you, I want to re-member you just like…*this*.'

Sorcha was glad that he entered her with that great powerful thrust, and glad when he began to move inside her, so that she could pretend her stifled cry was one of pleasure rather than pain.

Maybe it was better this way.

CHAPTER ELEVEN

'Is SOMETHING the matter, dear?'

Sorcha put the post down on the breakfast table and looked at her mother with a smile which felt as heavy as her heart. 'Wrong? No, of course not. Why should there be?'

Virginia Whittaker poured Earl Grey tea into bone-china cups and added a sliver of lemon. 'You just seem a little…out of sorts?' she observed delicately.

One sure-fire way of getting over something was not keeping it alive by talking about it, so Sorcha took the cup of tea with a bland smile.

'Oh, it's probably all the excitement of my short-lived career as a sauce bottle model,' she said airily.

'And nothing to do with the fact that Cesare di Arcangelo has gone back, I suppose?' questioned her mother shrewdly.

Just the mention of his name brought his dark, mocking face back into her mind with heartbreaking clarity, and yet their farewell seemed to mock her with its cold lack of passion. Two cool kisses on either cheek, followed by an equally cool look in his black eyes.

He had climbed into his sports car with all his stuff—including the brand-new silver beer tankard with his name inscribed on it, which everyone in the factory had clubbed together for and presented to him.

'Cesare's been very popular with the workforce,' Rupert had confided.

Sorcha had ached, and hearing things like that hadn't helped. The fact that everyone else thought Cesare was Mr Wonderful made her wonder what she had done wrong. She felt as if she had missed out—as if she had played it all wrong with Cesare. Except that relationships weren't supposed to be a game, were they?

And added to her sense of loss was the certainty that the factory was too small for more than one boss. This was Rupert's niche, not hers—and now it was too full of memories of Cesare for her to ever be able to settle. She certainly couldn't carry on living at home like this, but her flat was let out for the whole year. They had offered her a post in the new factory, but she didn't want to uproot herself and go and live in a part of the country where she knew no one—because that would surely only increase her isolation.

Her mother's voice broke into Sorcha's thoughts. 'And I suppose you must be missing your affair with him?'

The bone-china cup very nearly met an untimely end, and Sorcha put it down with a hand which was trembling.

'You…you *knew?* You knew I was having an affair with Cesare?'

Virginia sighed. 'Oh, Sorcha—of *course* I knew. Everyone knew. It was as obvious as the nose on your face—even though you did everything you could to try to hide it.'

So all that effort had been for nothing! Her attempts to make it seem as if it were not happening had been totally transparent—and in so doing she had lost the opportunity to spend a whole night with him.

'Maybe I'm not such a good liar as I thought I was,' she said, swallowing down the sudden salty taste of tears which tainted her mouth.

'Are you in love with him?'

'No.'

'I agree, Sorcha,' said her mother wryly. 'You're actually a hopeless liar.'

'Mum, I'm *not* in love with him. I'm… It's…*complicated.*' She sighed. 'We've got history and, yes, we're hugely attracted—but he wants the kind of woman who's docile and will fit in with whatever he wants, while I'm…'

Her voice tailed off. Just what *was* she? And what did *she* want? The things which had once seemed so important to her now seemed to have lost their impact. As if she had been seeing the world in a certain way and it had suddenly blurred and changed its focus without her realising it.

'I'm an independent woman,' she finished, with a touch of defiance. Someone who neither wanted nor needed anyone else—yet look what had happened, no matter how much she tried to deny it. She both wanted and needed a man who did not reciprocate her feelings.

Her mother sliced through a ripe peach. 'Has he been in touch?'

Sorcha shook her head. 'He phoned Rupert after he told him about the small business award we've been nominated for.'

'Well, that's good news, isn't it, darling?'

'I suppose so.'

'And even if things haven't worked out with Cesare there are plenty of other men. I can't tell you how many people have been coming up to me in the village and saying how it brightens their day when they pick up their sauce and shake you all over their omelette!'

Great, thought Sorcha. Nice way to be remembered.

Naturally, being nominated for a small business award was good publicity, and Sorcha was pleased for the company—and even more pleased to see how happy Rupert was.

'Cesare gave me the confidence to believe in myself and the business,' he had said quietly. 'And now I do.'

Bully for Cesare, thought Sorcha sourly.

She went through the mechanics of living—presenting to the world a close approximation of what Sorcha Whittaker was like. But inside it was like having something gnawing away at her and leaving a great, gaping hole. Had she once wondered if it was possible to feel as deeply as she had done as a teenager? Now she knew the answer certainly to be yes—but what she had not banked on was the level of pain, the aching deep inside her that she couldn't seem to fill with anything.

And then an invitation dropped through the letterbox— a stiff cream card, heavily embossed with gold, inviting Sorcha to a retrospective of Maceo di Ciccio's work in a prestigious gallery situated on the Thames in London.

'Are you going?' asked Emma, who was almost unbearable to be with—her 'loved-upness' so tangible that it seemed to be emanating from her in waves, even all these weeks after her honeymoon.

'I haven't decided.'

'Oh, do *go*, Sorcha—he might have included a photo of you, in your famous gingham apron!'

'Very funny.'

'And anyway,' Emma added mischievously, 'Cesare might be there.'

'Oh, *do* shut up,' said Sorcha crossly.

But he *might* be, mightn't he?

Was that why Sorcha took such inordinate care about her appearance—even going to the rather devious lengths of wearing a floaty skirt.

Just so he can put his hand up it? mocked the voice of her conscience and she drew herself up short— because, yes, that was the truth of it. Cesare liked women wearing skirts and dresses—he had said so— and here she was, conforming to his idea of what a woman should be. Wasn't that disgraceful?

But she didn't change. Instead she drove into London

with a fast-beating heart, and had to park miles away from her eventual destination.

It was a windy day, and the river was all silver as a pale, ineffectual sun struggled to make itself seen.

The gallery was beautiful—vast, with huge windows, and lit with the double dose of light which bounced off the restless water.

There were photos from every phase of Maceo's development as a photographer. Moody black and white shots of the backstreets of a city she took to be Rome, and countless pictures of the world's most beautiful women. He was good, thought Sorcha wryly.

In fact, he was more than good, she thought as she came across some of the tougher themes he'd handled: war and famine, natural and man-made disasters— photos which made you want to rail at the injustices in life.

And then—nerve-rackingly and unexpectedly—she came across a photo of herself. It was not, as Emma had teased, an advertising shot taken in the ghastly gingham apron, but a close-up taken when she hadn't realised that the camera had been trained on her.

She had been looking up, a look of consternation on her face, her eyes big and lost—as if something had just been wrenched away from her. And she knew just when it had been taken. When she had heard the door slam. When Cesare had jealously stormed out of the studio because Maceo had been getting her to pout and flirt outrageously.

She stared at the picture she made—a picture of longing and uncertainty, of a woman who was on the brink of falling in love again. But Cesare would not have seen that. He would only have caught the split-second before, when her face had assumed a seductive mask to sell a product. Yet here she was without the mask—and, oh, Maceo had managed to penetrate right through to the raw emotions beneath. Cesare was right—his friend had a real talent for seeing what was really there.

'Do you like it?' asked a velvety voice at her side, and Sorcha turned her head to see Maceo standing there, studying his own photo intently and then turning his head to look at her with his hard, brilliant eyes.

'It's…'

'Revealing?' he murmured.

'Possibly.'

She thought how edgy he seemed today, in his trademark black, with none of the flamboyant behaviour he'd displayed in the studio. Or was that because she no longer had the protective presence of Cesare in the background?

Suddenly she felt a little out of place. It struck Sorcha that Maceo had his own mask which he donned whenever he needed to. Everyone did. She just wondered what lay behind Cesare's. She looked around. Was there the slightest chance that he *might* be here?

Maceo raised his dark brows. 'Have you seen him?' he asked coolly.

If it had been anyone else she might have said, Who?—but it wasn't just Maceo's camera lens which stripped away the artifice, Sorcha realised, as those black eyes pierced through her.

'You mean he's here?' she questioned, her heart leaping with painful hope in her breast.

His mouth curved into an odd kind of smile. 'No. He isn't here. I meant his photo.'

Sorcha shook her head. 'No. No, I haven't.'

His eyes had narrowed and he seemed to be subjecting her to some kind of silent assessment. 'Come with me,' he said softly.

Sorcha followed him across the silent polished floor of the gallery, aware from the glances and the little buzz of the spectators that he had been recognised, but a small phalanx of assistants walking at a discreet distance kept any fans at bay.

He took her into a room that she hadn't noticed, a smaller one, with family photos—obviously his—and Sorcha had to bite back a gasp as she saw the terrible poverty in which he had grown up.

And then her gaze alighted on a group shot of some teenage boys in singlets and jeans, all with their arms folded, gazing with suspicion at the camera.

She saw Cesare immediately—to her prejudiced eye he looked the fittest and the strongest, and of course the most stunningly handsome of the lot. But how young he looked—extraordinarily young. And something else, too...

'How old was he when this was taken?' she questioned slowly.

'Eighteen.'

Eighteen. The age *she* had been that summer, when he had come to the house, when she'd felt so mixed and jumbled up inside, so frightened of the future and all the consequences of her choices.

Yet here on Cesare's face was the similar uncertainty of youth—the sense of standing on a precipice and not knowing whether you should step back to safety or take that leap of faith into the unknown. Had she imagined that he had never known a moment's uncertainty or doubt—even as a teenager?

Yes, of course she had. When she had met him he had been in his mid-twenties—polished and sexy and supremely confident. But that was just the external packaging.

What lay beneath?

When she'd turned down Cesare's proposal of marriage she had known that his pride had been wounded—but what about his heart? She hadn't even considered that, because she had only thought about how *she* felt. Why had she never credited him with having feelings like she did—of pain and hurt and fear of loneliness?

Just because he behaved in a shuttered way and didn't show his emotions, it didn't mean he didn't *have* them, did it? Why, she had never even stopped for a moment to wonder just *why* he behaved that way. She had never dared try to explore the substance of the man under the brilliant patina of charisma and success.

She had never allowed herself to consider that there was a chance that somehow they *could* be happy. And would she ever forgive herself if she didn't find out?

She stared at the photo of the teenage boy, knowing that she had to be willing to put her feelings on the line and run the risk that she might be rejected. The risk which Cesare had talked of didn't just apply to businesses, but to relationships, too. It was part of life. But this time a rejection would be final. A clean break. A sharp and terrible hurt, but one from which she could allow herself to heal properly and rid herself at last of the terrible ache of regret.

She turned to the photographer. 'Thanks, Maceo,' she said, a little shakily.

He shrugged. *'Ciao, bella,'* he said coolly.

He doesn't approve of me, thought Sorcha suddenly, and wondered what it was she was supposed to have done. But she wasn't going to let Maceo's opinion of her distract her from what she knew she had to do.

She rang the airline from her mobile and learned that there was a flight to Rome later that afternoon. Grateful to a college lecturer who had once told her to always carry her passport with her 'just in case', she booked it. Well, why not? she asked herself. What was the point in delaying?

She drove to Heathrow and parked, and there was time before the flight to buy some underwear, toiletries and a phrasebook—it wasn't until she was mid-air that Sorcha began to realise that this was pretty rash. But it felt better just *doing* something instead of moping around at home. Regrets were terrible things. They ate away at you and eroded your chances of finding peace and contentment.

But by the time she found a delighted taxi driver who was willing to take her out to Panicale, she was seriously beginning to question the wisdom of her actions.

Was she mad?

The motorway cut through huge patchwork mountains where toffee-coloured cows grazed and fields of sunflowers became more muted as the sun set and nighttime began to fall.

The driver was obviously labouring under the illusion that his cab was a sports car, and Sorcha tried to distract herself by staring out at the cloudy sky and wondering if she should have phoned Cesare to tell him she was on her way.

No.

She needed to see his face, his first instinctive reaction to her. Some heated things had been said in their conversation before he'd left—words which he might or might not have meant—just like some of the things she'd said.

And how was she going to explain her sudden bizarre appearance? She would be guided by him—if he scooped her up into his arms and told her that there hadn't been a moment when he'd stopped thinking about her...

She leaned back in the seat and closed her eyes. Oh,

please. They would hold each other tight, and she would have to show him that she *did* have a heart that loved and yearned and beat like a drum only for him.

And if he didn't?

That was the risk she ran—and anyway, it was too late to back out now, because the car was squeezing through a narrow stone arch over a track which seemed to bump upwards for ages. But there were the lights of habitation in the distance, and Sorcha's heart was in her mouth as the cab drew to a halt.

'Quanto e esso, per favore?' she asked.

The driver gave her a price, and it was expensive— but then the journey had taken close to two hours.

Sorcha remembered the other word she had learned on the plane. *'Per favore…attesa?'* Because she needed him to wait in case Cesare wasn't there—or in case the unthinkable happened and he didn't want to see her. Or he was with another woman.

'Si, signorina.'

The air was heavy and close, and Sorcha thought she heard the distant rumble of thunder. Tiny beads of sweat sprang up on her forehead and her hands were literally shaking as she walked across the soft grass towards the villa, where she could make out splashes of light which shone through an abundance of trees.

What was she going to say?

The door was open, and she stepped inside and heard voices and laughter and chatter and, incongruously, a baby crying. Her eyes opened in alarm.

What had she done? For a moment she almost imagined that Cesare had been living some kind of bizarre double life—that he had been conducting an affair with *her* while secretly flying back here to see his wife and child.

But she knew that he would never do that—in her heart she knew that Cesare was a man of principle and integrity, and that such a double betrayal would be alien to his nature.

So did this mean he was having some kind of *party?*

It certainly sounded like it.

She felt like someone in a film as she walked silently along the long corridor towards the sounds of merriment. As if she would find…

What?

The sound was coming from outside, on the far side of the house, and Sorcha walked through a vast kitchen and open-plan dining room to where she could see candles guttering on a table on the terrace.

Ignoring the small shout of consternation from a chef who was swirling flames around in a frying pan, Sorcha stepped onto the terrace to see a table set for dinner and four adults seated around it, plus a small child.

Five faces turned towards her, and the conversation dried up as if some celestial director had muted the sound. Only the child gurgled.

Sorcha barely registered the faces of the others— only distantly noting that one was male and two were female. How neat. How tidy.

Cesare was staring at her with an expression she didn't recognise. There was no smile. No word of welcome. Nothing but the cold glitter of disbelief in his black eyes.

'Madre di Dio!' he ground out beneath his breath, and rose to his feet.

CHAPTER TWELVE

CESARE stared at her and felt the great slam of his heart against his ribcage, its sudden powerful pounding as it leapt into life. 'Sorcha?' he demanded. 'What are you doing here?'

It was the greeting from hell—or at least from her very worst nightmare. Keep calm, Sorcha, she told herself as she felt herself sway a little. You have a get-out clause for just this eventuality—remember?

'There's a taxi waiting for me,' she said calmly, as if women just arrived from England at any old time and then turned straight back again. 'I'll…I'll go back to the airport.'

'Don't be so absurd,' said Cesare, but the coolness in his voice remained. 'I will go and dismiss him. Sit down—you look terrible. Luca will pour you some wine. This is Sorcha, everyone.'

He spoke in rapid Italian and the other man immediately stood up to pull out an available chair for her—at the end of the table, naturally, as far from Cesare as it was possible to be.

Sorcha didn't want to sit down. She wanted some giant hand to magic her away from here, from the bemused and frankly unwelcoming expressions of the people around the table. But she was feeling distinctly shaky, and she also recognised that it would look utterly ridiculous if she just disappeared again.

'Here.' Luca pressed a glass of red wine into her hand and Sorcha sipped it gratefully, nodding a kind of greeting at their collective faces, as if trying to resurrect a little bit of social grace in a situation which certainly didn't feature in any etiquette book.

They were all Italian—and why would they be anything else?

One of the women said, 'You have travelled far?'

'From…England, actually.' How bizarre it sounded.

It seemed difficult to follow that, and no one else said a word. They all sat there in an awkward silence and waited for Cesare to return from dismissing the taxi. He seemed to take for ever, but when he did, he was holding aloft a plastic carrier bag which was filled with shampoo, conditioner and knickers. In the darkness, Sorcha blushed.

'Your luggage, I believe?' he drawled, and deposited it by her chair. Then he said something in Italian and some of the frost in the atmosphere seemed to evaporate—but only by a fraction.

He shot her a look. She had taken him by surprise,

and it was not a familiar role for him to be cast in—especially in front of other people. She was on *his* territory, and she must understand that they did things differently here. If she was expecting him to drop everything and leave the table in order to…what? Why was she here?

A smile curved his lips. 'My friends were concerned that you might be some kind of stalker—some disgruntled ex-girlfriend—but I reassured them that I was unlikely to offer a glass of wine to anyone who posed a threat.'

She knew that he was trying to salvage a fairly impossible situation, but Sorcha could have curled up and died. Yet how else must it look to these sophisticated people?

Because sophisticated they certainly were.

'Let me introduce you,' Cesare said wryly. 'Luca you've met—and this is his wife, Pia, with Gino, my godson.' His black eyes softened as he glanced at the toddler, and then his gaze travelled to the other guest—a woman in black silk, with a blunt-cut raven bob and shiny lips the colour of claret. 'And this is Letizia…'

How easy it was to notice the absence of a wedding ring on the woman's finger, the way she looked up at Cesare and then at Sorcha, the unmistakable body language which said, *He's already taken!* Sorcha met her bright, hard dark eyes.

'Hello,' said Sorcha.

'Do you speak Italian, Sorcha?' asked Letizia guilelessly.

'Unfortunately, no—I don't.'

'Oh, well. Then you will have to suffer our English.' Letizia gave a tinkling little laugh. 'It will be good for us to practise—*si*, Cesare?'

'Effettivamente,' Cesare murmured, his gaze capturing Sorcha's as he lanced her with an impenetrable look. 'I'm *fascinated* to know what has prompted this unexpected visit—and at such an extraordinary time.' He glanced over to the doorway, where a chef was standing with his hands on his hips, looking as if he was about to do battle. 'But, like all great chefs, Stephan is a little temperamental—and as he is just about to serve the entrée it will have to wait until afterwards.'

He raised his eyebrows in imperious query, as if daring her to do anything other than sit there and be guided by him. 'Unless it is so urgent that it cannot wait, Sorcha?'

Oh, yes—sure she was going to blurt it all out *now*.

I think I love you, Cesare. I know how stupidly I've acted, and so I've rushed over here to see if our relationship has any future.

The answer was glaring her in the face as clearly as if he'd spelt it out for her. He was having dinner with a cluster of his mates, which may or may not be part of a packed social calendar. But whether it was or it wasn't didn't really matter—far from sitting around the place moping about her, or even thinking about her, Cesare was living his life.

He had moved on.

'No, that's fine,' she said lightly.

It was the worst meal Sorcha had ever had to endure—and because everyone kept forgetting to speak English she felt more and more of an outsider as every second passed.

But she pushed the food around her plate and tried to keep smiling. At least she was opposite Gino—who was the sweetest little thing and the most amenable of all the guests.

Cesare sipped his wine thoughtfully and stared down the table as she poked a fork uninterestedly at a piece of lettuce. He had never seen her so…

He shook his head. *Why was she here?* Did she have business in this part of Italy? No, of course she didn't. He had heard of travelling light—but three pairs of lacy panties and a toothbrush?

His mouth hardened. Had she decided on a whim that she wanted him? Was that why she had turned up out of the blue like this? Had she been hoping to find him alone and act out some wild sexual fantasy of walking in and pretending that he was a stranger and making hot, silent love to him?

Meeting the burning look of censure in his eyes, Sorcha quickly looked down at her plate. How could she have had the temerity to turn up here like this and try to convince him that in the space of a few days she had undergone a massive change? That she had suddenly discovered she wanted to jack in her supposedly precious career and settle down to a life of cosy domesticity *with him?* Or at least to work out some kind of mid-way compromise. As if he even cared!

Because he hadn't fulfilled his part in her fantasy. *He hadn't asked her to*. He hadn't been sitting, waiting to fling his arms around her and lift her up into the air, to whirl her round and tell her that he loved her and had missed her.

That was only make-believe.

The reality was that he was sitting, laughing and joking with his friends, and it was like seeing a different side of him. In England he had been her powerful and autocratic lover, yes, but never a permanent fixture in her life—he had just dipped in and out of it as mood and circumstance took him. The dark, enigmatic foreigner who always seemed to stand out like an elusive rare breed.

Whereas here he seemed to have become real—it was as if she was watching a black and white photo suddenly begin to glow with glorious colour.

'You are staying long, Sorcha?' asked Letizia suddenly.

'I…' Sorcha glanced up at Cesare, sending out a silent appeal that he come to her rescue, but his black eyes remained flinty and obdurate. 'No,' she finished.

An awkward silence fell over the table, broken only by a distant low rumble of thunder.

Letizia had succeeded in making her feel like the kind of desperado who would stoop to any means to ensnare a captivating and eligible bachelor like Cesare. The kind of woman who would jump on a plane and turn up announced.

They said that eavesdroppers never heard any good

about themselves—well, maybe gatecrashers fared no better. For all she knew, he might have been planning to spend the night with Letizia.

Her face paled as she realised that she was trapped. She had let the taxi go. Beneath the table, her fingers gripped convulsively at the heavy linen napkin. Surely Cesare would not be so insensitive as to put her in one of the spare rooms while he took the luscious Letizia off to his own to spend the night making love to her?

But why shouldn't he? Whatever he and Sorcha had had between them was over—or at least Cesare thought it was. They were not bound by any word or convention. No promises had been made, nor vows.

The clap of thunder was still distant, but loud enough to startle them. The baby began to cry as the candle flames started to dance manically.

'*Caro,* the storm!' said Pia to her husband.

A drop of rain as warm as bathwater and as big as a euro plopped down onto Sorcha's hand.

Pia stood up. 'We must go.'

'Stay,' said Cesare. 'Don't drive in it.'

'If we go now we'll miss it,' said Luca. 'It's miles away.'

'Not that far,' warned Cesare, with a glance skywards.

Another drop of rain fell and one of the candles went out with a little *hiss*—like a villain suddenly disappearing through a trapdoor at the pantomime. And in the urgent scurry with which people began to scramble to their feet Sorcha heard Letizia ask Cesare a question in a low voice.

'*No—va,*' he said to her.

Sorcha was not a betting woman, but she would have staked a fortune on the certainty that Cesare was telling Letizia to go.

Because an unexpected and unwanted guest had turned up?

She said goodbye to them all as the wind began to whip at the tablecloth, but decided to stay behind on the terrace and help Stephan clear the table. At least she could make herself useful—and she wouldn't have to see whether Cesare was kissing Letizia…

Raindrops were thundering onto the wooden table now, napkins and bread were getting sodden, and as she ran back to the table for a return journey she saw a tall, dark figure appear in the doorway. Her sleeve caught a crystal glass and sent it crashing to one of the flagstones, splintering into a hundred glittering shards. She bent down towards it.

'Don't touch it!'

His voice rang out and was caught up by the gathering wind. Sorcha looked up into his face—his dear, beloved face—which was now as hard and as forbidding as granite. His words sounded as if they were little bits of the stone he had chipped off and flung at her.

He strode over to her and caught her by the wrists, but it was an unequivocal capture—there was no tenderness or softness as his fingers bit into her flesh.

'And now you'd better start giving me some kind of explanation!' he ordered.

CHAPTER THIRTEEN

SORCHA stared at Cesare as the rain came down in great sheets and lashed across their faces, but he didn't seem to be aware of the weather—nor of the fact that if he hadn't been gripping her wrists she might have fallen.

All she could see was the whiteness which had appeared beneath his olive skin, and the way the rain-drops had made his eyelashes into little points, so that his eyes looked like dark stars. But there was no smile nor welcome on his face, just the glitter of accusation and of challenge.

'Well?' he demanded, when she did not answer him.

Her breath was coming in shuddering and painful gulps, and the clouds of jealousy which threatened to engulf her were darker than the stormclouds which were hurling down their contents. She thought about what might have happened if she hadn't turned up here tonight and she felt faint. 'Were you going to sleep with her?' she moaned.

His fingers gripped her even tighter. 'Who?'

'Who? *Who?* Letizia, of course!'

Cesare's eyes narrowed, and suddenly he wanted to hit out at her—to hurt her back as she had hurt him, and maybe make these feelings go away. The world was a dull and predictable place without Sorcha, but at least it wasn't full of pain, of torment and uncertainty.

'What *right* do you think you have,' he flared, and even though the rain was striking his face like hammer-blows he barely felt it, 'to just turn up here *out of the blue* and ask me questions like that?'

Right? No right at all. She should have done that thing people always recommended when you went to see a doctor—writing all your questions down in some coherent sort of order to avoid wasting time by saying the wrong thing or making a fool of yourself. And yet the question had released something—it was like loosening some dark, dank floodgate which, once open, couldn't be shut again.

All she could feel was the deluge of raindrops as they thundered down onto the terrace, and the beating of her heart and the terrible wrench of pain there. 'Would you have done?' she whispered.

Her words were lost in the storm, but he read them as they were framed by her trembling lips and he hauled her inside, into the dry, where their bodies dripped water into puddles which lay on the wooden floor.

'Nothing has happened between Letizia and me. But what do you want me to say?' he demanded. 'That the thought of sleeping with her hadn't crossed my mind? Then I'd be lying! That she isn't ready and willing to? Then I'd also be lying! Or that I am going to spend the rest of my life in celibacy because I could never seem to get it right with you? Well, that would be the biggest lie of all, Sorcha.'

Red-hot anguish caught her by the throat so that her words came out like a torrent of lava. 'Maybe I want you to lie!'

He laughed, but it was a mirthless and bitter sound. 'That is, as you say…tough,' he grated. 'There are many things you can say about our relationship—but at least no one can say it wasn't honest.'

She heard the tense he'd used. Past tense. She swayed. It was over.

His black eyes flickered over her, but he didn't loosen his grip. He could feel the rapid thready beat of her pulse beneath the pressure of his fingers. Witch. *Witch.* 'You still haven't told me why you're here.'

And Sorcha knew then that her jealousy—though agonising and very real—was yet another emotional wall she had been trying to hide behind. And wasn't that the mark of a woman who wasn't brave enough to fight for what she wanted?

This wasn't about pride or possession—not any more. And it wasn't about social convention either—about a woman never declaring her feelings for a man before he had indicated his, as if matters of the heart were like some kind of bidding war. This was about telling this man how she really felt about him—because she would never forgive herself if she didn't.

'I'm here because my life seems empty without you.

It's like you lit something in my world and now the light's gone out.' She drew a shuddering breath, because this was the hardest thing of all. To open her heart to him—to leave herself open to the possibility that he might not want her. 'I'm here because I think I love you.'

Cesare stilled, like an animal in the jungle at the dead of night who had heard the sudden rustle of something unknown in the undergrowth. *Love?*

He thought of the times women had declared love for him in the past—but never with that conditional word. I *think* I love you. The word should have made it less believable, and yet somehow it did the exact opposite— for it showed human fragility as well as fearlessness.

He stared at her, at the way her wet hair streamed down around her shoulders, the way her wet dress hugged her body—a water nymph, just like the first time he had ever set eyes on her—and he felt a powerful pull of longing which went bone-deep.

But the barriers he had built around his heart were too high to be toppled by a single word. He lanced her look. 'Maybe you just miss my body the way I miss yours?'

Sorcha licked a raindrop from her lips. Was that bravado she heard lurking behind the mockery of his words? Or was she crediting him with a softness which wasn't really there?

She thought of the eighteen-year-old Cesare in Maceo's photos—of all the hopes and fears in his young face. Of how she'd always thought him strong and in- vincible and somehow immune to the pain of living.

Maybe he didn't want her. Or maybe he didn't want her on the level of anything deeper than just good sex. But she would never know unless she had the courage to follow this through. Now.

Sorcha's heart was beating painfully as she pulled her hands free from his grip and placed one palm softly against his wet cheek.

The candles on the terrace had long been blown out by the wind, but the darkness was illuminated by a fork of lightning, so that everything in the room was silver and black.

Show him, she thought. Just show him how much you care.

'I think I love you,' she said again, and she put her arms around him.

She felt him stiffen, but he did not move, and she uttered a silent prayer as she held him closer, tightening her arms around his soaking body. Please know that this isn't sexual, she prayed. Know that it's because I love you and I want to cherish you—to comfort and protect you as women have always done with their men—no matter how strong or proud or arrogant they may be.

For a while he just stood there, stiff and unmoving, but gradually he made a little sound in the back of his throat and his arms went round her, like a man who had suddenly caught hold of a lifebelt. But his words contradicted his gesture.

'You have chosen the wrong man,' he said harshly, against her wet hair. 'You know that, don't you?'

Sorcha felt the salt taste of her tears as she shook her head. 'No,' she whispered. 'I don't.'

But Cesare didn't trust the torrent of feelings which holding her like this was threatening to unleash.

'You need to get dry,' he stated matter-of-factly, gently pushing her away from him. 'Come with me.'

Sorcha could have wept as he led her down a long corridor to an old-fashioned bathroom—but what choice did she have other than to go with him and submit to getting dry? She could hardly claim that she would prefer to catch a debilitating chill if only he would *look* at her properly.

He was quiet and absorbed as found her a giant warm towel and gave her one of his T-shirts.

'Put this on,' he said abruptly. 'I'll go and make us some coffee.'

And then he left her, struggling and feeling more than a little foolish as she stripped off her soaking clothes and rubbed the big towel over her shivering flesh. The T-shirt came to halfway down her thighs, and her nakedness beneath it made her feel vulnerable. But she felt vulnerable in other ways too—and the heart was a far less resilient organ than the rest of the body.

She found that he had changed into a dry pair of jeans and was just putting two mugs of coffee onto a tray. He glanced up.

'You look shattered, *cara*,' he said slowly, his voice sounding distant against the still-raging storm.

Their eyes met. Could he read the silent appeal in

hers? Or was he simply choosing to ignore it? And if so—what did that tell her? She had come all the way out here, hadn't she? Her pride would not let her throw herself down and beg him to want her, to offer her something from the heart if he had nothing to give. 'I am pretty shattered,' she agreed.

'Then let's take this through and go to bed.'

His eyes and his voice and his body language indicated nothing other than practicality. If it was emotion she had been praying for, then it looked as if she was going to be disappointed.

She followed him into a bedroom which was darkened by creaking shutters which rocked in the storm, and he drew her down onto the bed and into his arms, covering them both with a blanket.

For a moment Sorcha held her breath, but even though he was holding her close to his warm chest—as if he were shielding her from the elements outside—she still felt as lost as if she were wandering around outside in the storm.

He hadn't told her how he felt about her. He hadn't mentioned anything about whether they had any kind of future—but she told herself that wasn't the reason she had confessed her feelings. She'd said it because she had needed to—and because he'd needed to hear it. Even if they were destined never to be together she knew she would never have forgiven herself if she hadn't.

But her heart ached as they lay there while the wind raged and the storm lashed and the sound of thunder split the sky. Tight in his arms, her head on his shoulder while he stroked her hair, Sorcha stared at the dark shapes around the room until her eyes began to grow tired, and then her eyelids drifted down and she slept.

When she awoke, it took a moment or two for her to remember where she was—and with the calmness of morning came a sense of disbelief. Had she really just flown out here on a whim and told Cesare that she loved him?

She looked at the man in the bed beside her and moved a little. But Cesare was still sleeping. She wriggled away from him but he didn't stir. How ironic it was that she should have longed for so long to sleep with him, and that—when it had finally happened—the reality had been nothing like her dreams. They had shared the same bed with a chasteness which now seemed to mock her.

She went to the bathroom and washed her face and hands, and then, her head and her heart still full of uncertainty, went outside.

In the fresh, rain-washed light of the morning in the aftermath of the wild storm the villa looked exquisite. It was all so very beautiful—and so unexpected.

Sorcha had never imagined that roses could grow close to olive trees—but there were fragrant pale pink roses with water still dripping from their petals as they curved over an arbour which led from the house, and an olive grove glinted silver in the distance. The vineyard lay to the other side of the villa, with its rows upon rows of fruit-laden vines. The grass was green, and so were the huge mountains which provided such a stunning backdrop.

Sorcha felt a lump well up in her throat as she began to walk—because in the clear light of day what had happened yesterday seemed like a strange kind of dream. Almost as if she shouldn't really be here—that she would open her eyes and find herself back in England, putting on a sharp suit and getting ready to go to work.

She clenched her fists by her sides and willed the tears not to spill from her eyes as she stared out at the beautiful Umbrian countryside.

Lazily, Cesare stirred.

He had been having the craziest dream.

He stretched his arms above his head and murmured, and then his eyes snapped open as he turned his head to the empty space beside him and the indentation of where her head had lain on the pillow.

Had he dreamed it?

He sat up in bed and it all came back to him, like a jigsaw taking shape as all the pieces were added. Sorcha turning up in the middle of the dinner party. The storm. The broken glass. Sorcha telling him…

His eyes narrowed.

Sorcha telling him she loved him.

And him doing a pretty passable imitation of a clam.

He found still-damp soap in the bathroom, and the

plastic bag full of her things still outside on the terrace, but of Sorcha there was no sign. He felt the skin-chill of apprehension—even though logic told him she couldn't have gone far. That they were out in the middle of nowhere.

But the logic on which he'd relied all his life suddenly seemed hopelessly inadequate—because Sorcha was strong and resourceful. And proud. Who could have blamed her if she'd decided to walk the few kilometres up the mountain into Panicale, where someone would telephone for a taxi to come out to her? What if she had? *What if she had?*

Unexpectedly, he felt his heart twist with pain.

She had laid her emotions bare for him to see last night—and he had responded with less interest than he might have given to a new business strategy.

Because strategies were safe, and you knew where you were with them—whereas the way she made him feel was…

Scary.

Yet he hadn't given a thought to how *she* must be feeling…to what it must have cost her to come out here like that and tell him what he meant to her. She had made a gesture of humility—stripped away all her pride to tell him how much she cared.

And what had he given her back?

Nothing.

Standing on the terrace, looking down at the silver gleam of the olive groves, he saw something bright moving into his line of vision and his heart missed a beat—because it was Sorcha. Walking towards him, barefooted and wearing a dark T-shirt of his, with her bright hair contrasting against it and cascading down her back, like a beautiful waterfall.

As she grew closer he could see that her eyes were even greener than the lush grass. But they were shadowed with wariness.

'I thought you'd gone,' he said softly as she approached.

'I was…' What? Wondering whether she was in line for the prize of Idiot of the Year. She bit her lip. 'Cesare—'

'I thought you'd gone,' he whispered, and he shook his head like a man who was just emerging into the bright clear day after a subterranean holiday. He reached out and caught her hands in his, turned them over in his palms and looked at them, and then back up at her dazzling emerald eyes.

'I don't know how to do this, Sorcha,' he said softly.

Sorcha's gaze searched his. 'What?'

'To tell you about the emotion you stir up in my soul.' He stared at her, as helpless then as he'd ever felt in his life, and shrugged his shoulders—as if the movement could shift the intolerable weight which lay on them. 'I don't know why.'

She gripped tightly onto his hands, never wanting to let them go. 'Don't you, Cesare? Don't you really?'

He knew what she was doing. On an intellectual side he could see. She wanted him to confront his demons—

to let them out so that they might fly away and torment him no longer. But was it really that simple?

'Tell me,' she whispered, aware of being on fragile ground. One false move and all would be lost.

'People used to pity Maceo and envy me,' he said slowly. 'Because he had come from the slums while I was brought home to a mansion—but you know, Maceo needed nobody's pity. The home he grew up in was a *real* home. With a mother who was there and a father who came home.'

'And you didn't have that?'

He shook his head. 'My father was rich beyond most men's wildest dreams—but it never seemed to be enough. It was as though he needed to go out and earn more and more, to fill some kind of hole that could never be filled.'

And Cesare had done the same, Sorcha recognised. History had repeated itself, as it always did. 'And your mother?'

'Oh, she was very beautiful—and restless. She did not want a world dominated by a baby when her husband was flying all round the globe chasing achievements. She wanted her taste of the high-life, too…'

His voice tailed off and she saw the furrows which deepened his brow. Sorcha drew in a deep breath. It was as if Cesare had drawn the outline of a picture, and now he needed her help to colour it in. And if they were to be a couple, then that was what couples did, wasn't it? They helped one another. They were there for one another. They laid feelings on the line because those feelings mattered—they didn't pussyfoot around or worry about how it might look, or whether they would be hurt.

'She wasn't there for you?' she said.

He nodded, sensing that it was not censure he heard in her voice, but a fair evaluation of the facts. And in confronting those facts he found they somehow assumed less dominance, less power to hurt. 'No, she wasn't there. There were other people to care for me, but it wasn't the same.' He drew in a deep, shuddering breath as he did the unthinkable and confronted his past head-on. 'Maybe that's why it isn't easy for me to show…love,' he said shakily, and gave her a look like a lost little boy. 'Because I haven't had much practice.'

Sorcha stilled. 'Cesare?' she said breathlessly.

He stared down at her. 'I really thought you'd gone when I woke up this morning.'

Her eyes were still wary. She looked into his face—but she wasn't a mind-reader, and she wasn't going to second-guess him for the rest of her life.

'Do you *want* me to go?'

'Go?' He lifted her hand to his mouth and kissed each fingertip in turn, his eyes never leaving her face. 'I never want you to go away again, *cara mia,* because I think I love you, too. And I really must kiss you now.'

It was the first time he had kissed her in his native land, and it was quite unlike any other kiss they'd ever had—for it was a declaration and a seal, a farewell to past misunderstandings and a celebration of all that lay ahead of them.

When it was over, Sorcha bit back the tears which were shimmering in her eyes as she saw all the possible obstacles in their way. 'But how will we work it, Cesare? How can we be together?'

'Somehow,' he promised. 'We can live here—or in England. We *could* live apart, but I don't want that.'

'Me neither.'

His arms tightened around her, and for the first time Sorcha felt the shimmerings of true physical intimacy.

'Now that I've got you, I never want to let you go,' he whispered. 'The logistics are just details. The important thing is us.'

Us.

Such a tiny word, and yet such a big one—the most important word in any vocabulary—English *or* Italian.

EPILOGUE

A LOOK of pride made his black eyes gleam, and Cesare smiled. 'You look beautiful,' he murmured.

'But you can't see me properly!' Sorcha whispered back with a smile. 'Now, shhh—here's the priest.'

Ivory tulle hung over her face like a creamy water-fall, and the bouquet she carried was of pale pink and frilly roses—the closest match Sorcha could get to those which grew around the Villa Pindaro, where she had found her heart's desire on a clear morning after a mountain storm.

Behind her stood Emma as matron of honour. Her sister was newly pregnant and glowing like a lightbulb, and holding her hand was little Gino who, at the age of four, was deemed old enough to be a pageboy. He was behaving wonderfully—apart from the occasional lapse into solemn thumb-sucking.

Sorcha and Cesare hadn't rushed into marriage—they hadn't felt the need to—and they had made so many big life-changes in order to be together that they wanted to enjoy their wedding in a peaceful state of mind. And you couldn't rush peace of mind.

Sorcha had left England and gone to live in Italy—but it had been no great wrench nor an agonising decision. The world had shrunk and travel was easy, and it had felt like the place she both needed and wanted to be—the place she'd decided they would bring up their children, if they were lucky and blessed enough to have them.

Sorcha had jettisoned her career with the family firm— 'Been there, done that, and wasn't particularly brilliant at it,' as she'd said to Maceo. The corporate rat-race no longer held any appeal. Sometimes you just had to do something in order to get it out of your system.

Instead she had set about becoming competent in the business of running an Italian estate. She had learned about the harvesting of the precious olives and the making of di Arcangelo wine. She'd taken lessons in Italian and grown fluent, and had just started giving English classes to the children in a nearby village.

And Cesare had wound down his corporate life, too. He found that he no longer wanted to restlessly travel the globe, making more money than he would ever need. His life was with Sorcha, and she had built for him the first real home he had ever known. She had shown him how to love, and he had discovered—as with every other thing in his life—that he happened to be exceptionally good at it!

He turned now and smiled tenderly at the woman who would soon be his wife. So far so good. The only flies in the ointment were the banks of paparazzi camped outside the church—but he had only himself to blame for asking Maceo to be his best man!

The Whittaker house was ready for another wedding reception and looking glorious—everything was just about as perfect as it was possible to be. For the first time in his life Cesare was looking forward to the rest of it.

'I love you, Sorcha,' Cesare whispered, just before the priest began to speak.

And Sorcha was glad this wasn't a fairytale, because it would now be ending.

Instead of just beginning.

BOUGHT BY
A BILLIONAIRE

BY
KAY THORPE

Kay Thorpe was born in Sheffield. She tried out a variety of jobs after leaving school. Writing began as a hobby, becoming a way of life only after she had her first complete novel accepted for publication in 1968. Since then she's written over seventy-five, and lives now with her husband, son, German shepherd dog and lucky black cat on the outskirts of Chesterfield in Derbyshire. Her interests include reading, hiking and travel.

CHAPTER ONE

At least he hadn't refused outright to see her, although he must be aware of why she was here. Aware of curious glances from staff in the vicinity, Leonie kept her face blank of expression. Vidal's arrival, along with her father's absence, would have given rise to some speculation, but she doubted if the full facts were known as yet.

The man who emerged from what had been her father's office looked far from happy. Leonie couldn't blame him for avoiding her eyes. She only hoped he hadn't lost his job as a result of not realising what was going on.

She waited on tenterhooks for the summons to the inner sanctum herself, dreading the moment of confrontation. It was two years since she had last seen the man she was about to beg for forbearance on her father's behalf. Two years since she had told him he was the last man on earth she would ever consider marrying. If he still held a grudge against her for that put-down there was little chance of his complying with her plea, but she had to try.

The woman seated at the desk her father's secretary normally occupied was new to her; she remembered him saying he'd had a change about a month ago. She looked across at Leonie as the intercom buzzed, curiosity written large in her eyes. 'You can go through now,' she said.

Leonie got to her feet, steeling herself for what was to come. It was on the cards that she would be emerging from the office again in a couple of minutes with Vidal's boot— metaphorically if not physically—behind her. Not that he'd be anything but within his rights in telling her to go take a running jump, so to speak.

It was some time since she'd visited her father at work.

Spacious and well-lit, his office overlooked the river. Leaning negligently against the windowsill, lean and lithe body clad in a silver-grey suit of impeccable cut, Vidal Parella Dos Santos regarded her in silence for a lengthy moment, his tautly sculpted features unrevealing.

'You've changed little,' he observed in excellent Cambridge-acquired English. 'But then, looks such as yours are unlikely to deteriorate.' He indicated the chair set her side of the wide desk. 'Please be seated.'

'I'd as soon stand,' Leonie answered. She drew a steadying breath, meeting the dark eyes full-on. 'I'm sure I don't need to tell you how I feel about what my father's done. He abused your trust in him, and deserves to pay the price for it.'

'But?' Vidal prompted as she hesitated.

'But prison would kill him,' she said.

One black eyebrow lifted sardonically. 'So what are you suggesting? That I allow him to get away with embezzlement?'

Leonie put everything she knew into keeping a steady head. 'I'm asking you to just give him time to put things right again. He can repay what he owes by remortgaging the house.'

'And how would you propose that he even arranges a mortgage without a job?' The smile that crossed the hard-boned face when she failed to answer immediately was almost humorous. 'You expect me to reinstate him too?'

'He's unlikely to get another job at all if you prosecute,' she pointed out. 'Which means he's never going to be in a position to pay back. Obviously it would have to be in a lesser capacity.'

'One denying him any further opportunities to tamper with accounts, you mean?'

Leonie caught herself up, only too aware of being baited. 'It makes more sense than putting him in a cell.'

Vidal studied her strikingly lovely face, framed by the heavy fall of Titian hair, lowering his gaze with deliberation down the shapely length of her body, then back again. She tilted her chin, green eyes sparking as they met his once more. It was still there: the covetousness that had so alienated her in the past. What this man wanted he was accustomed to getting. Her refusal to marry him had been met with total disbelief at first, followed by cold fury when she'd added insult to injury by saying what she had. There had been no need to go that far, she had to acknowledge now. It said something for him that he hadn't taken it out on her father at the time.

More than could be said for her father for certain.

'Did he send you to plead his case?' Vidal asked.

She shook her head. 'This is my idea. I don't condone what he's done, but I'd hate to see him in a prison cell myself. I'm sure it can be taken for granted that he won't be doing any more big-time gambling.'

There was a lengthy pause. Leonie wished she could tell what was going on in the arrogant dark head. She was still here. That in itself gave her some hope.

'You think him ready to carry on here in the circumstances?' Vidal asked at length. 'So far only one other person knows the truth of the matter, but even if he were sworn to secrecy there would be speculation.'

Leonie had been holding her breath without realising it, letting it out now on a cautious sigh. 'Something he'd just have to live with. Part of the price to be paid.'

Vidal straightened away from the windowsill, six feet of vital Portuguese masculinity. 'I need time to consider,' he said. 'I'll give you my answer tonight. My suite.' He shook his head as she opened her mouth to protest, a hard glint in his eyes. 'Eight o'clock. Unless you'd prefer to settle the matter here and now.'

She knew exactly what he meant: the same settlement she would be facing at eight, if she went. There was little point in pleading with him. If she wanted to succeed in her aim, then *she* paid the price too.

She made no effort to conceal her aversion as she looked at him. 'I suppose I should have anticipated this.'

Broad shoulders lifted, his expression unrelenting. 'I'm due some recompense, I believe, but the choice is entirely yours.'

Leonie turned without another word and left the office. She gained the lifts, looking neither right nor left, pressing to descend. Thankfully the cage was empty when it arrived. Facing a sea of faces would have tested her to the limit.

One thing was certain: there would be no renewal of the marriage proposal tonight. Vidal would be seeking to humiliate her as she had humiliated him two years ago. There was one very good way of doing that: by making her submit to him. The very thought of it made her cringe inside, but if it meant keeping her father out of prison she could live with it. She would have to live with it.

It was raining when she got outside. Lacking an umbrella, and unwilling to have the pale beige suede suit she was wearing ruined, she sought refuge in a nearby coffee shop. Others had done the same thing, limiting table space, but she found a seat at the window bar, gazing unseeingly out at the hurrying crowds as she thought about the man she had just left.

One of Europe's leading industrialists, at the age of thirty-five Vidal Parella Dos Santos was regarded as something of a phenomenon. Born into Portuguese aristocracy, he could have idled his way through life any way he chose. Leonie had met him for the first time some weeks after her father had become chief accountant of the London company. She'd been drawn to him at first, she had to admit: few women could fail to find his looks alone an attraction. What she'd taken against was his arrogant assumption that he could have any woman he wanted for the mere asking. It had come as a shock when her refusal to sleep with him had resulted in a proposal of marriage, but she had been under no illusions. All he saw, all he coveted, was the outer shell. He knew nothing of the person she was inside, nor wanted to know.

Once he'd tired of her she would have been discarded, like all his other women.

Her father knew nothing of the proposal. Since losing her mother four years ago, he had shown little interest in anything except work—or so she'd believed. Exactly when the gambling habit had started she wasn't sure. Long enough to have gone through more than eighty thousand pounds of company money, at any rate. Like most gamblers, his losses had far outweighed his gains.

He wasn't going to prison, she vowed. Vidal could have his pound of flesh, if that was what it was going to take. There was always the chance that he would renege on the deal, of course, but she somehow doubted it. Whatever else he might or might not be, his reputation as a man of his word once given was widely known.

It was gone four by the time she reached the Northwood Hills home she still shared with her father. At twenty-six, and earning a decent salary, she could afford a place of her own, even if only to rent, but he refused to move somewhere smaller, and she couldn't bring herself to leave him to rattle around the house in solitude. Not that he might have any choice but to sell up if the worst did come to the worst.

Stuart Baxter was seated at his desk in the study, playing listlessly with the executive toy Leonie had bought him as a joke last Christmas. He looked up at her entry, eyes lacklustre, expression downcast. He'd looked much the same when he'd told her the truth last night.

'I still haven't heard anything,' he said dully. 'I keep expecting to find the police at the door any minute!'

'It may not come to that.' Leonie did her best to sound upbeat. 'I've been to see Vidal. Obviously he's not exactly over the moon about it all, but there's a good chance that he won't be prosecuting. Even a chance that he'll keep you on, if you arrange to pay back the money you've taken.'

Stuart gazed at her in silence for a lengthy moment, a variety of expressions chasing across his face. 'How on earth did you manage that?' he asked at last. 'You hardly know the man!'

Leonie crossed her fingers behind her back. 'I appealed to his better nature.'

'He didn't give the impression of having one when I saw him yesterday.' Stuart paused again, obviously at something of a loss. 'What exactly did you say to him?'

'I gave him my assurance that you'd chop your fingers off rather than risk gambling again,' she said. 'You wouldn't, would you?'

The smile was wry. 'I've learned my lesson on that score, believe me!' He shook his head, still bemused. 'It's more than I could ever have hoped for. More than anyone could hope for!' He hesitated before adding tentatively, 'I suppose everyone knows by now?'

'Only one, apparently, although there'll no doubt be some talk among the staff. Anyway,' Leonie added hardily, 'facing gossip has to be better than going to prison, doesn't it?'

'Yes, of course. Don't think I'm not grateful!' He shook his head again. 'I can still hardly believe he's even considering not prosecuting, much less keeping me on! Did he give any indication of when he might let me know his decision?'

'You should know by tomorrow,' she said, closing her mind to the possibility that it could still all go wrong.

She left him to think about it, heading upstairs to her bedroom. It was a relief to be alone for a while. By eight o'clock she had to be in complete possession of herself, focussed on one thing, and one thing only—getting her father off the hook he'd forged for himself. Easier said than done, when every instinct in her fought against what was to happen, but there was no other choice. Vidal's pride must be satisfied.

Despise him though she did, there was no denying the physical pull he still exercised. She'd felt it the moment she set eyes in him again. There had been media reports linking him with various women over the past couple of years, but none of them had lasted long. If she'd been fool enough to marry him she would very likely have fallen by the wayside herself long before this, with the only difference being that she could, had she been so inclined, have taken him for enough to keep her in comfort for the rest of her life. Some would call her a fool for not seizing the opportunity.

The only foolish thing she'd done was to get involved with him at all, she reflected ruefully. It was hardly as if she'd been unaware of his reputation where women were concerned.

She made no effort when it came to choosing an outfit for the evening, opting for a plain grey skirt and white blouse over her least glamorous underwear. She was allowing herself no emotionalism at all over this affair. It was the only way she was going to get through it.

She had booked a taxi to take her back into town. Expensive, but she didn't feel like facing another train journey. Allowing for all eventualities, she told her father she was meeting a girlfriend from work, and might spend the night at her flat.

Vidal kept permanent hotel suites in several cities. Drawing up outside the Mayfair edifice he graced with his presence when in London— knowing exactly what she faced in there—Leonie felt like some high-class prostitute. There wasn't, she supposed, all that much difference when it all boiled down.

Already in possession of the suite number, she was at least able to avoid asking at reception. The suite itself was on the top floor. She steadied herself with hard purpose before knocking on the solid mahogany door.

Vidal opened it, regarding her with lifted brows as she stood there silently waiting. Dressed now in trousers and casual shirt, he looked no less formidable to her than earlier.

'To the minute,' he observed. 'Come in.'

The doorway was wide. Even so, he was uncomfortably close as she stepped past him into the spacious living area. The place had been redecorated since her last visit—that was her first, totally irrelevant thought. The colour scheme was now a gracious symphony in mingled blues and greys, with touches of scarlet, the carpet underfoot stretching away like a silver-grey sea to the beautifully draped windows. An arrangement of fresh flowers on a side table gave off a delicate scent.

'Nice,' she commented, determined to appear on top of the situation. 'They do you proud.'

'For what it costs, so they should,' came the dry response. 'But you're not here to discuss the décor.'

'True.' Leonie turned to look him in the eye, hating him for what he was forcing her to do; hating herself for doing it. 'I want your assurance re my father before anything takes place between us.'

Vidal slanted a lip. 'You'd take my word for it?'

'Oddly enough, yes,' she said, hoping her faith in at least that aspect of his character wasn't misplaced.

The slant increased. 'Then you have it, of course. A drink before we eat, perhaps?'

'Eat?' She was totally thrown for a moment. 'I thought…'

'You thought I had but the one thing in mind,' he finished for her as she let the words peter out. There was derision now in the dark eyes. 'My sins are many, but crude I have never been.'

'What else would you call this whole…arrangement?' she asked.

'A mutual benefit,' he returned imperturbably. 'You scratch my back and I'll scratch yours—isn't that the saying here? Very appropriate in the circumstances, don't you think?' He didn't wait for any response. 'What will you have to drink?'

About to decline the offer, Leonie abruptly changed her mind. If Vidal was intent on drawing this out, she was going to need some extra stimulus. 'I'll have a gin and tonic.'

He waved a hand in the direction of the nearest sofa. 'Make yourself comfortable.'

That, she thought caustically, was a laugh in itself. She felt like a cat on hot bricks. Her eyes followed him almost involuntarily as he crossed to the drinks cabinet, registering the fluid movement of his body, the ripple of muscle beneath the fine cotton of his shirt, the firm male hemispheres. He must work out regularly to keep himself in such trim, she reflected, unable to keep her physical responses totally under control. Out of bed, *and* in it!

She had taken a seat by the time he had the drinks poured. He made no attempt to sit down beside her, but chose a chair set at right angles, crossing one leg comfortably over the other. The action pulled up his trouser leg enough to reveal a narrow area of bare, bronzed skin. He would be that colour all over, came the thought, hastily thrust aside.

'So what do you suggest we talk about while we wait for our meal to arrive?' he asked. 'Or perhaps it should be my place, as host, to open the conversation?'

'I really don't care,' she said, fighting to maintain a composure threatening to disintegrate any moment.

'So tell me how you enjoyed your trip to Paris last month.'

Green eyes widened in startled question. 'How do you know I was in Paris last month?'

'I've made it my business to know all your movements over the past two years,' he returned without turning a hair. 'I know, for instance, that there isn't now, and hasn't been, any serious relationship with a man.'

'You've been spying on me?' She was too stunned at the moment for anger.

The dark head inclined. 'I prefer to call it taking an interest. *Had* you become involved with anyone, it would have been a short-lived affair.'

'Oh, I see.' The anger was coming through now, bringing her to the edge of her seat, eyes stormy. 'Having had the temerity to refuse you, there was no way I should be allowed to find anyone else!'

'Correct.' There was no note of apology in his tone. 'Did

you really think I was going to simply forget the things you said to me? Do I need to remind you of what you did say?'

Leonie bit her lip, the memory only too clear in her mind. She'd gone overboard in an effort to blot out any temptation to say yes—to burn all bridges in effect. Telling him he was the last man on earth she'd ever consider marrying had been the least of it. Even now, the invective she'd used to ram home the message made her curl up inside.

'So I went a little too far,' she said stiffly. 'I admit that. But it's no excuse for what you've been doing. People go to jail in this country for stalking someone.'

The shrug was dismissive. 'Considering that you yourself never noticed you were under surveillance, I doubt if any such accusation would be taken seriously. Anyway, the question is of little importance now. I've found other means of achieving redress.'

'The word you're looking for is revenge,' she retorted, taking a hold on herself. 'Hardly an honourable aim!'

'But satisfying.' Vidal straightened as a knock came on the outer door. 'Dinner, I believe.'

The waiter who wheeled in the loaded white-clothed trolley was unobtrusive in his movements, transferring the contents to the table in an off-set dining area without speaking. He looked happy enough, however, with the size of the tip Vidal handed over.

'Come and eat,' the latter invited when the door closed in the man's wake. 'You're fond of seafood, if I recall.'

The last thing Leonie felt like at present was eating, but there was nothing to be gained by refusing. She got up, unsurprised by the unsteadiness in her lower limbs, and went to the table, passing by the door leading to the bedroom on the way. In an hour or so they would be in there doing what she was here to do. Whether Vidal would be prepared to let her leave immediately afterwards was open to question, but the ordeal had to be over some time. All she cared about—

all she'd allow herself to care about—was getting her father back on track.

As anticipated, the meal was excellent, though so far as Leonie was concerned she might as well have been chewing on sawdust. Vidal allowed her just one glass of wine, declaring his wish to have her *compos mentis*, not falling asleep on him.

'You're actually admitting that a woman *could* fall asleep on you?' Leonie asked with deliberation, drawing a brief smile.

'Only under the influence of too much alcohol.'

'It must be great,' she murmured, 'to have so much confidence in one's abilities!'

For the first time there was a genuine amusement in his eyes. 'Unlike a woman, any man lacking confidence in that particular ability could find himself devoid of it altogether. An unfair difference in physiology.'

'Meaning a woman can pretend to be aroused?'

'Precisely.' Dark eyes glinted. 'Not that I anticipate any problem in that direction.'

'Being the expert you are.'

The sarcasm left him unmoved. 'If you think to annoy me, forget it. I intend enjoying every moment of our time together. That means that you enjoy it too. And you will.'

Leonie bit back a caustic retort. She could vow to remain physically unresponsive to him, but the way her body reacted to his very presence made it unlikely. All she could do was keep those responses to the barest minimum.

The meal ended with a chocolate mousse that melted in the mouth and was nigh on impossible not to get pleasure from. Leonie took her time eating it, savouring every mouthful. Vidal watched her without comment, though with no sign of impatience, his whole attitude one of a man totally at ease with himself. She longed to disrupt that equanimity, but could think of nothing short of another burst of invective that might do the trick. With her father's fate still in the balance, she couldn't afford to take any risks.

Finished at last, she laid down her spoon, eyeing him across the width of the table with conflicting emotions, both hating the thought of what was to come, and yet undeniably stirred by it too: mind not strong enough to exercise full control over matter, she concluded ruefully.

'So, let's get it over with, then,' she said. 'The sooner I'm out of here, the better!'

Vidal linked both hands behind his head, leaning back in his chair to view her with irony. 'Time is of no importance. We have the whole night ahead of us.'

Leonie had been more than half expecting it, but that didn't mean she had to accept it without question. 'If my humiliation is all you're after, you don't have to go to such lengths,' she said. 'In fact, you've already succeeded.'

'Suggesting that I should be content to let it go at that?' He shook his head. 'I've waited too long for this moment. I should mention, too, that if you hoped to deter me by dressing like some secretary, you were sadly mistaken. I find the severity of your clothing a tantalising contrast with what I know lies beneath.'

'You have no idea what lies beneath!' Her indignation was ridiculous in the circumstances, Leonie knew, but she was too incensed to care. 'I didn't allow things to get that far between us!'

His smile was slow, his enjoyment at her discomfiture obvious. 'I don't need my eyes to tell me what my hands have already discovered. Your skin is smooth as silk, your breasts firm and full, your waist slender above the curve of hip that so excites a man, your—'

'Stop it!' Leonie's cheeks were burning, her whole body tingling. 'I don't want to hear any more!'

'You'll be hearing a lot more than that before the night is over,' he said. 'Speech can be as much a part of lovemaking as action.'

'You call what you've got in mind making love?' she retorted scathingly.

His lips slanted again. 'Had I been capable of what *you* apparently have in mind, I would have taken you that way two years ago. As I already told you, I intend you to enjoy our time together as much as I will myself. But not quite yet,' he added. 'First a brandy, I think, and a little music to set the mood. Perhaps we may even dance.'

Leonie held her tongue, unwilling to set herself up for any further ridicule. Whatever Vidal's intentions, she had no choice but to go along.

He saw her seated on the same sofa she had occupied earlier, switching on some hidden player on his way to get the drinks. Soft music filled the room. Nothing Leonie recognised, but soothing, she had to admit.

This time Vidal took a seat at her side, clinking his glass against hers in mocking salute. 'Pleasant dreams!'

'I hope you have nightmares,' she retaliated weakly, drawing another laugh.

'I'll let you know in the morning.'

'I'm intended to stay the *whole* night?' she asked, already knowing the answer.

'But of course. I look forward to breakfast together on the balcony, if the weather still allows it. Were we in Portugal now, there would be little doubt of it. June is a delightful time of year, the air warm, the fields filled with flowers, the whole ambience one of peace and plenty.'

There were times, Leonie had noted in the past, when his speech became a little more formalised, his accent more pronounced. Times when he both looked and sounded a different person. She stole a glance at the firmly moulded profile, lingering for the briefest of moments on the sensual curve of his mouth before dragging her attention back to the glass in her hand.

She hadn't wanted the bandy, but she lifted it to her lips now, swallowing half the contents in one gulp. The glow was

instant, spreading through her like fingers of fire. She made
to down what was left, to have the glass taken from her and
placed on the low table before her, along with his own.

'Brandy is meant to be savoured not tipped straight down
the throat,' he admonished. 'Or were you simply seeking
courage?'

'Courage for what?' she countered. 'I'm not afraid of you.'

'I think fear of yourself more likely,' he returned. 'You
want me—you always did want me—but you can't bring
yourself to acknowledge it. This way you can lay the blame
for any weakness on the effects of alcohol.' He put a fingertip
to her lips as she made to speak, his own curving as he felt
her involuntary tremor. 'No disputes. I'll have you say the
words before we're through.'

'I'd as soon cut my tongue out first!' Leonie spoke through
gritted teeth, fighting to stay on top of her warring instincts.
His touch stirred her senses; there was no denying that. She
had an almost irresistible urge to take the fingertip into her
mouth, to savour the masculine taste of it.

Vidal removed the temptation by moving the finger, sliding it gently along the line of her jaw and up behind her ear
in a caress that set every nerve-ending in her body aquiver.
It took everything she had to keep from dragging his hand
away; to sit there expressionlessly holding the dark gaze.

'A woman of some will-power,' he observed, 'but not by
any means invincible.' He took the caressing finger away,
getting to his feet. 'Come.'

She stood up, steeling herself afresh as he turned her about
to press her ahead of him clear of the sofa and table. The
music had softened still further. Vidal turned her again, this
time into his arms, hands sliding behind her back to hold her
close. The heels she was wearing brought her eyes on a level
with his mouth. His breath was warm on her cheek, the subtle
male scent of him filling her nostrils as he began to move in
slow cadence to the rhythm. Her nipples tingled as they
rubbed against the hardness of his chest, springing to life. He

would feel that reaction; he couldn't fail to feel it. Not that she could do a damned thing about it.

'*Bonito*,' he murmured softly.

He dropped his hands further down her back, bringing the vital centres of their bodies into closer proximity. Leonie bit down hard on her lower lip as he moved her hips so that she just barely brushed against him. He was aroused already, if not fully as yet then certainly well on the way. Fight it though she might, she was part-way there herself. He knew it too.

'I think the time has come,' he murmured.

Leonie put up no resistance as he led her across to the bedroom. The bedside lights were switched on, casting a warm glow across the wide expanse of the king-sized bed while leaving the rest of the room in semi-darkness. Vidal made no attempt to turn on extra lights, affording her some relief at least.

He took her face between both hands, searching the striking features as if to commit them to memory, his eyes dark pools. The first touch of his lips was unexpectedly gentle, teasing rather than asserting, brushing a way through the barrier she tried to keep going. His tongue felt like silk, exploring the soft inner flesh with infinite sensitivity. Leonie felt her senses begin to swim, her will-power to start draining away. If she was going to make any kind of stance at all it had to be now, came the thought, before she went under completely.

Leaving one hand cupping her nape, Vidal dropped the other to seek her breast, encircling her tingling, peaking nipple for a brief moment before moving again to unfasten her shirt buttons with dexterity and slide inside to find bare flesh. His touch was like fire on her skin, fingers penetrating beneath the flimsy lace covering of her bra to close possessively about the firm swell. Leonie gasped at the flooding sensation, clinging to the fast-fading remnants of her will-power like a drowning man clutching a straw.

The shock when he removed the hand and put her abruptly

from him was immense. Eyes wide and dark, she gazed at him in mute question.

'Cover yourself,' he said brusquely.

She did so, fumbling at the buttons with nerveless fingers. If it had been his aim to arouse her, then reject her the way she had rejected him, he had acted a little prematurely for total humiliation. Unless he'd changed his mind about the whole thing.

'Is this your way of telling me the deal is off?' she got out.

Face devoid of expression again, he shook his head. 'A change of plan. I find myself unwilling to settle for just the one night. When I return to Portugal, you will be coming with me.'

Leonie found her voice, amazed by its steadiness. 'You really think I'll consent to becoming your mistress?'

The laugh was short. 'So there's a limit to the sacrifice you're prepared to make for your father?'

She bit her lip, caught between two fires. 'For how long?' she managed at length.

Something flickered in the dark depths of his eyes. 'I want no mistress,' he said. 'Two years ago I asked you to marry me. Today, I demand it.'

CHAPTER TWO

LEONIE stared at him in stupefaction. When she did find her voice it sounded as if it were coming from the bottom of a well. 'You can't be serious!'

'I was never more so,' Vidal assured her hardily. 'For two long years I've tried to put you from my mind—to tell myself that no woman is worth losing sleep over. But it's been of little use. I made you an offer I'd never made to any other woman, only to have it thrown back in my face as though it were an insult. I have the opportunity now to make you eat your words.' The pause was brief. 'The final choice still remains with you.'

'It's emotional blackmail!' she accused, in no doubt as to his meaning. 'You're asking too much!'

'No more than you're asking of me in continuing to employ a man who stole from me,' came the unmoved return. 'Of course, you could always allow him to make the decision for himself.'

There would be no question of which way that decision would go, Leonie knew. Her father would be devastated if he knew what she was facing. The question of whether Vidal would actually call in the police if the money was paid back was debatable, but he certainly wouldn't be prepared to reinstate him, or give him a reference, which would effectively put paid to his career.

Vidal made an abrupt movement. 'I'll leave you to think it over.'

Leonie sank to a seat on the edge of the bed as the door closed behind him, her nerves in tatters. Any appeal to his better nature was going to be a waste of time: he didn't have a better nature. But marriage! How could she possibly go along with that? Especially when offered in a spirit of revenge for past offences.

There was a cheval mirror a few feet away. She caught a glimpse of herself, shirt only partially buttoned, hair tumbled from the hands run through it. She could still feel the imprint of his lips on hers, the hardness of his body against her—the deep down stirring at the memory. He was right about one thing: she had wanted him two years ago and she wanted him now. Despising him as a person made no impact on her senses.

She'd felt that impact the very first moment she'd laid eyes on him. She'd called in at the office to invite her father to lunch, to be told by his secretary that he was in conference with the company president. The inner office door had opened almost as she said it, framing a man whose expression registered open appreciation as he viewed her…

'I've been looking at the photograph on your father's desk for the past half-hour,' he said. 'It fails to do you full justice.' He moved forward, holding out a hand, his smile devastating. 'I'm Vidal Parella Dos Santos.'

Leonie took the hand, murmuring a response, aware of a tingle like a small electric shock as his fingers closed about hers. After all she'd heard and read about the man before her it was hardly surprising to find him exuding such pure animal magnetism. Women throughout Europe had been subject to it.

She turned her gaze on the man at his back. 'I was hoping we could have lunch together, Dad.'

'Sorry, darling, I'm going to be tied up for at least another hour,' Stuart answered regretfully.

'In which case, perhaps you'll allow me to take you to lunch in your father's stead?' offered Vidal. 'It would give me the greatest pleasure.'

Leonie's instinct was to refuse, but a stronger force held sway. It was, after all, only lunch. 'That's very nice of you,' she said.

The smile came again, equally disturbing in its effect. 'It takes little effort to be nice to a beautiful woman.'

Leonie caught her father's eye, reading the message there without difficulty. He was as aware as she was of Vidal's reputation. Not that she had any intention of becoming one of his conquests.

'I'll see you later, then,' she said lightly. 'Don't work too hard!'

They went to a restaurant she had never visited before, but where Vidal was welcomed by name and escorted to a table by the *maître d'* himself. The place was well populated, the dress code very much upmarket. Leonie was glad she'd chosen to wear a new lemon suit. While not exactly designer label, it looked the part sufficiently well to pass muster to all but the most discerning eye.

'I gather you're a pretty frequent visitor here?' she remarked when they were seated.

'Whenever I come to London,' Vidal agreed. 'They know my tastes.'

In women too, no doubt, she thought with a cynical edge. She wouldn't be the first he'd brought here, by any means. She studied him as he ran his eyes down the menu, taking in every superbly carved, olive-skinned detail of his face, the breadth of shoulder beneath the fine grey suiting, the lean, long-fingered hands with their well-tended nails. So far as outward appearances were concerned he had it all. Even without his position and wealth, he would never have to fight for female companionship.

As though sensing her scrutiny, he glanced up, catching her before she could look away. 'Do I meet with your approval?' he asked smilingly.

'You're a handsome man,' she answered, refusing to be thrown. 'You must be accustomed to attention.'

The dark head inclined in mock humility. 'A matter I owe to my ancestry. The Dos Santos males have always been fortunate.'

'Do the Dos Santos women share the same inheritance?'

'Some. Not all.' He paused, studying her in turn. 'You've little of your father in you. Your mother must have been a very beautiful woman herself.'

Even after four years, mention of her still brought a pang. 'How did you know she was dead?' she asked.

'I make it my business to know a top employee's background,' he said. 'I understand you still live with your father?'

'That's right.' Leonie saw no cause to explain her reasons. He should be able to work them out for himself. She dropped her eyes to the menu in front of her. 'I'd like the whitebait to start, followed by the trout, please.'

'A woman of decision!' He applauded. 'I believe I'll have the same. You're content to leave the choice of wine to me?'

Green eyes widened innocently. 'Of course. Men know so much more about wine!'

The smile that curved his lips wrought havoc on her heart-strings. 'Mock me at your peril,' he warned. 'I may find it necessary to exact penalties.'

Flirting with a man of Vidal's calibre was hardly to be recommended, but it was too enjoyable a pastime to be abandoned. 'I'll bear it in mind,' she said demurely.

She'd fully intended to plead other commitments after lunch, but when the time came she found herself agreeing without demur to his suggestion that they take a ride on the river.

'You may not believe it, but this is the first time I've ever done this,' she remarked when they were afloat.

'I find it very easy to believe,' Vidal returned. 'Few of us appreciate the readily available. There are parts of Lisbon I've never visited.'

'I know the Dos Santos headquarters are in Lisbon, but is it your main home too?' Leonie ventured.

'Not the city itself. I live at Sintra, some thirty or so kilometres to the northwest.'

'Your own place?'

'Of course. Reconstructed from the remains of a fourteenth century monastery.'

Her eyes lit with interest. 'Really?'

'And truly,' he mocked. 'Not that you'll find any ghosts from the past still in residence. They were all driven out by the clamour of modern machinery.'

'You planned the restoration yourself?'

'With the invaluable aid of an architect friend who was able to tell me what was and wasn't possible. It was finished three years ago, so the new stonework has weathered in. I employed a landscaping company to design the grounds surrounding it.'

'Does your family live in the same area?'

'The Dos Santos estates are in the Douro Valley. Beautiful, but too isolated for my tastes. There's more than one branch of the family surviving,' he added, anticipating her next question.

'My father's cousin has land adjoining. There are relatives on the island of Madeira too. They own several hotels there.'

'So you're not the only one who chose to go into business rather than sit around enjoying the fruits of inheritance?' Leonie remarked lightly.

The comment drew a quirk to his lips. 'A very poetic way of putting it, though correct in essence. I leave the latter way of life to my cousins.'

Leonie would have liked to know more, but the warning flags were out. She would be doing herself no favours by delving any deeper into the life of a man she was unlikely to be seeing after today.

The thought alone brought a rare despondency. He came across as so very different from the image she'd formed via media reports. She was drawn to him in more than just the physical sense.

They left the boat at Greenwich, and took a taxi back to where they'd left the car. By then Leonie was even less inclined to call time on the day. She'd never gone short of male attention, but none of the men she'd met had radiated the same charm. Vidal made her feel she was the one person in the whole world he wanted to be with. Deep down, she knew it was all part of his technique, but she turned a deaf ear to the cautionary voices.

Drinks in a Mayfair wine bar, followed by an invitation to dinner in his hotel suite, made his intentions clear enough, but she chose to follow the same reckless path, driven by an inner, irresistible need. Life was for living. With a man like Vidal, the experience could only be good.

The suite was sumptuous, the food superbly prepared, the conversation scintillating. They ate out on the balcony, finishing off the meal with brandies.

Feeling positively euphoric, Leonie got up and went to the balustrade to look out over the sparkling panorama. '"When a man is tired of London, he is tired of life",' she quoted softly.

'Samuel Johnson knew a very different London, I think,' Vidal observed. He was at her back, hands sliding about her waist to draw her closer, lips parting the hair at her nape to nuzzle the tender skin. 'The night is beautiful, but you surpass it,' he murmured. *'Eu quero, meu querido!'*

Leonie had taken off her jacket earlier. T e thin blouse she was wearing beneath offered little defence gainst the hands now sliding up to cup her breasts. She felt her nipples peak beneath the gentle caressing motion of his thumbs, a shudder run the whole length of her body. A core of heat rose from some central spot, radiating outwards to encompass her whole being. She felt as if she were floating, her legs too weak to support her.

Vidal turned her towards him, face dark but for the glitter in his eyes as he bent his head to find her lips. The kiss was a revelation, drawing an instant and overwhelming response. She could feel his heat, the burgeoning hardness against her thighs. He'd removed his jacket too. The fine silk of his shirt moulded to the muscularity beneath, emphasising every masculine line.

'Come,' he said softly.

It was only then, as he took her hand to lead her back indoors, that she began to come to her senses. This was nothing new to him. Nothing special, the way it was for her. She was just another easy lay—another notch on his bedpost.

He turned his head to view her in some surprise as she pulled sharply free of him. 'Is there something wrong?' he asked

'I'm no one-night-stand!' she jerked out

Dark brows drew together. 'Is that how you believe I see you?'

'Well, isn't it?' she challenged. 'You had this in mind from the first, didn't you?'

'I was under the impression that we both of us knew where we were heading,' he returned levelly. 'You gave me no cause to doubt it up until now.'

Leonie felt the warmth run up under skin. She sought refuge from the truth in anger. 'You take too much for granted! I accepted an invitation to dinner. I didn't realise I'd be called on to pay for it in kind.'

Vidal viewed her in silence for a moment or two, a deep down spark in his eyes the only indication of emotion. 'I apologise for the error,' he said at last. 'I thought you a woman of the world.'

She'd gone out of her way to give that impression, Leonie had to admit. Anger gave way to shame for a moment. The fault was more hers than his.

'I'm sorry,' she said thickly. 'I got a little carried away. I'm not in the habit of it, believe me.'

The expression that crossed the sculpted features was difficult to define. 'You were right,' he said. 'I do take far too much for granted. Perhaps we might begin again?'

Leonie shook her head, ousting temptation before it could swamp her. 'I really don't see any point. We come from different worlds. I'll stick to my own in future.'

'Your choice, of course.' Vidal indicated the open glass doors, face impassive now. 'I'll order you a taxi.'

Leonie went ahead of him back into the room, steeling herself to stay in control as she watched him pick up the telephone.

'It will be waiting for you,' he said, replacing the receiver. 'Charged to my account.'

No doubt an arrangement of long standing, she thought. 'I can pay for my own transport,' she declared stiffly.

He inclined his head. 'You must naturally do as you see fit.'

He came over to pick up the jacket she'd tossed over a chair-back before dinner, holding it out for her to slide her arms into. She did so as smoothly and swiftly as possible, vitally aware of his closeness, and of her hammering pulses. If she'd carried on the act a little longer they would have been in bed by now, with the question of right or wrong purely academic. It took everything she had to restrain the urge to throw caution aside.

Vidal saw her to the suite's outer door. It was still impossible to read anything in the dark eyes as she met them for the final time.

'It was an enjoyable day,' he said.

'But a disappointing night,' she responded, determined not to give way to any last-minute wavering.

The smile was unexpected. 'No matter. Sleep well, *namorado*.'

What the last meant, Leonie had no idea. Nor did she care to ask. She heard the door close as she made for the lifts.

Crossing the hotel lobby was an ordeal in itself. She was certain that the receptionists on duty were watching her every step. The taxi was waiting, as promised. She gave the address and slid inside, grateful for the closed glass partition precluding any conversation. It was going to be a costly ride all the way out to Northwood, but she had no intention of crying off from paying—even if it did probably mean that the driver would gain double fare.

It was close on midnight when she reached home. As anticipated, her offer of the metered charge wasn't rejected. Her father came out from the study as she let herself in, his expression only too easy to read.

'You didn't go back to your office this afternoon,' he said.

Leonie donned a smile, a light tone. 'No. Vidal fancied a trip on the river. We had dinner together too.'

'Just dinner?'

'Just dinner,' she assured him, smothering any resentment at the catechism. 'He's been the perfect gentleman.'

Stuart looked relieved. 'Good. It isn't that I don't trust you to keep a steady head,' he hastened to add. 'I was just a little concerned that he might attempt to take advantage, that's all.'

'Well, he didn't.' She could say that with truth, considering the way he'd accepted the rejection. A first for him too, she didn't doubt. 'I'm going straight up,' she declared, stifling a spurious yawn.

'I'll be up myself in a few minutes,' Stuart returned.

Leonie kissed his cheek in passing, mounting the stairs feeling anything but happy. She'd probably turned down the experience of her life tonight, and for what? Hanging fire for

Mr Right was all very well in theory, but what if he never turned up?

She spent a restless night, rising to a day that held little sparkle. The more she thought about the previous night, the more gauche she felt. She'd acted like some naïve teenager rather than a grown woman. Vidal must consider her totally immature.

Was it too late, she wondered, to contact him and apologise for giving the wrong impression? She had no idea what his itinerary was, but he'd still be in his suite at this hour. She wanted desperately to see him again. He was like no other man she had ever met. So what if he did have a reputation? At thirty-three, and single, he was hardly going to live like a monk. They'd been so well attuned until she'd come over all moral. Given the opportunity, the relationship might even have developed into something worthwhile.

She was still grappling with the temptation when she went down to breakfast. Her father was reading the morning newspaper.

'I think you should see this,' he said, handing a sheet over as she took her seat at the table. 'Just in case there's any doubt remaining.'

The photograph leapt out at her: Vidal, resplendent in evening dress, alongside a young and beautiful woman who looked vaguely familiar. According to the accompanying write-up Vidal had refused to accept responsibility for the child she'd recently given birth to, leaving her with a ruined modelling career, and destitute. She didn't believe in abortion, she claimed plaintively. All she'd ever asked from him was support.

Leonie swallowed thickly on the lump in her throat Knowing him for a philanderer was one thing; this was something else. What kind of man turned his back on his own child?

'I wasn't planning on seeing him again,' she said.

'Good.' Stuart sounded relieved. 'He'll be gone in a couple of days, anyway. He never spends long in any place.'

His name wasn't mentioned again.

Leonie did her best to cast him from her mind altogether—failing because her body refused to play ball. She could still feel the pressure of his lips on hers, the touch of his hands on her skin; still smell the emotive masculine scent of him. She despised herself for the weakness.

The day went by slowly. Emerging from the office at five-thirty to see Vidal leaning against the bonnet of a silver Mercedes was a shock that left her momentarily speechless. She could only gaze at him, aware of the interest aroused in those around her as he straightened.

'I remembered you mentioning your company name,' he said. 'I need to speak with you.'

'About what?' she asked, recovering enough of her poise to achieve a reasonable control of her voice.

He had to be conscious of the spectators, but his attention never wavered from her face, an amber spark deep down in his eyes. 'Not here.'

Not *anywhere* with you! she thought, but the words failed to materialise. 'I really don't see the point,' she heard herself saying instead.

'Indulge me,' he said.

Leonie hesitated, reluctant to cause further speculation among the onlookers by walking away as her every instinct advised. They would all know who he was, of course. His face had been splashed across too many papers and screens for them not to know. She was going to be faced with a barrage of questions tomorrow, regardless, but it would call for less explanation if she simply went with him now.

He took the hesitation itself as agreement, turning back to open the front passenger door. Leonie slid into the leather seat, reaching automatically for the belt as Vidal moved round the front of the car to gain the driving seat.

'You're parked on double yellow lines,' she said.

'I know,' he answered. 'There are times when the law has to be broken.'

He forced a passage out into the traffic stream, ignoring the furious hooting. Leonie stole a glance at him, unable to do anything about the toe-curling impact. It was unfair that one man should be given so much in the way of looks.

What he could possibly have to say to her she had no idea. Another apology, perhaps, for taking too much for granted last night—even though he'd had some cause. It seemed unlikely, yet she could think of no other explanation for his looking her up. Not that it would make the least bit of difference to her view of him after reading what she'd read this morning.

'Where are we going?' she asked as he turned onto Park Lane.

'My suite,' he said, jerking her upright.

'If you think…'

'I'm not about to repeat last night's error in judgement,' he declared. 'What I have to say to you requires privacy.' He shook his head as she made to speak. 'This is neither the time nor the place to discuss it.'

He was right about that, she had to admit. The evening traffic was heavy, road sense in short supply. A driver needed no distractions. She subsided again reluctantly, even more confused.

They made the square eventually. Vidal drove straight down into the hotel's underground car park. Another couple joined them in the lift. Leonie saw the way the woman looked at Vidal, then back at her own partner, as if comparing the two. Not that there was any comparison.

The other two got out at the fourth floor, leaving them to ascend to the fifth in a silence Leonie had no intention of being the first to break. She would listen to whatever it was he had to say, but he wasn't going to sway her opinion of him. Certainly not after that morning's revelations.

It was gone six-thirty by her watch when they reached the suite. She'd told her father she'd be going straight home tonight, though she rarely made it before seven. She'd give him a ring as soon as she got out of here, she promised herself. He tended to worry if she failed to put in an appearance when she'd said she would, imagining all kinds of mishaps. A leftover from her childhood days.

Vidal invited her to take a seat, lifting his shoulders in a philosophical shrug when she declined. Dressed today in trousers and a fine white cotton sweater, dark hair showing a hint of curl in its thickness, he was achingly alluring. Leonie steeled herself to stay on top of the emotions he still aroused in her.

'So?' she said.

A smile touched his lips as he surveyed her. 'You remind me of a stag at bay,' he said. 'Ready to do me damage should I make one false move. You need have no fear. I'm willing to wait.'

Green eyes fired a whole shower of sparks. 'You'll be wasting your time!'

'It's mine to waste,' he returned. 'Not that I intend a lengthy engagement.'

The wind taken completely out of her sails, Leonie gazed at him blankly. 'What are you talking about?'

'Our marriage,' he said. 'I want you to be my wife.'

Leonie knew a sudden urge to laugh. Pure hysteria, she thought dazedly. From last night to this was too much of a jump for her mind to make.

'What kind of game are you playing now?' she got out.

'I'm not in the habit of playing games,' he said. 'Certainly not of this nature. I've waited a long time to meet a woman I could contemplate spending my life with. A woman who values herself enough to overcome her more basic urges. You wanted me last night in exactly the same way that I wanted you, but you refused to give way. You never have, have you?'

Leonie felt her face flame. 'That's none of your business!'

Vidal smiled and shook his head. 'It's very much my business. My wife must have known no other man. It's one Dos Santos tradition I've no quarrel with. I'd prefer a quiet wedding. And as soon as can be managed.' The dark eyes acquired a tawny spark again as he studied her. 'I found last night frustrating enough.'

Leonie found her voice, amazed by its steadiness. 'Does the word love figure in your vocabulary at all?'

'Of course,' he said. 'Though perhaps not the "at first sight" kind written about in books. The real kind takes time and knowledge to develop.'

He paused, a faint line appearing between his brows as he waited for some response from her. 'Do you have nothing to say to me?'

She drew a deep shuddery breath, fighting a sudden mad inclination to simply go along with it all. 'I've got plenty to say,' she forced out. 'I wouldn't marry you if you were the last man on earth!'

The shock that sprang in his face would have been laughable if she'd felt at all like laughing. The possibility of rejection had obviously never occurred to him. Not so surprising, she supposed, considering his status as one of Europe's most eligible bachelors, but that in no way excused his sheer arrogance.

The anger sweeping her was as much a defence against any lingering doubts as an expression of repulsion. She drew herself up to her full height, fists clenched at her sides, eyes scornful. 'If you want the truth, I'd as soon consort with a worm than a womanising, baby-abandoning low-life like you! I must have been mad to let you anywhere near me to start with. Talk about scraping the barrel!'

She stopped there, apprehension taking over at the look in his eyes. Danger shimmered in the air between them.

He turned abruptly and made for the drinks cabinet, pulling down the shelf with control to reach for glass and bottle. The whisky he poured was at least a double measure. He tossed it back in a single gulp, standing there with his back to her, tension in every line of his body.

'I think you'd better leave,' he said.

For a moment she hesitated, ashamed of the sheer viciousness of her attack. It took the memory of the newspaper item to drive all regret from her mind. Somewhere out there was a woman caring for his child. Maybe not the only one, for all she knew. He merited no apology.

He was still standing there when she closed the door on him.

It hadn't been true, Leonie reflected painfully, coming back to the present. Not that part, at any rate. The woman had just been trying it on, losing her case when a blood test proved that the baby couldn't be his. Not that it made him any less of a rake.

The ultimatum he'd just presented her with was still hard to take in. No marriage contracted under such circumstances could ever become meaningful. He would be condemning them both to a loveless union simply to salve his pride. He had to see how utterly useless a gesture it would be.

He was seated on one of the sofas, a drink to hand, when she finally nerved herself to go through. He watched her expressionlessly as she moved towards him.

'There has to be some other way of handling this,' she said. 'Why would you want a wife who hates you?'

'You don't hate me,' he declared without undue emphasis. 'You feel the way you've always felt about me. The same way I feel about you. We're meant to be together. If this is the only way of achieving that, then so be it.'

'Forsaking all others?' she asked. 'Or are Dos Santos wives expected to turn a blind eye?'

The shrug was brief. 'A matter of learning to trust.'

'Trust *you*!' She put every ounce of derision she could muster into the words. 'That will be the day!'

Vidal shrugged again. 'Time will tell.' He paused, lifting a questioning eyebrow. 'Do I take it we have an agreement?'

'Do I have any choice?' she asked bitterly.

'Not if you want your father to keep his job.'

Leonie sat down heavily in the nearby chair, mind grappling with the implications. 'What am I supposed to tell him?'

'That's entirely up to you,' he responded. 'The truth, if you like. I'd doubt it would make any difference.'

Her head lifted, eyes blazing green fire. 'Yes, it would! He'd never go along with it!'

'Then you'll simply have to convince him that it's what you want. You could say, for instance, that I asked you to marry me two years ago but you weren't ready then to take the step. You've spent the last two years regretting your decision, and are happy to be given a second chance.'

'He'd never believe it!'

'Why not? He was aware of the attraction that flared between us the moment we met.'

Leonie gave a short laugh. 'He'd hardly consider that enough to precipitate an offer of marriage from you!'

'How could he know what my reaction would be? We come from different cultures.'

There was never a truer word, Leonie reflected, searching his face for some sign, however slight, of vulnerability. A hopeless task, of course. Vidal had no weak spots. Many women would be over the moon to have the opportunity she was being offered. If she were totally honest about it, the physical attraction he still held for her made the decision a little less fraught. It was doubtful if the marriage would be long term, anyway.

'You win,' she said thickly.

There was no reaction that she could perceive in the dark eyes. 'I'll begin arrangements tomorrow. I'm due in Munich the day after, but I'll curtail the visit as much as is possible. We can be married three weeks from now, and travel to Lisbon immediately after.'

Leonie felt her heart jerk. Her expression drew an ironic smile.

'You didn't imagine I'd be content to set up a permanent home here?'

She hadn't got that far, she acknowledged helplessly. 'It can't possibly be as quick as that,' she declared, looking for any delaying tactic. 'There's my job, for one thing.'

'Tell them you're leaving,' came the uncompromising reply. 'If there's any financial penalty it will be taken care of. I won't wait longer than three weeks for you. The strain is already telling on me.'

'I doubt if you'll have any difficulty easing it,' she said with purpose.

He made no perceptible movement, yet his posture somehow hardened. 'There will be no others.'

And pigs might fly! she reflected. One woman was never going to be enough for him, even over a limited period. Especially one whose sexual experience was nil!

Not that she'd stay that way for long, came the thought, sending a sudden frisson down her spine.

'If we're waiting till after the marriage, I assume I'm free to go now?' she said, blanking out any dissenting voices.

For a moment he seemed on the verge of disputing that assumption, then he inclined his head. 'For now. You can tell your father the news tonight, if you wish—or you can wait until the morning and we can tell him together.'

'You mean to come to the house?'

The smile was dry. 'I think your father and I have some matters to discuss before he returns to his job. I'll arrange a taxi for you.'

He got to his feet, heading for the telephone. Leonie watched him with a sense of *déjà vu*. Just what she was going to tell her father, she had no idea. How could she possibly convince him that her decision to marry a man she hadn't even seen for two years had nothing to do with his own predicament?

It was a long and fraught journey back to Northwood. Relief held the upper hand for a moment or two when she arrived home to find her father had already retired for the night, though the problem was going to be no less in the morning. Somehow or other she had to find the right words before Vidal's arrival.

It was still difficult to believe it was all really happening. She kept thinking she was going to wake up any minute and find the whole thing was a bad dream. She supposed she should be grateful that Vidal actually wanted to marry her, when he might simply have demanded she become his mistress for however long he chose.

None of which helped her sleep well. She rose heavy-eyed at seven, still with no clear idea of how she was going to give her father the news. He was already at breakfast when she finally went down, although not eating a great deal, she noted.

'I thought you were staying out last night,' he said. 'You must have been late getting in.'

'Fairly,' Leonie agreed. The only way, she decided resignedly, was to come right out with it. 'I didn't actually tell you the truth about where I was going last night,' she said. 'I went to see Vidal again. He'll be coming here this morning to see you.'

Stuart looked at her uncertainly, obviously struck by something in her tone. 'To tell me what?'

'That you can keep your job.' She drew a steadying breath. 'And to tell you we're going to be married.'

Thunderstruck was too mild a word for the expression on her father's face. 'You're what?' he got out.

'I know it must come as a shock to you,' she said, fighting to maintain an element of composure, 'though it isn't as out of the blue as it must seem. He actually asked me two years ago. I turned him down that time, but I've always regretted it.'

'Two years ago?' Stuart Baxter looked even more bewildered. 'But you only met him the once!'

'Twice,' Leonie corrected, aware of how crazy it all sounded. 'He proposed the day after we met.' She forced a smile. 'I felt much the same way you're feeling now. That it wasn't possible for anyone to make a decision like that so quickly. Especially a man like Vidal. I didn't have the courage to go with what I felt for him then. What I still feel for him.'

Her father gazed at her in silence for a lengthy moment, confusion giving way to perturbation. 'You're saying you're in love with him?'

Leonie held his gaze, willing herself to reveal no uncertainty. 'Yes.'

There was another pause, another change of expression, this time to one of suspicion. 'Are you doing this for me?'

Her laugh sounded hollow even to her own ears. 'Dad, much as I love you, I couldn't contemplate tying myself to a man I had no feelings for. What you did brought us together again, that's all. I *want* to marry him. More than anything!'

'He's no good for you, pet!' It was a cry from the heart. 'You know what kind of man he is!'

'I know what kind of man he's made out to be,' she returned. 'As a bachelor, he's been entitled to play the field. That's not to say he'll continue doing it after marriage,'

'Leopards don't change their spots. I know it's a cliché,

but it's based on fact. I can't believe you're really serious about this!'

'I am,' she assured him. 'Very serious. I want you to be happy for me, Dad. Happy for us both.'

'I'm trying,' he said. 'I'm really trying. I just find it—' He broke off, shaking his head. 'When were you thinking of?'

Leonie drew another deep breath. 'Within three weeks. And quietly. Vidal doesn't want any publicity.'

'Three weeks!'

Get it all over in one go, she thought, steeling herself. 'We'll be living in Portugal, of course. Vidal's main home is in Sintra, near Lisbon. We're not planning on a honeymoon.' *She* certainly wasn't. 'We'll be going straight there afterwards.'

'You planned all this last night?' Stuart both looked and sounded at a total loss.'

'That's right.' Leonie let herself relax a little. The worst was over. She attempted a smile, a lighter tone of voice. 'Vidal doesn't hang about.'

'Not in any sphere, apparently. What time will he be here?'

'I'm not sure,' she hedged. 'Definitely this morning.'

'What about your job?'

'I'll be leaving, naturally.'

'Just like that?'

Her shrug was meant to convey a wry acknowledgement. 'Needs must, I'm afraid.'

'Because Vidal says so?' Stuart viewed her in perplexity. 'Are you going to let him rule your whole life?'

'It would be a bit far to commute from Lisbon,' Leonie pointed out, trying to make a joke of it. 'Anyway, I'm hardly going to need a job. I'm marrying a multimillionaire.'

'That isn't you talking,' he protested.

'It's me talking nonsense,' she responded, rueing the comment. 'I'd marry Vidal if he didn't have a penny to his name! I'll be really sorry to leave you on your own,' she added truthfully, 'but it had to happen some time. Anyway, Portugal isn't all that far away. We'll be able to visit both ways.'

'Of course.' The agreement was subdued, his attitude one of unwilling resignation.

Leonie stretched a hand across the table to cover one of his, doing her best not to give way to the temptation to blurt out the truth. 'I know it's a shock, Dad, but I do know what I'm doing.'

'I hope so,' he said. 'I really do hope so.' He pushed back his chair and got to his feet. 'I'll be in the study.'

She let him go without protest. He needed time on his own to come to terms with it all. She needed it herself, if it came to that. By the time Vidal arrived she had to be in a frame of mind to go along with anything and everything he said.

The following couple of hours went by slowly. With ten o'clock come and gone, she began to wonder if he'd changed his mind about the whole thing. The sound of a car drawing into the drive a little before eleven dispelled that notion. A Mercedes again, she noted from the drawing room window. The latest model no doubt.

She went to open the door before he could ring the bell, unable to deny the customary tug on her stomach muscles as she viewed the decisive features.

'Dad's waiting for you in the study,' she said without pre-amble. 'I told him what to expect.'

'Leaving little to discuss,' Vidal responded dryly. 'Five minutes should be enough to say what I have to say.'

'You're going to read him the Riot Act again, I suppose?' she said, closing the door again.

Vidal gave a short laugh. 'I intend him to understand that our marriage buys him no further immunity, yes.'

'I'm sure he already knows that.' Leonie was hard put to it to keep a civil tone. 'He's facing a difficult time all round. I'd be grateful if you didn't lean on him too hard.'

Vidal made no reply. Wearing a dark grey suit today, he

looked every inch the hard-headed businessman. She bit back any further appeal, tapping lightly on the study door before opening it.

'Vidal's here, Dad.'

She left them to it, going to the kitchen to make coffee. There was no sound from the study when she went back along the hall with the tray. Five minutes, Vidal had said, but it was already fifteen. What they could be talking about she couldn't imagine.

Another five minutes went by before the two men put in an appearance. Stuart looked subdued, Vidal impassive.

'I've made the arrangements for Monday three weeks from now,' said the latter. 'I'll be travelling to Munich this afternoon in order to be through with business matters by then.'

Giving her three whole weeks to rearrange her life, thought Leonie sardonically. She kept both expression and voice under strict control. 'I'd have thought the register office would have been pretty heavily booked this time of year.'

Vidal smiled, seemingly at ease. 'I was offered a cancellation. Did you inform your employers?'

'Not yet,' she admitted. 'I can't do it over the phone. I'll go in this afternoon.'

Stuart started to say something, breaking off with a helpless little gesture as if in recognition of the futility. 'It's going to be very short notice for your family,' he observed. 'Will any of them be attending the wedding?'

'It's doubtful,' Vidal replied smoothly. 'They do little travelling. We'll visit them at the first opportunity, of course. The ceremony will be at ten o'clock. I have reservations on a flight from Heathrow at four.'

'So soon!'

The shrug was brief. 'I see no reason to linger. Naturally you'll be welcome to visit any time you wish.'

'Thanks.' The older man managed to keep his tone from reflecting any sarcasm.

Vidal drained his coffee cup, setting it down again as he rose. 'I have to go. You'll see me to the door, Leonie.'

It was more of a statement than a request, and with her father looking on she was in no position to object. She kept a smile pinned to her lips as she accompanied him from the room, losing it only when they were out of both sight and sound.

'Was it really necessary to be quite so cavalier?' she asked with some asperity, drawing an ironic glance.

'You think me inconsiderate where your father's concerned?'

She bit her lip. 'A consideration that comes at a price.'

'True.' His tone had softened. 'You find it such a high price to pay?'

Leonie met his eyes, wishing she could penetrate the unfathomable darkness. 'I suppose many would consider it no price at all for what I'll be gaining.'

'I believe many would,' he agreed. 'I don't claim any mitigating factors. I used the situation to my own ends. Just don't try pretending you feel nothing at all for me. It may be no more than a physical reaction at present, but you've yet to know me in any depth.'

He drew her to him to kiss her with an ardour that elicited an involuntary response. She had to stop herself from clinging to him when he finally lifted his head.

'You see,' he murmured, 'there are compensations.'

Of a kind, she thought hollowly, watching him walk to the car.

CHAPTER THREE

VIEWED from the air, the landscape was a montage of rolling hills and mountains riven by numerous rivers. A landscape bathed in sunlight for the most part. They would be landing in twenty minutes, the pilot had announced just now.

Flying first class was a new experience. An excellent experience, Leonie had to admit. She stole a glance at the man at her side, to see the dark head at rest against the padded cushion. His eyes were closed, his face relaxed, though there was no slackening of muscle along the firm jaw line

The past few weeks had been a rollercoaster ride, fast and furious and non-stop!

Her company had put no serious obstacle in her way when she'd handed in her resignation, although curiosity had been rife.

Vidal had returned from Munich, as promised. They'd spent the Saturday morning buying rings, both engagement and wedding.

She took a surreptitious look at her left hand, where the sparkling three-stone diamond hoop nestled above the beautifully engraved gold band. Worth a fortune, the pair of them, she didn't doubt, but still totally alien to her. The Senhora Parella Dos Santos, that was her new title. She wondered if she would ever come to view it with anything approaching familiarity.

The wedding ceremony itself had been less of a cold and clinical affair than she had anticipated. It had been a relief to emerge from the register office and find no lurking photographers. Vidal had booked a table for three for lunch, but her father had backed out from accompanying them. He ap-

46

peared to have accepted the situation with good grace, though Leonie doubted if it was wholly true. She'd promised to keep in regular touch, starting with a phone call as soon as they arrived safely at her new home.

Tonight Vidal would introduce her to the bedtime rites. She'd be a liar if she tried to make out that she viewed the prospect with loathing, she acknowledged, turning her gaze on him again. The feelings he aroused in her were all that had kept her going these past weeks.

'Analysis complete?' he asked, startling her as she had thought him genuinely asleep.

'I wouldn't presume to be capable of plumbing your depths,' she retorted, gathering her wits.

He turned his head to look at her without lifting it from the rest, expression enigmatic. 'You think I have depths to plumb, then?'

'Everyone has,' she said. 'Of one kind or another. You weren't born despising women.'

Dark brows lifted. 'You believe that's what I do?'

'Basically, yes.' Having begun this, she wasn't about to back down. 'We're there to be used. Your reputation bears that out.'

'Reputations,' he said, 'are often illusory.'

'Meaning the media make it all up?'

'Embellishment is a journalistic skill learned early in a career. I always credited you with more intelligence than to take everything you read in a newspaper as a hundred per cent correct.'

Leonie bit her lip, knowing he had a point. 'If I'd been all that intelligent I'd have steered well clear of you two years ago!' she declared in an attempt to keep her end up.

'If you had, your father might be in a very different position today,' Vidal returned equably. His eyes roved her face, devouring every feature, the look in them causing her heart to beat faster. 'It took time, but I got my way in the end. I look forward now to a long and happy life together.'

'Can a marriage contracted the way ours was ever be happy?' she asked, still doubting the 'long'.

'Given the will, there's no reason to doubt it,' he said. 'We'll be spending the rest of the week at the *quinta*,' he added. 'A time to get to know one another a little better.'

'In more ways than the one, you mean?'

'In more ways than the one,' he agreed, ignoring the satire. 'We found a great deal in common the day we sailed the river together. You were at ease with me then.'

Recalling the way she'd felt that day, 'at ease' wasn't exactly the way she would have described it, but she knew what he meant. There had been a compatibility in tastes: a liking for classical music, for theatre, for books with meaningful content. Looking back, it was amazing how much ground they'd covered during those few hours together.

'What happens next week?' she asked. 'Do I take it you'll be flitting round Europe?'

'Next week we travel to the Douro,' he said. 'I have to introduce you to my family.'

Catching a certain tension in his voice, Leonie slanted a glance. 'I take it they do know you're married?' she queried in sudden suspicion.

'Not yet,' he admitted. 'Nor are they likely to approve.'

Pride raised flags in her cheeks. 'You mean they may think I'm not good enough to join the Dos Santos clan?'

The smile that touched the firm mouth was wry. 'Snobbery isn't confined to any one race. They have fixed ideas of continuance where the bloodline is concerned. But faced with a *fait accompli*, they have no choice but to accept my choice of bride.'

'You had no right to spring this on me now,' she said tautly. 'How am I supposed to act?'

'As yourself,' he responded. 'Your spirit will see you through.'

Right at this moment, her spirit was at its lowest ebb. She turned her head back to the window, looking down on the unfolding landscape with a sense of entrapment. Coping with a marriage contracted under duress was bad enough; facing an antagonistic family into the bargain went beyond the pale.

The landing was smooth, disembarkation even more so. Vidal carried no luggage other than a laptop computer, leaving Leonie to assume that he kept a full wardrobe at all of his bases. She had expected no chauffeur-driven limousine, because she couldn't imagine him allowing anyone to drive him, but the white Mercedes Roadster was certainly impressive enough. He put the top down as they left the airport environs.

There was a lot to be said for wealth, she thought, cocooned in soft leather. A lot to be said for open-topped cars too, in this climate. She would be living in luxury from now on—or at least for as long as the marriage lasted. In other circumstances she'd consider herself blessed.

They skirted the city to head into rolling hills, passing whitewashed villages and rich manors to the Serra de Sintra. There was a village right at the base of the mountain, but Vidal continued on through, the road now rising and winding round the lushly forested mountain to reach a small, spilling township dominated by the huge medieval palace at its centre.

'Sintra,' he said. 'Not far now.'

The *quinta* lay some half a kilometre outside the town, reached via a winding driveway through the trees. Sparkling white in the evening sunlight, it was built to follow the lie of the land, descending the hillside in steps. The bell tower occupying a prominent position on the upper level was a fitting reminder of the monastery that had once occupied the site.

'It's superb!' Leonie exclaimed, too overwhelmed by the place to be parsimonious in praise of it. 'It's a wonder you can bear to leave it!'

'I'd find my life a little too curtailed on a permanent basis,' Vidal responded. He took her cases from the boot, along with his laptop, indicating the flight of stone steps leading up to a solid oak door. 'Lead on.'

Leonie did so reluctantly. The door opened before she reached it, the plump, motherly woman who stood there giving her an obviously surprised once-over before directing attention to the man now at her side and asking him something in Portuguese.

Vidal answered at some length in the same language, bringing a look of astonishment to the woman's face.

'This is my housekeeper, Ilena,' he added for Leonie's benefit. 'She speaks no English.'

'While I speak no Portuguese,' Leonie returned, smiling helplessly at the woman in lieu of a greeting. 'You might have prepared me! Her too, for that matter.'

She might as well have held her breath for all the notice he took of the admonition. Ilena stood back as he ushered Leonie ahead of him through the door, her expression readable in any language. It was apparent that she had only just learned of her employer's marriage. A further example of his inbuilt arrogance.

The entrance hallway was bright and spacious, the floor stone-tiled. Archways gave access to rooms on either side, a staircase to the next level. Weathered beams laced the ceilings, in perfect keeping with the antique furnishings.

Vidal handed over both suitcase and laptop, murmuring something Leonie couldn't catch. Not that it would have done her a lot of good if she had been able to hear.

'Through here,' he invited as Ilena made for the stairs. 'A drink first, I think, then an early dinner.'

Lunch was several hours away, but food was the last thing

on Leonie's mind right now. Under normal circumstances, the idea of spending even a week in such surroundings would have filled her with delight—only what about this situation was normal?

Beamed like the hall, with a wide stone fireplace at one end, the room invited one to sit and relax in the comfortable sofas and chairs. There was carpet underfoot in here, the colours faded to a soft glow. The paintings hung about the white stone walls were obvious originals even to her untrained eye.

Vidal sloughed his suit jacket, slinging it casually over a chair-back and following it with his tie. 'What would you like?' he asked.

'Why not champagne?' she returned, determined not to give way to the homesickness already beginning to eat her up inside. 'If you have it.'

Showing no perceptible reaction, he touched what she took to be a bell push set into the arm of a chair. 'It will take a few minutes. Why don't you sit down?'

She sank into the nearest chair, already regretting the rider. Of course he would have it. He would have anything one cared to ask for.

The young man who appeared in the archway was dressed in the dark trousers and white shirt of the serving classes, though there was nothing whatsoever servile in his cheerful expression. He took the order and departed, returning bare minutes later bearing a bottle of Krug and two champagne flutes on a silver tray.

Vidal opened the bottle without difficulty, and without spraying the entire area. Leonie took the glass he poured from him, tremoring to the mere touch of his fingers. The ring on her finger sparkled a myriad of colours as it caught a stray shaft of sunlight.

Vidal raised his own glass to her. *'Para melhorar o conhecimento!'*

'What exactly does that mean?' she asked.

'To better acquaintance,' he said.

'Of a very limited kind.'

'A fundamental kind,' he corrected. 'The essence of any relationship between a man and a woman in the beginning.'

'Only a man would see it that way.'

He laughed. 'You consider friendship a better basis?'

'I consider it just as vital.' She was getting into her stride, casting off any inclination towards soft-pedalling. 'Apart from one or two shared tastes, we're as far apart as two people can be. You've no idea what kind of person I really am. All you see is…what you see. If I didn't look the way I do, you'd never have given me a second thought.'

'That's probably true,' he agreed calmly. 'Would you have been attracted to me that first day had I been fat and balding?'

Leonie lifted her chin. 'I might.'

Laughing, Vidal shook his head. 'You're a lovely liar, but still a liar! As to knowing what kind of person you are beneath the surface, that, as I said earlier, will come in time— as you'll learn about me.'

She was wasting her breath trying to get at him that way, Leonie acknowledged resignedly. Maybe he was right. Maybe she should accept things the way they were, and stop pining for an ideal.

'About this visit to your family,' she said. 'I doubt if I have the wardrobe to impress the aristocracy.'

'The aristocracy, as you think of it, ceased to exist more than thirty years ago,' he returned. 'Clothing is a matter of taste, and I find yours impeccable. However, Lisbon is an excellent fashion centre, should you still have doubts. I'll arrange accounts for you.'

There's no way I'll allow you to buy clothes for me, it was on the tip of her tongue to retort. She bit the words back on realisation of how ridiculous they would sound. Not that she intended taking advantage. What she had, she would manage with.

He took her on a quick tour of the house before they ate. There were four levels in all. They had entered at the second. The lower level, it appeared, was devoted to kitchen and staff quarters, the third to more living areas. The bedrooms were situated at the very top, the suite they were to occupy looking out to a magnificent view of the mountains, and across the coastal plain to the sea. A superb four-poster bed held central place in the white-walled bedroom with its separate dressing area, while beyond lay a beautifully furnished sitting room. The *en suite* bathroom had a Jacuzzi semi-sunk into the floor.

Her suitcases had been placed on trestles in the dressing room. She had the key in her purse, so there was no question of the unpacking having been done. Left, at her own request, to tidy herself before dinner, Leonie quickly changed from the suit in which she'd been married, into a simple button through dress. The wardrobes were vast. One contained nothing but suits, ranging from continental lightweights through to evening wear, another more casual clothing. The stuff she'd brought with her was going to look lost in the two left empty.

It would be all too easy to slip into this lifestyle, she acknowledged wryly. Money might not buy happiness, but it didn't exactly make for misery either.

They ate a light meal of salad and fish out on a flower-strewn terrace, overlooking the same view she had seen from the bedroom. The sun went down in blazing glory, leaving them to a scented twilight. Switched on automatically, soft lighting came to life.

Shirtsleeves rolled, collar open at the throat, Vidal looked totally at home. Which he should, of course. Leonie wondered how many women he'd entertained here. Ilena would know, but even if she could speak the language she'd hardly be asking her.

In a little while he would be taking her upstairs to bed. There was no sense of dread, she had to admit, just a growing anticipation. Divorcing one set of emotions from another was proving easier than she had imagined. She might not love him, but she certainly wanted him.

'How long has Ilena worked for you?' she asked, desperate for something to keep her thoughts in order.

'Since the place was finished,' he said. 'Before this I had a service apartment in the city.'

'You're considered something of a marvel in the commercial world,' she observed lightly. 'What does it feel like to have achieved so much in such a relatively short time?'

'Satisfying,' he admitted. 'Not that mine is any rags to riches story. I inherited one fortune from my paternal grandfather, another from the Parella side. On my father's death I'll be heir to the whole estate.' He gave a faint smile. 'I hope, both for his sake and my own, that it won't be for a long time to come.'

'Because you'd feel obligated to go back and live there?' Leonie hazarded.

'It would be expected. As the only son, I'm expected to do many things I've no wish to do. My mother was unfortunately unable to produce any more children.'

'Why blame your mother?' she said with some asperity. 'It could be your father's fault.'

Vidal's lips twitched. 'I'd hesitate to cast any doubt on his virility. Not that it's applicable. My mother developed a medical condition that made further pregnancies too risky.'

Leonie made an apologetic gesture. 'Sorry for jumping the gun. It must have been hard for them both.'

'Especially with cousin Bernado's four children for comparison.'

It was almost fully dark now, the stars beginning to twinkle against a sky turning to black velvet. She viewed him across the table with her pulse-rate ever increasing. Lit by the soft glow from the wall lights, his face looked carved from bronze, his throat a taut column within the open collar of his shirt. All she knew of him so far was the feel. She could only imagine how he would look devoid of all clothing.

'Are their reactions likely to be unfavourable too?' she asked, closing her mind to the image. 'Your cousins, I mean?'

'In some respects.' His tone was easy, but there was something in his expression that warned her not to pursue the subject. 'I think a brandy to finish the meal.'

It was her instinct to defy the unspoken edict, but she held the words back. Whatever she was called on to face, she would face when the time came. Right now, she had other matters on her mind.

He went to get the drinks, returning bearing both glasses and decanter. Leonie watched him pour the golden liquid, recalling the last time they'd drunk brandy together just weeks ago. It still didn't seem possible that so much could have happened in so short a time.

'What would you do if you found I wasn't *virgo intacta* after all?' she said without conscious volition.

The gaze Vidal rested on her face was devoid of concern. 'As I've already told you, if there had been any serious relationship with a man, I'd know about it.'

'Taking it for granted that I haven't indulged in any non-serious relationships?'

'Taking it for granted,' he agreed. 'It isn't in you to indulge in one-night affairs.'

'I was prepared to spend the night with you,' she reminded him.

His lips twisted. 'Only because you had little choice. I'm not proud of my behaviour that day. I allowed my desire for reprisal to overcome all other considerations. Fortunately, I came to my senses in time to stop myself from doing something I should have regretted.'

Leonie held his gaze. 'You've no regrets over what you *have* done?'

'Would you have accepted me any other way?' he countered, smiling briefly when she failed to answer. 'Right or wrong, it was an opportunity I couldn't allow to pass.' A spark sprang in the dark eyes as he viewed her. 'You're mine now!'

'You don't own me!' she protested.

'A feminist cry, if ever I heard one! What is it you say in your country—possession is nine points of the law?'

There was humour in his tone. Leonie subsided, aware of being teased. She took a sip of the brandy, feeling it slide smoothly down her throat. Only the best, of course. Something she would have little difficulty in becoming accustomed to, she had to admit. She knew a cautious lifting of spirit. Vidal had used her father's position ruthlessly, to get his way, but it was done now, and time to make the best of it—for however long it lasted. It could have been so much worse. She could have found him physically revolting.

Vidal set his glass down and took hers gently from her. His eyes were luminous. 'I find myself unable to wait any longer,' he said softly. 'Come, *meu querida.*'

Heart hammering against her ribcage, Leonie allowed herself to be drawn to her feet. She wanted this as much as he did.

There was no one around as he led her up through the levels. The whole place was quiet. The bedroom was lamplit, the satin spread rolled to the end of the bed, silk sheets turned back both sides. The sheer white nightdress she had bought on a whim was laid out ready. By Ilena, she presumed.

Vidal wasted no time on rituals. He turned her into his arms, his mouth passionate. Leonie responded instinctively, arms sliding about his neck, body pressing closer in search of the heat and hardness she remembered so well. No other man had ever been able to arouse her the way Vidal aroused her. She wanted to know it all—everything she had been missing all these years.

Dextrous fingers unfastened the buttons running down the front of her dress, sliding the material back over her shoulders to allow the garment to fall to the floor. Swung from the ground, she clung to him as he carried her across to the bed. He tossed the silk cover aside with a sweep of a hand to deposit her gently on crisp clean linen, viewing her slender curves clad only in skimpy lace bra and panties with eyes fired by desire.

'*Sem igual!*' he murmured. '*Você é meu!*'

Blood singing in her ears, Leonie watched him remove his own clothing. His skin looked like oiled silk in the lamplight, the muscular structure of his shoulders and upper arms beautifully defined. His stomach was flat, hips hard and lean, body smooth and almost hairless but for the dark curls caressing the essence of his masculinity.

Every fibre of her body was alive to the feel of his naked body as he slid down beside her, the masculine scent of him an arousal in itself. He was all muscle and power, his hands possessive as they removed the rest of her clothing and began a pilgrimage down the contours of her body, sending ripple after ripple of melting sensation through her.

His touch was like a butterfly's wings against the fluttering skin of her abdomen. Her breath caught in her throat as he reached the spot she had allowed no man before him to access, thighs tensing instinctively against the intimate intrusion for a brief moment before relaxing to the gentle urging. Her hips began moving of their own accord to his command, her whole being seized by the overwhelming need to find release from the delicious, agonising torment. A release that tore a heartfelt cry from her lips.

'That is only a beginning,' Vidal promised softly.

He moved his body further over her, supporting his weight on bent arms as he looked down into her lovely defenceless face framed within the spread of Titian hair across the white-ness of the pillow. The glow in the dark eyes was all-consuming. When he kissed her she responded blindly, pas-sionately, lips parting to the silky touch of his tongue.

She writhed beneath him when he left her lips to seek the firmness of her breasts, running his tongue over and around each quivering, peaking nipple until she felt she could bear no more yet wanted him never to stop. She ran her hands into the thickness of his hair, back arching involuntarily, her heartbeats like thunder in her ears. Her thighs parted to the full potent weight of him, hips rising a little to facilitate his entry, the gasp drawn from her lips at the first gently probing contact smothered against his skin.

He took it slowly, carving a passage by degrees, until he filled every last inch of her, the pain so fleeting it was come and gone in the same instant. The feel of him so deep inside her was exquisite. She wanted to stay like that for ever. A desire overridden by a swift-rising fire as he began to move, her body following his into the age-old rhythm. The great rolling wave of pure sensation that caught her up at the peak made her cry out. Vidal climaxed almost immediately after, poised for a timeless moment above her before collapsing into her arms.

He was first to find his voice. Head at rest on her shoulder, body weight adjusted to allow her to breathe, he sounded at peace with the world. 'I knew the first moment I saw you how it would be between us,' he murmured. 'We were made for each other, you and I.'

Right now, Leonie could find no quarrel with that state-ment. She had never felt such utter gratification in her life before. Worth waiting for, was her last fading thought as she drifted into sleep

The bed at her side was empty when she awoke. The win-dows were opened on a morning drenched in sunlight and heady with scent from the massed banks of flowers ranging the hillside.

Leonie lay for a moment or two savouring the memory of the night's lovemaking. It had been everything she could have hoped for; more than she had ever imagined. The product of experience on Vidal's side admittedly, though even that knowledge failed to dampen her spirits to any degree. There was a great deal more to marriage than a good sex life, but it was a step on the way. Vidal had said there'd be no others. If he stuck to his word they might even stand a chance of forming some deeper commitment.

It was gone nine, she saw from the bedside clock. What time Vidal had risen she had no idea. She would have welcomed being woken with a kiss. For starters at least, came the thought, stirring a response deep down inside.

The nightdress she'd never got round to donning was on the floor. She got up to retrieve it, more than a little self-conscious in her nudity. If Vidal walked in now she would be overcome with embarrassment, regardless of what had passed between them. A state of mind she'd no doubt get over in time.

Showered, she dressed in cotton trousers and a sleeveless T-shirt, sliding her feet into flat sandals. A couple of gardeners were at work on the beds, she saw from the window; she could hear them chatting away. It was open to doubt if any of the staff spoke English, which make it imperative that she gain at least a basic knowledge of Portuguese as soon as possible.

She'd totally forgotten to call her father on arrival, as she'd promised to do, she realised. He would be at the office by now—or should be. There was a telephone here in the bedroom, and another in the sitting room. She chose the latter, taking a seat in one of the superbly comfortable armchairs as she dialled the number direct.

The connection went through without a hitch. She was transferred immediately to his office line.

'I waited all evening for you to call,' he said.

'Sorry,' Leonie proffered. 'I was a bit overcome with it all. How are things, anyway?'

'Settling down,' he acknowledged. 'Although I'm not sure I trust Simon to keep his mouth shut.' He paused, as though waiting for her to say something else, adding tentatively, 'Are you...all right?'

'I'm fine,' she assured him. 'I'm sitting here in the most wonderful house, in the most wonderful spot, still hardly able to believe it's my home!'

'I can hardly believe it either,' he said. 'It all happened so fast.' There was another pause, a subtle change of tone. 'You certainly sound happy enough.'

'I am.' Right now she could say that in all honesty, the imperfections relegated to the very back of her mind. 'I really am, Dad!'

'Is Vidal there with you now?' he asked.

'No, he left me to catch up on my sleep.' She did a hasty review in the realisation of how that might sound in the circumstances. 'It was such a long day yesterday, what with the travelling and all.'

Stuart gave a brief laugh. 'I'm sure. What are you planning on doing today?'

'I'm not sure,' she hedged. 'I have a lot of exploring to do. The whole area is a World Heritage site. It's absolutely beautiful! You must come and visit.'

'Some time, perhaps.' He hesitated before adding gruffly, 'You'd tell me if things started going wrong, wouldn't you?'

Leonie kept her tone light. 'What could possibly go wrong? I'll phone in a couple of days or so. Take care, Dad. I love you.'

She replaced the receiver before he could say anything else. He might have an inkling that all wasn't quite as it should be, but so long as she kept reassuring him he'd accept it.

A sound from the bedroom brought her head round to the connecting door, which she'd left open. Expecting Vidal to appear in the frame, she had a greeting all ready on her lips, the words dying away as Ilena put in an appearance instead. The housekeeper was carrying a tray, and said something in Portuguese. Leonie caught only *mestre*, but the tray bore the makings of a continental breakfast. If *mestre* meant Mr, or, maybe more likely, Master, then Ilena was probably trying to convey that he'd sent her up with it. It would have been better if he'd brought it up himself, but perhaps that was expecting a little too much.

'*Obrigado,*' she said, dredging up one of the very few words she knew for certain in Portuguese. 'Thank you, Ilena. I'm very grateful!'

If the latter words didn't get through, the accompanying smile gained a faint response. Ilena deposited the tray on a low table, poured a cup of fragrant coffee, and departed. Leonie couldn't blame her for feeling less than happy with the situation. The shock in finding her employer married must have been great.

Not nearly as great as the shock her new in-laws were going to get, came the thought, hastily discarded before it could begin to weigh too heavily. Next week was next week. The here and now was what mattered.

The coffee was excellent, the accompanying croissants and preserves more than adequate. It was almost ten-thirty by the time she finished, with still no sign of Vidal. She took the tray with her when she went downstairs. Lifts would have ruined the design, she supposed, and the stairs would certainly keep one fit, but they must tax someone Ilena's age.

She left the tray on a table in the lower hallway, reluctant to venture into the staff quarters. She wondered how many people Vidal employed at the house. Ilena would more than likely live on the premises, with others coming in on a daily basis. So far she'd seen the two gardeners, plus the young man who had served the champagne last night—Paulo, Vidal had called him.

Where Vidal himself was she couldn't begin to think. After the way he'd been last night, she had anticipated—well, she wasn't sure exactly what she had anticipated, but being left on her own like this certainly wasn't it. Even if she could find someone to ask where he might be, the language barrier made it impossible.

She was standing there irresolute when Paulo came up from the lower regions. *'Bom dia, senhora,'* he greeted her, and then, in halting English, 'You wish something?'

Relief swamped her. She wasn't totally incommunicado after all. 'Where is Senhor Dos Santos?' she asked, enunciating the words clearly.

'He go to the town,' the youth answered.

'Town!' Leonie gazed at him in bewilderment. 'You mean Lisbon?'

'Town, yes,' he confirmed. 'To his…' He searched for the word he needed. 'Offices,' he concluded triumphantly. *'Negócio.'*

Leonie didn't bother asking what the last meant. She felt totally let down. Her first impressions had been correct after all. Vidal had no feeling whatsoever for her beyond the physical desire he'd demonstrated so vibrantly last night. Any tenderness he'd shown had been purely the product of technique. Today it was business as usual.

The house felt suddenly oppressive. She made her way outside, heading for a lower terrace away from the men at work higher up. The morning sun was hot, the shade afforded by an overhanging tree welcome. Seated on a stone bench, she surveyed the superb view with lacklustre eyes.

So what had she really expected? she asked herself ruefully. Vidal might appear at times to have a softer side to his nature, but it was all surface. He'd proved that this morning. What the staff must be thinking, she couldn't imagine.

It made little difference in the long run. There was no get-out clause attached to the contract. At least not from her side. The way she saw it, she had two choices: she could accept the situation as it was, and enjoy at least one aspect, or she could pay him out by turning frigid on him. The last might be the hardest choice, considering the way he made her feel, but it was the only weapon she had.

The sound of an engine brought her mind into sharp focus again. She straightened abruptly as a car came into view around the curve in the drive, its open top revealing the driver to be a woman about her own age. Sending a shower of gravel over the border, the newcomer brought the vehicle to a skidding stop on the forecourt.

Black-haired, good-looking, and seductively shaped in a tight-fitting T-shirt, she gazed at Leonie, obviously disconcerted.

'*Quem são você?*' she said.

'I'm sorry,' Leonie answered. 'I don't speak Portuguese.'

'You are English?' Though heavily accented, the words were clear enough, and the disconcertedness even more pronounced. 'What are you doing here?'

There was only one answer Leonie could give. 'I'm the owner's wife. I live here.'

'Wife!' The other looked first stunned, then disbelieving. 'I think you joke with me!'

'It's no joke.' Leonie could say that with feeling. 'Who are you, anyway?'

Dark eyes flashed. 'I am Sancha Barreto Caldeira! Where is Vidal?'

'He went out.'

'When is he to return?'

It was more of a demand than a simple question. Leonie

felt her hackles rise. 'I've really no idea,' she said. 'Perhaps I can give him a message for you.'

'I leave no messages!' She sounded vicious. She slammed into gear, turning the car in a gravel-crunching circle.

A woman of a somewhat volatile nature, Leonie judged, watching the vehicle career back down the drive. Not one to take rejection easily, for certain. If, as appeared likely from her attitude, she was on more than just friendly terms with Vidal, then she was justified in feeling badly done to. It made *her* feel no better about him for certain.

She was still sitting in the same place when he returned some twenty minutes or so later, bringing the Mercedes to a controlled stop in front of her.

'*Bom dia,*' he greeted her smilingly. 'You're fully rested?'

Leonie kept her tone even, determined not to give way to the emotions boiling up inside. 'Fully.'

She waited until he'd alighted from the car before adding, 'You had a visitor a short while back.'

'Is that so?' Leaning against the bonnet, arms casually folded, Vidal regarded her with quizzically lifted brows. 'Did they leave a name?'

'Sancha, something or other.' Leonie looked for some sign of perturbation in the lean features, but his expression remained easy. 'She seemed a little put out to find me here.'

Amusement lit the dark gaze. 'Only a little?'

'Meaning she has cause for more?'

'A matter of opinion,' he said. 'As with many women, Sancha reads a great deal too much into very little.'

'Meaning you don't consider sleeping with a woman grants her any kind of entitlement?'

'One of the things I find difficult to understand about the English is this habit of referring to sexual relations as "sleeping",' Vidal returned smoothly. 'To answer the question, I consider her due no more from me than I'm due from her.'

'No more than I'm due myself, in fact.'

His brows drew together as he surveyed her. 'What is it you find missing from our relationship?'

'Emotion,' she said. 'What happened between us last night was simple lust, nothing more. I won't pretend to have hated it at the time, but it doesn't alter the fact that we've no other feelings for each other.'

'Is all this because I left you alone this morning?' Vidal asked softly.

'Not at all,' she lied. 'I was grateful for the opportunity to get things into perspective.'

Vidal hadn't altered his position, but there was little trace of amusement in his eyes now. 'And what conclusion did you reach?'

She steadied her nerve, blanking out any inclination towards backtracking. 'That I might be stuck with the marriage, but I don't have to play the part of docile wife.'

'Let me be sure I have your meaning correctly,' he said after a lengthy moment. 'You're saying you no longer intend indulging this lust you spoke of?'

Leonie lifted her chin. 'That's right.'

His laugh was derisive. 'Judging from last night's performance, you could no more take that stance than I could myself!' He straightened away from the car. 'I'll leave you to think on it.'

He drove off in the direction of the garages tucked away round the curve of the hillside. Leonie swallowed on the hardness in her throat. She hadn't intended going quite that far; the words had been dragged from her. Refusing to sleep with him outright was out of the question, of course. While she doubted he would stoop to using force, her father's future still rested with him. The only thing she could do was put every effort into controlling her baser instincts. Vidal would gain little pleasure from making love to an inanimate block of wood.

CHAPTER FOUR

LUNCH was served on the same terrace on which they'd taken dinner last night. Leonie had contemplated giving it a miss, but decided that would be a futile gesture. She anticipated finding Vidal less than amiable after what she'd said to him, but he appeared oblivious to any strain between them.

'A change of plan,' he announced. 'I need to go to Zurich. We can go from there to the Douro.'

'What am I supposed to do in Zurich while you talk business?' Leonie asked.

His shrug was light. 'What most visitors do. It's a very historic city. I'll introduce you to Helen Bouche, the wife of one of my bank's directors. She'll be delighted to show you around. We'll be leaving in the morning, so you can replenish your wardrobe there, instead of here in Lisbon. You'll find Zurich an excellent fashion centre too.'

Clothes were the last thing on Leonie's mind. Vidal had taken nothing she'd said seriously, it seemed. Well, he'd learn. She was determined on that.

'So what would you like to do with the rest of the day?' he asked when she failed to make any comment. 'I'm completely at your disposal.'

Feeling the way she had felt this morning, she'd have found little difficulty in choosing a way of passing time. Right now, all she wanted to do was to pack her bags and head for home. Only she couldn't, could she? She was well and truly trapped.

They spent the afternoon exploring Sintra Villa. Lush with bougainvillea, gardenias and eucalyptus, and spanning five centuries of history, the place was magical. The conical chimneys of the National Palace dominating the skyline looked for all the world like a pair of enormous champagne bottles.

At this time of year, the labyrinthine streets were far from empty. Vidal hired a horsedrawn carriage to tour the granite slopes on which the older part of the town was situated. Leonie sat entranced by the diversity of the architecture, the superb views, the whole ambience of the place.

'I'd heard of it, of course,' she said. 'It's a place I'd meant to visit some day.'

She sobered in sudden recollection of the reason she *was* here, aware of the dark eyes on her face, the tolerant smile.

'You'll become accustomed to it,' Vidal returned. 'As you'll become accustomed to a different way of life. The *quinta* will be our base, of course, but I'll expect you to accompany me when I travel.'

They'd left the carriage to view the sweeping scene below from a vantage point. Leonie gave him a swift sideways glance. 'Won't you find that rather curtailing?'

The muscles about his mouth tautened momentarily, though his tone remained steady. 'If you mean what I believe you mean, I already told you there will be no others. Our marriage had an unfortunate beginning, but—'

'You call blackmail *unfortunate*!' Leonie put every atom of scorn she could conjure into her tone. 'I'd call it criminal!'

'Whichever, the marriage took place.' He viewed her flushed and angry face for a moment in silence, his expression enigmatic. 'Would it have made any difference to your feelings if I'd told you I loved you?'

'You don't believe in love,' she retorted. 'You told me so yourself two years ago.'

'What I meant,' he said, 'was that I didn't believe in the lasting quality of the kind based on physical attraction alone. I can't recall the exact words I used when I asked you to marry me the first time, but I thought I made it clear that my feelings for you took far more than that into account.

Obviously my command of your language isn't—or certainly wasn't—as good as I took it to be.'

'You didn't *ask* me to marry you,' Leonie retorted. 'You *told* me I was going to.'

'I was arrogant,' he acknowledged disarmingly. 'Your response left me in little doubt of that. Not that I believe I merited quite the degree of vitriol you produced.'

'I'd seen the item about that woman claiming you'd abandoned her and her child,' she defended. 'I know it wasn't true now, but I—'

'But you thought me the kind of man capable of it then,' he finished for her. 'Do you still?'

She shook her head. 'No.'

'Why not?' he asked. 'You know me no better in essence than you did two years ago.'

'I just…know,' she said, stumped for a better answer. She made an abrupt movement. 'Can we go back now? I need to pack some things for tomorrow.'

Vidal made no demur. He'd kept the carriage waiting. Seated at his side as they headed back to the starting point, Leonie went over everything he'd said these past minutes. She could believe there would be no others while their relationship was new, and her naïveté still a novelty, but she doubted if the idea of having her accompany him on business trips would be a long-term one. But then, the marriage itself was unlikely to be very long term.

However long or short a time it lasted, acting the ice maiden wasn't going to change anything, she acknowledged. Better, surely, to accept the limitations and just make the most of the rest.

Unlike the night before, Vidal showed no inclination towards early retirement. They passed the evening in desultory conversation—pleasant enough, but lacking any element of challenge. The wine Leonie had drunk with dinner, plus the brandy they'd finished with made her restless rather than relaxed. Even if she hadn't already decided her earlier retaliatory plan was a non-starter, she would have found it beyond her to keep it up, she reflected wryly, eyeing Vidal's lean length stretched out on the lounger at her side.

The tailored white trousers he was wearing were pulled taut at the groin, outlining the masculine shape. She touched the tip of her tongue to lips gone dry at the memory of last night's lovemaking. He'd taken her to heaven and back; she wanted desperately to go there again.

'What time will we be leaving in the morning,' she asked.

'Right after breakfast,' Vidal answered. 'I've an appointment at three. It may be necessary for you to travel to the hotel alone while I keep it. The Swiss consider punctuality all important.'

'Will they know who I am?' she said, not caring for the idea at all.

'Of course.' He sounded amused. 'Did you imagine I intended keeping the marriage a secret?'

'Considering you didn't even tell your own family yet, it wasn't beyond the realms of possibility,' she retorted. 'Assuming you still haven't, that is?'

He shook his head. 'To pre-warn is to pre-arm.'

'Anyone would think,' she scoffed, 'that you were afraid!'

He laughed, refusing to rise to the taunt. 'Something you must judge for yourself when the time comes.'

The time had come for *one* of them to make a move, Leonie decided, tired of the sparring. It was coming up to midnight. She put up a hand to hide a spurious yawn.

'If we're making an early start, I'm going to turn in.'

'A sensible idea,' Vidal agreed. He reached for his brandy glass as she got to her feet. 'I'll finish this first.'

The difference between his attitude now and his fervor last night was like a slap in the face. The kind of woman he was accustomed to making love to would be as experienced as he was himself, of course, with no hang-ups to overcome. If he was bored with her performance in bed already...

She left him sitting there and made her way up to their suite. Vidal still hadn't arrived by the time she was ready to get into bed. It was another twenty minutes or so before he finally put in an appearance.

She lay there on tenterhooks, pretending to be asleep already, while he undressed. There was another ten-minute hiatus while he took a shower. Lying on her side, Leonie held her breath as he finally slid into the bed at her back, her whole body tingling in anticipation of his touch.

Only he made no attempt to touch her. She could feel his body heat, smell the emotive masculine scent of him, but he remained on his own side of the bed.

'You're not asleep, so stop pretending,' he said at length. 'If you want me, you must show me. I've no intention of persuading you.'

Desire fought a battle with pride, losing because she couldn't find it in herself to give way so completely. 'As I told you this morning, *I've* no intention of playing the docile wife,' she retorted.

'You were speaking nonsense then, and you're speaking nonsense now.' His tone was surprisingly mild. 'I'll leave you to consider.'

He remained lying on his back, apparently untouched by the frustration she couldn't deny. What she'd wanted was to be persuaded, she admitted with shame. To be assured that Vidal still felt as passionately about her in at least that one sense. But he couldn't, could he, if he was prepared to deprive himself?

He underlined his lack of disturbance by falling asleep within minutes—at least to judge from his breathing pattern. It was another hour before *she* slept, and then only fitfully.

*   *   *

The flight was delayed, not reaching Zurich until close on two-thirty. Vidal put her into a taxi to go straight to the hotel, taking another himself for the banking district. He should be with her by five, he said.

Set about a crystal-clear lake, with distant views of snowy peaks, Zurich was one of the most beautiful cities Leonie had seen to date. She needn't have worried about recognition by the hotel staff. She was treated like royalty from the moment she gave her name at Reception.

The suite to which she was shown was sumptuous in every detail. Living like this was a real hardship, she reflected ironically, viewing the marble bathroom. Commonplace to Vidal, of course. He'd lived this way all his life.

There had been no hint this morning of anything untoward in his attitude to her. He'd been courtesy itself, in fact. But if she phoned her father now, and told him the truth, he'd have her on the next plane home regardless. The temptation to do just that was almost irresistible. They'd get through whatever Vidal chose to throw at them.

Except that it wouldn't be her he was throwing it at, of course.

Her case unpacked, she pinned up her hair and took a leisurely soak in the enormous bath. There were controls to turn it into a Jacuzzi, but she was in no mood for experimentation. The warmth, combined with the fact that she hadn't slept at all well last night, made her drowsy. With her head supported on the waterproof pillow looped over the bath edge, she allowed herself to drift, happy to be relieved of her problems for a while.

She awoke to the feel of water trickling slowly over her breasts. When she opened her eyes, it was to find Vidal seated on the wide bath-edge. He'd taken off the jacket he'd been wearing, but hadn't bothered to roll his shirtsleeves, his cuff dripping as he allowed the last droplets to fall.

'You've allowed the water to go cool,' he said.

Leonie sat up with a jerk, only just resisting the instinctive impulse to cover her vital parts with her hands in the time-honoured fashion. 'You said you wouldn't be here before five!'

'It's exactly fifteen minutes past five,' he returned equably. He stood up to reach for one of the thick Turkish cotton towels. 'I'd suggest you get out of there before you take a chill.'

'I can manage that quite well on my own, thanks,' she said, making no move. 'Just leave the towel on the rack.'

'What else would I have in mind?' he asked. 'I meant what I said last night. The word must come from you. We're invited to dinner with the Bouches. Just the two of us, so no formality.'

Leonie watched him from the room before pulling herself upright. Her foot slipped as she made to step from the bath. She only just saved herself from falling out of it. Poetic justice, Vidal would probably have called it, if he'd come back to find her measuring her length across the floor. He might, she thought ruefully, have had a point. She'd acted like some silly schoolgirl.

The same could be said of her threat to freeze him out. It had gained her nothing but frustration. From what he'd said just now, she was going to have to eat some humble pie if she didn't want to spend any more restless nights. A galling thought, but at least he didn't appear to have gone off her altogether.

Dried, she donned the fresh underwear she'd laid out ready, then went through to the dressing room to search out something suitable for the evening. The dress she chose was of a light summery style in figured lemon silk. Scoop-necked, and sleeveless, it fitted closely down to the waist, to fall in soft folds to her knees. She'd worn it only once before, to attend the engagement party of one of the girls at work. That had only been a month ago, yet it seemed ages since.

Vidal was watching a news item on television when she

went into the living room. He viewed her with confidence-boosting appreciation. 'Excellent,' he said.

'What time are we expected?' Leonie asked.

'Around eight. It's a half-hour drive.'

'You're hiring a car?'

'Already arranged. I take taxis only when unavoidable. Piers and I still have a few matters to discuss, but I'm sure you and Helen will find a lot in common.'

'Only if she speaks English,' Leonie felt moved to remark. 'My French is strictly schoolgirl. Not even very good schoolgirl either.'

'Helen is English,' Vidal advised. 'She met Piers four years ago, when she came to Zurich on holiday. They have a two-year-old son, with another child expected in seven months.' His tone was easy. 'The perfect family.'

A perfect start, she thought, with a pang of envy.

Vidal got to his feet. 'I'll go and take a shower myself now you're out of the bathroom.'

He left the television playing. Leonie took a seat, watching the screen without interest. At the very least she wouldn't have to struggle with the language tonight—assuming Piers spoke English too. She refused to dwell on what was to happen later.

The Bouche home lay in the forested, castle-adorned countryside outside the city limits. Stone-built, and set in its own grounds, it was everything Leonie would have expected of a Swiss bank director.

The Bouches welcomed them at the door. A vitally attractive man, Piers was in his early forties, his wife some ten years younger. Blonde-haired and pretty, she had an outgoing manner that soon put Leonie at her ease.

'I've been agog to meet you,' the other declared with engaging frankness. 'I'd begun to believe the woman didn't exist who could tie our friend here down!'

'I'd begun to despair of finding a woman I could bear to

be tied down by,' Vidal said lightly. 'Which is why I made certain of her before she could change her mind.'

'As if there was any chance of it,' Leonie put in, trying for an equally light note—though not quite succeeding, if the glance Vidal gave her was anything to go by.

'Our lives are all in the hands of fortune,' commented Piers in heavily accented English. He lifted Leonie's hand to his lips. 'Vidal is fortunate to have met with such a beautiful fate!'

Frenchmen were renowned for their lack of inhibition when it came to greeting women, Leonie reminded herself, seeing the unconcealed lust in his eyes as he raised them to hers. It wasn't to be taken seriously.

She would have liked to meet their small son, but he was already in bed. They ate a beautifully prepared meal out on a terrace overlooking a small lake. Helen was an excellent hostess in every sense. Leonie had a feeling she would cope just as easily with a dinner party for twenty.

She said as much after the meal, when the men had gone into a business huddle, leaving the two of them to entertain themselves. Helen laughed, lifting her shoulders.

'It's no problem. I just call in the caterers. I'd rather spend any spare time I have with André.'

'Does he know about the new baby?' Leonie asked, assuming that was the son's name.

'Oh, of course. We told him as soon as it was confirmed, to give him plenty of time to get used to the idea.' She patted her scarcely rounded stomach. 'He wants a brother, but both Piers and I would like a girl this time. Do you want children yourself?'

'I hadn't got round to thinking about it yet,' Leonie prevaricated.

'I suppose it is a bit soon, although I imagine Vidal will be under pressure from the family, considering he's the only son. I gather you didn't get to meet them yet?'

'No.' Leonie kept her tone easy. 'We're going to the Douro next.'

Helen laughed again. 'Business first. Trust a man!'

'I always thought Frenchmen put romance before everything,' Leonie commented, drawing a smile.

'An impression most of them like to give. They're a smooth-talking race. If you weren't married to a very important client, you'd be on the receiving end yourself. Piers could never resist a beautiful woman.'

'You don't mind?' Leonie asked after a moment.

'It's the way he is.' Helen sounded matter-of-fact about it. 'The way most men are, if we're realistic about it. Unlike us—or some of us, at any rate—they can indulge their appetites without emotional attachment.'

Leonie made no comment. The summing-up was too close to home for comfort. All the same, there was no way she could ever bring herself to accept it the way Helen apparently did.

'Have you met the Dos Santos family yourself?' she asked, steering clear of any further introspection.

'Few people have. They rarely move far from their own little empire, it seems. I don't wonder Vidal got out. He's hardly the type to relish confinement.' She paused. 'They know about the wedding, of course?'

Leonie briefly contemplated a lie, abandoning the idea on the realisation that Vidal may already have told Piers. She shook her head. 'Not yet.'

'Oh?' Helen looked nonplussed. 'It's going to be quite a shock for them, then.'

That, Leonie thought, was set to be the understatement of the year. 'They'll get over it,' she said, adopting a positive note. 'They don't have any choice.'

'Meaning they're unlikely to approve.' Helen nodded sagely. 'Piers' family felt much the same about him marrying outside his own nationality to start with, but they soon came round. You and Vidal are ideally suited.'

'He told Piers you wanted to do some shopping while you're here,' she added on a brisker note. 'They're due to visit some project or other tomorrow, but I'm free all day. I could pick you up from the hotel at ten.'

'What about André?' Leonie hedged, reluctant to be drawn into something of so little interest to her at present.

'He has a nanny.'

Leaving his mother to do what? Leonie wondered fleetingly. 'It's very good of you,' she said, resigning herself to the inevitable in the certain knowledge that reluctance on her part would look distinctly odd.

'No problem at all,' Helen assured her. 'Shopping is my favourite pastime!'

'As my statements constantly prove,' put in Piers from his seat some distance away, causing Leonie to wonder just how much of their conversation had carried across. She did a hasty review, finding nothing of any particular note—although Vidal might well object to her summary dismissal of his family's concerns.

Not that she really cared, anyway, she assured herself. She'd spoken nothing but the truth.

'How long do you plan on staying in Zurich?' she asked him on the way back to the hotel.

'One more day,' Vidal answered. 'Two more nights.'

Leonie winged a glance, taking in the tilt at the corner of his mouth. If he thought she couldn't hold out against him he was going to be sorely disappointed, she vowed wrathfully, sidelining her earlier considerations. She'd managed for years without sex.

Only because she hadn't known the full extent of what she was missing, whispered the treacherous little voice.

'And in the Douro?' she queried, turning a deaf ear again.

'As long as it takes for them to accept our marriage as irrevocable.'

'With me as pig in the middle!'

Vidal laughed. 'I doubt you'll allow yourself to be diminished in any way.'

'You can count on *that* much, at least,' she responded.

He made no comment. Leonie stole a glance at the lean profile, feeling the instant impact on her senses. She was fighting a hopeless battle, she acknowledged resignedly. One hurting her far more than it was hurting him.

It was coming up to midnight when they reached the hotel. Vidal offered her first use of the bathroom, again without a flicker of irony. He made no comment when she emerged wearing both nightdress and negligee.

Leonie took off the latter to get into the bed, lying motionless on her back, gazing at the figured ceiling. Like some sacrificial lamb pinned out for the slaughter, came the thought, bringing a wry smile to her lips. The only sacrifice she was being called on to make was to her pride, and that seemed of little importance right now. Vidal had awoken her to a whole gamut of emotions. She yearned to run them again.

He was wearing the bottom half of dark silk pyjamas when he returned to the bedroom. As on the night before, Leonie found herself holding her breath as he slid between the sheets at her side—willing him to make the move himself.

He didn't, increasing her frustration to unbearable limits as the minutes ticked by. Throat dry, she finally gave in, her voice gravelly in her ears.

'You don't need to persuade me.'

'Actions speak louder than mere words,' came the level response. 'Show me how much you want me.'

Leonie swallowed hard on the vituperative retort that was her first impulse. She'd begun this; it was up to her to finish it.

Without giving herself any further time to think about it, she turned towards him, pressing her lips to the smooth skin of his shoulder as her hand sought the masculine shape within the thin silk. The breath hissed between his teeth as her fingers closed about him, his response immediate. Following an instinctive sensual urge, she began a slow caressing movement, relishing the sudden sense of power. She'd been happy on their wedding night to take all he could give her, but lovemaking was a two-way affair; she was just beginning to appreciate that.

Vidal ran a hand into the thickness of her hair as she kissed her way up the column of his throat to reach his mouth, caressing the tender skin at her nape with a touch that sent quivers down her spine. His lips were pliable beneath hers. She played with them as he had played with hers two nights ago, brushing, nibbling, teasing them apart with the very tip of her tongue—inhibition suddenly and heart-racingly a thing of the past.

'I want you,' she whispered huskily.

He turned her under him in a swift surging movement that took her by surprise, framing her face between his hands to kiss her with a passion that elicited instant response. Her thighs parted to the potent pressure applied, the material of her nightdress a barrier she deplored.

Only not for long. Vidal lifted himself from her to remove the garment, along with his own, easing down over her again to begin the incursion she craved. He watched her face as they came wholly together, the look in his eyes dispelling any doubts she'd harboured about his lack of desire for her. She wrapped long, slender legs about him, lost in the driving power of his loins.

'You're a woman of many surprises,' he said softly when the world had steadied again. 'You almost robbed me of control altogether back there.'

'I doubt if you'd ever allow that to happen to you,' Leonie answered, equally softly.

'There's a first time for everything.' There was a pause, a change of tone. 'It was brutal of me to put you in such a position.'

'It was silly of me to take the attitude I did,' she returned after a moment.

'But understandable, perhaps, in the circumstances. I should have waited at least until you awoke before leaving.'

If the marriage had been a normal one, based on love, he probably would have done, she thought.

'It made me feel totally inadequate,' she admitted, seeing no gain in pretence. 'I was, of course. Still am.'

His mouth curved at the corners. 'You were far from inadequate the first time; even farther from it this. You give me the greatest pleasure a man could know.'

How many women had he said that to? she wondered. How many women might he say it to in future?

Not that it made any difference to the emotions soaring through her as he put his lips to hers again.

CHAPTER FIVE

HELEN arrived prompt on the hour to pick her up. Vidal had presented Leonie with a platinum credit card already made out in her married name. The Open Sesame to anywhere and anything, Helen observed.

They took a taxi to the main shopping area, leaving her car in the hotel's underground park. One of the most expensive shopping streets in the world, the Bahnhofstrasse was a world away from Leonie's normal haunts. As Helen had intimated, the name elicited instant recognition.

Faced with top-name designer wear in abundance, plus the wherewithal to indulge, Leonie gave in to temptation. Prices were never discussed. Those with a need to know such things stuck to the more modest end of the street at Bahnhofplatz, or the complex of ShopVille, Helen said. As the wife of a multimillionaire, she scarcely needed to worry about such matters, Leonie was bound to concede.

They broke for a late luncheon in a *haute-cuisine* restaurant with sweeping views of the lake. The ambience was superb, the staff attentive to a fault, the food sublime. Leonie took herself to task for wishing they were somewhere just a little less formal.

'I should have worn one of the new outfits,' she commented, only half jokingly. 'This suit doesn't do the place justice.'

'The suit's fine,' Helen assured her. 'It wouldn't be what most people see when they look at you, anyway.' She lifted quizzical eyebrows at Leonie's expression. 'I'm being complimentary not bitchy.'

Leonie had to laugh. 'From you, I'll accept it. Is this one of your favourite haunts?'

'It might be, if Piers didn't keep my card accounts under review.' She gave a mock sigh. 'A distinct disadvantage to being married to a banker! I never got round to asking you last night,' she added, 'but how did you and Vidal meet?'

Leonie kept her tone easy. 'My father works for one of his companies. I called in on him one day when Vidal happened to be there.'

'It must have been fate for both of you, then.'

'I suppose it must.' Leonie looked for some other topic, anxious to avoid any further probing. 'Vidal said you met Piers when you came here on holiday?'

'True. We ran into one another—literally—on a street corner. We were both driving at the time, me in a hire car, him in his Porsche. My fault entirely, although I wasn't ready to admit it, of course. Anyway, we finished up having dinner together, and it just went from there.' The pause was brief. 'I realise what I said last night about him shocked you a little.' She smiled and shook her head as Leonie made to speak. 'I might have felt the same way at one time, but—'

She broke off as a woman who had paused at their table greeted her in voluble French, then responded in the same language with a fluency Leonie envied. Clad *haute couture* from head to toe, her blonde hair pinned into a smooth French pleat, the newcomer looked as if she'd just stepped off the catwalk.

Helen turned her attention across the table again, an odd gleam in her eyes. 'This is Simone Dubois,' she said, switching back to English. 'Leonie Parella Dos Santos,' she added, completing the introduction.

The Frenchwoman's almost too perfectly moulded features underwent a sudden and disconcerting change of expression. 'Dos Santos?' she repeated.

'That's right. Vidal's brand-new wife.' Helen's tone was

bland, but the gleam still lurked in her eyes. 'Gorgeous, isn't she? Not that you'd expect anything less, of course, Vidal being the connoisseur he is.'

Leonie's automatic smile and word of greeting withered beneath the icy regard. Without another word, the woman stalked away to join the party she had temporarily abandoned. Helen gave a low, satisfied laugh.

'How are the mighty fallen!'

'Why did I get the freezing treatment?' Leonie asked, already suspecting the answer.

'Because she'd probably give her eye-teeth to be where you are!'

'Married to Vidal, you mean?'

'You bet!' Helen caught herself up, looking a little uncomfortable. 'It might be best if we forget her.'

Leonie lifted her shoulders, doing her best to sound matter-of-fact about it. 'I'm not going to fall apart over Vidal's past affairs. Who exactly is she, anyway?'

'The Dubois are big in property. Simone is a company executive. On paper, at any rate.'

'You've known her a long time?'

'I only know her at all through Vidal,' Helen admitted. 'They were having dinner at the same restaurant where Piers and I were dining a few months ago. Vidal insisted that we join forces for the evening—much to Simone's disgust. From the way she asked after him just now, she's seen little of him since.'

'I gather you don't care for her very much?' Leonie ventured.

'Not one iota! She's one of those women who can set any other woman's teeth on edge just by being there.'

Leonie knew what she meant. She'd met one or two herself. Simone wasn't the first of Vidal's ex's she had run into, and very likely wouldn't be the last.

She avoided looking in the other woman's direction when

they left the restaurant, but she could almost feel the dagger in her back. She wouldn't be human, she defended herself, if she didn't feel just a little elated by the fact that she had the man the other had coveted.

For now, came the mental rider, bringing a certain deflation.

Helen was all for revisiting the stores, but Leonie felt she'd indulged quite enough for one day. They were back at the hotel by four. Helen declined an invitation to come up to the suite.

'I hope it won't be too long before you're this way again,' she said before getting in the car.

Leonie hoped not too. They might disagree on certain matters, but all in all she felt she'd found a friend.

She reached the suite to find that most of the things she'd bought had already been delivered. Vidal arrived while she was still sorting through them, eyeing the mass of bags with a dry smile.

'I see you had a good day,' he observed.

'I didn't realise just how much I'd bought,' Leonie admitted.

He laughed. 'With Helen in charge, I'm not surprised. I'll get them to send someone up to pack them for you while we're at dinner.'

'I can do that myself,' she protested. 'There's plenty of room in my bag.'

His shrug expressed a tolerant resignation. 'As you prefer. We have a midday flight to Porto.'

The reminder of what she faced tomorrow brought sudden despondency. 'What I'd really prefer is not to be dropped on your family like a bolt from the blue!' she said. 'It's going to be bad enough as it is, knowing how they're likely to react. A few hours' prior warning would at least give them time to come to some kind of terms with it all.'

'Better the short sharp shock,' Vidal returned unequivocally. 'You'll cope.'

'So you keep telling me.' She refrained from further persuasion, recognising adamancy when she heard it, though no closer to understanding the reason for it. 'Do they speak any English?'

'Of course. Although you may find their use of it very much more formal than mine.' He moved to take her by an arm and turn her towards him, holding her lightly as he looked down into her eyes. 'You're my wife. Nothing and no one can alter that!'

Certainly not her, with her father's whole future at stake, Leonie reflected. She still placed no reliance on the long-term chances of this marriage of theirs, but she had to admit that she wasn't exactly desperate to regain her freedom any more. With a lover like Vidal, and a lifestyle she could never in her wildest dreams have imagined, who would be?

Spectacularly beautiful, the valley became more and more sparsely populated the further inland they went, the spilling hillsides given over to terraces of vines interspersed with the occasional olive grove, the mountains a misty backdrop against a sky already deepening in hue.

'How much further?' Leonie asked.

Vidal kept his attention on the narrow, twisting road. 'Fifteen minutes.'

Fifteen minutes to gather herself for the meeting she dreaded. Damn him for putting her through this! she thought.

'Just what am I supposed to say to them?' she demanded.

'You need say nothing,' came the steady return.

'You mean I just stand there like a dummy?'

'Your beauty speaks for itself.'

'Bosh!' she retorted, in no mood for soft soap.

His mouth curved. 'So inelegant a phrase from such sweet lips!'

'Stop it!' Her voice had a tremor in it, only partly of anger. 'It's no joking matter! I'm the alien here. Why should they accept me?'

'Because they have no choice.' Vidal's tone was flat now, the humour flown. 'It may take a little time to convince them that the marriage is irrevocable, but convince them I will.'

It was a moment or two before Leonie could bring herself to say it. 'You really intend it to be permanent?'

Vidal shot her a swift glance, his surprise evident. 'What else did you think was my intention?'

She lifted her shoulders, not looking at him. 'I believed you were simply taking advantage of my father's situation.'

'To use you as a sex slave?' he suggested. 'If that had been my only aim, marriage would not have been offered.'

'So maybe I misjudged you,' she said, not by any means convinced. 'In that sense at any rate. Nothing can change the fact that you blackmailed me into marrying you.'

'I used the only persuasion available to me,' came the unmoved response. 'I make no excuses.'

'And you'd really be prepared to have my father charged with embezzlement if I walked out on you?'

There was a pause before he answered. When he did speak, the flatness was back in his voice. 'If that was the only way of keeping you from doing so, then yes.'

A bare week ago it would certainly have been the governing factor, Leonie admitted. Now, it was nowhere near as clear-cut.

She said no more, taking a firm hold on herself as he turned the car between huge iron gates to head up a gravelled driveway winding through woodland. However difficult this proved to be, she had to handle it.

Set high on a landscaped slope, majestic in the late-afternoon sunlight, the building that came into view as they rounded a bend drew a gasp to her lips. Crenellated towers lofted both ends of a long central section, pierced along both upper and lower floors by tall arched windows framed in what appeared to be gold, the whole appearance majestic.

'It's a castle!' she exclaimed.

'A palace,' Vidal corrected. 'The Palacio de Mecia. Built in the 18th century by one of my forebears, and named in honour of his wife.'

'I thought you said the aristocracy was no more,' Leonie queried dazedly.

'Their titles were lost, but some retained the land. The Dos Santos vineyards are world-renowned for the quality of port they produce.' He gave her a curious glance. 'What were you expecting?'

'Nothing like this,' she acknowledged. 'I knew the Dos Santos family was wealthy, of course, but a *palace*!'

'A small one. Many are larger.'

This one was more than big enough for her, Leonie thought. It was ridiculous to allow the grandness of the place to increase her nervousness about meeting the inhabitants of it, but there was no doubt that it did.

Vidal swept the hired Mercedes round the final curve to bring it to a stop on the wide forecourt. A central fountain gushed sparkling falls over stone bowls. Leonie opened her door with some reluctance to get out, stiff from the long drive.

Her heart jerked as an elderly man clad in a formal dark suit appeared at the top of the imposing flight of granite steps fronting the building. His questioning expression altered to one of out and out pleasure as Vidal alighted from the car.

'Senhor!' he exclaimed. '*É bom vê-lo!*'

Vidal answered in the same language, his smile and tone expressing a fond familiarity with the man. His name was Artur, Leonie gathered. A long-time family retainer, from the sound of it.

She gave him a smile herself in passing, a murmured, '*Bom dia.*' Vidal made no attempt to introduce her. But then, he was hardly going to make a servant the first recipient of the news, she reasoned.

The stone-arched doorway gave access to a grand entrance hall running all the way through to the rear of the property, where double glass doors offered a glimpse of sky. Polished to shining perfection, the terracotta-tiled floor seemed to stretch for ever. Golden chandeliers hung from the vaulted ceiling, complementing the grand piano and other lovely old pieces spread around.

The navy and white suit Leonie was wearing was Chanel, but it still felt inadequate to the surroundings. She braced herself as Vidal drew her forward to open a door on the left.

The room within made little initial impression, her attention riveted on the couple seated in it. Too much like Vidal in looks to be anyone else but his father, the man was the first to overcome his initial surprise at their appearance, coming to his feet to speak in tones of obvious reproof.

Vidal slid an arm about Leonie's shoulders. 'I saw no purpose in it,' he said levelly. 'I wish you to meet my wife, Leonie. She speaks no Portuguese as yet.'

Leonie had heard the phrase 'a deafening silence', but had never until now appreciated it. 'Hello,' was all she could come up with.

A beautiful woman still, dark hair showing no hint of grey, her mother-in-law conquered the shock that had rendered her momentarily speechless, rising from her chair with an expression on her face that left little doubt of her feelings. She spoke in Portuguese, but Leonie needed no translation to get the gist of what she was saying. Oddly, the disapproval expressed so forcefully put her on her mettle.

'I intend learning the language, of course,' she said the moment the other drew breath, 'but in the meantime I'd very much appreciate it if we could speak English. I realise what a shock it must be for you both,' she continued as both pairs of eyes turned her way. 'It's all happened so fast, I can still hardly believe it myself!'

'When did the wedding take place?' asked Senhor Dos Santos before his wife could speak again.

'Four days ago, in England,' Vidal answered. 'A civil ceremony, but a binding one.'

Eyes smouldering, his mother let rip with another torrent, totally ignoring Leonie's request—totally ignoring her. It took her husband to quieten her, his gesture that of a man accustomed to command.

'What is done is done,' he said. He came to take Leonie's hand in his, lifting it to his lips. 'You are very beautiful!'

Like Vidal's own, the dark eyes were impenetrable, his true feelings concealed. She murmured her thanks for the compliment, relieved when he released her to turn back to his wife. He held up a staying hand again as the latter made to speak. *'Não mais!'*

No more to be said, Leonie guessed. For now, at any rate. Judging from the glitter in her mother-in-law's eyes, the battle was by no means over.

'I'm truly sorry you're unhappy about the marriage,' she said impulsively. 'I'll make every effort to be worthy of the name.'

'You already are worthy of the name!' Vidal declared with some force.

'Your parents know nothing about me,' she returned. 'Why should they be expected to take it on trust?'

'It appears we have no choice,' Senhor Dos Santos interposed. 'But there are certainly matters to be discussed. Come, take a seat.'

Leonie forced herself into movement, choosing one of the brocade sofas. Vidal lowered himself at her side, close enough for her to feel his body heat. She kept her attention fixed on his father, who was still standing, trying to disregard his mother's unmitigated hostility.

'What would you like to know, *senhor*?'

'Perhaps your family name, to begin,' he said.

'It's Baxter,' she acknowledged. 'Though it's hardly going to mean anything to you. My father is an accountant, my mother is dead, and I'm the only child. I'm twenty-six years old, with a degree in Sociology, and I've worked in public relations for the past five years. That's about it,' she finished.

From the expression on her face, Senhora Dos Santos was in no way mollified by the potted history. Not that Leonie would have expected her to be. It hardly came across as an illustrious background. The fact that she was of foreign blood would be a drawback in itself.

The man she had been addressing studied her for a lengthy moment in silence. She held his gaze without flinching.

'You love my son?' he asked.

There was only one possible answer she could give, face burning as she did so. 'Of course.'

'And you?' he queried of the man at her side.

'What kind of talk is this?' his wife demanded fiercely, this time obviously not about to give way. 'You will not shame us!' she fired at her son. 'The marriage must be dissolved!'

'It will not.' Vidal spoke quietly but unequivocally.

She drew in a harsh breath. 'Does honour mean nothing to you?'

'The promise was yours not mine,' he returned. 'I see no dishonour. The old ways are long gone.'

Bewildered, Leonie said tentatively, 'I don't understand.'

Senhora Dos Santos turned on her like a virago. 'You will be silent! You have no place here!'

'My wife's place is wherever I am.' Vidal still hadn't raised his voice, but there was steel in it.

'Will someone please tell me what's going on!' Leonie was past being polite, eyes flashing green fire as she regarded the man she had married. 'Vidal?'

It was his mother who answered, her tone icy now. 'My son is committed to marriage with his cousin, Caterina. He—'

'An arrangement I had no part in making,' Vidal interposed flatly. 'One I never had any intention of fulfilling, as I attempted so many times to tell you. Caterina must look elsewhere for a husband.'

'Where is she to find one now?' demanded the *senhora*. 'She has wasted the best years of her life waiting for you!'

'With no encouragement from me.' Vidal wasn't giving an inch. 'There will be no shortage of suitors when it becomes known one is sought for her. The Dos Santos name alone is enough to draw them.'

His mother broke into Portuguese again, to better express her feelings. Vidal listened impassively. Leonie marshalled her reserves, fighting the immediate urge to get up and flee from the place. Believing she was facing mere disapprobation on the suitability front was one thing, hearing what she'd just heard something else entirely. She felt used, in every sense of the word.

Senhor Dos Santos put a stop to the tirade once more with a few short words. 'I think it best that the two of you leave us for the present,' he added in English to his son. 'Your rooms, as always, are ready for you.' He shifted his gaze to Leonie, expression as unrevealing as Vidal's own. 'You will find them adequate for two.'

Leonie didn't doubt it. She inclined her head stiffly, and rose along with Vidal, keeping a tight rein on her tongue as they moved to the door. Only when they were outside in the hall, with the door closed again, did she let go, tone scathing.

'Not just a blackmailer, but a jilter too!'

'There can be no jilting where no promise was given,' Vidal responded levelly. 'The arrangement was made when I was eight years of age. At no time since have I expressed agreement.'

'There's such a thing as a tacit agreement!'

'I believe the word tacit means unspoken. As I already said, I tried many times to convey my feelings on the subject.'

'Obviously not hard enough!'

The shrug was brief. 'When words fail, action is the only course left. If you'd married me when I first asked you, the problem would have been long resolved.'

'It could have been resolved long before that,' Leonie returned shortly. 'You've known enough women over the years!'

'None I could contemplate marrying, until I met you.'

'Oh, of course! A Dos Santos bride must be a virgin!'

'Among other things.' Vidal made an abrupt movement. 'This is no place to discuss matters. We'll go to my rooms.'

Staircases rose from either side of the hall. Leonie accompanied him in silence up the left hand one, too churned up inside to take much note of her surroundings as they traversed a long corridor. Vidal's suite of rooms occupied the whole middle floor of one of the twin towers. He ushered her into a spacious salon lit by windows on three sides.

'My home when I'm here,' he said. 'Now yours too.'

'Home is where the heart is,' she retorted, 'and mine's far from here!'

Vidal moved to where she stood, taking her face between his hands to look long and deep into her eyes, tiny amber lights flickering in his. 'Are you sure about that?' he asked softly.

This close to him, every nerve in her body alive to his mere touch, she was sure of nothing. It took a real effort to overcome the urge to sink into his arms and just accept things the way they were.

'There's a world of difference between love and lust,' she got out. 'I can hardly claim to feel nothing at all for you, but that's just chemistry. I could never love a man who'd do what you've done—to me, *and* to this Caterina.'

Eyes impenetrable again, Vidal released her. 'I plead guilty to the one accusation,' he said brusquely, 'but not the other. Would you have had me commit myself to a woman I feel nothing for to comply with an outdated custom?'

Leonie hesitated, torn between two fires. 'No,' she admitted at length. 'But did you ever try to talk to your cousin about it?'

'It would have been of little use if I had.'

'You can't know that!'

Vidal shook his head impatiently. 'The question no longer arises. She's free now to marry whomever she chooses. And a choice she'll have, despite my mother's fears.'

'Only from among those attracted by the Dos Santos name, according to what you said downstairs,' she reminded him. 'Hardly a bright prospect.'

'Perhaps better than she would have faced with me.' Vidal sounded as if tolerance was fading fast.

Leonie stood irresolute as he turned away to cross the room to a carved cabinet set against the wall, reminded by the very way he moved of the time two years ago when she'd refused his offer of marriage. Without that newspaper article to set her against him, she might well have said yes then. Where would they be now, she wondered, if she had?

'Is there really any point in staying on here?' she said hollowly. 'You've done what you set out to do.'

'We stay until they accept the marriage,' came the short return. 'You would like a drink?'

About to refuse, Leonie changed her mind. She certainly needed some kind of stimulant. 'Vodka,' she requested, plumping for the first thing that came to mind. 'Neat,' she added recklessly

She sank into the nearest chair, only now taking stock of the room. Unlike the lower floor, the décor here was light and airy, the furnishings a pleasing mix of the old and the new, artwork kept to a minimum. Huge leather sofas were set at right angles to the vast stone fireplace. No fire burned there at present, though she could imagine crackling logs and leaping flames in the winter months.

Vidal brought the glasses across, but didn't take a seat himself. The silence stretched between them like something tangible. Concentrating on the glass in her hand, Leonie could still see him on the periphery of her vision,

'When might we be expected to put in an appearance again?' she asked.

'Dinner will be soon enough,' he said. 'By then, I hope my father at least will have reconciled himself.'

'There might be more chance of your mother coming to terms with it if I'd come up with a rather more upmarket background,' she suggested. 'The daughter of an accountant hardly cuts it.'

'Her view would be the same no matter whose daughter you were. She lives in the past.'

Leonie looked at him directly, taking in the twist to his lips. 'But you care about her?'

'Of course I care about her. That doesn't mean I have to live the life she chooses for me.'

'How old is Caterina?' she queried after a moment.

'A year older than yourself,' he said. 'The arrangement was made at her birth.'

'If you've never spoken to her about it, how do you know she doesn't feel the same way you do?'

'If she does, she hides it well.'

'While you've always made your feelings perfectly obvious to her?'

'I think my absence alone speaks for me,' he returned. 'If she had an ounce of spirit in her, she would have refused to wait for so long.'

'Perhaps she thought you were worth waiting for.'

The irony drew a faint smile. 'Then she'll be disillusioned. You'll no doubt be meeting her soon. The family will be over in force once the news reaches them.'

Leonie dreaded the thought of it. 'You don't care who you hurt, do you?' she accused. 'Just so long as you get what *you* want!' She drained the glass, putting it down with a thud on the low table before her and thrusting herself back to her feet. 'I'm going to unpack!'

Vidal made no move to follow her.

Equally large, the bedroom was right next door. Leonie eyed the king-sized bed with disfavour. Demanding to be allocated another room was obviously out of the question, but she'd sleep in a chair rather than share a bed with Vidal again after this. She hated him for what he'd done—both to her and to his cousin. Facing the latter alone was going to tax her to the limit, to say nothing of the rest of the family.

The wardrobes contained the usual selection of men's clothing, although Vidal had brought a bag along with him this time. Any pleasure Leonie had found in the clothes she'd bought in Zurich had flown. She ignored them all in choosing something to change into for the evening, opting for a plain black tunic that summed up her mood. She could drop Vidal even further into the mire by telling them all the truth about their marriage, but that would also mean admitting to her father's misdeeds.

It was only three days since she had telephoned him, she realised with a sense of shock. It seemed much longer. Her life back home had been so settled, so uncomplicated. Here, she was in constant emotional turmoil. Any faint hope she might have entertained of reaching a closer relationship with the man she had married had flown. He was without a heart.

She was standing at a window looking out over the extensive landscaped grounds when Vidal finally came through to the room. He didn't hesitate, coming straight over to turn her into his arms. The kiss lacked any element of tenderness.

'I won't be disparaged by my own wife!' he declared in a low tone when he lifted his head. 'You'll show me some respect!'

'Respect has to be earned,' she said, steadying herself. 'You treat people abominably!'

Something flared deep down in his eyes. 'Including your father?'

She bit her lip, but refused to back down. 'There was no compassion involved. You used him to your own ends. Not only to salve your pride where I was concerned, but to kick your family in the teeth. Having done that, why rub their noses in it? If—'

She broke off as the strong mouth suddenly tilted. She was finding nothing in the least humorous in the situation. 'Don't you dare laugh about it!' she snapped.

'An involuntary reaction,' he said. 'You use words so descriptively.' He sobered, jaw tautening afresh. 'They accept you, or we lose contact altogether. It's as simple as that.'

Leonie held her tongue as he turned away, recognising the futility. However difficult the situation, she had to deal with it.

CHAPTER SIX

SPACIOUS though it was, the *salon* looked crowded with people. Leonie hesitated in the doorway, propelled forward again by Vidal's hand in her centre back. She put a smile on her face, willing herself to at least appear in control. Despite what he'd said earlier about the family coming over in force, she hadn't really expected to be faced with them all tonight.

Vidal performed introductions with an aplomb she envied, seemingly oblivious to the atmosphere. Three of the younger element were male, two of them with wives in attendance. Not all Dos Santos women shared the family looks, she recalled Vidal saying at lunch that very first day. Though far from ugly, Caterina's face was unlikely to launch any ships. More her mother's daughter than her father's.

Oddly enough, of them all, she was the only one to offer any degree of warmth in her greeting. Her parents and brothers made little attempt to hide their true feelings. Leonie stiffened her backbone and rode it out.

With twelve at table in the panelled dining salon, and much of the conversation carried on in Portuguese regardless of Vidal's request that English be spoken, dinner was far from an enjoyable meal. Leonie picked at the various dishes with little appetite. Catching Caterina's eye across the table at one point, she was surprised to receive a tentative smile. She smiled back involuntarily, cheered by the lack of censure from one with most reason to direct it. There was a possibility that Caterina might have been no more eager to marry Vidal than he her.

Ranging in age from mid-twenties to early thirties, the three brothers had all of them inherited the Dos Santos looks to varying degrees. The eldest, bearing the name of Roque, was the closest in facial resemblance to Vidal, though lacking—to Leonie at least—the latter's magnetic attraction. She could sense his gaze on her from time to time, discomfiting in its brooding intensity.

Seated at her side, Vidal showed no discomfiture whatsoever. Leonie felt like kicking him on the ankle, just to gain a reaction. She'd never forgive him for landing her with this, she vowed.

Her father-in-law had little to say throughout the meal. His announcement at the end of it silenced all other voices.

'If this marriage is to be recognised, it must be sanctified,' he declared. 'Arrangements will be made.' He held up an imperious hand as Vidal made to speak. 'You will not deny me this too.'

It was a statement, not a question. Leonie held her breath as she waited for Vidal's reply.

'I find no objection,' he said levelly. 'Providing arrangements can be made without too much delay.'

'It will take whatever time it takes,' came the controlled response. 'Your business affairs must wait.' He directed his attention to Leonie. 'You have family other than your surviving parent?'

The focus of all eyes, Leonie slowly shook her head. 'No.'

'Then your father must travel alone.'

Speech broke out around the table as he resumed his seat, all of it in Portuguese, and none of it, according to tones and expressions, favourable. Leonie looked helplessly at Vidal, who gave a brief shrug, signifying acceptance. It was, she supposed, the least he could do in mollification.

If a church blessing went any way towards mending the rift he'd created, she had no quarrel with it herself, although she didn't care for the idea of exposing her father to the hostility still coming across in waves from most people at

the table. Her mother-in-law's attitude certainly hadn't altered.

It was some relief when the cousins left right after the
meal. Vidal elected to take their leave too. Copying what
she'd heard, Leonie offered a muted, *'Boa noite,'* doubting
if her pronunciation alone would impress anyone. Senhor
Dos Santos responded civilly, his wife not at all.

Vidal made no comment on the way to the tower. Pacing
at his side along the wide, thickly carpeted corridor, Leonie
tried to put her thoughts in order. For her, little had actually
altered. Left high and dry after so many years of waiting,
Caterina was the one deserving of sympathy. True, she hadn't
appeared to be suffering too deeply, but who could tell what
was really going on inside? She'd been led to believe from
childhood that she would one day become Vidal's wife.

'I suppose you might have found it a little easier to go
along with the arrangement if Caterina's looks had come up
to your standards!' she said flatly.

'Her looks have no bearing,' came the steady response.

'I don't believe that. Mine certainly did.'

'So I appreciate beauty in a woman,' he acknowledged.
'That doesn't mean I consider it the only factor of any importance. Caterina has the sweetest nature of any woman I've
ever known, but she has no conversation, no knowledge of
the world. The farthest place she's ever travelled to is Porto.
Even if I'd never had a life of my own, away from here, she
still wouldn't have been enough for me.'

'Can any one woman ever be enough for you?'

'Only time will tell.' His tone had shortened. 'Enough of
the catechism!'

There were shades of his father's imperialism in the latter
command. Leonie quashed her instinctive reaction, unwilling
to make an issue of it.

They had reached their destination. Vidal opened the tower
door for her, ushering her through to the narrow hall from

which staircases led to both upper and lower floors. He made straight for the bedroom, leaving her with little option but to follow him. She'd vowed earlier to sleep in a chair rather than share a bed with him again, but the mood he was in, she doubted if he'd accept any such move.

'Will it really be necessary for Dad to be here for this ceremony your father's insisting on?' she asked as he took off his suit jacket.

'As your only representative, yes,' came the unequivocal answer. 'What objection would you have?'

Her chin lifted. 'None, providing he isn't given the third degree!'

'My father will almost certainly want to know more of his history than you outlined.'

'Including his immediate history?'

Vidal cast an ironic glance. 'The only person who could raise that aspect would be your father himself, which I very much doubt. He'll be treated well, I assure you. Dos Santos hospitality has never been found lacking.' He registered the pointed lift of her brows with a faint smile. 'The circumstances are rather different.'

'Is your mother ever likely to feel any differently about my suitability as a Dos Santos bride?'

'In time, perhaps, when you've proved yourself.'

'Proved myself how?'

'It remains to be seen.' Vidal sounded suddenly weary. 'I have arrangements of my own to make tomorrow. Fortunately, I have people I can rely on to keep things running smoothly for a time.'

'How long do you think we'll be here for?' Leonie asked.

'No longer than absolutely necessary.'

Shirt unbuttoned, he slid it off, tossing it carelessly over a chair. Leonie felt the spasm in her inner thighs as he flicked open the buckle of his belt, the warmth uncurling from the pit of her stomach. There may come a time when he could undress in front of her without stirring any response, but that time certainly wasn't yet.

His skin looked golden in the lamplight, the muscle clearly defined. He slid off both shoes and socks before removing his trousers, slinging the latter over the same chair-arm as his shirt. The silk jockey shorts left little to the imagination.

'Are you going to stand there all night?' he asked.

'I'm just not used to…all this yet,' she said, unsurprised to hear the huskiness in her voice.

The smile that touched his mouth was in no way derisive. 'By "all this", I assume you mean undressing in front of me?'

Her return smile was wry. 'Ridiculous, I know, to be self-conscious about it when—'

'When you've lain nude in my arms,' he finished for her. 'When I've kissed and caressed every inch of your body, as you have mine. The feeling will pass, but in the meantime…'

She stood her ground as he came to her, meeting his lips with gratitude that he hadn't laughed at her outmoded modesty. The tribulations of the past few hours paled into insignificance before the tidal wave of emotion sweeping over her. His hands were gentle, easing the long back zip of her dress and sliding it the length of her body, seeking and opening the clip of her bra without fumbling, and tossing it aside. The rest of their garments followed. Leonie drew in her breath as he lowered his head to circle each tingling, peaking nipple with the very tip of his tongue, a low cry torn from her lips at the touch of his teeth on the tender nubs, so light and yet so agonising.

He came back to her mouth, kisses deepening, demanding, drawing a fevered response, hands cupping her buttocks to bring her into full and devastating contact. Then he was lifting her, sliding into her, filling her with his maleness. Legs wrapped about him, Leonie gave herself over to the exquisite sensations coursing through her body, lips parting in a silent scream as she reached the peak.

They were lying on the bed when she came back to earth, Vidal propped on an elbow above her, the smile on his lips reflected in his eyes as he studied her face.

'Assim bonito, assim sensual, assim totalamente irresistible!' he said softly.

'You're difficult to resist yourself,' she murmured, latching onto a word she could understand. 'How come it's the same in Portuguese as in English?'

'Derived from the same source.' He kissed her very gently on the lips, the smile widening at her involuntary tremor. 'Am I forgiven for—how does the saying go?—throwing you in at the deep end?'

The way she felt right now, she could forgive him almost anything, she thought languorously. 'They say it's the best way to learn to swim,' she returned. 'I dare say I'll survive the shock.' She hesitated, reluctant to mar the moment, yet unable to let it go completely. 'I suppose Caterina will too.'

'She appeared far from distraught tonight,' Vidal observed with some truth. 'Perhaps I've been deluding myself all these years in thinking she wanted the marriage herself.'

'Does that hurt your pride?' Leonie teased, drawing a laugh.

'I think it might survive the blow.'

'I doubt if her family will adjust any too quickly.'

'They have no other choice.'

Vidal dropped another light kiss on her lips, then heaved himself upright to get to his feet. Leonie watched him as he made for the bathroom, stirred by the play of muscle across his back as he eased his shoulders, the lean hipline and taut thighs. A fine figure of a man in any language.

Regardless of everything he'd done, her feelings for him already went deeper than mere physical attraction, she acknowledged. What she doubted was the depth of his feelings for her. He wanted her now, but how long would that last?

The sound of running water indicated he was taking a shower. She was tempted to go and join him, but lacked the self-confidence to take that degree of initiative. In any case, she was so luxuriously comfortable lying here, so utterly replete. In a little while…

She woke with a start, disorientated for a moment or two. It was daylight, she realised with a sense of shock. She must have gone out like a light last night.

Like that first morning, she was alone. It could have been Vidal closing the bedroom door that had woken her, she supposed. She sat up slowly, running an automatic hand through her tumbled hair as her eyes sought the bedside clock. It was still barely seven. Where Vidal could be going at this hour she couldn't imagine. It was surely far too early to start ringing round and making arrangements for others to take over his business affairs.

On the other hand, he probably saw no reason why he should wait until a more reasonable hour. He was up, therefore so should they be. She wondered what reason he would give for his absence—if he considered it necessary to give any reason at all. It may be assumed he was taking a belated honeymoon.

Fat chance of that, the way things were, she thought. Vidal's father was at least making an effort, his mother none at all. At some point she would have to face her alone. Not something to be looked forward to.

She slid from the bed, donned the light silk robe she hadn't got around to wearing last night, and headed for the bathroom. The long mirror set into one wall revealed a couple of eyes smudged with the mascara she hadn't removed. She creamed it off, hoping Vidal hadn't seen it this morning. He wouldn't, she was sure, have been at all impressed.

Showered, she donned the robe again, to return to the bed-room and find something to wear, choosing a plain white skirt and a simple green blouse as the least likely to offend any house rules. She was brushing her hair into order when Vidal came into the room.

Dressed in jeans and sweatshirt, his jaw still bearing overnight stubble, he set her pulses hammering regardless.

'You were up and about early,' she said, trying for a casual note.

'Things to take care of,' he returned equably. 'You look fresh as the morning dew!'

Leonie laughed, half expecting him to come over and follow up the compliment with a kiss, but he made for the bathroom instead. Deflated, she pulled herself up sharply. There was more to think about than sex. A great deal more! She had her own phone call to make for a start.

She doubted if her father was going to regard the invitation—if it could be called that—to attend the sanctification of their marriage with any great enthusiasm. He would be totally out of his depth with these people—as she was herself.

It was still only half past seven. Uncertain of where to go, she took a seat by an opened window to wait for Vidal. The morning was glorious, the sun already clear of the belt of pine trees backing the spreading lawns, warming the old stonework. Mountains reared in the middle distance against a clear blue sky. The whole place still took her breath away.

Vidal emerged minus the stubble. This time he came straight over to her, perching on the arm of her chair to part the fall of her hair and put his lips to her nape. Warmed by the gesture, Leonie leaned back instinctively against him, the subtle scent of aftershave tantalising her nostrils.

'What happens today?' she asked.

'Today we do whatever you wish to do,' he said. 'The village nearby is holding a festival. We could spend an hour or two there if you like.'

'I'd love to.' The way she felt at the moment, Leonie was happy to go along with anything he suggested. 'I'll have to phone Dad first, though,' she added, sobering again at the thought.

'Better to wait until we know when the ceremony is to be,' Vidal advised. 'It may take several days to arrange. Are you ready to go down?'

She wasn't, but it had to be faced some time. Maybe her mother-in-law would have mellowed a little overnight, she thought without much hope.

Breakfast was eaten on the covered, stone-arched terrace which ran the full length of the central section of the building. Leonie refused Vidal's offer to order something cooked for her, happy with the fresh fruit, hot rolls, bagels and preserves already laid out.

The cushioned chairs set about low tables afforded both comfort and a view of the gardens. With no one else around to mar the moment, she was able to relax, to enjoy the peace and tranquility.

One leg propped casually across the other, Vidal looked relaxed too. His face was a sculptor's dream, she thought. Not just his face either. His body was superb. If his father was anything to go by, neither looks nor lean fitness would alter much with age. If she was still around by then.

'How old were you when you first left here?' she asked.

'Eighteen,' he said. 'To go to Cambridge. I never returned. Not in any lasting sense.' He looked across at her, gaze roving her features with undisguised pleasure. 'You think I should have stayed to fulfil my duty?'

Leonie shook her head. 'I can't imagine you living any life but the one you do. Anyway…'

'Anyway?' he prompted as she broke off.

She had been about to say they would never have met otherwise, but that came close to acknowledging that her own life might have lacked something if they hadn't.

'Nothing important,' she said lightly.

Vidal didn't press it, though the smile hovering about his lips suggested he might have an idea of what had been in her mind. Leonie wondered where she might be if they really had never met. No man she'd known during the last two years had stirred any real interest, but if she'd had no one to compare them with it could have been a different story.

She sat up straighter in her chair as Senhor Dos Santos came out through the doors leading from the great hall. He was dressed casually himself, in trousers and open-necked shirt, but still appeared redoubtable.

'Bom dia,' she proffered before he could speak. 'That's about all I can manage at present, but I'll learn.'

'The effort is appreciated,' he returned with no discernible irony. 'You slept well?'

Catching Vidal's eye, Leonie was hard put to it to maintain an outer insouciance. 'Very, thank you. I'm not quite sure what to call you,' she added.

'Sogro will suffice for now,' he said.

'It means father-in-law,' Vidal supplied as his parent went to select food and drink for himself. 'Mother-in-law is *sogra*. Not that I think she would appreciate the familiarity at present.'

Leonie could imagine. She'd yet to be recognised as a legitimate Dos Santos to start with. She couldn't visualise a time when relations between the two of them would be anything like they should be, though there was every chance that she wouldn't have to worry about it all that long.

Having chosen a solitary roll and coffee, Senhor Dos Santos took a seat. 'The ceremony will take place in two days' time,' he said. 'Only family and those closest to us will attend.'

'That doesn't leave my father much time to arrange things,' Leonie felt bound to protest. 'I haven't even contacted him yet.'

'I'll arrange a flight for tomorrow,' Vidal stated calmly, 'and have him met in Porto.'

'Even if there's a flight, there may not be any seats.'

'In which case I'll charter a plane.' He levered himself to his feet. 'I'll see to it now.'

Leonie controlled the urge to stop him from leaving her alone with his father with difficulty. It had to happen some time. The latter made no immediate comment. It was left to her to break the silence between them.

'I truly am sorry for all the trouble this has caused you. If I'd known…'

'If you had known of his commitment to another you would have refused my son's offer of marriage?' Senhor Dos Santos queried as she hesitated.

She bit her lip, stuck for an honest answer. 'I can't claim that,' she said at length. 'I don't consider an arrangement made for him when he was just a boy binding in any way.'

'Then why indicate otherwise?' came the flat demand. 'You have no cause to apologise for an issue you knew nothing of. The fault is Vidal's and his alone that Caterina is now left abandoned.'

'She didn't appear all that concerned last night,' Leonie ventured. 'Perhaps she wasn't all that keen on the idea herself.'

Surprisingly, the comment drew no angry response. 'There is nothing to be gained from dwelling on the matter,' he said. 'You are part of this family now. Perhaps you will persuade Vidal to visit a little more often in the future.'

There was a far better chance of it now that the pressure was off, she thought. She considered asking if her mother-in-law was likely to want further visits from her wayward son at all, in view of her feelings, then decided it wasn't her place to ask.

Vidal returned in a surprisingly short time to report that he'd secured a seat on a flight from Heathrow at nine-forty.

Leonie rose with some reluctance to go and phone her father with the news. They were an hour ahead of Greenwich time here, so he wouldn't have left for the office yet.

She got through without difficulty. His greeting held a hint of reproof. He'd obviously expected another call before this.

'I'm at Vidal's family home in the Douro,' Leonie said. 'His father has arranged to have the marriage blessed in church, the day after tomorrow. You have to be there too.'

'I can't just drop everything!' he exclaimed.

'You can if the boss says so,' she returned. 'He's booked you on a flight to Porto from Heathrow. Nine-forty tomorrow morning. You'll be met at the airport and brought out here. Prepare yourself for a bit of a surprise. His parents live in a palace. Not quite as big as Buck House, but impressive enough.'

'Are you being serious?' Stuart asked suspiciously.

'Never more,' she assured him. 'I'd better warn you too that approval is in short supply, especially where Vidal's mother is concerned. I'll fill you in on the reasons why when I see you, but don't expect any red carpet.'

'Sounds real enticing.' Stuart was obviously doing his best to keep curiosity under control. 'I'll be there. Just don't let them get you down.'

'I've no intention,' she said.

Reluctant to venture into any of the rooms, she'd used a telephone in the hall. Turning to see Vidal's mother standing at the foot of the staircase a few feet away was something of a shock. How much of the conversation had she over-heard? she wondered.

'You lured my son into this marriage!' the older woman accused.

Leonie took a firm hold on herself, choosing her words with care. 'Do you really believe Vidal the kind of man to be taken in by a woman?'

The answer came with vitriol. 'Men are all too easily

blinded by a beautiful face! Caterina has so much more than that to give. He will come to realise it for himself.'

'I don't think so.' Leonie did her best to maintain a level tone. 'In fact, I'd go so far as to guarantee he won't. He considers Caterina a lovely person, but just not right for him.'

'While you, the daughter of a mere accountant, are so?'

'Daughter of the chief accountant of one of your son's companies, to be exact.'

'Your father is in my son's employment?' The tone was even more derogatory.

'And proud of it.'

Grateful might be a more apt word considering, Leonie acknowledged. What might be said if the truth were known, she dreaded to think. But one thing she refused to knuckle under to was disdain. An accident of birth had placed the Dos Santos family in the position they occupied. It made them no better than others.

'My father is a good man!' she declared. 'And, whether you like it or not, *I'm* Vidal's wife, not Caterina!'

Face taut, the other turned abruptly away to open the nearest door and disappear into the room beyond, closing the door behind her with a force that set the chandeliers jangling. Not exactly an endearing exchange, Leonie reflected ruefully.

'Did you get through?' Vidal asked from the terrace doorway, making her jump.

'All arranged,' she assured him, jolting herself into movement.

'You look unsettled,' he observed shrewdly as she came up. 'Are you sure there's no problem.?'

'I'm afraid I just had a run-in with your mother,' she admitted, certain he'd hear about it from her anyway. 'I may have been a bit…impolite.'

Vidal's lips twitched at the corners. 'Where did she go?'

'In there,' indicating the room. 'I thought it best to leave well alone for now.'

'Very wise. She'll come round to it in time. She has no choice.'

'You can't bend everyone to your will,' Leonie rejoined. 'She's a very strong-minded woman. She may decide to disown you.'

'My father won't allow that.'

'Meaning no woman rules the roost in the Dos Santos hierarchy.'

'It depends on the kind of rule she wishes to apply. No woman respects a man who gives way to her every whim.'

'No man has the automatic right to make decisions for both,' she countered. 'Marriage is supposed to be a partnership, not a take-over!'

'If partners hold opposing views, one of them has to take the lead. Did you want more coffee?'

Leonie shook her head, aware of the futility in further discussion—if the foregoing could be called that. Vidal's views were too entrenched to be undermined with mere words. The time to stand her ground would be when there was something worth standing it over.

'I should go and tell your father everything is arranged,' she said.

'He'll have taken it for granted.'

The humorous spark in the dark eyes drew a reluctant smile to her lips. 'I suppose I asked for that.'

'A little,' he agreed. 'It's impossible to resist teasing you when you blaze at me the way you did just now. But then, a rose without thorns would be too easy to pluck.'

Only a Latin could coin a phrase like that without sounding ridiculous, Leonie thought as he held open the door for her.

CHAPTER SEVEN

SMALL though the local village was, the festival lacked nothing in colourful atmosphere. Every form of transport possible had been used to form a procession of wonderfully decorated floats. Stalls lined the main street, laden with produce, with trinkets, with leatherwork and pottery. Music filled the air.

'No particular event,' Vidal said when Leonie asked what was being celebrated. 'Festivals take place throughout the summer in just about every town and village in the region.'

He lifted a hand in greeting to one of the stallholders, answering the man's smiling comment with a word and a smile of his own.

'What did he say?' Leonie asked curiously.

'He was wishing us good fortune,' Vidal supplied.

'So word has got around already?'

'The house staff will have lost little time in spreading the news.'

Leonie gave him a swift glance. 'Are you saying everyone knew you were supposed to marry Caterina?'

'If the arrangement was ever a secret, it wouldn't have remained one for long. Some may look on you with disfavour.'

'As the foreign hussy who stole you away from one of their own?' She gave a short laugh. 'If the truth were only known!'

'There's nothing to stop you from making it known.' Vidal's tone was level enough, but his jaw had tautened.

'Exposing Dad? I'm hardly going to do that.'

'Then don't threaten,' he advised. 'I told you I was prepared to go to any lengths to keep you with me.'

Leonie regarded him in silence for a moment, registering the only too familiar flutter in her lower abdomen as she searched the decisive features. 'I suppose I should be flattered.'

His lips slanted. 'So you should.'

Standing there amid the milling throng, they were drawing attention, some of it indulgent, some not. Leonie smiled at a woman carrying a small child, to receive a scowl in return. One of Caterina's supporters, she assumed. At some point she had to get Caterina on her own and discover what she really felt about it all—if only for her own peace of mind.

'I'll be glad when this is all over and we can go back home,' she said wearily.

'You regard the *quinta* as home already?' Vidal queried.

'It's *your* home,' she returned. 'I have to look on it the same.'

'Not necessarily. It's just a building.'

Leonie gazed at him with drawn brows, oblivious for the moment to the people around them. 'Are you saying you'd just as happily live elsewhere?'

'If you expressed a dislike for the place.'

'Who could possibly dislike it?' she said. 'It's absolutely beautiful!' She paused, searching for the words. 'It's certainly home as opposed to here, but my real home is back in England—and always will be.'

'Always is a long time,' came the mild reply.

Time wouldn't make any difference, she thought, even if she was given it. Not to that aspect, at any rate. However long she lived in this country, it could never be anything to her but a foreign land.

Vidal made no further comment, drawing her attention back to the colourful parade. Leonie wondered if he really would have abandoned the *quinta* if she'd professed to hate the place, or had simply been saying it knowing full well she didn't. Either way, the question was immaterial.

They ate a light meal of fish, salad and crusty bread at a little tavern on the outskirts of the village, washing it down with sparkling white wine. Afterwards, Vidal took her on a tour of the vineyards. They were vast, spreading across the terraced hillsides in a sea of green. The cousins had their own yards, though they weren't as expansive.

'Would marriage between you and Caterina have consolidated the two?' Leonie felt moved to ask.

'I doubt if that was the intention,' Vidal returned.

'So it was more of a blood thing?'

He shrugged. 'It's of no importance now.'

Let it go, his tone implied, creating in her a stubborn disinclination.

'What will happen if you're still unwilling to take over the estate when your father dies?'

'Hopefully, that won't be for a long time yet.'

'Even so, it—'

'The decision will be mine, and mine alone.' Vidal spoke with quiet but unmistakable authority. 'Would you like to see the winery?'

Leonie bit back a caustic retort, settling for a shake of the head. There was no point getting uptight about something she was unlikely to be involved in.

It was just the four of them at dinner that evening. Whether Senhora Dos Santos had received orders from her husband there was no way of knowing, but she appeared to be making some attempt to come to terms with the situation.

'You must dress appropriately for the ceremony, of course,' she said at one point. 'No trousers.' The last in tacit disapproval of the silky trouser suit Leonie was wearing. 'And certainly not white! A simple cream dress would be most suitable, if you have such a garment?'

'I think I might have the very thing,' Leonie acknowledged, running through a mental inventory of the things she'd bought in Zurich. 'It's Versace, so it should come up to scratch.'

Her mother-in-law frowned. 'What is meant by that?'

'Sorry.' Leonie did her best to look penitent. 'It means it should be highly suitable. Very plain, very classy.' Very expensive, she could have added. 'What about the language? Assuming everything will be in Portuguese, how will I make any responses?'

'I'll write them down for you to practise,' Vidal put in easily. 'You'll soon pick the language up.'

If her prowess with French in school was anything to go by, Leonie doubted it. Some people had an ear for other languages; some didn't. She definitely belonged to the latter category.

'It seems you might be right about your mother coming round,' she commented later, when they were alone. 'She was almost affable tonight.'

'My father will have pointed out the futility in taking any other course,' Vidal responded.

'You mean he came the heavy?' she said. 'Like father, like son!'

He gave her a quizzical glance. 'You consider me a tyrant?'

'I wouldn't go as far as that, but you do tend towards autocracy at times.'

'Which you find objectionable?'

'Which any woman with any spirit at all would find objectionable,' she retorted with sly purpose. 'A quality you found lacking in Caterina, I believe?'

A wicked light sprang in the dark eyes. He reached her in a couple of strides, swinging her up to dump her flat on the bed and stand over her threateningly. 'You dare to taunt me, woman!'

Laughing, Leonie held up her hands in mock surrender. 'I claim immunity!'

'*I* claim a penalty,' he declared.

Leonie wasn't loath to accept what he had in mind. *Anything* he had in mind along these lines, she thought as he lowered himself to her. There was nowhere else she would rather be right now.

Stuart Baxter arrived at three, as overwhelmed initially as Leonie had been. He was greeted with courtesy by her father-in-law, with restraint by her mother-in-law.

'A better reception than *I* got from her,' she said wryly in the bedroom he had been allocated. 'Talk about fire and brimstone!'

'If they were dropped on the way I was, it's hardly surprising,' Stuart commented. 'I'm still getting over the shock myself.'

'There's more to it than just that,' Leonie admitted. 'Vidal was supposed to marry his father's cousin's daughter. Arranged when he was just a boy. He's made every effort to quash the whole idea these past few years, but it was still taken for granted.'

Stuart regarded her pensively. 'So he decided to present them with a *fait accompli*?'

'That wasn't the only reason he married me,' she said.

'I'm sure of it. But he still used you.' He paused, registering the wariness in her eyes. 'Is there anything you're not telling me?'

'Such as?' she prevaricated.

'Such as the possibility that you've realised you made a mistake?'

'I made no mistake,' she denied.

'So you really do love him?'

'Of course.' She made the assertion without hesitation,

sensing uncertainty on his part. 'He's everything I could possibly want in a man.'

'And you're sure of his feelings for you?'

'Of course,' she said again, shutting out the dissenting voices. 'He waited two years for me, didn't he? What more proof could there be?'

Stuart smiled faintly, and shook his head. 'Not a lot, I agree. Lucky for me that he feels that way. Otherwise I'd probably be rotting in jail. I gather his parents don't know the whole story?'

'Of course not.' Leonie was beginning to feel like a stuck record. 'No one else knows.' She hesitated before saying tentatively, 'Did you repay the money yet?'

'The bank came through the day before yesterday.' He sounded a little defensive. 'It's all squared away.'

'And Simon?'

'He's keeping a tight lip so far.'

'Tell him Vidal will have him out on his ear if he doesn't keep it that way!'

Stuart gave her a doubtful look. 'You reckon so?'

'I know so,' she claimed recklessly. She gave him an impulsive hug. 'I'm so glad you're here, Dad!'

'I wasn't given much choice,' he pointed out. 'I think it will be a long time before your husband and I form any family closeness—if ever. Not that I'm complaining.'

He had no room to complain, Leonie thought, hoping against hope that he really had learned his lesson. Any bargaining power she'd possessed with Vidal was already used up.

The evening was less fraught than she had anticipated. A charmer when he set himself out to be, her father made every effort to lighten the atmosphere. Senhora Dos Santos unbent far enough to favour him with a faint smile when he apologised for not being able to speak the language with self deprecating humour. With English so widely spoken, it was perhaps understandable that the English themselves found it unnecessary to learn any other languages, she condescended.

'Why didn't you tell her you speak both French and Spanish?' Leonie raged at him when she got him alone for a few minutes before retiring for the night.

'Why bother?' he asked mildly. 'I'm not out to impress. I'm just glad Vidal has a life away from this kind of semi-feudal existence. Although, as the only son, I suppose the time will come when he'll be expected to take over. How will you feel about that?'

'It's too far in the future to worry about just yet,' Leonie temporised. 'You have to see the *quinta*,' she added, to change the subject. 'I doubt if we'll be staying on very long once this ceremony is over. You could even travel back with us for a couple of days.'

Stuart gave a short laugh. 'I'm sure Vidal would go a bundle on that. Anyway, I'm booked on a flight home Tuesday.'

Vidal's presumption in booking the return flight made her blood boil. So far as he was concerned her father was an employee, and to be treated as such.

'I'm surprised you didn't have Dad on a flight back to-morrow night.' she accused in the privacy of the bedroom. 'You obviously can't wait to get rid of him!'

'He has commitments,' Vidal returned levelly. 'So have I. We'll be leaving on Tuesday too.'

'Is business all you think about?' Leonie snapped.

The dark eyes slid the length of her body and back, coming to rest on her stormy face with a spark in their depths. 'In what way do you feel deprived?' he asked. 'Do I not satisfy you?'

'I'm not talking about sex!' she declared. 'I'm sure you're the world's greatest expert!'

The smile was brief. 'With no basis for comparison, how would you know?'

'Practice makes perfect,' she shot back, 'and you've certainly had enough of that!'

'No more than many my age. A great deal less than some. Sex plays a vital role in a man's life, but it doesn't fulfil every need, doesn't exercise the brain. So, yes, my business interests are important to me. That's something you have to accept.'

'For what difference it makes,' she said after a moment, trying to sound as dispassionate about it as he did.

Vidal made no reply to that. He didn't need to, she reflected hollowly. He'd made his feelings—or lack of them—perfectly clear.

Decked out in flowers, the little church was heady with perfume. Standing at Vidal's side, Leonie mouthed the responses he had taught her when called on to do so, listening to the padre's incomprehensible chanting without emotion. She felt no more married when the service was finished than she had a week ago, emerging from the register office.

As Senhor Dos Santos had said, only family and a few close friends had been invited to attend. The party returned to the palace for a luncheon fit for royalty, spilling out onto the terrace afterwards replete with food and wine.

Seeing Caterina slip back indoors at one point, Leonie followed on impulse, catching up with her as she paused halfway down the hall to run light fingers over the yellowed ivory keys of the grand piano.

'Do you play?' she asked.

'A little,' the other answered shyly. 'Do you play yourself?'

'Some.' Leonie paused, not quite sure how to say what she wanted to say. The only way, she decided, was straight out. 'This can't be easy for you, when you've waited so long.'

Caterina's smile was a reassurance in itself. 'It is a relief to me,' she admitted. 'A very great relief. Vidal is a man for whom I have the greatest respect, but I have no desire to be his wife.'

'Then why haven't you made it clear?' Leonie asked.

'It was not my place,' came the simple reply. 'I could only trust in Vidal's determination. I am happy that he has made his own choice. You are far more suited to him than I could ever have been. I have no understanding of his world.'

'But you're not against marriage itself?'

The smile came again. 'Not with the right person.'

'Then I hope you find him,' Leonie said with sincerity.

The glow that suddenly shone in the other eyes enhanced her whole face. 'I already did find him.'

'Caterina!' Roque called from the terrace doorway. *'A mãe está procurando!'*

The glow disappeared, leaving a dark void. 'My mother wishes me to go to her,' Caterina translated for Leonie's benefit. 'I wish you and Vidal much happiness together.'

Roque remained by the door as his sister moved down the hall towards him. Leonie sat down at the piano and played a few tentative notes, mulling over what had just been said. The question was whether the man Caterina wanted to marry felt the same way about her. And, if he did, would he be considered acceptable by the family? At twenty-seven, and shorn of any obligation towards Vidal, she should now feel free to live her life the way she chose, but there was no certainty of it.

Semi-feudal, her father had called the Dos Santos lifestyle. He was right too—at least regarding certain aspects. And Vidal himself still subscribed in part.

'You play well,' Roque commented, giving her a shock as she hadn't heard him approaching. 'Although I fail to recognise the piece.'

'It was nothing in particular,' Leonie answered, gathering herself. She looked at him as he moved into view, struck once again by the total failure of the looks he shared so closely with Vidal to make any impression whatsoever on her senses. 'I didn't realise you were there.'

'I thought it time I got to know my new cousin,' he said. There was open admiration in his eyes as he scrutinised the striking face turned up to him. 'It is understandable that Vidal should have chosen you in preference to my sister. I would have done the same in his place. Your hair rivals the sun in its glory!'

Leonie turned an involuntary splutter of laughter into a cough. That was a bit over the top, even by Latin standards. 'Thank you,' she said demurely. 'You're very kind.'

'It is never difficult to be kind to a beautiful woman,' he responded.

Vidal had said something similar to that the first time they met, she recalled with a pang. Little had she known then of the effect he was going to have on her life.

'I should be getting back,' she said. 'Vidal is going to wonder where I've got to.'

Roque looked piqued, obviously unaccustomed to having a woman show so little desire for his company. 'I studied the piano myself,' he said. 'I would be honoured to play for you before you go.'

To refuse would be downright discourteous, Leonie told herself. Roque was making an effort to be friendly in his own fashion. 'I'd be honoured to have you perform for me,' she returned, tongue in cheek.

She slid from the ornate stool, standing to one side as he took her place. Eyes never leaving her face, he began to play, fingers rippling over the keys. He was good, Leonie had to admit. Better than good, in fact.

'That was beautiful!' she applauded in all sincerity when he finished the piece. 'Chopin, wasn't it?'

His smile was ironic. 'You find it surprising that I should have classical tastes in music?'

'Not at all,' she denied. 'Something else you share with Vidal.'

'Something else?' he queried.

'You must realise how much alike you look. Vidal doesn't play, of course. At least, I don't think he does.'

An odd expression crossed the handsome features. 'You would surely know if he did?'

Leonie gave a laugh, regretting the remark. 'There are all kinds of things we still have to learn about each other. If I'm surprised about anything,' she added lightly, 'it's that you're still unmarried yourself.'

'Jorge and Angelo are both of them easier to please than I am,' came the smooth return. 'The woman I finally select must be exceptional in every way. Vidal is fortunate to have you as his wife.' He lifted a hand to cover hers where it rested on the keyboard's side, fingers caressing. 'I hope he proves worthy of you.'

Smile fixed, Leonie tried not to make too much of the gesture, withdrawing her hand without haste. 'I'm sure of it,' she said. 'And now I really must get back.'

The terrace doors were ajar. Left that way by Roque, she assumed. Talking with Angelo, and one or two other men close by, Vidal gave her a hardened glance as she emerged into the sunlight. He was annoyed with her for deserting the party, she took it, although she'd only been gone about fifteen minutes. She gave him a smile in return, refusing to be apologetic about it. At least she could settle any guilt he might be feeling over Caterina for good and all now.

Her father was talking with her father-in-law, the conversation quite amicable from what she could tell. Caterina was seated with the rest of the women in the party in a group at the far end of the terrace. Leonie contemplated going to join them, unaware that Roque had emerged from the house at her back until his hand came to rest on her shoulder.

'You would like some more champagne, perhaps?' he asked.

'I've had enough, thanks,' she said, wishing he'd take a hike. 'I don't have much of a head for it.'

Roque laughed. 'You have a most entertaining way of expressing yourself.'

Leonie refrained from voicing the peppy response that sprang to mind. 'I think it's time I paid my respects to the ladies' circle,' she said instead.

She found herself the focus of all eyes as she moved along the terrace. She had an almost irrepressible urge to give a little royal wave right and left.

'Caterina tells us you are accomplished on the piano,' her mother-in-law commented as she slid into a seat with a smile all round. 'You must play for us tomorrow, when we visit with our cousins.'

'I'm really not all that good,' Leonie protested, wondering how she'd managed to give Caterina any other impression. 'Anyway, I believe Vidal is planning to leave tomorrow.'

'He cannot do that!' His mother sounded outraged. 'Do we mean so little to him that he cannot spare us a few more days of his time?'

'I'm sure you mean a great deal to him,' Leonie soothed, wishing she'd kept her mouth shut. 'It's just pressure of business.'

'He must have people who can deal with his business affairs in his absence.'

'Yes, but—'

'Then there is certainly no cause for his immediate return. You will tell him so.'

You tell him so, Leonie thought, bridling at the peremptory tone. She couldn't say it, of course. Her relationship with her mother-in-law was too fragile to risk alienating her still further. She would pass on the message, then it would be up to Vidal himself to decide.

Both in their early twenties, Jorge and Angelo's wives regarded her with cool curiosity. Leonie dredged the names Madelena and Brianca from memory, but couldn't recall which belonged to which. They neither of them spoke more than a few words of English, making it nigh on impossible to communicate. In addition to Caterina's mother, there were three other women present, all of them married, none of them extending much warmth in the way of greeting. It was possible, of course, that they were taking their cue from their hostess.

Leonie schooled herself to show no discomfiture.

'Please do carry on with what you were all talking about,' she urged. 'I might even be able to pick up a few words.'

'You must study the language with care if you wish to be understood,' Senhora Dos Santos chided. 'Vidal must employ a tutor for you. When you next visit, I shall expect to find you fluent.'

'I'll do my best, 'Leonie promised, thinking it was possible that she might never have to prove herself. The other would be the first to cheer, she was sure, when the marriage broke up. Which it would, once her appeal for Vidal had run its course.

Caterina looked as though her thoughts were elsewhere. There was an air of serenity about her. If any obstacles were put in the way of the happiness she sought with a man other than the one chosen for her, it was to be hoped she would have the courage to defy them, Leonie reflected. She'd certainly encourage it herself if she got the chance.

'If you'll excuse me, I have to go to the bathroom,' she said to her mother-in-law, weary of the struggle to maintain her own composure.

Senhora Dos Santos inclined her head stiffly. From her disdainful expression, Leonie gathered that such delicate matters were not mentioned in public. She didn't care. Escape was her priority.

She made her way indoors once more, pausing for a moment to contemplate her options. How long all this was going to go on for, she had no idea. It was possible, she supposed, that it would extend into the evening. She could snatch no more than another fifteen minutes on her own without appearing totally uncouth.

She turned her head sharply as the terrace doors were opened again, half expecting to see Roque following her in. Vidal viewed her with raised brows.

'You were expecting someone else?'

'Who else might I be expecting?' she asked. 'I just got a bit fed up with the general attitude out there.'

'With Roque the exception?'

His tone drew a line between her own brows. 'What's that supposed to mean?'

'You spent some considerable time alone with him earlier. I wasn't alone in noting it.'

'I was with Caterina,' she said, eradicating any trace of defensiveness from her voice. 'Roque came to tell her she was wanted by their mother. He played me a piece on the piano, that's all. He's actually a quite superb pianist.'

'He was caressing your hand when I saw him,' Vidal observed. 'You were making no effort whatsoever to stop him.'

'I don't play the outraged heroine scene over a simple gesture,' Leonie retorted, fast losing tolerance. 'Anyway, if you thought something was going on, why didn't you start shouting the odds there and then?'

Relieved of the jacket of the fine dark suit his mother had deemed suitable apparel for the ceremony, cream silk shirt open at the throat, Vidal looked relaxed on the outside, but the glitter in his eyes was a giveaway.

'I wouldn't give Roque the satisfaction,' he said. 'You'll stay away from him!'

The time to stand her ground would be when there was

something worth standing it over, she had told herself yesterday. That time, she decided, was here and now.

'Don't tell me what to do!' she snapped back. 'I'm no sweet little submissive!'

The glitter increased. 'You'll do as I say!'

'Otherwise what?' Leonie challenged. 'You'll expose my father for what he is? Do that, and you lose any hold you have on me!'

She stopped there, struck by the sudden blanking out of all expression from the dark eyes. When he spoke it was in flat, unemotional tones. 'We have guests. It will be considered the height of discourtesy for both bride and groom to desert them together.'

In which case he shouldn't have followed her, Leonie thought mutinously, though she found herself moving forward regardless as he opened the outer door once more. Her own instincts were to avoid any further dalliance with Roque, but she could hardly avoid him altogether. The sooner the day came to an end, the better.

People began leaving gradually soon after, with the cousins the last to depart, around six-thirty. Probably hoping for an invitation to dinner, Leonie thought, relieved when it wasn't forthcoming. One branch of the Dos Santos family was enough to deal with. While still objecting to the caveat, she steered clear of any one-to-one farewell from Roque.

'Vidal seems to hold a real grudge against him,' she commented to her father.

'According to his father, the two of them were always alienated, even as boys,' he returned. 'We got on surprisingly well this afternoon. Unlike his wife, he accepts the situation. Not that he can do any other if he wants to see his grandchildren. Assuming you'll be having some, that is?'

Leonie gave a laugh, unsurprised by the hollowness of it. 'We've only been married a week, Dad!'

'I'm talking future plans, of course. I'd like grandchildren myself. Otherwise I'm looking forward to a pretty lonely old age.'

'You're not even fifty yet,' Leonie observed. 'It isn't too late to meet someone else.'

Stuart gave her a swift glance, his expression uncertain. 'You're saying you wouldn't mind if I did?'

'Because of Mum?' She shook her head. 'That would be a very selfish attitude. I know how you felt about her, but it's been four years. She wouldn't have wanted you to spend the rest of your life on your own.' She paused, eyeing him in sudden suspicion. 'You have, haven't you? Met someone, I mean?'

His smile was a little self-conscious. 'It's only been a few days.'

'But you obviously like her.' Leonie fought down an undeniable pang. 'How did you meet?'

'I went to the theatre the night you left. Shirley had the seat next to me. She's a widow in her early forties, with one son twenty years old. He's at university, so she's very much on her own too. She has her own house in Holburn.'

'You must have done a lot of talking,' Leonie commented lightly. 'What does she look like?'

'Nice,' he said. 'Not glamorous, just…nice. Good figure for her age,' he added judiciously.

Leonie pulled a face at him. 'I see you've got your priorities straight!'

He grinned back. 'Don't begrudge an old man a little titillation.'

'You're far from old.' She had to laugh. 'The starting point, I believe. I hope it works out for you, Dad,' she added. 'I really do. You deserve to be happy.'

'What I deserve is where I'd be if it weren't for you,' he returned with wry inflection. 'However you feel about Vidal, I doubt if you'd have married him quite so quickly in normal circumstances.'

Leonie kept her voice steady. 'In normal circumstances we might never have got together again at all. Anyway, you've paid your dues. It's time to move on. I look forward to meeting Shirley.'

'You'll be coming over soon?'

'Very soon,' she promised recklessly. 'You're hardly a world away. If Vidal can't make it, I'll come on my own.'

'You'll go nowhere on your own,' declared the latter, who had approached their corner of the terrace unnoticed by either. Both face and voice were taut. 'Did you tell my mother we'd be staying several more days?'

'Actually, *she* told *me*,' Leonie responded, bristling instinctively at the tone of the question.

'But you saw no reason to dispute it?'

'I didn't think it was up to me to do that. Would it be such a sacrifice anyway?'

'Meaning *you* think we should extend our time here too?'

She had absolutely no interest in spending extra days in her mother-in-law's company, but she was too riled by his attitude to play the placatory card. 'It might show some consideration after what we've put them all through, yes.'

'Then of course we must stay.' The tone was silky now, but the line of his mouth didn't alter. 'I'm going to take a shower.'

Stuart whistled under his breath as his employer departed. 'I think your lord and master is just a bit peeved!'

'Don't call him that!' Leonie snapped back, regretting it the moment the words left her lips. 'Sorry,' she proffered. 'I'm not feeling very humorous right now.'

'As jokes go, it wasn't in the top category,' her father acknowledged. 'Vidal obviously doesn't take too kindly to having decisions taken out of his hands—even by his wife.'

'Especially by his wife,' she said tartly. 'In his view, women have no right to a mind of their own.'

It was a moment or two before Stuart replied, 'I'm sure that's not true.'

The concern in his voice shamed her into retraction. 'No, of course it isn't. I'm being stupid. It's his family. He should be the one to decide.'

'On the other hand, I think you have a point about consideration. It must have taken some doing to get everything together in a couple of days. Especially in the circumstances. Valente—'

'Valente?' Leonie queried.

'Your father-in-law invited me to call him by his given name. As I was saying, he told me he found the shock of the marriage difficult to deal with, but realised that alienation was the only alternative to acceptance. If he can make the effort, so can Vidal. Time I was thinking about a shower and a change of clothes myself,' he added. 'It's less than an hour to dinner—if we're eating at the same time as yesterday.' He got to his feet. 'What about you?'

'The same, I suppose,' she said reluctantly, in no mood to face Vidal again.

They went indoors together, parting halfway along the upper corridor, where Stuart's room was situated. Leonie could hear the shower running when she gained the bedroom. It was possible that Vidal had been waiting for her to put in an appearance. He hadn't finished hauling her over the coals for certain.

She chose a dress at random from the selection in the wardrobe, along with fresh underwear. The shower had stopped by the time she finished. She steeled herself as the bathroom door opened, ready for anything Vidal cared to throw at her—metaphorically speaking.

He was nude but for a smallish towel slung about his hips when he emerged, dark hair ruffled and glistening still with moisture. His skin had a golden lustre as he passed through the shaft of sunlight angling in through a window.

'All yours,' he said levelly, indicating the room he'd just left.

Nonplussed, Leonie gazed after him as he headed for the dressing area. 'Is that all you have to say?'

'What else would you have me say?' he rejoined without turning his head. 'You made your point. I was being inconsiderate.'

There was no answer she could think of. None, at least, that didn't include backing down herself. She wasn't ready for that.

CHAPTER EIGHT

STUART left for the airport at ten. Leonie found saying good-bye again even more of a wrench than the first time.

'Is everything all right?' he asked softly as he hugged her. 'With you and Vidal, I mean?'

'Fine,' she assured him. 'Just fine!'

She'd overdone it, she knew, when she saw his expression, but with Vidal himself close by he could hardly say anything else.

The two men shook hands in businesslike fashion. Leonie found it difficult to imagine any other kind of relationship between the two. They did have one thing in common, though, she thought cynically: embezzlement and blackmail were both criminal acts. At least her father had gone some way towards redeeming himself by replacing the money he'd stolen.

Vidal had made love to her last night as though this alter-cation had never happened. She'd responded because she couldn't help herself, but there had been little tenderness be-tween them. In what was becoming the pattern of her life, he'd been gone when she woke this morning. She hadn't seen him until breakfast, where she'd admittedly ignored him. Childish tactics, she acknowledged ruefully.

She turned back to him as the car bearing her father dis-appeared down the long winding driveway, willing herself to be natural. 'Nice of you to come and see him off with me. I'm sure it was appreciated.'

'My father would have thought it strange if I'd left you to do it alone,' he said.

'And we mustn't give him any idea that things aren't all

they seem, of course,' she retorted, dumping the natural act. 'It would be a real shock for him if he discovered what you're really capable of. He might even disown you.'

'It's possible.' Vidal studied her with a cynicism of his own. 'You're not without fault yourself in agreeing to the terms I set out.'

'You gave me no choice!' she protested.

'You had a choice. Saving your father from prosecution was far from your only reason for making the one you did. You wanted what you'd been yearning for since the moment we met; what you'd been looking for since you first became aware of your sexuality. You remained a virgin as long as you did because you'd only found one man who could heat your blood to fever-pitch, and you were unwilling to settle for less. If you'd married me two years ago, we—'

'If I'd married you two years ago, we'd be long divorced by now,' Leonie cut in bitingly. 'Lust fades with nothing to back it.'

There was a hint of cruelty in the curl of his lip. 'Then we must obviously make the most of what we have while it lasts.'

He turned to go back indoors, leaving her standing there feeling utterly depressed. As marriages went, this one left just about everything to be desired.

More of a manor than a palace, the other Dos Santos residence was still impressive enough. The family greeted them *en masse*, joined by two small boys belonging to Angelo and Brianca, who hadn't been deemed old enough to attend yesterday's ceremony. They spoke no English at all, and found Leonie's attempts at communication highly amusing, collapsing into fits of giggles. They were despatched to bed in a nanny's care.

They weren't the only guests. Leonie counted twenty people in all about the long polished table sparkling with silverware and crystal. Dinner was a stomach-swelling eight courses. Wearing a figure-hugging gold Estrada, she took very small helpings of everything, but even so would have given a great deal to ease the side zip.

Devastatingly handsome in a cream tuxedo, Vidal had been placed between two of the non-family female guests on the opposite side of the table. He'd been aloof all day. Roque had the seat on Leonie's right. He applied the major share of his attention to her during the course of the meal, making no secret of his admiration. He was a man accustomed to having women eating out of his hand. Irked by Vidal's whole attitude, she played up to him a little.

He stuck close when they retired to the salon after the meal. Leonie had totally forgotten about her mother-in-law's notion that she should entertain the company on the piano. She contemplated refusing, on the grounds that she was nowhere near talented enough to perform in public, to have that idea scotched by Roque's proprietary approbation. She daren't even glance in Vidal's direction.

The compilation of Andrew Lloyd Webber numbers she managed from memory seemed to go down reasonably well. She at least got through without hitting any wrong notes. Focused on escape, she suggested Roque should play next, enthusing over his vastly superior ability. He kissed her hand before taking the seat she vacated.

He played non-classical pieces himself, but with an expertise that sparked real enthusiasm from the gathering. Leonie applauded along with the rest.

'You really are good!' she exclaimed when he returned to his original seat at her side.

'I am good at everything I do,' came the reply, accompanied by a wicked sparkle that drew an involuntary smile to her lips.

'I'm sure of it,' she said.

Doors leading from the salon to the open terrace had been

left open to the wonderfully warm night air. Although it was already past midnight, people had begun moving outside. Vidal was engrossed in conversation with one of the women he'd been sitting with at dinner, eyes riveted to her face. A woman he knew pretty intimately, if she was any judge, Leonie thought, watching him for a moment, if not all that recently.

She became aware that Roque was speaking to her, turning back to him with a murmured apology. 'Sorry, I was miles away.'

He nodded understandingly. 'Your true home is miles away. I asked if you would like to step outside for the air.'

Sensing attention from her mother-in-law, if from no one else, she was about to refuse, but another swift glance in Vidal's direction beat discretion into second place.

'Nice idea,' she said.

More than one pair of eyes followed their progress across the wide room, but she was past caring what the owners of them might be thinking. She'd had enough of their disparagement.

Those who had already retired outdoors had formed a group. Roque made no attempt to join it, steering her down a flight of stone steps to the beautifully laid out gardens. The sky was clear of cloud, the moon riding low but offering enough light to see by. Leonie sniffed pleasurably at the air.

'That smells like night-scented stock!' she exclaimed.

'You would need to ask the gardeners the name of the plant,' Roque answered, obviously with little interest in horticulture. 'Your perfume is so much more entrancing.'

'Chanel No 5,' she said. 'Always a favourite—when I could afford it.'

'You had financial difficulties before you married Vidal?' he asked.

Regretting the unstudied remark, Leonie made haste to clarify it. 'Not in any meaningful sense.'

'Then you love him?'

'Of course.' How many times had she responded to that same question that same way? Leonie wondered. It seemed like dozens. 'I don't care about his money,' she added truthfully.

'He is a very fortunate man.'

'You already said that yesterday.'

'The truth can bear repetition.' There was a pause, a change of tone. 'You must know of the reputation my cousin has acquired. Does it not concern you?'

'Do you mean, do I worry that he may still be drawn to other women?'

Her factual tone drew a surprised glance. 'Yes.'

'Men being the way they are, I'd say it's inevitable.'

'And you would have no objection?'

'What the eye doesn't see, the heart doesn't grieve over.' She was spouting utter nonsense, Leonie reflected, but better that than allow emotions she'd shoved down deep to surface. 'The woman he's talking with in there is an old flame, I gather?'

'A former lover, yes.' Roque sounded suddenly sorrowful. 'A woman *I* might have married had he not come between us!'

'It must have been a long time ago if he left home at eighteen.'

'It was no more than two years ago, when he came on one of his visits. The moment he knew I was—' He broke off, shaking his head. 'It was always the same. *He* was always the same! I would hate for him to deceive you as he has deceived others.'

'Perhaps the boot might be on the other foot?' she rejoined.

Roque's brows drew together in puzzlement. 'The boot?'

'What's sauce for the goose—or should it be the gander in this case?' Her laugh sounded anything but natural in her ears. 'Sorry, I'm confusing you. They're just sayings, meaning what one can do, so can another.'

'You would take a lover yourself if you believed Vidal was being unfaithful to you?' Roque sounded intrigued now.

Leonie pulled herself up with a jerk. The man at her side had no love for Vidal. Allowing herself to be influenced by anything he said about him was shameful. Being out here with the man at all was shameful.

'I think this conversation has gone far enough,' she declared. 'I'd like to go back to the house now. Now, please!' she repeated, when he showed no sign of halting his footsteps. 'Unless you'd prefer I went back alone?'

This time she got a reaction, though hardly a congenial one. Without a word, Roque turned and began retracing their path, face set in lines that did little to enhance his looks. If his aim had been to undermine her trust in Vidal, he needn't have bothered, Leonie could have told him, because she didn't have any to start with.

She felt her heart sink when they came in sight of the house and she saw Vidal on the terrace steps, looking as if about to set out in pursuit. He watched the two of them coming without moving, the only sign of emotion in the tension along his jawline.

'Mina,' he said softly to Roque, and then, to Leonie herself, 'We're leaving.'

She accompanied him without protest, conscious of the watchers along the terrace. He took her into the house via another door, and along a corridor to the entrance hall. They had travelled here in separate cars, as Vidal refused to be driven by the chauffeur. Still without speaking, he put her into the front passenger seat, then walked round the front of the vehicle to slide behind the wheel.

'I don't have my purse and wrap,' Leonie felt moved to murmur as he brought the engine to life.

'They'll be brought,' he said.

By his parents, she presumed. Her behaviour tonight was hardly going to improve their opinion of her as a suitable wife for their son. But then, what would?

'Whatever you've got to say, I wish you'd just say it!' she burst out when nothing more was forthcoming. 'So I went for a walk with your cousin. Big deal!'

'You spent the whole evening cavorting with him,' Vidal returned hardily.

'I was not *cavorting*!' she denied with heat. 'It wasn't my idea to sit next to Roque at dinner. Not that you looked too unhappy with the partners you were given, if it comes to that. Especially the one you were slavering over the last hour!'

They had left the grounds and were heading along the narrow lane leading back to the main roadway. Vidal slowed the car to take a series of bends, hands steady on the wheel. 'Antonia is an old friend.'

'A very *close* friend, from what I hear! You certainly didn't waste much time finding solace after I turned you down two years ago. Straight out here and into her arms—regardless of who might get hurt in the process of boosting your ego!' Leonie was past caring what she said, intent only on piercing the armour he'd donned. 'I wondered why a man like Roque was still unmarried, and now I know! You took the woman he loved!'

'Love isn't a word Roque knows anything about—unless applied to self,' came the unmoved rejoinder. 'Antonia remains unmarried because she's never found a man she could contemplate spending her life with.'

'Including you?'

'That I wouldn't know. I never saw her as a potential wife.'

'Just a *friend*.' Leonie let the sarcasm rip. 'And, of course, you never went near her two years ago.'

'On the contrary. We spent a lot of time together during the three days I was here.'

'But you didn't sleep with her, naturally?'

The strong mouth slanted. 'I've told you before, I find that particular euphemism ridiculous. Sleep, no. Have sexual intercourse, yes. We were two adult people, neither of us tied at the time. If Roque had meant anything to her, she would have told me.'

'Pillow talk, you mean.' Leonie was doing her utmost to stay on top of the forces gathering inside her. 'It never occurred to you that you might be the one stopping her from turning to anyone else?'

'No.' Vidal kept his eyes fixed on the road—what could be seen of it. 'What other ideas did Roque plant in your head?'

'Nothing I didn't already know. Your reputation is hardly a secret. Your father told Dad you and Roque had been alienated since you were boys.'

'True.'

'Any particular reason, or just simple boyhood rivalry?' she asked when he failed to add to the statement.

The smile was faint and humourless. 'Some might view it that way. The fact that I stand to inherit everything he covets for himself could have a bearing.'

'But he's hardly going to be left destitute.'

'Money is only a part of it. My father has overall control of both estates, which means that I will too when the time comes. To say nothing of the properties we own throughout the region.'

'Might he have believed your marriage to Caterina would bring the two of you closer?' Leonie ventured after a moment.

'If he did, he was wrong. We may bear a physical resemblance, but we could never become brothers.'

He turned the car out onto a wider road, empty of other traffic at this hour. Several moments elapsed before he spoke again, voice still controlled. 'You're attracted to him?'

Leonie sighed, abandoning any remaining antagonism. 'Not in the least. I was simply kicking over the traces. Not just to get at you. I'm sick of the way your mother regards me. If I were here by choice…'

'And not by compulsion?' Vidal supplied as she let the words trail away. 'What difference would it make?'

'None, I suppose.' She was suddenly weary of the whole discussion—if what had passed between them these last few minutes could be called that. 'As it's unlikely I'll be seeing her again after this, it isn't really important.'

Vidal gave her a swift glance. 'Why would it be unlikely?'

'Why would it be anything else?. You've achieved your aim, which was to quash any possibility of marriage with Caterina.'

'You think that's the only reason I married you?'

'I think you seized on Dad's situation to kill two birds with the one stone, as the saying goes.'

They were approaching the Palacio de Mecia gateway. Vidal waited until they were through and heading up the drive before making any response, face austere in the moonlight.

'Whatever the motivation, you won't lose by it.'

She already had lost by it, she thought hollowly, giving up on the fight. Loving a man who could do as Vidal had done was crazy, but then, love itself was a crazy emotion. One thing was certain: however long or short a time his desire for her lasted, he'd never know how she really felt about him. That much pride she could preserve.

The staff had apparently retired for the night, though the hall and staircase lights had been left on, as had those in their suite. Despite the hour, Leonie made no protest when Vidal suggested a nightcap before retiring themselves. Alcohol was no aid to sleep, but she was in no mood for that anyway.

'For someone who feels the way you do about Roque, you

were very controlled back there,' she remarked as she took a glass from him.

'I saw no reason to supply the audience with entertainment,' he said. 'Nor to give Roque the satisfaction of achieving what he'd set out to achieve.'

'Which was what, exactly?'

'To make me angry enough to do as I have always refused to do where he's concerned, and fight. To Roque's way of thinking, it's the only way to prove manhood.'

'Some might agree with him.'

Dark brows lifted ironically. 'Including you?'

She shook her head. 'The last thing I'd accuse you of is cowardice.'

'How can you be so sure?' he asked. 'I might be a quivering mouse inside.'

Her laugh was the first genuine one of the evening. 'And pigs might fly!'

He gave a mock frown. 'I appreciate the vote of confidence, although I'm not sure I care for the association.'

'You should take it as a compliment,' she said. 'They're pretty high up the intelligence scale.'

Looking at him, seeing the amber lights in his eyes again, she let the relief of at least being back to where they'd been a couple of days ago wash over her. If he didn't love her now the way she wanted him to, then it was up to her to make it happen, she reflected in sudden surging determination. Forget the beginning, and work towards a happy end.

She got to her feet before she could change her mind, taking his glass from his unresisting hand to deposit it along with her own on the nearest surface.

'Let's go to bed,' she said softly.

Facing her in-laws at breakfast next morning was a trial, though Senhor Dos Santos offered no verbal condemnation. His wife, however, suffered no such restraint on her tongue.

'Have you no honour at all that you make such an exhibition of yourself?' she stormed. 'Did the vows you made to my son mean nothing to you?'

'Don't you think you're getting the whole thing a bit out of proportion?' Leonie responded, resenting the implication.

The retort created near apoplexy. 'No, I do not! Your place was with your husband!'

'Then I should surely have been placed with my husband,' Leonie felt bound to point out. 'Not that I consider I did anything outlandish. You were the one who set me up to play the piano, *senhora*. All I did was ask someone more competent to take over.'

'And afterwards invite him to take you into the gardens!'

'Bastantes,' Senhor Dos Santos put in mildly.'It is up to Vidal if he wishes to reprimand his wife.'

'Already taken care of,' Vidal returned calmly.

Leonie met his eyes, unable to stop her lips from quirking in response to the humour lurking there. She'd been reprimanded all right. Twice! They'd had little more than a couple of hours sleep.

Catching the glance, her mother-in-law spread her hands in a gesture only too easy to read. Having a son apparently untroubled by his wife's lack of proper decorum was obviously beyond all reckoning.

'So what's on the agenda for today?' Vidal enquired when no further criticism was offered. 'Assuming you still want us to extend our time with you, that is?'

'Of course,' his father answered. 'I wish you to take a tour of the yards with me. You have yet to meet Javier Alvares, who replaced Rodrigo as manager last year.' He held up a hand as Vidal made to speak. 'I am only too well aware of your lack of interest in estate affairs, but there will come a time when you can no longer turn away from your responsibilities. However far in the future that might be.'

Leonie donned a smile as Vidal glanced her way. 'I'll be

fine,' she assured him. 'I'll even behave,' she added with mock humility, drawing a reluctant grin.

'That will be a day to remember!'

His mother made a sound of disgust, adding something in Portuguese before stalking off indoors. Making her peace there—or trying to—would be one way of passing the time, Leonie acknowledged wryly. The woman could hardly be blamed too much for views implanted in her since birth.

'Sorry about this,' Vidal proffered before leaving. 'It's easier to just go along.'

'Your father's right, though,' Leonie felt bound to say. 'Who else is there to step into his shoes? What's to stop you running both empires, anyway?'

He eyed her speculatively for a moment. 'I may be too old by then to run even one.'

'In which case you can put managers in both and enjoy retirement,' she returned lightly. 'It comes to everyone in the end.'

He took her face between his hands the way he'd done many times before, smoothing back the radiant hair from her temples to scrutinise every vibrant feature, the look in his eyes a boost to her spirits. '"Age shall not wither her"',' he quoted softly.

If she could arouse the same degree of emotion in his breast as she could lust, she'd be home and dry, Leonie thought, meeting his lips.

The day stretched before her like a desert after he'd gone. She nerved herself to go and find his mother, determined to at least try to reach some understanding. One of the staff who had some English directed her to a small salon, where she found her mother-in-law writing letters. The greeting she received was anything but encouraging, but she ploughed on regardless.

'I came to apologise for my behaviour last night,' she said, with all the sincerity she could muster. 'You were right. I shouldn't have gone off like that with Roque.'

The older woman eyed her in silence for a lengthy moment, looking just a little nonplussed. 'Why did you not say this earlier?' she asked.

Leonie made a wry gesture. 'I was on the defensive. I knew I was in the wrong, but I didn't want to admit it. I suppose I'm just not used to being answerable to anyone but myself.'

'You are answerable to your husband.' The tone was severe.

'I know.' Leonie kept both tone and expression rueful. 'He made that clear last night. I really am sorry, *senhora*. Not just for last night, but for everything. I realise how unsuitable I must seem as a wife for your son, compared with Caterina.'

'There is nothing you can say that will cause me to change my mind about that suitability,' the other declared. 'However, as my husband has said, what is done is done. All I ask is that you conform to our ways when you are here.'

'I will.' Whether she would be called on to keep that promise was still a matter for conjecture, Leonie could have told her. 'I do love Vidal,' she added. 'I didn't marry him for any kind of material gain.'

Her mother-in-law looked sceptical. 'You claim to have no interest in his wealth?'

'If you mean do I find it a turn-off? Obviously not.' She gave a significant glance down at the beautifully cut linen dress she was wearing. 'It's great to be able to spend without having to think about cost. I'd be a liar if I tried to pretend otherwise. But it isn't everything by a long chalk!'

Senhora Dos Santos shook her head. 'There are times when the words you use are beyond my understanding, but I believe you are telling me that you would love my son whatever his position in life?'

'Yes.' It was a questionable claim, Leonie thought fleet-

ingly, because she couldn't know what kind of man Vidal
might have been if he'd been born to any other walk of life,
but this was no time to start philosophising. 'Completely.'

The scepticism was still there in the other eyes, though
somewhat muted. 'We shall see,' she said.

Unless Vidal became bankrupt, it was difficult to know
how she could prove herself, Leonie reflected. The question
may prove to be academic anyway, if he did eventually lose
interest in her.

A possibility she wasn't going to allow herself to dwell
on, she resolved. Faint heart never won anything.

She left the room feeling some minor inroad might have
been made. With three hours to go until lunch, and no other
form of entertainment presenting itself, it would, she decided,
be a good time to do a little more exploring.

So far she'd been no further than the immediate garden
area, but the grounds were extensive. She headed into the
woodland bordering the long drive, glad to be out of the sun
beating down from a cloudless sky. Douro summers were
baking hot and dry, the winters wet and cold, with distinct
demarcation lines between the seasons, Vidal had told her.
Unlike England, where snow in June and a heatwave in
November wasn't unheard of.

She felt a sudden wave of homesickness. Ridiculous, when
she'd only been away from home some ten days, but who
was to say how long it might be before she saw it again?
Vidal had been angry when he'd declared she would be going
nowhere on her own, but that wasn't to say he hadn't meant
it. He still held the whip hand where her father's future was
concerned.

The path she had been following through the trees was
apparently little used. She went right when it forked, emerging some few minutes later close by the open gates. About
to begin retracing her steps, she came to a halt as a figure
hove into view.

Caterina came to an abrupt stop herself, a variety of expressions chasing across her face before it settled into one of relieved recognition.

'I thought for a moment that you were some other person,' she said. 'You are the one I came to see. You—and Vidal.' She paused, a flush staining her cheeks. 'I have something to ask of you both. Something very important to me.'

Leonie put curiosity on the back burner for the present, settling for a reassuring smile. 'I'm afraid Vidal isn't here right now, but he should be back for lunch.' She wasn't sure about that, but neither could she be sure he wouldn't be. 'Why didn't you drive in?' she added. 'Assuming you came by car?'

Caterina shook her head. 'I hold no licence to drive a car. I walked here.'

'But it must be all of ten miles by road!'

'There are shorter ways.' Her tone dismissed the subject as of no importance. 'If Vidal is not here, then I must come another day.'

'You could come and wait for him,' Leonie suggested. 'I'm sure a long cool drink would be welcome.'

'No!' The denial was emphatic. 'No one else must know I am here!'

Leonie studied her in some perplexity. 'Then how did you intend getting to see the two of us, anyway?'

'There is a side entrance to the tower where Vidal has his apartments,' Caterina answered. 'I hoped to find you there.'

A long shot to start with at this hour, Leonie thought. 'It's possible we won't be around for many more days,' she said cautiously. 'Perhaps you could tell me what you want to ask, and I can pass it on to Vidal. It might be the only chance you have,' she added, seeing the refusal forming on the other's lips.

Caterina looked torn by indecision. When she did finally incline her head in acceptance, it was with some reluctance.

Leonie had passed a stone seat set to one side of the path a few yards back within the trees. They would be out of view of anyone traversing the drive.

She led the way, uncertain if she was doing the right thing, but unwilling to just do nothing. Caterina took a seat at her side with diffidence, obviously still labouring under doubts herself. The green canopy above was silent. Too far on in the year for any birdsong claiming territory, Leonie imagined. They would all be too busy by now, feeding their young. She schooled herself to wait for Caterina to start the ball rolling.

'I have to go to Lisbon,' the latter said at length. 'I hope to travel with you and Vidal when you go.'

Leonie absorbed surprise with an effort. It was the last thing she would have expected to hear. 'Why is it necessary to be secretive about it?' she asked.

'Because I would not be allowed to go,' came the simple answer.

'You're twenty-seven!' Leonie protested. 'How can anyone stop you from doing whatever you want to do?'

The smile was faint. 'You speak from your own experience of life. As I failed to gain the husband chosen for me, I must marry whoever will have me. Approaches have already been made.'

'This isn't the Dark Ages!' Leonie burst out, bristling with indignation. 'No one can make you do that!'

'Force, perhaps not. But an unmarried daughter is a humiliation to the family name.'

To hell with the family name! was Leonie's instinctive reaction. 'So marry this man you told me about,' she said, harking back to their conversation just a couple of days ago. 'That way everyone is happy!'

The glow that had transformed the other woman's face on that occasion appeared once more, her eyes deep pools of emotion. 'To do that I have to go to Lisbon.'

'He lives there?'

'In spirit, yes. He has no earthly form.'

Gazing at her, Leonie felt realisation suddenly dawn. 'You mean you want to become a nun?' she said, in tones that drew another faint smile to Caterina's lips.

'You find that so shocking a desire?'

Leonie took a sharp hold on herself. This wasn't *her* life they were talking about. 'Not shocking, just…unexpected,' she managed. 'How long have you felt like this?'

'As long as I can remember.'

'But you'd still have married Vidal?'

'The promise was given at my birth. I had a duty to fulfil it. If I had access to the money it would take for me to go to the convent, then I would already be gone. As I do not, I can only appeal to Vidal. And yourself, of course.'

Taking into account the length of time Caterina had been forced to wait for Vidal to put paid to the whole antediluvian idea, he owed her at least that much, Leonie reckoned. If it was what she truly wanted, then it was what she should surely have!

'I'll speak to Vidal,' she said. 'He'll make whatever arrangements are necessary.'

'It must remain our secret,' Caterina urged anxiously. 'How will I know if he is in agreement?'

'He'll contact you somehow.' They were reckless promises to make, but Leonie was too caught up to care. 'Just leave it with me.'

Caterina took her hand in hers, lifting it to her lips in a gesture of gratitude. 'Thank you! I knew you would understand.'

She was a long way from understanding the desire to lock oneself away from the world in a convent, Leonie acknowledged, but that was another matter. She watched the almost too slender figure out of sight before stirring herself. Vidal would help his cousin. He *had* to help her.

CHAPTER NINE

THE men didn't return for lunch. The two women ate together on the terrace. Senhora Dos Santos seemed a shade more mellow, at least prepared to make some effort towards conversation, and Leonie listened to whatever she had to say without dissension. If that was what it took to get along with her mother-in-law, then so be it. She could surely put up with kowtowing a little on a temporary basis.

The older woman retired to take siesta after the meal. Leonie spent a couple of hours lounging with a book taken from the well-stocked library. There was a fair selection in English. Having command of both languages would open up a very much wider world of literature.

She'd acquired a few words of Portuguese herself over the past days, mostly via the staff. Certainly not enough to get by with on her own as yet, but better than anticipated. The difference, she supposed, between learning a language by rote and hearing it spoken every day.

Life here wouldn't be bad at all, she mused, if the feudal element, as her father had called it, was removed. Vidal could do that if he did eventually take over. If he didn't accept his role, someone would have to. If there was any chance at all of Roque getting in on the act, that would surely be the deciding factor.

It was almost six o'clock when the men finally put in an appearance. Vidal appeared in surprisingly good humour for a man who'd spent the greater part of the day doing something against his will. He also seemed on far better terms with his father.

'We reached an agreement,' he said later, when he and Leonie were changing for dinner. 'I'll do my duty when the times comes, providing I'm left to get on with my life in the meantime. He's only fifty-six now, and in fine health, so it's going to be at least another ten years before he even considers taking a back seat. As you said yourself, there's no reason why I should abandon my own interests entirely even then.'

'No reason at all,' Leonie agreed. She considered whether to launch her plea for Caterina here and now, deciding to hold fire until he was in a frame of mind to take a sympathetic viewpoint. 'Tycoons can tackle anything!' she added, tongue in cheek.

His mouth curved. 'Including a disrespectful wife!'

'I hang my head in shame,' she declared in mock humility, stepping back with a laugh as he made a move toward her. 'Pax! We're going to be late for dinner.'

'I'll deal with you later,' he promised.

She could wait, Leonie thought. Just!

The evening passed in relative harmony. Leonie kept a rein on her tongue, refusing to rise to provocation from her mother-in-law, real or suspected. Wholesale approval might be in short supply, but a little was better than none at all.

'What happened to this morning's disposition?' Vidal asked quizzically when they retired for the night.

Leonie smiled and shrugged. 'I decided to exercise some discretion for a change. Your mother has a right to her opinions.'

'You have rights too,' he said. 'Don't allow her to overcome them. My father admires your spirit.'

Green eyes widened in genuine surprise. 'He does?'

'He said so today. You're the first English woman he's ever had any real dealings with. Speaking of which,' he added with a glint, 'I have a score to settle with you myself.'

He did it in his own inimitable manner.

Lying supine and utterly satiated in his arms afterwards, Leonie had to make a real effort to bring her mind to bear on Caterina's problems.

'We had a visitor this morning,' she murmured. 'A would-be one, at any rate.'

Vidal nuzzled his lips into the hollow at the base if her throat, using the very tip of his tongue to stir her pulses afresh. 'Who?' he asked against her skin.

If he didn't stop that she was going to lose her thread altogether, she thought, feeling the heat beginning to rise again.

'Caterina,' she said, forsaking any idea of a lead-in. 'She wants us to take her to Lisbon when we go.'

That got a reaction. Vidal jerked his head up, expression incredulous. 'She wants us to what?'

'Take her to Lisbon,' Leonie repeated. 'To join a convent.'

For lengthy moment Vidal remained in suspended animation, looking down at her in stupefaction. 'Is this some kind of joke?' he demanded at last.

'Not unless Caterina's given to that kind of twisted humour,' she said. 'Which I very much doubt. It's what she wants, Vidal. What she's always wanted, apparently. If she stays here, she's going to be forced into marrying some man just to protect the family name. You wouldn't condemn her to that, would you?'

He thrust himself suddenly upright, running a distracted hand through his hair as he came to a sitting position on the mattress edge. 'It's a preposterous idea!' he exclaimed.

'The marriage, or the convent?' Leonie queried.

'The convent, of course! Maureo Guera is a good match for her.'

Leonie came upright herself, hair a flaming cloud in the lamplight. 'You knew about it?'

'It was mentioned today.'

'Just that—a mention? How thoughtful!' She was too angry now to pull any punches, disgusted with his acceptance of an arrangement she found so repulsive. 'This is Caterina's life we're talking about!'

'Which will be far better than the one she proposes to lead,' came the curt reply.

'That's your opinion, not hers! Are you saying she isn't entitled to a mind of her own?'

Vidal turned a quelling glance on her. 'It's a matter of what's best for her.'

'Which neither you nor anyone else has the right to decide for her! You refused to be driven into an arranged marriage yourself; why shouldn't Caterina take a leaf out of the same book? She's wasted enough years trying to please others. It's time she got to please herself!'

Vidal was looking at her as if at a problem picture, taking in the high spots of colour in her cheeks, the blazing eyes and tempestuous mouth, his own anger giving way to something less easily discerned.

'Why such passion for someone you barely know?' he asked.

'I'm against injustice, whoever's suffering it!' She took a grip on her temper in the realisation that losing it was gaining her nothing. 'You owe her your help, Vidal. You have to recognise that much.'

She paused, viewing the sculpted features in hope of seeing his expression soften—heart sinking when he remained impassive. 'Please!' she added softly.

He got abruptly to his feet, reaching for the robe tossed over a nearby chair. Nude herself, Leonie resisted the ridiculous impulse to draw the silk sheet up across her breasts as he turned back to her. The lamplight cast shadows across his face, outlining the hard male cheekbones.

'So what do you propose we do?' he asked expressionlessly. 'Assuming you have a plan?'

'I hadn't actually got that far,' she confessed.

A corner of his mouth turned down. 'Now, why am I surprised? I already told my father we'd be leaving tomorrow.'

'I'm sure he'll be only too delighted if you delay another day,' she said, trying not to let the irony get to her. 'I told

Caterina we'd find a way of letting her know what to do. We'll be on our own in the car. We could arrange a pick-up point somewhere.'

'And how is she supposed to smuggle baggage out with her?'

'If she's going into a convent, she's hardly going to need extra clothing. I believe everything is provided.'

'Taking it for granted that she'll be accepted, of course?'

'I can't see them turning anyone away. It wouldn't be Christian.' She made an appealing gesture. 'It's the right thing to do. You know it is!'

'A matter of opinion,' he said, 'but, as you pointed out, mine isn't the only one to be taken into account. I need a drink,' he added shortly.

'I could do with one myself,' Leonie proffered.

He shook his head. 'I have some thinking to do. You'd better get some sleep.'

She watched him go from the room, painfully aware that in championing Caterina's cause she might have put paid to her own. There had been nothing even remotely lover-like in the way he'd looked at her just now.

As predicted, her father-in-law accepted the change of plan with gratification, if a little surprise.

'You must show Leonie more of our environment,' he said to his son at breakfast. 'Perhaps a visit to Vila Real. The home of Mateus wine,' he added for Leonie's benefit. 'The Palace is open to the public. It has magnificent gardens.'

'Even better than the ones here?' she asked, drawing an appreciative smile.

'Even better.'

His wife had received the news without comment. Leonie had a feeling she would as soon have the parting over and done with. She'd accepted the marriage because she had no choice, but she would never wholly accept her son's choice of bride. Not that she might have to for all that much longer.

It had been an hour or more before Vidal had come back to bed last night. Leonie hadn't been asleep, and he must have known it, but he'd made no attempt to touch her. She'd slept fitfully, coming awake instantly when he'd got up at six-thirty. There were calls to be made, he'd said when she asked a tentative question. She should go back to sleep.

She hadn't, of course. She'd been showered and dressed by the time he'd returned. He'd seemed normal enough on the surface, but had cut her short when she mentioned Caterina's name. The matter, he'd said, would be dealt with.

She cast a swift glance in his direction now. His attention appeared to be fixed on the distant mountain backdrop, though she doubted if it was the scenery he was thinking about. If they were to take Caterina with them tomorrow, then a message had to be delivered to her some time today.

If. It was still very much the operative word. For all she knew, he had scotched the whole idea.

They set out at ten for the proposed trip to Vila Real. Only when Vidal turned off the main road to take the lane they had traversed two evenings ago did Leonie realise where they were really heading.

'You're going to tell them what Caterina's planning, aren't you?' she accused.

'I'm going to do what she should have done herself,' was the level response. 'How else are they to know what she wants?'

'You can't!' Leonie was desperate to stop this happening. 'She'll think I betrayed her!'

'Don't dramatise. If she's really serious about becoming a nun, I'll do what I can to help. But this plan the two of you concocted is ludicrous! She won't be forced into marrying Maureo.'

'Just coerced into considering it her duty—the same way she considered it her duty to wait for you.' Leonie was hard put to it to keep from letting fly. 'She doesn't have your strength of mind. If you'd seen her yesterday, you'd realise just how much of an effort it was for her to ask for help at all. She put her trust in me!'

'And you, of course, saw no reason to discourage her. Did it occur to you at any point to consider what might be thought if she simply vanished? It isn't unknown for women to be abducted.'

'Obviously she'd have left a note,' Leonie prevaricated, not about to admit that the thought hadn't crossed her mind. 'Anyway, it's immaterial now, isn't it?' The pause was brief, her voice taking on a beseeching note. 'Unless you'll change your mind?'

Vidal gave her a swift glance, lips twisting as he met the glimmering green eyes. 'I'm afraid I can't do that.'

'You mean you won't!' she flung at him, losing the battle. 'You might have escaped family commitments yourself, but why should Caterina? After all, she's only a woman!'

He made no answer. Viewing the unyielding profile, Leonie felt a powerful urge to hit out physically. There had been times these last days when she'd believed he wasn't nearly as case-hardened as his image, but she'd been wrong. She'd been wrong about loving him too. He wasn't worth loving!

'I hate you!' she said savagely.

There was cynicism in the brief smile. 'But not all the time.'

There was too much truth in that for comfort. It was entirely possible that hatred would take a back seat if he made any physical approach right now, she acknowledged ruefully. Caterina was far from the only one lacking will-power.

Roque was crossing the courtyard when they drew into it. He viewed the pair of them with undisguised hostility.

'To what do we owe such an honour?' he asked, his accent making heavy weather of the phrase.

Vidal replied in Portuguese, bringing a sudden frown to the other man's brow. He hesitated a moment before turning with obvious reluctance to go back indoors.

'You stay here,' Vidal instructed as Leonie made to open her door. 'Caterina has no need of a champion.'

Caterina had every need, if she was any judge at all, but she could hardly force him to take her with him. She subsided back into her seat, watching him frosty-eyed as he followed Roque through the wide main doorway. For all she knew he'd been lying through his teeth when he said he would do what he could to help his cousin. He could come back out here and tell her anything—even that Caterina had changed her mind.

If she was refused any further contact she'd know that probably wasn't true, but there would be little she could do about it.

The day was already hot. Even with the car windows down it was becoming uncomfortable sitting here. She contemplated running the air-conditioning, but there was a possibility of the unit overheating. After several minutes she got out of the car and found a shady seat by a side wall.

Whatever was happening in there, it was taking a long time, she mused, glancing at her watch. If Vidal had intended merely to warn them of Caterina's intentions it would be over and done with by now. She could hear no raised voices from within. But then, the walls were thick, the windows closed. All hell could have let loose without her knowing a thing about it.

She could defy Vidal's injunction and go on in, of course, but to what end? Her presence wasn't going to swing any votes.

Roque was the first to put in an appearance. He came striding over to where she sat, face suffused with anger.

'You did this!' he accused. 'You put this idea into her head!'

'It's entirely her own idea,' Leonie answered levelly. 'All I did was listen.'

'Then your time was wasted. She is going to no convent!'

Leonie came to her feet, too incensed to heed the glittering malice in the dark eyes. 'It isn't up to you to say what she can or can't do! You're her brother, not her keeper! All you should want is her happiness!'

'All *she* should want is what all women want,' he snapped. 'A man to keep her in comfort. Maureo Guera will provide her with everything she could ask for. All she has to do is provide him with a son. That is what she will do!'

'Over my dead body!' Leonie challenged, ignoring the fact that she wouldn't even be here after tomorrow.

'Leave her!' Unnoticed by either of them, Vidal was bare feet away. His tone was a whiplash.

Roque spun round to face him, answering in Portuguese, fury in both face and voice. Seeing them in close proximity for the first time, Leonie realised Vidal was actually the taller of the two by a couple of inches. The fitter too, judging by the tautness of his midriff compared with the distinct signs of rounding about the other. Eyes narrowed to blazing points of light, body balanced, he looked dangerously close to launching an attack.

'Don't!' she pleaded. 'He didn't touch me.'

The sneer that appeared on Roque's lips was a goad in itself, but Vidal held himself in check. 'You may get your wish one day,' he said, 'but not now.'

Roque shot another mouthful of obvious abuse after him as he moved to the car, but he showed no reaction. Leonie slid in beside him, sitting silently as he fired the engine and headed out the way they'd come.

'Do you still want to visit Vila Real?' he asked

'I suppose.' She waited a moment, glancing his way when he failed to say anything else. Not that she was any the wiser. 'Are you going to tell me or not?' she demanded.

'If you mean about Caterina, I explained the position.'

'And?' she urged.

'And left her to convince them of her seriousness.'

'She'll let them ride over her!'

'If she does, then her calling isn't strong enough. I told

her we'll be here at nine-thirty in the morning. It's up to her now.'

'With Roque around, what chance does she have?'

'Roque has no power to stop her leaving. No one has the power to stop her leaving—if she has the will to do it.'

And if she hadn't, he wouldn't be making any further approaches on her behalf, Leonie gathered from his tone. She could, if she was fair about it, see his point of view. Becoming a nun was a lifetime commitment. The vocation had to be strong enough to overcome all obstacles.

There was no point in further protests, anyway. It was, as he said, up to Caterina herself now. If she failed to put in an appearance in the morning, then that would be that.

'I think I've let the whole thing get a bit out of hand,' she said in subdued tones.

Vidal lifted his shoulders. 'You empathise with Caterina because you see a parallel with your own position. If I could be persuaded to free the one from her bonds, I might do the same for the other.'

'That never occurred to me,' she denied. 'In any case...'

'In any case, what?' he queried as she let the words trail away.

She'd been about to say she no longer wanted her freedom, but that would have left her too vulnerable. 'Nothing,' she said flatly. 'Can we forget about it for now?'

He inclined his head. 'By all means.'

Conversation took a natural enough flow from that point, but Leonie sensed a subtle difference in his manner towards her. It was all down to her that they were still here in the Douro when they could have been halfway to Lisbon by now, she reminded herself. Obviously he was going to be annoyed.

It was more than that, she knew. Whatever power she exercised over him, it wasn't inexhaustible.

As days went, she'd spent worse ones. The Mateus palace and gardens proved as magnificent as her father-in-law had indicated. She sampled the rosé wine at lunch in one of the town's many restaurants, and liked it.

'Not that I'm any connoisseur,' she said lightly.

'You don't need to be,' Vidal responded. 'Drink what appeals to you.'

'This certainly does!' She held up her glass to the light. 'Such a wonderful colour!'

Vidal viewed her across the table, lips smiling, eyes dense. 'A beautiful wine for a beautiful woman. My mother is quite fond of it too.'

'Nice to know we have *something* in common.' Catching his eye, she pulled a wry face. 'That sounded nasty, and it wasn't meant to be. I don't suppose we could ever really hit it off.'

'There are no certainties in anything,' he said. 'Would you like dessert?'

Leonie shook her head, wishing she could convince herself that everything was as it had been between them. Tonight might prove the deciding factor. They'd made love every single night since their marriage—apart from the one she'd sabotaged herself. If he was going off her, she'd know it.

It should have been apparent that Vidal's parents would be informed of their morning call, of course, but Leonie was unprepared for the reception they got on their return to Palacio de Mecia.

She and Vidal would take no further part in the affair, her father-in-law commanded furiously. The family would make their own decision over Caterina's future.

'Except that it is *her* future they're deciding!' Leonie burst out, infuriated herself by the castigation. 'Why should—?'

'I'll deal with this.' Vidal's tone was clipped, his face set.

He addressed his father in Portuguese, darkening the older man's expression still further and drawing a vituperative response. Standing by, his mother attempted to intervene, to be silenced abruptly by her husband's angry gesture. She glared at Leonie as if to say this was all her fault.

Which it was, of course. But Leonie was in no mood to play the repentant. While unable to understand a word of the exchange between the two men, it was obvious that Vidal wasn't going down that road either. It was his father who backed down in the end, throwing up his hands as if to divest himself of all responsibility and walking off. Looking a little lost for words herself, his wife followed him.

'I gather you refused to do as ordered?' Leonie said tentatively.

Vidal gave a hard shrug. 'The promise was made, and the promise will be kept, if it proves necessary.'

Which it very well might not, if Caterina had been subjected to bombardment of a similar nature, Leonie suspected. Only time would tell.

The atmosphere at dinner could have been cut with a knife. Leonie stood it as long as she could before finally letting go.

'I'm the one responsible for all this,' she declared with force. 'So blame me, not Vidal.'

'Do you think we are unaware of that?' said her mother-in-law frostily. 'You have been a source of trouble since you arrived!'

'If stirring a little life into an outdated society is causing trouble, then all power to my elbow!' Leonie fired back. 'Being married to your son doesn't make me in any way subservient. If you knew…'

She caught herself up, biting her lip. 'If we knew what?' prompted Senhor Dos Santos on a surprisingly mild note.

'Tell them,' Vidal invited. Both voice and face were impassive.

'If you knew how difficult it is to adjust to all this,' she supplanted weakly. 'You were all born to it. I've never known anything like it. I can never be the kind of wife you think Vidal should have. I'm just not made that way.'

From the expression in her father-in-law's eyes, he had a very good idea that it wasn't what she'd been about to say, but he let it pass.

'Our welcome was far from ideal,' he said. 'Shock is no excuse. Perhaps we should make a fresh start.'

'A little late, don't you think?' queried his son. 'We're leaving first thing in the morning.'

'It's never too late,' Leonie stated, not about to slap his father in the face with his offer. It was odds on that this would be the last visit she made here anyway, but they could at least part on reasonable terms. She cast a glance in her mother-in-law's direction, doubting if it would be any use, but willing to at least make the effort. 'Can we? Try again, I mean?'

The other looked anything but amenable. Only when her husband gave her a meaningful look did she stiffly incline her head.

'All's well that ends well.' Vidal made no attempt to disguise the satire. 'Brandy, anyone?'

The evening ended early by tacit consent. Leonie accompanied a silent Vidal to their quarters with a heart growing heavier by the second. It seemed incongruous that so short a time ago she would have welcomed the possibility of ending this travesty of a marriage.

'Why didn't you tell them the truth?' he asked in the bedroom.

'Because it's my father I'd have been betraying,' she said.

'Perhaps he deserves to be betrayed.'

'Not by me.' She held his gaze, wishing she could tell what was really going on in the dark head. 'I hope not by you either.'

He gave a short laugh. 'Why would I jeopardise an arrangement that suits me so well?'

He drew her to him, his kiss as passionate as it had ever been. Leonie returned it with mixed emotions. He obviously still wanted her, but for how much longer?

CHAPTER TEN

THERE was no mention of Caterina at breakfast. No mention of anything to do with the other branch of the family.

It was a very formal leavetaking by Leonie's standards, though she couldn't visualise her mother-in-law showing much emotion about it at the best of times. It was left to Vidal's father to express the hope that it wouldn't be too long before they came again. Vidal made the appropriate reply, though that was no guarantee of a joint return.

The sky was clouded over this morning, the heat sultry. Leonie let out pent breath on a faint sigh when Vidal took the same route as the day before, drawing a sardonic glance.

'You doubted my word?'

'I thought you might have had second thoughts,' she admitted. 'Do you really think she'll be ready to go?'

'That,' he said, 'is what we're about to find out.'

Now that it came to it, Leonie was uncertain as to what she wanted the outcome to be. If Caterina did enter the convent, then found the life didn't after all fulfil her dreams, then she herself would bear some responsibility for setting the whole thing into motion. The vows, once taken, were irrevocable, she believed.

There was no one in the courtyard when they arrived. No sign of life at all, in fact. Vidal turned the car fully around, coming to a stop at the foot of the steps leading to the closed main door.

'Aren't you going in?' Leonie asked after a moment.

Vidal shook his head. 'I told her to be out here at nine-thirty. She has three minutes.'

'You can't...' she began to protest, voice fading as she

viewed his unyielding expression. 'You know she isn't coming, don't you?' she said flatly. 'You never really believed she would!'

'No,' he agreed. 'She lacks the spirit to—' He broke off as the door above opened to emit the woman they were waiting for, his expression altering. 'Seems I was wrong, after all,' he murmured. 'A good thing I booked the extra seat.'

Carrying nothing but a small leather hold all, Caterina descended the steps to the waiting vehicle. Her face was serene, her whole bearing unfaltering.

'You will be in my prayers always,' she said, as Vidal got out to open a rear door for her. 'Both of you!'

'Isn't anyone coming out to see you off?' Leonie felt moved to ask.

'We said our goodbyes last night,' came the simple response. 'They have the address and telephone number of the convent if they wish to make contact.'

'You mean you've already been in touch with the convent?'

'But of course. They are waiting to welcome me. Are we to fly in an aeroplane?' she asked Vidal.

'A big one,' he assured her.

She gave a huge sigh. 'So many new experiences!'

The last of any note, Leonie thought. Yet that was only her viewpoint, of course. For Caterina, life was just beginning.

They landed in Lisbon at four. Caterina had sat entranced in her window seat throughout the flight. Vidal had suggested she spend the night at Sintra, but she'd asked to be taken straight to the convent.

It lay in the outskirts of the city, overlooking a small square. Dating back to the seventeenth century, the lovely old building was badly in need of repair, the golden granite walls scarred by time and pollution, the windows sagging.

Caterina saw none of it. To her it was home—the one place she wanted to be.

She refused to have them accompany her to the big iron-barred door. This was something, she said, that she had to do on her own. Leonie embraced her, and wished her well, aware that if it weren't for Vidal's obduracy she would never have achieved her heart's desire. After a slight hesitation he followed suit, murmuring something that brought a smile to his cousin's face.

'I will ask,' she said.

They watched from the car as she was greeted by a white-robed nun and drawn inside. Leonie swallowed hard on the lump in her throat as the door closed on her.

'It's a Carmelite order, isn't it?' she said. 'That means she'll never see the outside world again!'

'I doubt if she'll miss it,' Vidal answered. 'It's her choice. Her life. Be happy for her.'

'I am,' she said. 'At least, I'm trying. I just can't imagine incarcerating myself that way.'

'You'd never make a nun,' he rejoined. 'You're far too volatile.' He put the car into motion again. 'Time we were home ourselves.'

Leonie couldn't agree more. An age seemed to have passed since they'd left Sintra. She was eager to see the *quinta* again, to relax on the terraces with those superb views spread out below: to make love again in the bed where she'd lost her virginity that never-to-be-forgotten night.

Their lovemaking last night had been as good as ever. Physically, at any rate. She still sensed a difference in him, though she couldn't put a name to it. She slanted a glance at him now, stirred as always by the clean-cut masculinity of his face, by the powerful breadth of shoulder, the lean-fingered, well-shaped hands. She knew his body better than she knew her own—every sleekly muscled line of it.

'Keep looking at me that way and I'll finish up running into something,' he said softly. 'Save it, *querido*.'

She loved it when he called her darling in Portuguese. It seemed to mean so much more. It was going to work out, she assured herself. Everything was going to work out. If she said it often enough she might even get to believe it.

Ilena welcomed them home with a warmth extended to Leonie too. The latter was amazed to find she could actually recognise a word or two of the rapid-fire Portuguese.

'*É bom ser home,*' she said haltingly, dredging the depths. To Vidal, she added, 'How was that?'

'The accent needs work,' he returned lightly, 'but a reasonable attempt. Did you want to eat right away, or change first?'

'Change,' she said. 'I'm not all that hungry yet.'

Only for you, she could have added, except that she didn't need to, because she got him anyway, the moment they reached the bedroom.

'You're insatiable!' she murmured when the world slowed again. 'Utterly and completely insatiable!'

'We're two of a kind,' he rejoined softly, kissing the end of her small straight nose. 'This way, at least.'

'Not in other ways?' she asked, without opening her eyes.

'No.' It was a flat statement of fact. He rolled away from her to sit up and get to his feet. 'I'll go first.'

She couldn't have it plainer than that, Leonie thought painfully. Sex was one thing, love quite another.

She put the whole problem aside over the weekend, knowing he would be plunging back into business with a vengeance come Monday morning. As it was, he spent a fair amount of time on the telephone, plus several hours closeted in the room allocated as office space. He'd been away from it all for a week, she reasoned. It was only to be expected that he'd need to see exactly what had been going on in his absence.

Those times aside, she enjoyed every minute. On the Sunday, they drove to a beach along the Atlantic coast, descending mountains that made her doubt there could possibly be a beach below, until a gap between two enormous hills revealed the deep blue of the sea.

Vidal was a strong swimmer, but she kept pace with him, taunting him with a flash of rounded buttocks as she dived after a fish. He came after her like a devil fish himself, seizing her about the waist to bring her in close, wrapping his legs about hers so that she was held immobile, sealing her breath with his lips as they sank into the depths, her hair streaming behind her in a red-gold cloud.

They returned to the beach to lie in the sun until they dried, ate a leisurely lunch in the homely little restaurant, talked about all kind of things. What wasn't touched on was the future. Leonie schooled herself not to even think about it. What would be, would be.

After almost two weeks of near constant companionship, the following days were lonely. Vidal left before nine each morning, returning around six each evening. Things to catch up on, people to see, was all the comment he made.

Leonie spent a great deal of her time exploring the grounds and immediate vicinity. She enlisted Paulo's help in extending her scant vocabulary—first just one word at a time, then the odd sentence or two. He applauded enthusiastically the first time she managed to cobble a whole phrase together without help. Grammatically, it left a whole lot to be desired, but it was a step on the way, he said—or words to that effect.

'You're spending too much time with him,' Vidal declared shortly, after listening to her extolling the young man's virtues as a tutor. 'Ilena's concerned that he may misread your interest.'

'That's rubbish!' Leonie scoffed. 'He sees me as his employer's wife, nothing more.'

'He sees you the way any male past puberty sees you. At his age, the blood heats quickly.'

'Are you telling me to stay away from him altogether?' she asked after a moment.

The strong mouth widened briefly. 'I'm simply asking you to use a little discretion, so you can put the hackles down. I've arranged for a car to be delivered tomorrow, so you won't be confined any longer. You hold a licence, of course?'

'Yes.' Leonie was bound to admit that having transport of her own would be a boon, though the crunch was that she would *be* on her own. 'It's very thoughtful of you,' she added.

'Isn't it?' he agreed satirically.

The car arrived at ten. A sleek Mercedes convertible, it was a slightly smaller version of Vidal's own choice of vehicle. Left-hand drive, of course, but Leonie had driven on the right before this. She could hardly wait to try it out.

The call came through as she was changing from the dress she'd been wearing to trousers and shirt, as more comfortable driving gear. Stuart sounded concerned.

'I've been waiting for a call from you. I rang Palacio de Mecia, but they said you left last Friday.'

Today was Wednesday. He could be forgiven, Leonie acknowledged ruefully, for considering himself badly treated.

'Sorry, Dad,' she said on a penitent note. 'I should have called. I suppose you were told about Caterina?'

'What, about Caterina?'

'We delivered her to a convent in Lisbon. It turned out she'd always wanted to become a nun.'

'Lucky Vidal held out against the marriage, then. I gather the family weren't too keen on the idea?'

'Not exactly. I think Vidal will be in the doghouse for some time to come.'

'I shouldn't imagine that will bother him too much.' There was a short pause, a change of tone. 'How are things going?'

'Things are brilliant!,' she said brightly. 'Vidal just presented me with a brand-new Mercedes sports car. I'm taking it out for a test run.'

'Alone?'

'Vidal's at work. *Negócio*!' she added with a laugh. 'I know just about enough to get around now—with a little sign language thrown in. Don't worry, Dad. I'll be careful. You always said I was a good driver. How is it with you and...' she dredged her memory for the name '...Shirley?'

'So far, so good. Are you still intending to make that trip back?'

'Of course! And soon. I'll let you know in good time.'

'Keep in touch in the meantime,' he said. 'I need to know you're happy.'

'I am,' she assured him. 'Blissfully!'

She'd overdone it a little, she suspected, ringing off. Her father was no idiot; he was capable of reading between the lines.

Meanwhile, the car awaited. With most of the day ahead of her, why not drive down into Lisbon itself? A baptism of fire, maybe, but she'd be accustomed to the feel of it by the time she hit any heavy traffic.

The young salesman who had brought the car up had run her through the basic layout. He'd also offered to accompany her on a test drive, which she'd declined, by no means blind to the bold appraisal of her face and body. He'd said something that had drawn a salacious grin to the lips of the man who had driven up in his wake. She'd been glad to see the back of them both.

Like Vidal's own model, the car's exterior was white, in this case with dusky red leather upholstery instead of black. A beautiful machine, designed to draw eyes in its passing. Leonie got behind the wheel, studying the central control console. The salesman had left the roof up. She pressed a button, relishing the way the whole thing folded away smoothly and silently into its rear compartment.

The engine started with a purr, the twin exhausts giving vent to a low growl when she touched the accelerator. She put the gearstick into drive, and released the handbrake, edging forward with some caution to begin with, but acquiring confidence by the second as she headed down the long drive. Vidal had pointed out the tall white building that housed the Dos Santos headquarters as they drove through on Friday night. She might even pay him a visit.

Easy to think about, not so easy to accomplish, she found once she hit the city streets. The route through had seemed pretty straightforward with Vidal in the driving street; her attempt to reverse it proved anything but. Traffic was dense, allowing little time for consideration at junctions. When she finally found the business section it was more by luck than direction sense.

It was with real relief that she saw the Dos Santos logo as she turned into yet another busy thoroughfare. It was close on one o'clock already. With any luck at all she would find Vidal just about ready to break for lunch. The traffic up ahead had come to a stop for some reason. There was an underground car park to the building, Vidal had told her. She could see what appeared to be the entrance to it two cars' distance away.

The long white vehicle that suddenly emerged from it was only too familiar. Vidal edged his way into the traffic as it began to move again, forcing a gap to the tune of furious hoots from those held back. Dark-haired like himself, the woman at his side was talking to him, her whole attention fixed on him.

Leonie pulled herself together as the driver at her back tooted an irate horn of his own. Vidal hadn't glanced down this way, and was unlikely to spot her in the mirror with two other vehicles between them. She'd seen the woman only once before, but recognition had been instant. Sancha Baretto Caldeira was not someone easy to forget.

Vidal turned right at the next intersection. Leonie turned left, driving on automatic in more than the one sense. If he'd taken up with an old flame again, it was a pretty sure sign that his desire for her was on the wane, she thought hollowly. But then, why be surprised? It was what she had expected from the beginning. Their marriage had no foundation.

She found her way out of the city again somehow, not really caring where she went right now. Back at the *quinta*, she abandoned the car without a backward glance, heading indoors. Paulo was in the lower hall. His face lit up when he saw her.

'You have telephone call,' he announced, his English considerably improved over the last couple of days. 'Not now,' he added. 'Before.'

'Who?' she asked.

He shook his head. 'The lady leave no name. She said she will call once more.'

He probably meant she would call again, Leonie concluded. 'You're quite sure it was me she wanted to speak to?' she said.

'The *senhora*, yes.'

'How long ago? *Quanto tempo?*' she added as he looked a little baffled.

He held up both hands, fingers extended. Ten minutes, Leonie interpreted. The only person she could think of who might possibly be calling her was Helen Bouche. She murmured a word of thanks to the young Portuguese man, aware of his eyes following her as she headed for the stairs. Ilena was possibly right in thinking she may have been paying him too much attention, though it seemed of little importance right now.

The bedroom was no haven. Her face looked drained in the dressing mirror, eyes lustreless. She tried reasoning with herself. So Sancha had been in the car with Vidal, even possibly going for lunch with him. That didn't necessarily indicate a renewal of their affair.

If it had ever been terminated to start with.

It was closer to seven than six when Vidal put in an appearance. He made no attempt to explain his lateness, and Leonie certainly wasn't going to ask the reason.

'I gather you tried out the car,' he said over dinner. 'Where did you go?'

'Round and about,' she said vaguely. 'It's a wonderful machine!'

'You won't have had much opportunity to open it up yet.' His tone was easy. 'We'll take a ride together when I get back.'

Leonie gave him a sharpened look. 'Back from where?'

'I have to go to Munich again.'

'You said you'd be taking me with you on business trips,' she observed after a moment.

'Not this one. I need no distractions.'

None that she could provide, at any rate, came the thought. 'How long will you be away?' she asked, trying to maintain at least an air of composure.

He shrugged. 'Just the one night, if things go well.'

'How is it you do all the running around yourself? You surely have plenty of people qualified to handle any problems that crop up?'

'Several,' he agreed. 'Two of them will be accompanying me tomorrow.'

Male or female? it was on the tip of her tongue to ask. She bit the words back with an effort. 'When will you be leaving?'

'Early,' he said. 'The flight is at nine. I'll try not to waken you.'

'I'm surprised you don't have a company jet,' Leonie remarked. 'Or even two. Ready whenever you want one! You could even write them off against tax.'

'Already taken into consideration,' he returned dryly. 'What will you do with yourself while I'm gone?'

'Oh, potter around, read a book, play with my new toy. Maybe learn some more Portuguese,' she added with purpose.

Vidal's face darkened a fraction. 'From Paulo?'

'He's the only one here—apart from yourself, of course—with enough English to be of any real use to me. It's a reciprocal arrangement. I'm teaching him too.'

The glitter that sprang in the dark eyes was a warning in itself. 'Not any more. If you want to learn the language, I'll arrange for proper tuition.' He held up a hand as she made to speak. 'Don't defy me on this!'

'*Defy* you!' Leonie gave full rein to her derision. 'This is the twenty-first century, not the middle ages! You'll be asking me to wear a chastity belt while you're away next!'

'I'm asking you to use the common sense I know you have buried under all that feminist idiocy,' he said, still without raising his voice beyond its normal pitch. 'Paulo—'

'You weren't asking, you were instructing!' she broke in. 'Like father, like son! Except that I'm not your mother! I don't subscribe to the dominant male theme. I will do as *I* think fit!'

Vidal was silent for a moment, the regard centered on her lovely, turbulent face dispassionate now. 'Even if it means Paulo losing his job?' he asked at length.

Leonie drew a shaky breath, aware that her behaviour smacked more of the kindergarten than adulthood, yet unable to control the need to hit out. 'That's you all over, isn't it?' she fired at him. 'Do as I say, or someone will suffer! Fine! You win! The way you always win!' She flung her napkin on the table, knocking over her half-full wine glass and not caring a damn. 'I'm going to bed!'

'No, you're not.' Vidal spoke quietly still, but there was no doubting the purpose in his voice. 'You're going to sit there and finish your meal, and stop acting like some fishwife. *Sit*!' he commanded as she made to push back her chair.

She subsided reluctantly. Her limbs were probably trembling too much for her to stand steady, anyway. Not with fear: whatever his faults, he wasn't given to violence; she could vouch for that. The trembling was caused by emotional stress, built up over the course of the afternoon until it had to have an outlet. She loved a man who didn't know the meaning of the word—who probably never would know the meaning of the word. It was as simple as that.

'The wine can be attended to later,' he said, as she made an ineffectual attempt to mop the spill up. He reached across to right the upturned glass, then for the decanter to pour some more. 'Drink that, and calm down.'

She did so, grateful for the boost to her flagging spirits. She'd made a total fool of herself these last minutes. What was it he'd called her? A fishwife? The picture that conjured up was far from flattering.

'So?' he queried. 'Are you going to tell me what all that stemmed from?'

She could, quite easily, but she wasn't going to. Accusing him of seeing other women suggested jealousy, and jealousy was too much of a giveaway. Whether he really would denounce her father if she tried opting out of the marriage herself was open to question, but it still wasn't a risk she was prepared to take. She was committed for as long as he wanted it to last.

'I was just being stupid,' she claimed. 'And ungrateful. The car is wonderful!'

'I don't want your gratitude.' His tone had brusquened again. 'And you're far from stupid.'

'Not when I'm giving the feminist idiocy an airing.' She

raised a wry smile. 'Not that I ever liked being told what to do.'

He smiled himself briefly. 'That, I can imagine. I could perhaps have been a little more diplomatic.'

'No, you were right about Paulo. I should try to keep a certain distance between us. I'd hate to be responsible for him losing his job. He won't, will he?'

'Not unless he does something to merit it.'

Considering the way he'd looked at her this afternoon, it might be advisable to play it a little cooler from now on, Leonie concluded. She met Vidal's eyes across the table, her own veiled. 'Can we put these last few minutes behind us? I'm not proud of myself.'

The dark head inclined, more than a hint of irony in the slant of his lips. 'The feeling is mutual.'

If only! she thought achingly.

She came awake when he got up at six, watching through slitted eyelids as he stretched at the bedside before making for the bathroom. Lean and lithe, his body was superb in the morning light, the musculature well defined without being over-developed, like some.

She must have made a sound as he began to move away, because he glanced down at her, mouth widening as she gave up any pretence to still be asleep. He came back to kneel on the mattress-edge and press a kiss to her lips, a caress to her breast.

'Be good,' he murmured.

Leonie felt like being anything but right now. Sheer greed, considering last night's excesses. She stayed prone as Vidal moved away again, willing herself not to try delaying tactics. It would be a waste of time anyway. Business took precedence over sex.

She made out she really was asleep when he came back to the bedroom, rolling over only after the door had closed softly behind him. Tonight would be their first spent apart since their marriage. She would cope without the intimacies because she had to, but Vidal would be under no such restriction. Like a sailor, he would have female company available in every port of call. Munich would certainly be no exception.

If the morning dragged, the afternoon went even slower. Keeping Paulo at arm's length proved far from easy. Leonie resorted to telling him she was to have proper tutoring in the language in the end, which didn't go down at all well. But whatever he was feeling, he'd get over it, she assured herself, with not a little cynicism.

The follow-up to yesterday's phone call came in the shape of a personal visit. Superbly dressed in amber silk, a matching glitter in her eyes, Sancha made no attempt at small talk.

'I think you should know that I was with your husband only yesterday,' she declared.

Controlling her initial urge to have her forcefully evicted, Leonie regarded her with outer calm. 'I know.'

The wind taken completely from her sails, the other gazed at her in some obvious confusion. 'Vidal told you?' she asked uncertainly.

Leonie shook her head, hanging on to her poise by a thread. 'He didn't need to tell me. I was downtown myself yesterday, trying out the car he just gave me. I spotted the two of you.'

Dark brows drew together. 'You followed?'

Leonie lifted her own brows, as though surprised by the question. 'What on earth for? We're not joined at the hip!'

'The hip?' Sancha looked even more confused.

'It means Vidal and I have open views about marriage.'

'You have no objection to the involvement of others?'

'Affairs? Not at all. You know what they say about variety being the spice of life!'

From the expression on her face, Sancha was struggling with a concept totally new to her. Leonie was struggling too, lacking the stamina to keep the act going for very much longer.

'What did you imagine?' she asked derisively. 'That I'd leave Vidal to you?' She gave a laugh. 'Marriage wouldn't be on the agenda, I can assure you of that. You see, *I* understand him. The way someone like you couldn't even begin to match! If that's all you came to say, have a nice day,' she added, when no response was forthcoming. 'I don't think I need to have you shown out.'

The confidence she'd marched in with totally undermined, the Portuguese woman departed without another word. Leonie drew a shuddering breath, collapsing back onto the lounger where she'd been attempting to interest herself in a book. If she'd needed verification that yesterday's outing had been far from innocent, then she certainly had it now.

How she'd managed to come up with all that twaddle she'd just spouted, heaven only knew, though, if nothing else, it had given Sancha a poke in the eye. Thinking about the way Vidal had been with her last night, she felt thoroughly degraded. Nothing about their relationship was special to him. Nothing!

She went through the rest of the day like a zombie, the night wide awake for the most part. However bad the situation, she was still committed. Vidal wasn't going to let her go. Not until *he* decided it was time.

So far as she could see, she had two choices. She could either tell him about Sancha's visit, and suggest that he kept his other women under control in future, or she could turn a blind eye to the whole thing and continue to enjoy her own part in his life—if enjoy was the right word. He hadn't even bothered to phone her to say he'd arrived safely. That was how little she really meant to him.

She was still in a state of flux when he arrived home late the following afternoon. His greeting was reserved—almost detached. Yes, the meetings had gone well, he said when she asked, the problems were ironed out. This was a different man from the one who had left here the previous morning, Leonie acknowledged numbly. Something had happened, it was obvious.

He was distant all through dinner, speaking only when spoken to, and then in monosyllables. He waited until they both had a brandy to hand before dropping the bombshell.

'I've had time to give some serious consideration to our relationship,' he said. 'I think we should terminate the arrangement before it becomes too much of a habit. Your father won't suffer from it. You have my word on that. Neither will you, of course.'

'Why now?' Fighting to stay on top of emotions threatening to overwhelm her, Leonie was amazed by the steadiness of her own voice. 'So suddenly?'

The broad shoulders lifted, face revealing nothing. 'As I said, I've had time to think things through. I've treated you abominably. There are no excuses for that. All I can do is try to make some amends. The settlement will be generous.'

'I don't want your money.' Her throat was tight as a drum, her whole body one big ache. She put everything she knew into maintaining her grip, contempt in her eyes. 'It's enough to be regaining my freedom. I take it my father can keep his job too?'

'I already told you he won't suffer,' he said on a hardened note. 'And you'll take the settlement whether you like it or not.'

Her shrug was deliberated. 'I suppose I'm entitled to some compensation. Not that it's been all bad. I've learnt a whole lot from you. Should stand me in good stead.'

Something gleamed momentarily deep down in the dark eyes, then was gone, leaving them impenetrable as ever. 'You're taking this very well.'

'What did you expect?' she asked. 'That I was going to

cling to you, beg you to keep me with you? I'd need to be utterly besotted with you to go to those lengths.'

'And you're not, of course.'

'Never was, never could be. The only feelings you rouse in me are the physical kind. You're very good at that, I grant you. But then, you would be, wouldn't you? With all the practice you've had. One thing's for certain,' she went on before he make any response. 'Your parents are going to be delighted! They can start looking round for a more worthy bride.'

Vidal gave a short laugh. 'They may look.'

'But one marriage was enough? That's something we can agree on, at least.'

She drained her glass, swept back for a moment to the night she'd gone to the London apartment to plead for her father's future. A bare few weeks, yet it seemed a lifetime ago.

'I'll get some things together,' she said thickly. 'I can book into a hotel until I get a flight home. If you'll call me a taxi.'

Vidal came to his feet with her, a muscle jerking along his jaw line. 'That isn't necessary. We'll sort out a flight in the morning.'

'What did you have in mind?' she asked. 'A last night together?'

The muscle jerked again, but his voice remained controlled. 'The last thing I'd expect. I'll use another room.'

'It's your house. I'll use another room!'

He inclined his head. 'Take your choice.'

Leonie left him standing there. She had to go to the bedroom they had shared to fetch at least the basics for the night. The room she chose was as far from it as it was possible to get. Only when she was in there with the door closed did she allow the iron control to crumble, sinking to a seat on the bed with a sense of her whole life falling apart.

It was all so sudden, so drastic. It was as if the man she

had known these past weeks had been a figment of her imagination. Yet why be surprised? She had never put any trust in the long-term nature of their marriage. She was going home. That was what really mattered. Home!

The flight was late getting in. It was gone five by the time she cleared the airport. She stood another twenty minutes in line for a taxi, turning down an offer from the man in front of her to share one. The last thing she needed at present was male company. The last thing she was going to need for some time to come—her father the exception.

He'd no idea she was on her way home as yet. At least she could rely on a wholehearted welcome from him, with no demand for explanations until she felt ready to provide them. He already suspected the truth, anyway. The problem was going to be stopping him from blaming himself too much. Vidal had been right about that much: saving her father hadn't been her only driving force.

He'd insisted on driving her to the airport after securing a seat for her. He'd been withdrawn, aloof. He would be in contact, he'd said formally on parting. If he'd made any attempt to embrace her he would have received short shrift, but he hadn't. He'd walked away without a backward glance. A phase of his life over and done with.

Leonie had packed a single bag for the journey, taking only the clothing she'd bought and paid for herself. He could do as he liked with the designer gear, she'd told him. She had no use for it.

First priority would be finding a job, because she had no intention of relying on Vidal's magnamity. He could make whatever arrangements eased his conscience—if he had any—but he couldn't force her to accept them.

It was pelting with rain in Northwood. She was relieved to see the house lit up when she got there. With a suitcase to carry, and no umbrella to shelter under, she was drenched in the short journey from taxi to front door. There was a door key in her handbag, but fishing for it was too much trouble. She rang the bell instead, gearing herself up for the coming moments.

The woman who opened the door was a complete stranger. The two of them gazed at each other, mutually disconcerted. The former was the first to recover.

'It's Leonie, isn't it?' she said, adding with a shake of her head, 'Silly question! I was only looking at your photograph a few minutes ago!'

She stood back to allow Leonie entry, obviously at something of a loss. 'Your father's in the study. I'm Shirley, by the way. I don't know if he's mentioned me?'

Leonie made a valiant effort to sound natural. 'Yes, of course he has. You're exactly as he described you. I was expecting Dad to open the door, that's all. He doesn't know I'm coming.' She laughed, unsurprised by the brittle sound. 'I've a passion for stating the obvious!'

The older woman regarded her shrewdly. 'Bad journey, was it? You look exhausted. Why don't I go and put the kettle on, while you let your father know you're here? I'll bring coffee in for you both.'

Leonie found a smile. 'That would be so welcome.'

She slipped off the damp jacket of her suit, pulling a face as she caught a glimpse of herself in the hall mirror. 'I didn't realise I looked quite such a mess!'

'Just a bit damp, that's all,' Shirley assured her. 'Your hair is springing back already. Wonderful colour!' she added. 'I'd love to paint you some time.'

'You paint portraits?' Leonie asked in some surprise.

'Not professionally. Just a hobby. I'll put your jacket to dry, shall I? You go and find your father. He's going to be so glad to see you.'

And she him, Leonie thought. She went along to the study door as Shirley headed for the kitchen, pausing for a moment to gather herself before opening it. Stuart was seated at his desk, studying an opened file.

'Hello, Dad,' she said quietly. 'I'm home again.'

His head came up with a jerk, a whole range of expressions chasing across his face as he gazed at her.

'He did it.' he exclaimed in tones of disbelief. 'He actually did it!'

Leonie studied him uncertainly. 'What are you talking about?'

'Vidal, of course.' He got to his feet, coming round the desk to hug her close. 'I wasn't sure he had it in him!'

She hugged him back, still more than a little bewildered. 'To do what?'

'Let you go. I told him I was ready to turn myself in, if necessary, which would mean he no longer had any hold on you, anyway.' His tone was wry. 'I know why you married him. I've always known. I just didn't have the guts to face up to it at the time.'

Leonie pulled away to look at him in confusion. 'When did you speak to him?'

'I reached him in Munich a couple of nights ago.'

Her mind was racing now as she tried to fit the pieces together. 'He told me *he'd* decided it was time to call it a day.'

'Saving face. He isn't used to being on the losing side. I believe he really cares for you. What you could call poetic justice.'

Leonie could feel warmth beginning to flow through her veins. There was no absolute certainty that her father was right in his assessment, but every instinct was telling her so. It explained so much. If Vidal had been saving face, then so had she. Two of them too proud to give way.

'I need to make a phone call,' she said. 'I need to book a flight.'

Stuart searched her face in sudden appalled enlightenment. 'You really do love him, don't you?'

'Totally,' she confirmed. 'I know he's no holy angel, but I can't help it. If you turn out to be wrong about his feelings for me, I'll accept it. But he'll have to tell me straight.'

She was on the phone when Shirley brought the promised coffee in. The latter looked questioningly at Stuart, who lifted his shoulders resignedly.

'Eight-thirty tomorrow morning,' Leonie announced, replacing the receiver. 'I'll order a taxi.'

Her father shook his head. 'If it's what you really want, I'll take you myself.' He looked at Shirley, receiving a nod. 'In fact, we'll both take you.'

Meaning Shirley was spending the night, Leonie assumed. 'I'd like that,' she said. 'Very much.'

It was a pleasant enough evening—or would have been if she hadn't been consumed with impatience for it to be over. She would be revealing her own deeper emotions by going back, but if there was any chance at all of Vidal feeling the same way about her, she was prepared to make the gesture. There were other matters to be sorted too, of course—his association with Sancha being one of them—but they could wait. All she cared about at present was Vidal himself.

They were all of them up at five-thirty, arriving at the airport in good time for the flight. Leonie gave her father a hug at passport control, doing the same, impulsively, to Shirley.

'Don't you two go cocking this up,' Leonie said warmly. 'You're perfect together!'

'We'll do our best,' Shirley promised. 'I hope everything works out for you too.'

It was going to, Leonie assured herself. Whatever it took!

The flight was uneventful, the weather in Lisbon warm and sunny. She took a taxi from the airport, remembering the first time she'd been driven along this route. Vidal had been a totally unknown quantity then; she wasn't sure she knew him all that much better now. If she was proved wrong about the way he felt she stood to make a fool of herself, but that was a risk she had to take.

It wasn't until the taxi turned up the drive that she allowed herself to consider what she would do if Vidal wasn't home. The staff would obviously have been informed by now that she wasn't coming back. Ilena might even take it on herself to ban her from the house.

She was relieved to see his car on the forecourt. The one he'd given her was garaged, she assumed. Unless he'd already had it taken away. She'd asked him once why he didn't have a whole variety of luxury cars, as did most men in his walk of life. He had no interest in collecting status symbols for the sake of it, he'd said.

There was no one around to see her as she alighted from the taxi. She paid the driver the exorbitant sum asked without quibbling, more important matters on her mind than being taken for a ride. A Sunday morning somnolence lay over the place, the only sound to be heard the buzzing of bees. Even the cicadas were quiet.

Ilena opened the door to her, her homely face revealing confusion. Leonie didn't blame her. The poor woman must be wondering what was going on.

'I'm back,' she announced smilingly. 'Are you going to let me in? *Entrada*?' she added when the woman made no move.

That got a result. Ilena took the bag Leonie dropped to the floor, her face still reflecting uncertainty. *'O mestre está no terrace,'* she said.

The master was on the terrace, Leonie translated. Asking which one would only be prolonging the agony. She'd find him by a process of elimination.

She came on him laid out full length on a lounger, eyes closed against the sun filtering down through the overhanging

Jacaranda tree. The white shorts he was wearing revealed firmly muscled thighs, the downy coating of hair bleached golden. Leonie touched her tongue to lips gone dry, searching for the right words.

As if sensing some presence, he opened his eyes, the mask for once stripped from them as he gazed at her. When he moved it was with lightening speed, coming to his feet to pull her to him, arms enfolding her, lips finding hers in a kiss that left her in no doubt at all of his feelings.

'You came back!' he said gruffly.

'And I thought I was the one given to stating the obvious,' Leonie rejoined, trying to keep her voice steady. 'I had to come back. I left without telling you I loved you. Dad said—'

'Never mind your father!' Vidal searched her face, eyes piercing her soul. 'Say it again!'

'Say what?' she asked innocently, laughing as he made a threatening gesture. 'I love you,' she repeated. 'You put me through hell, sending me away like that.'

'I put myself through worse.' He smoothed the hair back from her face, the look in his eyes as they roved her vivacious features everything she had hoped for so long to see there. 'I used your father's position to force you into marriage because I knew it was the only way I was ever going to get you. I had two whole years of hell trying to find some means of bringing us together. I knew you wanted me, but it was never going to be enough. I wanted all of you, every last part. I wanted to hear you say what you just said to me—to know you meant it. You *do* mean it?'

'Vidal Parella Dos Santos with doubts?' she teased. 'Now, that's a first!'

She abandoned the whimsy, putting her lips to his in surging, overwhelming emotion, pressing herself closer to the hard masculine lines of his body, loving the power in the arms enfolding her.

'I want you,' she said softly. 'Now!'

They reached the bedroom without seeing anyone. The slatted blinds were drawn, casting shadows across the bed. Clothing shed, they merged together in total harmony, every touch, every caress a new experience, the culmination utter bliss.

'Why did you make me think you wanted me to go?' Leonie murmured when the first desperate need was assuaged.

'Pride,' Vidal admitted. 'I couldn't bring myself to tell you I loved you when I believed all you felt for me was desire. The whole time since we came together again I've thought only of myself—of *my* needs.' He raised himself on his elbows to look at her, tenderness in his eyes. 'You made me realise just how self-centered I was when you put so much into defending Caterina's rights. I'd robbed you of the right to make your own choices. Even then, I couldn't bring myself to let you go.'

'Until Dad put his oar in,' she said huskily. 'Did you believe he'd really do what he was threatening to do?'

'Yes, I did. He'd reached a point where his own interests became secondary to yours. He was ashamed, he said, of allowing you to go through with the marriage knowing you were doing it purely for his sake. He shamed me too.'

Leonie brought up a hand to smooth the firm lines of his mouth with a fingertip, her eyes luminous. 'So you came back and tossed me out on my ear!'

The smile was rueful. 'I was convinced that you could never, under any circumstances, love me after what I had done to you. Forcing you into marrying me, into sharing a bed with me, into sacrificing the virginity you'd saved for the man of your choice.'

'Saved, because I'd found no other man I wanted that way,' she whispered. 'Because all I could ever think about was how *you* made me feel when you kissed me, when you caressed me. How just looking at you made my pulses start racing, my mouth go dry, my stomach muscles tense up. I regretted the way I rejected you every day of those two years!'

'Then why did you not come to me?'

'I was convinced you must despise me for taking a media story at face value.'

'I could never despise you,' he said softly. 'You barely knew me. How could you be expected to know what was the truth? It would be an obvious untruth to claim there have been no other women in my life, but I've never loved another woman. Not this way.'

'Including Sancha?' She hadn't meant to say it; the words just came.

The expression that crossed his face was more one of surprise than guilt. 'Sancha?' he queried. 'What made you think of her?'

'I drove down into town on Wednesday to try out the car, and possibly to have lunch with you,' she said. 'I saw the two of you leave together.'

Vidal studied her for a moment, as if in some perplexity. 'Did you follow us?'

She shook her head. 'No. I didn't want to know where you might be going.'

'I dropped her off in the main shopping section,' he said. 'Then continued on to an appointment I was already late for. She came to the office to ask my advice on a business proposition she was considering.'

'And you believed that?'

'Not wholly. But I made it clear that any interest I'd shown in her in the past was over and done with.'

Prompting Sancha's visit next day to try driving a wedge between the two of them, Leonie surmised. Hell hath no fury, and all that. There was no point, she decided, in telling him about it. It had played little part in the end.

'You don't believe me?' Vidal asked, viewing her expression.

'Of course I believe you!' she assured him. 'I was just feeling a bit sorry for her, that's all. She lost you.'

'She never had me. Not in any way that counted. No one did.' He put his lips to her temple, feathering them down the line of her cheek to reach her mouth, the kiss so tender, so loving, it brought tears to her eyes. 'I have no need of any other woman now I have you,' he murmured against her lips. 'You fill my life, my heart, my every waking moment!'

She could take the latter claim with a pinch of salt, came the fleeting humorous thought. There would be many moments in his business affairs when he forgot he even had a wife!

It was possible that she'd have distractions of her own in the not too distant future, anyway. She'd realised only last night that she was over a week late. Lord knew how it could have happened, when they'd both been using protection, but she had a very strong feeling that it had.

Of course, there had been the night Vidal had insisted she made the overtures, she recalled. He hadn't used anything then.

'What are you thinking about now?' he asked, searching her face again.

'About how much I love you,' she said, tucking the rest away for another time. 'About how much I want you!'

'Again?' The dark eyes sparkled with laughter. 'And you call *me* insatiable!'

She wrinkled her nose at him. 'If you can't manage it, of course...'

The sparkle turned to a gleam. 'You'll pay for that slur, woman!'

Worth every penny, she thought as the waves started building once more.

EPILOGUE

GURGLING with delight at his own cleverness, the birthday boy wavered across the grass, watched over carefully by his sister, who took her two years seniority very seriously.

'Vitoria is a very caring child,' declared her grandmother approvingly.

She could also be a very wayward one at times, Leonie reflected with humour. Like mother, like daughter, Vidal had been moved to remark ironically, on more than one occasion. Both requiring a firm hand.

She cast a glance along the terrace to where the men were seated together, discussing who knew what? Nothing too serious, if the occasional burst of masculine laughter was anything to go by. Vidal looked the same now as he did four years ago, the superb bone structure of his face impervious to the passing of time. There was no hint of grey in the thickness of his hair, no slackening of muscle anywhere about his body. Certainly no diminution in his sex drive—as he'd proved both last night *and* this morning.

'What are you smiling about?' asked her mother-in-law curiously.

'Just thinking how wonderfully well everything has turned out,' Leonie answered in fluent Portuguese. 'Who would have thought it four years ago?' she couldn't resist adding.

The older woman gave a somewhat reluctant little smile of her own. 'I was wrong,' she admitted with unaccustomed magnanimity. 'You have proved yourself quite satisfactory.'

Coming from her, that was praise of the highest order! thought Leonie with an inner grin. The children had helped break the ice, of course. Named after her grandmother,

Vitoria had scored an instant hit. Providing Vidal with a son in addition had brought the final barriers tumbling down. With Marco as back-up, the future of the Dos Santos empire was secured for a long time to come.

Dependant, of course, on what Marco himself decided he wanted to do with his life, Leonie had added as a mental rider when the point had first been made.

Vidal himself had kicked against the commitments imposed on him, although he'd softened his attitude to the extent of taking an active, if intermittent part in the running of the estate. They visited Palacio de Mecia on a fairly regular basis these days, even in the harshest of winters.

Relations with the rest of the family had mellowed over the years. Especially since Roque had found himself a wife and moved to the other side of the country. Caterina was blissfully happy in her cloistered life, and the convent itself restored to its full glory by a huge donation from Vidal.

Leonie's father had married Shirley within two months of their meeting, and now shared the Northwood house with her. He still worked for Vidal, but was on the board as a director now, with shares in the company. The two of them could hardly be said to be close, but they got along well enough.

He and Shirley would have been here today too, but her son was recovering from a bout of glandular fever and needed her there. Leonie and Vidal planned to travel on to London from here for a couple of days to see them.

Marco had collapsed on his bottom, and was vigorously objecting to Vitoria's attempts to help him back to his feet, his chuckles turning to howls of rage when she stood back with hands on hips, telling him off.

Leonie got up and went to join them, sitting down on the grass to pull Marco into her lap, her arm about Vitoria's waist.

'What will Grandad think of all that noise?' she asked in

Portuguese, switching to English to add laughingly, 'My ears are ringing!'

'Ears don't ring,' declared her daughter in lofty tones in the same language. 'They only wear rings.'

'Wings!' said Marco, pointing at the gold hoops Leonie was wearing, sunny nature returned. 'Pretty!'

Leonie gathered him to her, drawing Vitoria down to plant a kiss on the bright head. Her daughter had inherited her colouring and looks, while Marco was emerging into the image of his father. As it should be, Vidal always said.

She looked up now to find him watching the three of them, the smile on his face expressing the same contentment she felt. She smiled back. It had all worked out, just as she'd always known it would.

Deep down, at any rate.

THE BEJEWELLED
BRIDE

BY
LEE WILKINSON

Lee Wilkinson lives with her husband in a three-hundred-year-old stone cottage in a Derbyshire village, which most winters gets cut off by snow. They both enjoy travelling and recently, with their daughter and son-in-law, spent a year going round the world 'on a shoestring', while their son looked after Kelly, their much loved German shepherd dog. Her hobbies are reading and gardening and holding impromptu barbecues for her long-suffering family and friends.

CHAPTER ONE

BETHANY glanced around her. The scenery on the high mountain pass was awesomely bleak and beautiful in the pearly grey light of an early February afternoon. For the first few miles, while the pass had run fairly straight and level between rock-strewn fells, she had seen a black Range Rover in the rear-view mirror. But over the last half mile or so it must have turned off into a side valley, because now she had the road to herself.

When she had set off to Bosthwaite earlier in the day to visit Mrs Deramack and look at some antiques, she had taken the main road but had taken this lonely route back especially to see more of the wild and rugged grandeur she remembered well from her one previous visit to the Lake District.

As she drove however, she thought back to that wonderful visit and remembered a lean, good-looking face with brilliant eyes and a mouth with the kind of male beauty that tied her insides in knots.

A face that had stayed fresh in her mind for the past six years.

Quiet and shy, she had been just seventeen at the time and on a family holiday with her parents. Returning from the west coast of Scotland, they had decided to spend one night in Cumbria on their way back to London.

They had been staying in Dundale End, and after dinner that

evening, encouraged by their landlady, 'You must go, my dears, everyone will be there…' they had gone to a concert at the small village hall. In front of a makeshift stage, rows of chairs had been arranged in a semi-circle, and it had been there, sitting on an uncomfortable plastic chair in the centre of the second row, that she had fallen in love for the first time. Love at first sight. The hot, crazy kind of love that had turned her chest into a bell and her heart into a clapper.

She had watched him walk in, tall and broad across the shoulders, casually dressed, he had an air of quiet confidence. Somewhere in his early twenties, he was a man not a boy, with a strong-boned face, thick corn-coloured hair and light, brilliant eyes.

With him had been an elderly couple and a girl about his own age, who addressed him as Joel.

Joel… Bethany had hugged the name to her as though it was some precious gift.

He exchanged greetings with many of the people there, which suggested he was a local. Bethany had wished fervently that she and her parents were staying here instead of going back to London the next day.

Try as she would, her eyes had been drawn to him more often than to the stage. On one occasion she had found him staring back at her with a quiet intensity that made heat spread through her entire body. Feeling her cheeks flame, she had looked hastily away, her curtain of long dark hair swinging forward, hiding her embarrassment.

As the show came to an end, finishing with prolonged and hearty applause, she had kept her attention fixed firmly on the stage.

Perhaps when everyone was on their way out they might meet, might exchange a word. Lovely evening… Are you on holiday…? But when she'd glanced back, the little group had gone. She'd felt bitterly disappointed.

Although she had told herself it was ridiculous to long for something that only *might* have happened, she had thought and dreamt about him for months.

The memory of that past innocent adoration warmed her and for a few precious seconds took her mind off this which was turning out to be a disaster.

In more ways than one.

That morning, after a poor night's sleep and an uncomfortable half hour spent sitting opposite her silent, still-angry boss, Tony, while they ate breakfast at the Dundale Inn, she had taken the main road to the valley of Bosthwaite to see Mrs Deramack.

It was, she had discovered, a dead-end valley, and the tiny, isolated hamlet of Bosthwaite was made up of a few widely scattered houses and a farm.

Finding the road—which was little more than a track—ran through the farmyard, she had stopped to ask directions.

After warning her, 'Old Mrs Deramack's a bit… you know…' Apparently at a loss for words, the farmer had tapped his forehead with a gnarled finger, before pointing out Bosthwaite House.

Bethany soon realized what he'd meant when the old lady informed her that though Joseph, her husband, had passed away some five years ago, he was still with her and would need to agree on the price of anything she parted with.

The antiques she wanted to sell were stored in the freezing cold, badly lit attic, and while she hovered at the bottom of the attic stairs talking to her husband as though he was still alive and with them, Bethany had gone through what seemed endless boxes and cartons.

When, chilled to the bone and cramped from so much squatting, her throat dry, clogged with the dust of ages, she had finished the last box, she pushed back a loose strand of dark hair and admitted defeat.

In an attempt to soften the blow, she had told the old lady that though there was nothing amongst her treasures that Feldon Antiques would be prepared to buy, there were other local dealers who might be interested. She had written down the names of two of them before getting into her car and driving away.

When she reached an old white-walled pub called The Drunken Pig, she had stopped to wash her face and hands and re-coil her long dark hair before ordering a refreshing pot of tea and an omelette.

While she ate she had studied her map and decided to take the mountain pass back to Dundale, rather than the main road.

From the start the landscape had been dramatic, but now it had become even more spectacular. On the left was a towering rock face and on the right, an abyss, as the ground dropped away precipitously.

A lot sooner than she had expected, the clear air had become hazy and twilight had started to creep in, while grey swirling mist began to hide the tops of the highest peaks.

She switched on the car's headlights and on a road way down in the valley below saw an answering gleam. Just that distant light, a reminder that she wasn't totally alone, was reassuring.

Even so, she found herself wondering a shade uneasily if she had been wise to take this deserted switchback route—though the Lakeland scenery was truly magnificent, and she loved it.

A love of the country that Tony Feldon, her boss, and owner of Feldon Antiques since the death of his father the previous year, had signally failed to share.

He had made no secret of the fact that he was a dedicated city man and couldn't wait to get back to London and 'civilization'.

When they had drawn up outside the Dundale Inn the previous night, he had glanced around at the dark fells and shuddered. 'It looks like the back of beyond! When I booked I should have made sure it was in town…'

She wondered why he'd booked it himself rather than leaving it to Alison, his general dogsbody.

'If we're forced to stay in this God-forsaken spot for two nights, it had better be worth it,' he muttered half under his breath.

'I'm sure it will be.' Hoping to keep him in a reasonably good mood, she added, 'There are some very fine lots listed in Greendales' preview catalogue.'

Taking their overnight bags from the car boot, he handed Bethany hers and agreed, 'That's true.'

As she followed him into the hotel and across the deserted lobby to the empty reception desk, he muttered, 'God, what a dump! It looks as if we're the only people staying here.'

'Well it *is* the middle of the week and out of season,' she pointed out.

He dropped his case on the carpet and brought his hand down hard on the brass bell that squatted on the desk like a metal toad. 'It might be the middle of the week and out of season,' he said irritably, 'but the blasted place is supposed to be *open*.'

Ignoring his bad temper and the scowl that marred his darkly handsome features, Bethany went on, 'And from what Mrs Deramack said when I spoke to her on the phone, it sounds as if she has some very good pieces of silver and porcelain.'

'Well, if she has, let's hope the old biddy doesn't realize *how* good, or she'll no doubt want the earth for them.'

'Do you intend to go and see her yourself?'

'No. I had a quick glance at the map. It's quite a way to Bosthwaite Valley, and I'll have more than enough on. I'll get a taxi to Greendales and you can take the car.

'If you think any of the items Mrs Deramack wants to sell are in our line, don't say too much and don't put a price on them. I'll do the negotiating myself, even if it means staying up here an extra day…'

Bethany frowned. His failure to give her a free hand rankled. She had worked for James Feldon, Tony's father, since she had left school at eighteen, and after his sudden and fatal heart attack, she had missed him a great deal.

She had liked and trusted the old man as much as she disliked and distrusted his son. His conviction that women were fair game made her hackles rise, as did his frequent suggestions— since Devlin had been wiped from the picture—that if she loosened up they could 'have a little fun together'.

So far she had managed to keep him at arm's length without too much bad blood, but if he didn't soon get the message and back off she would have to leave.

It was a depressing thought.

She still liked her job and when she wasn't actually travelling the shop was within easy walking distance of the flat in Belgravia that she shared with a friend.

Added to that, while she was working she was not only saving hard but buying up small items with a view to one day starting her own business.

Glancing round the still deserted lobby, Tony banged the bell a second time with unnecessary violence. 'Where the devil is everyone?'

A moment later an elderly woman appeared. 'I'm sorry if I've kept you waiting, but the desk clerk has gone home ill and there's no one to take his place… You have booked?'

'Yes, for two nights. The name's Feldon.'

Opening the register at what appeared to be an almost empty page, she confirmed, 'Ah, yes, here we are… Mr and Mrs Feldon. A double room on the ground floor. Number five.'

As she handed over the key, Bethany came to life. 'There's been some mistake,' she announced distinctly. 'I'm *not* Mrs Feldon, and I need a separate room.'

Catching a glimpse of Tony's furious face, she knew there had been no mistake. That was why he had made the booking himself, and that was what he had meant when he'd said, 'It had better be worth it'.

'Oh, I'm sorry,' the woman apologized. 'Well there's a single just down the corridor. Number nine, if that'll do.'

'That will do fine, thanks,' Bethany assured her crisply and, taking the key, marched in the direction the woman had indicated.

'Damn it all, Bethany,' Tony complained, following her to her door. 'Why did you have to insist on another room?'

She turned to face him, her clear grey eyes sparkling with anger. 'Perhaps it hasn't occurred to you that I don't *want* to go to bed with you?'

He was quite taken back. 'Why not? Plenty of other women do.'

Bethany raised her chin and replied, 'Then you should have brought one of them.'

'I wish I had, rather than bringing a prim and proper little Miss like you,' he snarled angrily.

As she turned away he said more moderately, 'Look, I'm sorry. Change your mind. God knows we could use some fun in a hole like this.'

Bethany was furious. 'For the last time, I don't sleep around, and if you don't stop pestering me I'll be forced to hand in my notice.'

She was invaluable to him and, reluctant to lose her, he muttered, 'There's no need to go to those lengths.' Then, petulantly, 'I don't know why you can't loosen up a bit. You're too old to act like some shrinking virgin. And it's not as if you're still engaged to that Devlin bloke…'

It had been some six weeks before their wedding when, returning early from a business trip to Paris, Bethany had dropped in to Devlin's flat and discovered him in bed with another woman.

Unable to believe his pleas that it had been a spur of the moment thing and would never happen again, she had given him back his ring and walked out.

'Just because you're still angry and bitter at the way he treated you,' Tony went on, 'it doesn't mean you have to take it out on all men.'

When she just looked at him coldly, he taunted, 'If you hadn't been so frigid he wouldn't have needed another woman…' When his cruel jokes elicited no response from her he swung on his heel, and a moment later she heard the slam of his bedroom door.

As she remembered Tony Feldon's harsh comments her mind wandered back to her broken engagement to Devlin that he had callously mentioned. She *had* been both angry and bitter at first. But she had soon discovered, or rather *realized,* that while her pride had been trampled on, her heart was virtually intact. And in retrospect she could see that she had only imagined herself in love with Devlin. In fact she'd only really been drawn to him in the first place because he reminded her a little of the blond stranger she had adored at seventeen…

A sudden savage wrench at the steering wheel and a thumping judder brought her back to the present with a shock.

Her heart in her mouth, she dragged the wheel over and steered to the side of the road away from the steep drop into the valley below.

On shaking legs she climbed out to find—as she had feared— that her nearside front tyre had burst.

Well, she would have to do something about it, and fast. It

was rapidly getting dark and the swirls of mist had changed to thick swathes that were now shrouding the peaks and threatening to roll down and engulf the pass.

Shivering in her fine wool suit, she pulled on her short jacket before going round to open the boot. Lifting the inner cover, she took out a jack, the spare wheel, the wheel brace and a foot-pump.

Though so far she had never been forced to change a wheel, when she had bought her first old banger, her father had insisted on her learning how to.

Now she was grateful. Only it didn't seem to be as easy as she remembered.

She was still struggling to put the jack in place when, miraculously, headlights appeared over the crest of the previous rise. A moment later a big black Range Rover, like the one that had followed her earlier, drew to a halt a few yards away.

As she straightened, a tall well-built man with fair hair got out.

Though she was dazzled by the lights, and with his back to them his face was in shadow, there seemed to be something oddly familiar about him.

'Need some help?' he asked.

He had an attractive voice, she noted, low-pitched and cultured with no trace of a local accent.

'Please,' she said gratefully.

The air was damp and raw and, clenching her teeth to prevent them chattering, she watched his broad back while he proceeded to change the wheel with a deft efficiency she could only admire.

Then, having tested the tyre pressure he put some air in with the foot-pump, observing, 'That ought to do it,' before stowing everything back in the boot and closing it.

'Thank you very much. I can't tell you how grateful I am.'

He wiped his hands on a handkerchief he'd taken from the pocket of his leather car-coat and, turning towards his own vehicle, said easily, 'I'm glad to have been of help.'

As the headlights shone full on him, for the first time she saw his face clearly. It was the face that had haunted her for the past six years.

No, it couldn't be! It was far too much of a coincidence. But even while she told herself it couldn't be *him,* she knew it was. And once again he was going to walk out of her life.

'I don't know what I would have done if you hadn't come along,' she said desperately.

'I'm quite sure you would have managed…' Then, briskly, 'I suggest we get going while we can still see the road.'

In the short time it had taken him to change the wheel the mist had begun to close in with ominous speed, rolling down the mountainside and starting to obscure the drop into the valley below.

A combination of cold, desolation and fear made Bethany shiver.

As though sensing that fear and desolation, he paused and asked, 'Do you know the pass at all?'

'No,' she answered in a small voice.

'In that case I'm going to suggest we team up.' He waited for her nod of assent before adding, 'My name's Joel McAlister.'

Her heart leapt in her chest, making her sound breathless, as she said, 'Mine's Bethany Seaton.'

'Where are you heading for, Miss Seaton?' His rich, smooth voice melted her heart.

Somewhat nervously, she replied. 'I'm staying at the Dundale Inn.'

'I'm heading for the Dundale Valley myself, though judging by how fast the mist's closing in, it's my bet we're not going to get that far.'

'Oh…'

Perhaps he mistook her little exclamation of excitement for panic, because he added quickly, 'But don't worry. If we can make it to the foot of Dunscar, which is about a mile away, there's a small hotel there. It's closed for the winter, but I understand the caretaker lives on the premises.' He went on automatically, 'Now, let's get moving. As it's too narrow here for me to get past, we'll have to take your car.'

Turning off his own vehicle's lights, he added, 'I'd better drive, as I know the road.'

When she made no demur, he opened the passenger door for her, then slid behind the wheel.

Bethany was barely able to see anything except the mist reflecting back the dipped headlights, yet he drove with a careful confidence that was reassuring. Though, truth to tell, rather than worrying about their safety, her thoughts centred on the fact that fate had brought him back into her life.

She was being given a second chance.

The chance.

At seventeen, she would have been too young.

But now, at twenty-three to his twenty-seven—twenty-eight? the timing was perfect.

Unless he was already married?

No! She pushed the awful thought away.

She and this stranger, who was no stranger, were *meant* to be together. She had never been more sure of anything in her whole life.

While they made their way down to Dunscar, her heart beating fast, she studied his profile in the glow from the dashboard.

His nose was straight, his jaw strong, the curve of brow and sweep of long lashes, several shades darker than his hair. At the corner of his mouth was a small dent, too masculine to be called a dimple, but surely it would become one when he smiled…

'Think I'm trustworthy?' Both his words and his voice held a hint of amusement.

Looking hastily away, she said as lightly as possible, 'I certainly hope so. Though it's a bit late to worry about it.'

When he said nothing further, she observed, 'You're obviously very familiar with this area, yet you don't have a local accent.'

He shook his head. 'No.'

'So you don't live around here?' Bethany toyed with the strap of her handbag, her nervous excitement getting the better of her.

'No. I'm based in London.'

Bethany breathed a sigh of relief. That was good news. Though London was a big place, it meant he was closer at hand than if he'd lived in Cumbria.

'Are you up here on business?' she asked.

He smiled wryly. 'You could say that...'

When he made no further attempt at conversation, afraid of spoiling his concentration, she relapsed into silence and, unwilling to be caught staring at him again, looked resolutely ahead.

After a while he remarked, 'Here we are,' and, turning left into grey nothingness, brought the car to a halt and doused the lights.

At first all Bethany could see was mist pressing damply against the windscreen, then ahead and to the right she saw a faint glimmer of light.

He came round to help her out and, an arm at her waist, steered her towards the dark bulk of the hotel and the glow of a lighted window.

Just that casual touch seemed to burn through her clothing, setting every nerve in her body tingling and robbing her of breath.

When they reached what seemed to be a small annex, the window lit, Bethany could see now, by an oil lamp standing on the windowsill, he stepped forward and knocked on the door.

It opened almost immediately, letting out a slanting beam of yellow light, and an elderly man in shirtsleeves and a pullover peered at them, his face startled.

'I'm sorry to disturb you, but we need a couple of rooms for the night,' Joel told him.

'The hotel's closed,' the caretaker said shortly. 'You'll have to go somewhere else.'

'Unfortunately that's not possible. The mist is much too thick.'

'The hotel's closed,' the man repeated doggedly, and made as if to slam the door.

Joel stepped forward and held it, saying something quietly but decidedly that Bethany didn't catch.

'All the rooms are shut up and there's no heating on in the main part,' was the surly reply.

'Well, I'm quite sure you can find us something,' Joel insisted pleasantly. 'In an old place like this there must surely be a room with a fireplace?'

'The manageress lives on the premises while the hotel's open, so there's *her* room. But the bed's not made up and the generator's not working, so there's no electricity…'

'Perhaps you'll show us?'

Grumbling about the cold and damp, and being scarcely able to walk for his rheumatism, the caretaker turned away.

Bethany noticed that Joel kept his foot in the door until the man returned, wearing a jacket and with a bunch of keys and a torch.

He closed the door behind him and, limping a little, led the way through the mist to a side entrance which gave on to a small tiled lobby.

The dank air seemed even colder inside than out.

At the end of a short corridor he opened a door and flashed the torch around a good-sized room furnished as a bedsitter.

They glimpsed a divan bed, a basket piled with logs next to a stone fireplace, a wooden table and chairs, a couple of deep armchairs and, through a door that was standing a little ajar, a tiled bathroom.

'This will do fine,' Joel assured him briskly. 'A couple of pillows, a few blankets and a candle or two are all we'll need.'

'There's bedding and towels in the cupboard and an oil lamp and matches on the chest of drawers,' the caretaker said grudgingly.

'Thanks.' Some notes changed hands before Joel suggested, 'Perhaps you could manage a bite to eat and a hot drink for the lady?'

The man stuffed the notes in his trouser pocket and, sounding somewhat mollified, said, 'I'll see what I can do.' He went, leaving them in total darkness.

As Bethany hesitated uncertainly, Joel's level voice ordered, 'Stay where you are until I've located the matches.'

A moment later she heard the brush of a footfall as he moved unerringly through the blackness, then the scrape and flare of a match.

With an ease that seemed to speak of long practice, he lit the oil lamp, adjusted the flame and replaced the glass chimney. In a moment the room was filled with golden light.

His clothes—smart casuals—looked expensive, his shoes handmade, but, taking no heed of either, he squatted by the hearth and began to set the fire.

She watched as his long well-shaped hands placed first sticks and then split logs on a bed of flaming kindling.

Glancing up, he said, 'You're shivering. Come and get warm.'

Needing no further encouragement, though truth to tell the shivering was due as much to excitement as cold, she went and sat in the low armchair he'd pulled closer to the fire.

Putting her big suede shoulder bag on the floor by the chair, she stretched her numb hands to the leaping flames.

'Feet cold?' he queried, looking at her suede fashion boots.

'Frozen,' she admitted.

Piling more logs on, he suggested, 'They'll get warm a lot quicker if you take your boots off.'

Recognizing the truth of that, she tried to pull them off but they were high and close-fitting and her hands had pins and needles.

'Let me.' Crouching on his haunches, he eased off first one and then the other, before rubbing each foot between his palms.

His touch scattered her wits and made her pulses race. At a deeper level it also made her feel cared for, cherished, and at that moment she would have lost her heart to him, if it hadn't been his already.

Gazing at his bent head, she noticed that his thick fair hair still had minute droplets of water clinging to it. She wanted to dry it and cradle his head to her breast.

'That better?' he asked when he'd rubbed some life back into her slim feet.

'Much better, thank you,' she answered huskily.

'Good.'

He had an olive-toned skin at odds with his fairness, and a smile that almost stopped her heart. As he looked into her face she saw that his eyes weren't the pale blue she had imagined, but a light silvery green. Fascinating eyes...

He rose to his feet just as the door opened and the caretaker returned, a torch in one hand and a plastic carrier bag in the other.

Plonking the bag down on the kitchen counter, the man said shortly, 'There's everything you should need in here. The cooker runs on bottled gas and you'll find a kettle and crockery in the cupboard.'

'Thanks… And goodnight,' Joel said.

With a grunt, the man turned and shambled away.

The thought of a hot drink was a welcome one and Bethany had started to rise when Joel ordered, 'Stay where you are and get warm. I'll rustle up a drink and a sandwich.'

Devlin, worried about protecting his macho image, would have sat down to be waited on, Bethany thought. But Joel, confident about his masculinity, clearly had no worries on that score.

Within a minute the gas was lit, the kettle was on and two mugs were waiting.

When he had closed the curtains, shutting out the grey mist that pressed like a wet grey blanket against the glass, Joel began to unpack the carrier. There was a jar of instant coffee, a plastic carton of milk, a tub of sunflower spread, an unopened pack of cheese and a small sliced loaf.

'Hardly a feast,' he commented, 'but quite adequate, so long as you like cheese and coffee and you don't take sugar.'

'I do, and I don't,' she answered.

He gave her a lazy smile that made her heart quicken and, taking off his short car-coat, tossed it over a chair. 'In that case we don't have a problem.'

As soon as the kettle started to sing, he made the coffee and handed her one of the steaming mugs.

Sipping it gratefully, she watched while, with cool efficiency, he made a plate of sandwiches and, carrying that and two smaller plates over to the hearth, put them on a low table.

The heat of the coffee banishing the last lingering inner coldness, she said, 'I don't think I need this any longer,' and, rising to her feet, made to take off her coat.

He helped her off with it, then, pulling up a chair, joined her in front of what was now a blazing fire and, offering the plate of sandwiches, urged, 'Do make a start.'

'I'm not very hungry.'

When he continued to hold the plate, though she felt too pleasantly agitated to eat, she took a sandwich just to show willing.

'That's better.' He smiled at her.

His teeth gleamed white and even and his smile held such charm that her heart began to beat faster.

Despite the emotional upheaval, after the first few bites her usual healthy appetite kicked in and she found herself enjoying the simple fare. Or, rather, enjoying the fact that she was sitting in front of a blazing fire sharing a plate of sandwiches with the man who had lived in her heart and mind and dreams for so long.

It was almost too wonderful to be true, and she felt like pinching herself to make sure that the whole thing wasn't just another dream.

CHAPTER TWO

'MORE?' Joel queried when the plate was empty.

Replete, Bethany shook her head with a little sigh of contentment.

Noting the sigh, he raised a well-marked brow and teased, 'That bad, huh?'

'As a matter of fact I've thoroughly enjoyed them,' she said, made breathless by his teasing smile.

'I thought at first that you might be too concerned to eat.'

'Concerned?'

'About spending the night with a total stranger.'

He wasn't a total stranger. She had known him for six years. But she could hardly tell him that. He would think she was mad.

Aware of his eyes on her, she said jerkily, 'I'm not at all concerned.'

'You seem a little… shall we say… flustered?'

Not knowing quite what to say to that, she remained silent until he queried, 'So what brings you to these parts?'

'I'm here on business.'

The mention of business broke through the spell his presence wove, reminding her that she ought to let Tony know she couldn't get back.

Reaching for her bag, she took out her mobile.

Joel gave her an enquiring look.

'I must just call the Dundale Inn and let Tony know I can't get back tonight.'

'I'm afraid you'll be wasting your time,' Joel told her. 'You won't get a signal here.'

'Oh…' As she glanced around, wondering if there was a phone she could borrow, he added lightly, 'And knowing we're marooned together with just one bed, might give him a sleepless night.'

'He wouldn't be worried.' But, remembering his attempts at seduction, she found her colour rising. The intimacy that 'marooned together with just one bed' implied, and thinking a strange man might succeed where he'd failed would make him *furious*.

Watching her companion note that blush, she added hastily, 'Tony's my boss.'

'I see,' Joel said in a way that showed he didn't see at all.

'I—I mean he's not my boyfriend.'

'Well, either way, if he has any sense he won't be expecting you back on a night like this.'

He was no doubt right, Bethany thought, and abandoning any idea of phoning, dropped the mobile back into her bag.

Stretching long legs towards the fire, Joel asked idly, 'What kind of business are you in?'

'Antiques,' she answered quietly, still a little overawed by his presence.

'Your own business?'

She shook her head and her hair, listened in the candlelight. 'No. Tony, my boss, owns Feldon Antiques.'

'Of course,' Joel murmured.

'But I am picking up small, affordable pieces that Feldon Antiques wouldn't touch, with a view to one day starting my own business.'

'You're the buyer?'

She hesitated. Respecting her judgement and knowledge of antiques, a year before his death James had made her the firm's buyer, trusting her to buy at a keen but fair price.

Since Tony had taken over, however, though he relied on her to seek out and identify the rarer items they dealt in—items they sold on to collectors worldwide—he hadn't allowed her to put a price on them.

But she was still the official buyer, she reminded herself, and answered firmly, 'Yes.'

'Does the job involve much travelling?'

'An occasional visit to Europe or the States.'

He raised an eyebrow and questioned, 'So what do you think of The Big Apple?'

'I think New York's wonderful. I remember first falling in love with it when as a young girl I saw *Breakfast at Tiffany's*.' Bethany smiled at the memory.

He grinned. 'And I remember falling in love with Audrey Hepburn.'

For a little while they discussed their favourite old films, then he harked back to query, 'Presumably with your job you put in long hours?'

'Yes, but then I get time off in lieu. This week I'll be in the shop on Wednesday, then I've got until Monday off.'

'What sort of things do you look out for when you're on your travels?'

She thought for a moment then replied, 'Silver and porcelain mainly, but really anything that's rare and valuable.'

'Like this pretty bauble, for instance?' He touched the bracelet she wore, an intricate gold hoop set with deep red stones.

Her heart beating faster, she looked down at his hand, a strong, well-shaped hand with long lean fingers and neatly trimmed nails.

'How did you come by it?' There was a strange note in his voice, an undercurrent of… what? Anger? Condemnation?

But when she looked up the only emotion his face was showing was polite interest, and she knew she must have imagined it.

'Someone brought it into the shop. Though I originally intended it for my collection I loved it on sight, so I decided to keep it.'

'I'm a complete ignoramus when it comes to things like this,' he remarked, turning it round on her wrist. 'I've no real idea how old it is—my guess would be Victorian?'

Only too aware of his touch, she strove to sound cool and unmoved as she told him, 'It dates from the early eighteen hundreds.'

A shade breathlessly, she added, 'Often that kind of bracelet was accompanied by a matching necklace and earrings, which would have made it a lot more valuable. I would have loved a set, but unfortunately it was sold as a single item.'

'May I ask what kind of price a thing like this would fetch?'

She told him what she'd paid for it.

A muscle jumped in his jaw as if he'd clenched his teeth, but his voice was even as he remarked, 'I would have thought—as it's gold and rubies—that it was worth a great deal more than that.'

She shook her head. 'Had it been gold and rubies it would have been, but the stones are garnets.'

'They look like rubies. I always understood that garnets were transparent?' he pursued.

'They are. It's the way these stones are set that makes them look like rubies. Even the seller thought they were.'

'I see.' His expression relaxed.

There was a short silence before he changed the subject by saying, 'I suppose you must meet some interesting people in your line of business?'

Noting how his thick, healthy-looking hair had now dried to its natural ripe-corn colour and longing to touch it, she answered distractedly, 'Yes, you could say that.'

When he waited expectantly, she added, 'The old lady I went to see this morning looked as if she'd stepped out of the pages of some period novel.

'She was dressed all in black, with jet earrings, and was still talking to her husband, who'd been dead for over five years.'

Joel smiled, then, his voice casual, queried, 'She had some antiques she wanted to sell?'

'An attic full,' Bethany said drily.

'Did you find anything worth having?'

She shook her head. She had been hoping to discover something rare and valuable, both for the old lady's sake and—needing to appease Tony's anger—her own. But the 'antiques' had turned out to be, at the best, collectibles, at the worst, junk.

'No valuable silver or porcelain?'

Wondering why he was displaying such interest, she answered, 'The only thing we might have considered buying was a Hochst group of porcelain figures. But unfortunately it had been damaged and mended so badly that it's virtually worthless.'

Leaving his chair to pile more logs on the fire, he remarked, 'So it was a fruitless journey.'

'I'm afraid so.'

In reality it had been anything but. She was with Joel at last and they had the whole of the night in which to get to know one another.

Watching his broad back, noticing how the fine material of his dark sweater stretched across the mature width of his shoulders, she felt a fluttery excitement in her stomach.

The fire blazing to his satisfaction, he gathered up the

crockery and put it on the draining board before washing his hands.

While they talked, almost imperceptibly the light from the lamp had got dimmer, and beyond the glow from the fire shadows were gathering.

Picking up the lamp, Joel moved it from side to side gently. 'I'm afraid we're almost out of oil.'

After a quick search through the cupboards he said, 'There doesn't appear to be any more, so it's a good thing it's almost bedtime.'

He filled the kettle and put it on the stove, remarking, 'It might not be a bad idea to get the bed made up while we can still see what we're doing.'

Recognizing the truth of that, she went to the cupboard and took out bed linen, pillows and a duvet.

Instead of presuming it was woman's work and leaving her to it, as some men would have done, Joel came to help.

The moment she moved away from the fire the cold air had wrapped around her, and she began to feel thoroughly chilled.

As they made the bed together, seeing her shiver, he remarked, 'The duvet appears to be a reasonable weight, so it should be warm enough in bed.'

Suddenly focusing on the fact that there was only the *one* bed, she felt her stomach start to churn.

Picking up her excitement and apparently interpreting it as alarm, he said, 'Don't worry, the bed's all yours.'

In a strangled voice, she queried, 'Well, if I have the bed, where will you sleep?'

'I'll make do with the armchair and a blanket.'

'There aren't any blankets, and only one duvet.'

Sounding anything but worried, he said, 'In that case I'll have to keep the fire well stoked...

'Now, as I estimate that the lamp has only a few minutes' burning time if we're lucky, you'd better have the bathroom first.' Tongue-in-cheek, he added, 'There's soap and towels, but I suppose you don't fancy a cold shower?'

'You suppose right,' she said with feeling.

He grinned. 'A kettle of hot water?'

'Absolute luxury.'

'Not a difficult woman to please.'

'The only thing I mind is not being able to clean my teeth,' she admitted.

Opening the nearest cupboard, he produced two cellophane-wrapped courtesy packs each containing a disposable tooth-brush and toothpaste. 'As to all intents and purposes we're hotel guests, I suggest we borrow a couple of these.'

'Wonderful.'

He handed her the packs, then carried the lamp and the kettle through to the bathroom and set them down on a shelf.

'Will you manage at that?'

'Very well, thank you,' she said gratefully.

'Then I'll leave you to it.' He went out, closing the door behind him.

Bethany cleaned her teeth in water so cold it almost made them ache, then slipping off her bracelet, washed in half a kettleful of hot water, leaving Joel the other half.

It was so cold in the bathroom she could see her breath on the air, but just the knowledge that he was close at hand made her feel warm inside. Being together like this, she could almost imagine they were married.

When she had finished, she hastened back to the fire to comb out her long dark hair while he took her place in the bathroom.

When he returned he brought the oil lamp, which was on its last expiring glimmer, and the empty kettle.

'Generous woman,' he remarked, adding, as he refilled the kettle and lit the gas, 'I thought you might like a hot drink before we turn in?'

'I would, please.'

Having washed their two mugs and made coffee, he came to sit beside her again, stretching his long legs towards the hearth.

The lamp flame had finally died, leaving the rest of the room full of shadows and making the circle formed by the flickering fireglow cosy and intimate.

Their coffee finished, she had just taken a breath to ask him about himself when he invited casually, 'Tell me how you got into the antiques business.'

'It was something I'd always wanted to do. Though my father is an accountant, he's always been fascinated by old and beautiful things. A fascination he passed on to me, along with quite a bit of knowledge, so when I left school I got a job with Feldon Antiques in London.'

'London's a big place… and I'm quite sure we've never met. It's just…'

Studying her lovely heart-shaped face in the firelight, the long-lashed grey eyes and dark winged brows, the neat nose and generous mouth, the determined chin that added such character, he went on with a half smile, 'I have the strangest feeling I've seen you somewhere before… You have a face I seem to recognize. To remember…'

When, suddenly transfixed and with her heart racing wildly, she just gazed at him, he went on, 'But perhaps you don't know the feeling of something half-remembered…?'

As she held her breath a log settled with a rustle and a little explosion of bright sparks.

'Maybe it was in my dreams that I met you…' He reached out and ran a fingertip down the curve of her cheek to the little cleft in her chin. 'Maybe in some dream I've kissed your mouth, held you close, made love to you…'

Tracing her lips, he added softly, 'It's what I've wanted to do since the first moment I saw you…'

Caught up in the magic, she sat quite still while her heart swelled and every bone in her body melted.

'It's what I want to do now…' he added softly and, leaning forward, touched his mouth to hers.

His kiss was like no other she had ever experienced before. It held all she'd ever wanted—the delight, the excitement, the warmth and comfort, the sheer joy of belonging.

As her lips parted beneath his, he deepened the kiss until she was on fire with longing, a quivering mass of sensations even before he rose and, lifting her to her feet, drew her against his firm body.

When, still kissing her, he began to run his hands over her, she leaned into him, making soft little noises in her throat.

Even the feel of the cold air on her skin when he removed her clothes and the coolness of the sheets when he lifted her into bed didn't break the spell he'd woven.

And when he slid into bed beside her and drew her against the naked warmth of his body it was like coming home.

He was a good lover, strong, masterful, passionate, yet those qualities went hand in hand with skill and caring, a boundless generosity. Not once but twice he sent her sky-rocketing to the stars with an effortless ease, before gathering her into the crook of his arm and drawing her close.

Snuggled against him, all passion spent, her body sleek and satisfied, her mind euphoric, she knew she had never been so wildly happy, so blissfully content. She was with him at last.

Thinking how wonderful it was that he was under the same kind of spell that she was under, that the enchantment was mutual, she slipped into sleep saying a silent but heartfelt prayer of thanks.

* * *

When Bethany awoke, just for a second or two she was completely disorientated, then memories of the previous night, of Joel, came crowding into her mind filling her with gladness.

Sighing, she reached out to touch him. The space beside her was empty and cold. Pushing herself up on one elbow, she looked around in the semi-darkness.

There was no sign of him and though her clothes still lay where they had been discarded, his had vanished. But, of course, he would be in the bathroom getting washed and dressed.

The fire, though still in, had burnt low and, her naked body goosefleshing, she got out of bed and began to hurriedly pull on her own clothes.

As soon as she was dressed she piled on some logs and went to draw back the curtains. The fog had cleared but the morning was gloomy and overcast with a sky the colour of pewter.

Wondering what time it was, she glanced at her watch. Almost a quarter past nine.

She grimaced. Tony would be livid. He had made it abundantly clear that if they didn't need to stay another day he wanted to make an early start back to the great metropolis.

But even the thought of how furious he would be when she turned up so late and with nothing to show for her visit to Mrs Deramack failed to spoil her new-found happiness.

Though, as yet, she still knew little about Joel except that he came from London, they were together at last. Lovers. In love for ever. A glowing future ahead of them.

While she waited for him to emerge, she put the kettle on, rinsed two mugs and spooned instant coffee into them, before going back to the fire.

Reaching for her capacious bag, she flipped it open and started to unzip the compartment that held her comb and cosmetics.

But something—it looked like the corner of a facial tissue—

was caught and the zip had jammed, though it had seemed all right the previous night when she had replaced her comb.

And her mobile wasn't in the pocket she usually kept it in, but no doubt she had been too excited to care where she put it.

A little frown of concentration marring her smooth brow, she worked the zip free, then, having combed her hair, took it up into its usual gleaming coil.

As she clipped it into place, it began to impinge on her consciousness that, apart from the crackle of burning logs and the kettle starting to sing, everywhere was silent. There wasn't another sound. No movement. No running water. And when she'd put the kettle on it had been cold.

Trying to subdue a sudden, completely unreasonable panic, she went and tapped on the bathroom door. 'Joel… Will you be long?'

There was no answer.

She threw open the door to find the room was empty.

He must have gone across to have a word with the caretaker, she told herself, and, judging by how low the fire had been, he'd been gone for some time, so no doubt he'd be back at any moment.

When another five minutes had passed with no sign of him returning, an icy vice began to tighten around her heart.

But after all they had shared the previous night, he wouldn't have just gone. Walked away without a single word. He *couldn't*.

Of course! All at once the solution struck her. He'd gone to fetch his car. If he had woken her up, she could have driven him there. Though the road had been too narrow at that precise spot for any manoeuvring, there must surely be *somewhere* on that stretch a car could turn round.

When the kettle boiled she made a single cup of coffee and drank it sitting in front of the fire.

After another half an hour had crawled past she knew with

dreadful certainty that he wasn't coming back. Perhaps, subconsciously, she had known from the very beginning.

Joel had gone for good. Had gone without a word. Without so much as leaving a note.

He had walked in and out of her life like some wraith. All she knew about him was his name and the fact that he came from London. He might even be a married man.

Gripped by an icy coldness, a pain so intense she might have been in the grim embrace of an iron maiden, she could neither move nor breathe.

Last night had meant nothing to him. Just a seized chance. A one night stand. All the talk about seeming to know her, to recognize her, had just been part of his seduction technique.

Perhaps he had believed Tony was her lover? Had decided she was easy?

Well, she *had* been, she thought bitterly. Stupidly, idiotically easy.

In love with a dream, she had behaved like some silly little adolescent who hadn't yet learnt to curb her impulses and respect herself.

She stood for a long time staring blindly into space before she was able to move, to find her coat and bag and make her way to the car.

The keys were in the ignition where Joel had left them the previous night. Thinking of how excited she had been when they arrived here, how hopeful, she felt as if a knife was being turned in her heart and was forced to lean against the car until the worst of the agony had passed.

Then, her usual graceful movements clumsy, she got into the driving seat and, leaning forward, rested her forehead on the wheel.

After a moment or two, as if so much pain had caused a protective shield to drop into place, she raised her head and, neither thinking nor feeling, her entire being numb, drove back to Dundale like some automaton.

It was almost twelve by the time she reached the Inn to find Tony pacing the lobby, every bit as enraged as she had imagined.

'So here you are at last! I wondered what the devil had happened to you. Have you any idea how long I've been waiting?' he demanded angrily.

Her voice curiously flat and lifeless, she said, 'I'm sorry. I'm afraid I overslept.'

'Overslept!' He uttered a profanity. 'So where the hell did you sleep?'

Briefly, she explained about the burst tyre and the mist and having to spend the night at a hotel that was still officially closed for the winter. She didn't mention Joel.

'Why didn't you let me know?' Tony sounded even more exasperated.

'I couldn't get a signal,' she said shortly, and was pleased when he grunted and left it at that.

'So how did you get on with old Mrs Deramack? Any good stuff?'

She shook her head.

He swore briefly.

Making an effort at normality, she asked, 'How about Greendales? They seemed to have some extremely nice things.'

'They did,' he admitted grudgingly, 'but their reserve prices were a damn sight too high. Private sales make a lot more sense…'

Bethany was aware that, translated, that meant *a lot more money*. James Feldon had cared about antiques. All Tony cared about was the bottom line.

'That's why I was hoping the old lady had something worth our while. As it is, the trip's been a waste of time. And now you've managed to sleep in,' he added nastily, 'it's been a waste of a morning too.'

'I'm sorry,' she said again.

'I hope you weren't expecting to have lunch before we start?'

'No, I'm not at all hungry. I'll just fetch my things.' She couldn't wait to get away.

Except for a short stop to refuel and have coffee and, in Tony's case, a packet of sandwiches, they drove straight back to town. Still in a foul mood, apart from occasionally cursing another motorist, Tony barely uttered a word.

It was a relief in one way, but it allowed too much time for brooding. The numbness had passed and, her thoughts bleak as winter, Bethany found herself going over and over everything that had happened the previous night. Picking at it. Dissecting it. Exposing the pain, so that it was like doing an autopsy on a living body.

By the time Tony dropped her at her flat she was feeling like death and only too pleased that Catherine, who was an airline stewardess, was away until the following week and she had the place to herself.

Quite unable to stomach the thought of food, even though she'd had nothing to eat that day, Bethany made herself a pot of tea and sat down to drink it. She would have an early night. She needed the blessed oblivion of sleep.

Tomorrow, though her beautiful dreams had turned to dust, she would have to get up and face the day as if nothing had happened. If that were possible.

But it *had* to be. She must *make* it possible.

She recalled a motto in one of last year's Christmas crackers: *When your dreams turn to dust, Hoover.* It seemed appropriate.

Her tea finished, she was heading for the bedroom when the phone rang.

For a moment she considered not answering. But old habits died hard and, before she could make herself walk away, she had picked up the receiver.

'Hello?'

'So you're back…'

It was Michael Sharman. Over the last few months she had got to know and like him and they had been out together on quite a number of occasions but she saw him as nothing more than a friend.

'Bethany?'

She wasn't in the mood to talk to anybody. She sighed, 'Yes, I'm back.'

'It doesn't sound like you.'

'I'm a bit tired.'

He went on regardless, seemingly oblivious to her overwhelming tiredness. 'I tried to phone you earlier. Been home long?'

'No.'

'Care to go out for a spot of supper?'

'I don't think so, Michael.' She wasn't in the right kind of mood to go out.

'Why not?' he asked.

'I was just on my way to bed.'

'Bed?' he exclaimed, surprised. 'But it's barely eight o'clock. Look, what if I pop round now and pick you up?'

'No, thank you. I'm tired.' Then, aware that she'd sounded a bit curt, she added apologetically, 'I'm sorry. I guess I'm even more tired than I thought.'

'Sure I can't change your mind? Going out might be just what you need to liven you up.'

'I doubt it.'

He was a young man who was used to getting his own way with women. But this woman was special, not like the rest, and he didn't want to spoil his chances.

'In that case,' he said reluctantly, 'let's make it tomorrow night.'

'Well, I—'

'What if I pick you up around seven? We'll go to the Caribbean Club and have a good time.'

Before she could argue, he was gone.

Sighing, she replaced the receiver.

If she found she couldn't face it, she would just have to call him and put him off.

But what would she do if she did stay at home? What was she *likely* to do?

Mope. Which would get her precisely nowhere.

Going out with Michael had to be preferable.

After first thinking him somewhat cocky and immature, she had come to enjoy his company and almost envy his carefree, sybaritic attitude to life.

They had first met when, after inheriting his grandmother's house and its contents, he had brought a blue and white porcelain bowl into Feldon Antiques, saying he needed to raise some ready cash.

Bethany, who had been in the shop at the time, had thought the bowl was Ming, which would have made it extremely valuable. But an expert on Chinese porcelain that Tony had later taken it to had identified it as Qing, which made its value a great deal less.

However, it was still worth a considerable amount and Michael had been more than happy to part with it.

After selling them the bowl, he had produced several smaller items which Tony had dismissed but Bethany had been pleased to buy for her collection.

The bracelet Joel had admired had been one of them.

But where was the bracelet?

A moment's thought convinced her that she had taken it off

in the bathroom the previous night before getting washed. She hadn't noticed it that morning, nor had she given it a thought, but she had had other things on her mind.

Just to be on the safe side, she found her shoulder bag and searched through it, but there was no sign of the bracelet in its capacious depths.

She must have left it at the hotel.

It was a blow, even though she hadn't really *expected* to find it—looking in her bag had been an act of sheer desperation.

If it were possible, her spirits sank even lower. Until then, despite all the pain, she hadn't shed a single tear, but, as though leaving her bracelet was the last straw, she began to cry.

She cried until she had no more tears left, then, feeling empty, drained, hollow as a ghost, showered and crawled into bed.

In the morning she would have to try and get in touch with the caretaker…

Following closely on that thought came a sense of helplessness. She didn't even know the name of the hotel they had stayed at. All she knew was that it lay at the foot of Dunscar.

But if she contacted the nearest information centre, supposing there was one open in early February, they should be able to give her the name of the place…

After a night spent tossing and turning, Bethany got up feeling heavy-eyed and heavy-hearted. Though she had no appetite, before setting off for the shop, she made herself eat some breakfast—a triumph of common sense over despair.

It was a bleak, grey morning that perfectly matched her mood. The only bright spot was when Tony, still noticeably surly, announced that when he'd dealt with the morning's mail he was going out and would be gone for the rest of the day.

After working several weekends in a row, she was entitled to three days off, which meant she wouldn't have to come in again until Monday, and, as things were, she could only be glad.

In their absence, her colleague Alison had been her usual efficient self and there was no backlog of work.

With nothing pressing to do, Bethany set out to find the name of the hotel at the foot of Dunscar. The area's central information bureau was open and able to tell her that it was called The Dunbeck. They even provided the phone number.

Somewhat heartened, she dialled the number.

There was no answer.

Though she tried periodically for the rest of the day, she met with no success.

Just as she was about to close the shop a couple of browsers came in and it was turned six before she was able to lock up and leave.

By the time she reached her basement flat, tired and frustrated, it was almost six-thirty and Michael would be picking her up at seven.

CHAPTER THREE

FEELING anything but sociable, Bethany was tempted to ring and put Michael off, but better sense prevailed. It would do her a lot more good to go out than sit at home brooding.

Her decision made, she drew the curtains against the dark, frosty night and went into the bathroom to have a quick shower.

Dried and scented, she touched a mascara wand to her long lashes and glossed her lips with pale, shiny lipstick. Then, as though making up for her previous lack of enthusiasm, she donned her best dark blue cocktail dress and fastened pearl studs to her small, neat lobes.

Leaving her hair falling loosely around her shoulders in a dark silky cloud, she was ready when the bell rang.

She opened the door to find Michael was waiting beneath the lantern, a bouquet of crimson roses in his hand.

'Wow!' he exclaimed at the sight of her. 'You look fantastic!' Then, handing her the flowers, 'I hope you like roses?'

'Thank you, I do. They're lovely. If you come in for a minute I'll put them in water.'

Following her inside, he leaned against the kitchen counter while she stripped off the cellophane and found a vase to arrange the roses in.

Slimly built and a couple of inches taller than herself, he was

well-dressed and well-groomed, a personable young man with
dark curly hair and more than his fair share of charm.

From a wealthy background and with a private income, he
was, she supposed, quite a catch.

Watching her arrange the flowers, he queried, 'Was it a successful trip?'

She shook her head. 'Not very.'

'I thought you seemed depressed. Oh, well, let's forget our
troubles and go and have a good time.'

Wondering what troubles he had in what she had hitherto
regarded as a carefree life, she locked the door behind her and
followed him up the basement steps to his red Porsche.

During an evening spent dancing and dining at the Caribbean
Club, Bethany did her best to hide her misery and appear
cheerful. But, despite all her efforts, Michael picked up her low
spirits.

When they returned to their table after a slow foxtrot, he
remarked sympathetically, 'You really *are* down, aren't you?'

Feeling guilty, she said, 'I'm sorry if I've spoilt your evening.'

He shook his head. 'Of course you haven't spoilt it.' Then,
with a sigh, 'I wasn't exactly ecstatic to start with.'

'You have a problem?'

'Too true… I'm in a mess. I need a substantial sum of money
and I need it fast.'

Catching her look of surprise, he said, 'If you're thinking of
what I got for the bowl… I invested it in a new stage show that
was looking for backers.

'If it comes off, it should make everyone involved, me
included, multi-millionaires.

'But there's still months to go before it's due to open, and I
learnt today that they're running out of cash.'

He sounded so despondent that Bethany's heart went out to him.

'Can't they find extra backers?'

'They've tried, but once it gets around that a project is rocky, no one wants to take that risk. So one way or another, I've just got to come up with some more cash.'

'What about your grandmother's house?'

'Unfortunately I can't sell that.'

'You're fond of it because it was the family home?'

'God, no! Now all the staff are gone, apart from a cleaning lady, it puts me in mind of a mausoleum. I was rattling round the blasted place like a grain of rice in an empty tin until my stepbrother suggested I could move in with him for a while...'

'So you're living with your stepbrother?'

Michael shook his head. 'It didn't work. All he wanted to do was keep an eye on me. He started to tick me off about the hours I kept, so I'm bunking with a mate of mine in a very small flat.'

Gloomily, he added, 'I was hoping to rent a place of my own but my allowance won't stretch to it.'

Then, with a sudden flare of temper, 'I could afford to *buy* a flat and still have a tidy bit left if I was able to put the blasted house on the market.'

Seeing her puzzled frown, he went on, 'But even when things are through probate, thanks to the terms of the will, I can't sell it before I reach the age of twenty-five. That's in two years' time. Until then my stepbrother has control.'

'Couldn't your family help out in the meantime?'

'He's the only family I have left.'

'What does he do?'

'He's an entrepreneur,' Michael said sourly. 'As well as owning JSM International, he has a finger in a great many different pies.'

'So he's a lot older than you?'

'Only six years.'

Seeing her surprise, Michael explained. 'He made his pile young by buying up failing businesses, putting them on their feet again and selling them at a hell of a profit.'

'Well, surely he'd help if you asked him?'

Michael's laugh was bitter. 'You have to be joking! The last time I was forced to ask him for extra cash, he grudgingly paid off my debts. But when I asked him for a bigger allowance, he said it was high time I got a job.

'I pointed out I hadn't been trained for anything.' Miael sighed and went on, 'He offered me a position in his Los Angeles branch. I'm sure the climate would be great, but who in his right senses wants to be tied to an office five days out of seven?

'My only hope is that amongst the rest of my grandmother's antiques there's something really valuable... I suppose you wouldn't be prepared to take a quick look and advise me?'

'Of course. When would you—?'

'Tonight,' he broke in eagerly. 'We can call in there on the way back to your flat...'

Bethany's heart sank. Tired and headachy, it was the last thing she wanted to do, but feeling she owed it to him, she agreed, 'All right.'

Having signalled the waiter, he paid the bill, collected their coats and hurried her out to the waiting car.

In spite of the traffic, in a matter of minutes they were drawing up outside his grandmother's elegant porticoed townhouse in Lanervic Square.

Michael let them in and, closing the door behind them, switched off the alarm.

As he led the way across the spacious hall to a vast and silent living room, Bethany began to realize why he had described the place as a mausoleum.

At first glance all the furniture appeared to be antique, and there were several glass-fronted display cabinets crowded with Chinese pottery and porcelain.

Staggered by the sheer amount of stuff, she stared at it in silence.

After a minute or so, Michael asked eagerly, 'Do you think there'll be something I can raise a good amount on?'

'Almost certainly. How many pieces do you want to part with?'

'One… Two, at the most. Otherwise it might be—' He broke off abruptly.

'Examining even a few pieces is going to take time and care,' Bethany said, 'so it would make more sense to come back tomorrow.'

He took her hand. 'I've a much better idea… Why don't you stay the night?'

Before she could refuse, he had pulled her close and was kissing her with an ardour that just for a second or two swamped her, then she tried to draw away. But his arms were wrapped tightly around her and he was so much stronger than she had imagined.

She was gathering herself to struggle in earnest, when all at once she was free and Michael, his startled face an unbecoming brick-red, was goggling at something behind her.

Turning to follow the direction of his gaze, she saw that there was a tall fair-haired man with wide shoulders lounging in the doorway.

Feeling as if she'd walked slap into a plate glass window, she found herself staring at Joel.

Michael was the first to break the silence with a stammered, 'H-hell… you startled me.'

'So I see,' Joel said smoothly.

With a hint of bravado, Michael asked, 'What are you doing here?'

'I could ask you the same question.' A bite to his tone, Joel added, 'Only the answer seems obvious. Unless I have the wrong end of the stick?'

All the colour draining from his face, Michael stammered, 'Well I—I just brought Bethany in to… to… see where I used to live.'

Joel glanced at her as if he'd never met her before in his life and, his little smile contemptuous, drawled, 'Really?'

'There's nothing wrong with that, is there?' Michael blustered. 'In any case we were just on the point of leaving.'

'Then I'll say goodnight to you both.'

Throughout the little exchange, shocked and stunned, incapable of coherent thought, Bethany had stood there, transfixed, her wide eyes on Joel's face.

Now she found herself hurried out of the house and across the pavement to the red Porsche as if the hounds of hell were baying at their heels.

'That's blown it!' Michael exclaimed as he slid behind the wheel and started the car. 'He must have overheard everything. What rotten luck for him to walk in just at that minute.'

While Bethany was still fumbling to fasten her seatbelt, they set off with a whoosh that threw her back in her seat.

'Was that…?' Her voice failed. She swallowed hard and tried again. 'Was that your stepbrother?'

'Yes, for my sins. And now you see what I mean?' he went on as he joined the traffic stream. 'See what a swine he is?

'He's always been an arrogant bastard, but now he holds the purse-strings he thinks he rules the world and other places.

'Well, at the moment he might have the whip hand. But one of these days I'll be my own master. I won't have to kowtow to him any longer…'

During the silence that followed, Bethany made an attempt to gather herself and come to terms with the almost unbelievable.

It seemed so strange, so bizarre, that Joel was Michael's step-brother. She felt as if fate was playing the jester. Mocking her. Making fun of her. Having a game at her expense.

Meeting him again out of the blue like that had shaken her to the core. But what had disturbed her even more was the way he had looked at her. As if she'd crawled from under a stone. As if he held her in contempt.

Obviously he had heard Michael asking her to stay the night and presumed they were already lovers. After what had happened in the Lakes, he must have thought her immoral. A woman who had no principles, who would sleep with a man she knew nothing about, a man she had only just met.

If he'd respected her at all, he wouldn't have left the next morning without a single word.

It was the old double standard. Yet somehow it still held sway.

Her unhappy thoughts were interrupted when the car drew up outside her flat.

Michael got out and accompanied her across the pavement. When she paused at the top of the area steps, he asked, 'Can I come in?'

It was the last thing she wanted. She felt much too churned up. Too agitated.

She was about to make some excuse when he added, 'God, do I need a brandy!'

As a rule, when he was driving he made a point of not drinking but, glancing at his face in the glow from the street lamp, she could see that he really did need something to steady him.

Turning, she led the way down the steps and unlocked the door. He followed her into the cosy warmth and threw himself into one of the comfortable linen-covered armchairs while she took off her coat.

Finding a glass, she poured a measure of brandy from a bottle Devlin had brought for some party or other and handed it to him.

'Thanks.' He downed it in a single gulp and held out his glass for more.

'You're driving,' she reminded him.

'Just a small one,' he coaxed.

Putting the bottle back in the cupboard, she said firmly, 'I'll make some coffee.'

'You're acting like a wife,' he accused.

Ignoring that, she said, 'You don't want to risk losing your licence, do you?'

'God, no!'

While he stared moodily into space she made a pot of good strong coffee and handed him a cup, before sitting on the couch.

He took a sip, then, putting the cup down so that it rattled in the saucer, asked abruptly, 'Suppose we get married?'

'Married?' she echoed blankly.

'Why not? You know I'm mad about you. You've got everything I've been looking for in a woman. We could have a lot of fun together.'

She shook her head emphatically. 'The whole idea is ridiculous.'

'What's so ridiculous about it?' He sounded hurt. 'I may not have much money at the moment, but I *will* have plenty. I don't have to work for a living. I have a top-of-the-range car...'

It occurred to her to wonder how, if his allowance was 'a mere pittance' as he'd claimed, he could afford to own and run a car like that.

But he was going on. 'The family I belong to is an influential one, and you'd have a place in society.'

Thinking about Joel, she said, 'I'm sorry, Michael, it's out of the question.'

'Why is it out of the question?'

Agitation brought her to her feet. 'W-well for one thing, I don't love you.'

'Give it time and you might change your mind.'

'I'm sorry, Michael, it just wouldn't work.'

He got up and, taking her shoulders, said seriously, 'Look, don't say anything now. Sleep on it.' With an attempt at a grin, he added, 'Perhaps by morning the idea will seem a little more appealing…

'Tell you what, have lunch with me and give me your answer then.' Snatching a quick kiss, he let himself out.

She sank back on the couch, her mind a confused jumble of thoughts. Before she could begin to sort out that confusion, she heard his footsteps returning and his knock at the door.

Glancing around to see what he'd left, she went to open it. As soon as the latch was off, the door was held to prevent her shutting it again and a man that *wasn't* Michael brushed past her. Closing the door behind him, he set his back to the panels.

Both her heart and breathing seemed to stop as, for the second time that night, she found herself staring at Joel.

Then, her heart starting to race wildly, she stammered, 'W-what are you doing here? How did you know where I lived?'

'I followed you home,' he admitted shamelessly.

'What do you want?'

'I want to talk to you.' His voice was as cool as his silvery-green eyes.

When she continued to stand gaping at him, he said, 'I presume we're alone?'

Making a great effort to pull herself together, she said, 'Yes.'

'Good. Suppose we sit down?'

Bethany forced her shaky legs to carry her across to the couch once more.

Joel waited politely until she was sitting down before removing his short car-coat and taking the chair opposite.

Wearing casual trousers and a black polo-necked sweater that made his hair seem even fairer, he looked dangerously attractive.

His mere presence overwhelmed her but, not wanting him to gain the upper hand, she took a deep breath and asked as steadily as possible, 'What do you want to talk about?'

His eyes fixed on her face, he said, 'Knowing Michael, I strongly suspect he's going to ask you to marry him…'

Then, reading her expression correctly, 'Ah, I see he's already asked you. I hope you haven't accepted.'

Ruffled by the casual arrogance of his manner, she looked him in the eye and said shortly, 'That has nothing to do with you.'

He laughed mockingly. 'That's just where you're wrong. It has *everything* to do with me. *What answer did you give him?*'

Her eyes fell beneath his and she shook her head.

'I haven't given him a final answer yet.'

'Good.' Joel's voice held satisfaction. 'When is he expecting one?'

'Tomorrow, when he picks me up for lunch,' Bethany said quietly.

He looked her directly in the eye. 'You'll say no, of course.' It was an order.

Refusing to be intimidated further, she lied, 'I haven't made up my mind yet.'

His tone became angry. 'Well, get this into your pretty little head, there's no way I'll allow you to marry him.'

'You might have some financial control over Michael's life,' she said furiously, 'but you can't stop him marrying whoever he wants to marry. And you certainly can't tell *me* what to do.'

There was silence for a second or two, then Joel spoke.

'That's quite true. If you're determined to marry him, I can't stop you. All the same, it would be a sad mistake.'

'Why are you so against it?' she asked without stopping to think.

He raised a level brow.

Flushing, she supplied her own answer. 'Because you think I have no morals.'

'Now, why should I think that?' he asked mockingly.

'Because…' She stopped, her colour rising.

'Because you've slept with both of us?'

'That's not so.'

'Don't tell me that holding you in my arms, feeling your naked body against mine, making love to you, was just a dream!' he said with a smirk.

Hating the derision in his voice, she said thickly, 'I haven't slept with Michael.'

'Never?'

'Never.'

Joel raised an eyebrow, as if questioning her response. 'I heard him invite you to stay the night.'

'If he hadn't kissed me when he did, you would have heard me refuse.'

'Playing hard to get? Or would *Tony* have objected?'

Bethany was furious. 'Tony is my boss, not my boyfriend.'

'That's what you said before.'

'But you don't believe me.'

'I might have done if, at the Dundale Inn, you hadn't been booked in as Mr and Mrs Feldon.'

Taken aback, she demanded, 'How do you know that?'

He answered her question with a question of his own. 'It's the truth, isn't it?'

Taking a deep breath, she said, 'Yes, but Tony had made the booking without my knowledge…'

It was quite obvious that Joel didn't believe her. Even so, she ploughed on. 'He was hoping to "have a little fun" as he put it—'

'So presumably he's used to *having a little fun*.'

Bethany lifted her chin. 'Not with *me*, he isn't. I don't even like him. But since I broke my engagement he's been trying to get me to go to—'

'Who were you engaged to?'

She saw by his face that she was digging herself in deeper. 'His name was Devlin.'

'Why did you break it off?'

'I came back from a business trip to find him in bed with another woman.'

When she said no more, Joel prompted, 'So your boss has been trying to get you to "have a little fun" but so far he hasn't succeeded…'

Bethany crossed her arms in a gesture of defiance. 'No, he hasn't.'

Joel smiled wryly, and she knew so exactly what he was thinking—*yet you let a perfect stranger seduce you*—that he might have spoken the words aloud.

She bit her lip.

'To have booked a double room he must have been fairly confident,' Joel pursued.

'His confidence was misplaced,' she said shortly. 'When I discovered what he'd done, I insisted on having a separate room.'

'Really?' he drawled.

'Yes, really. If you'd checked further you would have found that I slept in number nine. On my own,' she added for good measure.

'That couldn't have pleased our Lothario.'

'No, it didn't. He called me prim and proper.'

With a sardonic gleam in his eye, Joel remarked, 'I certainly wouldn't call you prim and proper. Quite the opposite, in fact… But do go on.'

Feeling her face grow hot, she added hardily, 'I told him I didn't sleep around and—'

Joel gave a little bark of laughter. 'I suppose it depends on what you mean by "sleep around".'

She felt the prick of angry tears and was forced to blink. 'You think I'm easy, don't you? That's why you don't want me to marry Michael.'

'I don't want you to marry Michael for a variety of reasons,' he informed her coolly.

'Such as?'

His mouth a little wry, he admitted, 'Perhaps I'm jealous. Perhaps I want you for myself.'

Hardly daring to believe it, she stared at him in silence, the breath caught in her throat.

Rising, he took her hand and pulled her to her feet. Bethany was tall, but at over six feet he had a good five inches on her.

Looming over her, he looked at her with a quiet intensity that made heat spread through her entire body. Then, with deliberation, he brushed the pad of his thumb across her lips.

As she read the intent, the purpose, in his face, a shiver ran through her. The hammer blows of her heart threatening to break her ribs, she backed away a step or two until she stopped by the wall, whispering, 'Don't. Please don't.'

'Don't what?' he asked, closing in on her.

'Kiss me,' she said desperately. 'I don't want you to kiss me.'

He put a hand each side of her head, trapping her there. 'But of course I'm going to kiss you. You know perfectly well you want me to.'

His voice soft and seductive as silk, he went on, 'And I've been thinking of nothing else since I last saw you.'

He took her heart-shaped face between his hands to hold her head still while he kissed her, teasing first with his tongue, then nipping gently at her bottom lip.

At first she made an effort to keep her lips pressed tightly together, but after a few moments, unable to help herself, they parted beneath that skilful coaxing.

With a little murmur of male satisfaction, he took instant advantage.

His kiss was long and lazy, yet with a leashed hunger that scattered her wits and swamped any attempt at rational thought.

After a while he lifted his head and looked into her face. Her eyes were closed, long lashes making dark fans on her cheeks, her lips dewy, a flush of colour lying along her high cheekbones.

Almost wonderingly, he murmured, 'You're quite exquisite. You have the kind of beauty that men often dream about but are seldom lucky enough to find…'

Pleasure running through her that he thought her beautiful, it barely registered when he added almost to himself, 'If the inside matched, you'd be one of the most perfect things nature ever created…'

Sliding one hand beneath the silky fall of dark hair, he cupped her nape and drew her head forward until his mouth had captured hers again.

Exploring, tantalizing, dominating, by turns, his kisses sent shivers of delight and excitement coursing up and down her spine.

While he kissed her, he moved his hands caressingly over her slender curves, tracing her hips and buttocks, her waist and ribcage and the soft swell of her breasts.

He brushed a nipple lightly and, feeling her shudder, whispered into her mouth, 'I want to take you to bed and strip you naked, to pleasure you until you're a quivering mass of sensations in my hands. I want to feel your body against mine, to make love to you until you're mindless. Then I want to do it all over again…'

Somewhere, buried deep, the still, small voice of common sense warned that she should send him away. If she let him make love to her now, after the way he'd walked out on her, it would only reinforce his belief that she was easy.

But, even as she tried to hold on to that thought, she could feel it slipping away, feel her resolve weakening as his mouth moved against hers and his hands brought every nerve ending in her body zinging into life.

Though she knew virtually nothing about him, she knew with absolute certainty that out of all the men in the world *this* man was the one she had been waiting for, the other part of her, the part that finally made her whole. He was her love, her destiny.

Though it sounded like a sentiment from some romantic movie, it didn't make it any less true.

When he stooped and, one arm beneath her knees, the other supporting her shoulders, lifted her high in his arms, on fire for him, she made no protest.

Her bedroom door was ajar and, having shouldered it open, he carried her inside and, setting her down carefully, switched on the lamp. Then, slipping off her shoes and dress and slip, he led her over to the bed and laid her on it, before swiftly stripping off his own clothes and sitting down beside her.

The last time he had removed her clothes it had been almost dark and cold enough to make her skin goose-flesh even though he'd been fast and deft.

This time it was comfortably warm and, the glow from the bedside lamp gilding the smooth creaminess of her flawless skin, he undressed her slowly, savouring each moment.

First he unhooked her bra and tossed it aside, pausing to admire her firm, beautifully shaped breasts with their dusky pink nipples.

Next came her silk stockings—one of her few extravagances—which he rolled down her long slender legs slowly, erotically, pausing to massage first one foot and then the other, kneading and stroking, working between her toes, finding previously unknown pressure points.

The feelings he engendered were amazing, each toe sensitive to his touch, each one turning into an erogenous zone, making her nipples firm and her stomach clench.

By the time he removed her lacy panties, she was eager to feel his weight. But, clearly in no hurry, though he was obviously aroused, he moved his attention to her shoulders, stroking and caressing, following the line of her collarbone to the hollow at the base of her throat.

Having lingered there as though reluctant to leave, his fingertips went on to trace the curve of her breasts and the warm cleft between them.

As his mouth took the place of his fingers, a slight stubble accentuating the sensations, she quivered with anticipation. But, as though determined to tease, while he explored the soft firmness with his tongue and lips, occasionally nibbling gently, he avoided her nipples.

She was in an agony of suspense before he began to lave first one and then the other, causing spasms of pleasure to run through her. When his mouth finally closed over one dusky peak, sucking and tugging slightly, and his fingers teased the other, the sensations were so exquisite that she began to gasp and squirm.

Wondering dimly how he could hold back for so long and eager to feel his body against hers, eager for his possession, she moved her hips with an instinctive invitation as old as Eve.

Lifting his head, he smiled and, and as though in answer to her question, told her, 'The more the sensations build, the more intense and prolonged it makes the pleasure for both of us…'

One hand following her ribcage down to her flat stomach and past the nest of dark silky curls to the moist, silken warmth of her inner thighs, he murmured, 'But I think we're almost there…'

For a moment or two he inched her closer to the brink and she was almost mindless when he finally lowered himself into the cradle of her hips.

Unable to help herself, she cried out as his first strong thrust sent her tumbling and spinning into the abyss of pleasure.

It took a long time to fall and she was still quivering with ecstasy as she heard his groan and felt the weight of his head heavy on her breast.

When the heated bliss changed to a glowing warmth and their heartbeats and breathing returned to something like normal, he drew away, leaving her momentarily cold and alone. Then, having switched out the light, he gathered her against him and settled her head on his shoulder.

Once more all was right with the world and within moments she was asleep.

After a while he awoke her with a kiss.

Her heart overflowing with love and gratitude that miraculously everything had come right, she nestled against him and returned his kiss.

This time their love-making was just as intense, but different. He moved with maddening slowness, withdrawing to the very tip then pressing back again, sending shuddering thrills through her.

Then, as she abandoned herself to the slowly spiralling bliss, the rhythm grew faster and he drove deeper until, her fingers knotted in his hair, her back arched, the night exploded like a rocket into a thousand bright sparks and she cried out at the intensity of the shared pleasure.

For a while she lay blind and transfixed, her fingers unconsciously stroking his hair, savouring his weight and the glorious waves of release surging through her body.

She wanted to cling to this moment, to make it last for ever, but almost before he lifted himself away she had drifted into a blissful sleep.

CHAPTER FOUR

WHEN Bethany awoke it was to a singing happiness. The instant awareness that Joel was back in her life. The precious knowledge that, in spite of everything, he still wanted her.

She turned to him in the dimness, only to find that once again the space beside her was cold and empty. Her heart lurched sickeningly. Even as she tried to reassure herself that he would be in the bathroom, something in the quality of the silence convinced her she was alone in the flat.

Pushing herself upright, she glanced around. Sure enough, his clothes were gone.

But that needn't necessarily mean he had walked out on her for a second time. The bedside clock showed it was almost nine forty-five. Perhaps he'd had to go because he had pressing commitments.

But, if that was so, why hadn't he at least told her he was going?

He might not have wanted to wake her.

Oh, stop clutching at straws! she told herself angrily. He had gone because, apart from taking her to bed when the opportunity arose, he had absolutely no interest in her. She was less than nothing to him.

She felt a return of the numbing despair she had felt previously. Maybe he had only made love to her so he could tell

Michael, make it clear to the younger man exactly what kind of woman she was?

Perhaps if she had told him the truth, that she hadn't the faintest intention of marrying his stepbrother, he wouldn't have made such a determined attempt to seduce her.

And it had been determined. But if she had held out against him, refused to allow herself to be seduced a second time, would he have thought any better of her?

Possibly not.

But she would have thought better of herself.

As it was, having made the same mistake twice, she would just have to live with it. Try to forget about Joel, put the whole sorry mess behind her and carry on as best she could.

All she wanted to do at the moment was hide away with her misery, but in less than two hours Michael would be calling for her.

She would have to phone him, she thought in a sudden panic, tell him she was ill…

But that was chickening out. Or, at the best, only a temporary solution. Michael was a persistent young man who wouldn't be easily deterred, so what she *must* do was talk to him face to face and make it clear that they had no future together.

Getting out of bed, she headed for the bathroom, feeling cold and lifeless inside, her limbs as heavy as her spirits.

A hot shower, while it warmed her flesh, did little to dispel that inner coldness and she huddled into a towelling robe as she cleaned her teeth.

When she was dressed in a suit the colour of mulberries and a cream shirt, she coiled her hair and stood before the mirror to pin it into place.

With a flawless skin and dark brows and lashes, she normally needed very little in the way of make-up. But now the sight of herself looking like a ghost, with a pale face and hollow cheeks, had her reaching for her cosmetic case.

She had just finished applying a dab of foundation, a little blusher and a touch of lip-gloss when, without warning, the bedroom door opened.

With a gasp, she spun round.

Joel stood in the doorway looking handsome and relaxed and entirely at home. 'Sorry,' he said easily. 'Did I startle you?'

After a moment of stunned disbelief, life and warmth flowed back in a rush. 'I—I thought you'd gone,' she stammered.

'Because I had things to do, arrangements to make, I left quite early. It seemed a shame to wake you, so I borrowed a key to get back in again if you happened to be still asleep.

'I've been rather longer than I'd anticipated, so I'm glad to see you're dressed and ready. All you need to do is pack a case.'

'Pack a case?' she echoed blankly. 'Why do I need to pack a case?'

Sounding as if he was talking to a not-very-bright child, he told her, 'Because you're spending a long weekend with me.'

As she gaped at him, he urged, 'You want to, don't you?' Though it was phrased as a question, he seemed very sure of her answer.

Knowing that if she meekly agreed he might think the worst of her, she shook her head. 'I—I can't.'

'Why not? The other night you told me you had some days due to you.'

'Yes, I do, but I—'

'Then let's get moving. I'll explain everything later. Where do you keep your travel case?'

Excitement running madly through her veins, she said, 'In that cupboard.'

Almost before the words were out, he had opened the cupboard door and taken out one of her small cases. Tossing it on to the bed, he said, 'Throw anything you might need into that. Oh, and don't forget to pick up your passport.'

Always neat and organized, she swiftly found and packed undies, a nightdress and negligée, a couple of changes of clothing, a simple black cocktail dress and a few accessories.

Looking extremely elegant in well-cut trousers and a soft leather jacket, he leaned against the door jamb, one ankle crossed lazily over the other, and watched her.

Having closed the case and zipped it up, she gathered up her coat and shoulder bag and announced breathlessly, 'I'm ready.'

He straightened, saying approvingly. 'An efficient, focused woman, I see.'

As he picked up her case and began to shepherd her towards the door, suddenly remembering, she blurted out, 'Oh, Michael is expecting me to be here.'

'You can phone him as we go.'

One hand at her waist, Joel hurried her out of the house and up the area steps.

By the kerb, a sleek silver limousine was waiting, a shaft of cold winter sunshine that had pierced the low cloud glancing off its polished bonnet.

As they crossed the pavement a uniformed chauffeur jumped smartly out and held open the passenger door.

As soon as she was installed, Joel handed the chauffeur her case and said, 'Let's hope the traffic's not too bad. Time's tight. If we get delayed we may miss our slot.'

Sliding in beside Bethany, he reached to fasten both their seat belts and a moment later they were on their way.

She had just got her breath back and was about to ask him where they were going, when his mobile rang.

With a murmured, 'Excuse me,' he took it from his pocket and answered briskly, 'Joel McAlister.'

The call was a lengthy one and when it was over he said, 'Sorry about that.'

Dropping the phone back in his pocket, he went on, 'I don't usually let business intrude on my private life, but there's an important deal going through that I've really needed to nurse.

'As I had to be on the spot in person in case anything went wrong, and I wanted to spend these few days with you, I decided it would be admissible, for once, to mix business with pleasure.

'However, everything is going smoothly. Which means I can focus entirely on you.' He smiled into her eyes.

His look was so direct, so intent, it was more like being kissed than looked at. It made her head swim.

He moved a fraction and without conscious volition her eyes closed and her lips parted in anticipation of his kiss.

When it didn't come, flustered, she opened her eyes to find he was still looking at her, an amused, faintly mocking smile hanging on his lips.

As the colour rose in her cheeks, he said softly in her ear, 'If I gave way to the temptation to kiss you I might lose control and I don't want to shock Greaves. He's a pillar of the church and a happily married man.'

Knowing he was making fun of her, she blushed even harder and, turning her head away, stared resolutely out of the car window.

Was she doing the right thing throwing caution to the wind and going off like this with a man she still scarcely knew?

But what was the point of asking herself that? Though she was taking a big risk, though she knew full well it could all end in tears, she had chosen to be with the man she knew she loved.

Or perhaps she'd had no choice? Maybe she was so under his spell that she couldn't help herself?

The thought was an uncomfortable one, and a shiver ran down her spine.

'Cold?' he asked solicitously.

'No… No, not at all…' She smiled weakly.

'If you're sure,' he murmured.

Realizing she'd sounded as uptight as she felt, she made a conscious effort to relax, observing, 'I still don't know where we're going.'

'New York.'

'New York!' Surprise made her jaw drop. If she'd had to hazard a guess it would have been Paris or Amsterdam. 'Why New York?'

'My mother was from New York, and most of my business interests are Anglo-American, so now it's my second home. I thought you might like the idea.'

'Oh, I do… It just seems a long way to go for a weekend, and the flights can be awkward—'

'I have a private jet standing by,' he broke in smoothly, 'which greatly facilitates matters.'

Well, it would, she thought, and decided dazedly that when Michael had said his stepbrother was as rich as Croesus he hadn't been far wrong.

Guiltily reminded of Michael, she reached into her bag for her phone.

As though he'd forgotten their earlier conversation, Joel raised an eyebrow at her.

A shade awkwardly, she said, 'I really must talk to Michael before he sets off.'

His silvery-green eyes cool as a glacier, Joel asked, 'What explanation do you intend to give him for not being there?'

'I don't really know,' she admitted. She couldn't bring herself to tell him about Joel. 'But I can't just let him call and find me out.'

She dialled Michael's mobile and, when he answered promptly, blurted out, 'I'm sorry, but I won't be able to have lunch with you.'

'Why won't you?' he sounded cross.

'Something's cropped up and I'm going to be away for the weekend.'

'What's cropped up? Where are you going? Damn it, Bethany, the least you can do is explain.'

'Well, I—'

Taking the phone from her hand, Joel turned it off and dropped it into his own pocket.

Giving her a glinting smile, he said, 'You've told him you're not going to be there. Why make it complicated by trying to explain things?'

A little miffed by his high-handedness, she said, 'Don't you think he's entitled to an explanation?'

'You mean a truthful one?'

She felt her cheeks grow warm. The last thing she had wanted to do was tell Michael the truth.

'Perhaps he's *entitled* to one,' Joel went on caustically. 'But wouldn't it be *unsettling* for him, to say the least, to be told that the woman he's hoping to marry is going off to New York for the weekend with his stepbrother?'

Bethany bit her lip. She had always avoided dealing in lies and deception, but now she seemed to be caught up in that kind of situation. A situation she was totally unprepared for.

The events of the last few days had been so strange and unsettling, so wonderful in some ways, so traumatic in others...

'By the way,' Joel pursued as they reached the airport environs, 'when exactly did Michael ask you to marry him?'

'Last night when he took me home.'

'Not before you went up to Cumbria?'

'Certainly not... Surely you don't think—' She broke off.

'Don't think what?'

When, biting her lip, she stayed silent, he urged, 'Do go on.'

Taking a deep breath, she said, 'Think that if Michael had

already proposed and I'd had the slightest intention of marrying him, I would have…'

'Slept with me?' he finished for her. 'As you didn't know then that Michael and I were related, what was there to have stopped you?'

The impact of his words sent her reeling. He really *did* believe she was promiscuous. Something inside her, a hope for the future, a surviving dream perhaps, shrivelled up.

As they came to a halt at the terminal, he said with satisfaction, 'We've had a pretty good run through. We ought to be able to complete the formalities and take our slot with no hassle. Then, thanks to the time difference, we should be in Manhattan by early afternoon.'

'I've decided I've made a mistake. I don't want to go with you,' she informed him jerkily.

With no change of expression, he said, 'I'm afraid it's much too late for second thoughts.'

Setting her teeth, she repeated, 'I've no intention of going with you.'

He smiled, but it was sharp and it was fierce. 'So what do you intend to do?'

'I'll get a taxi back to London.'

'What's made you change your mind?'

'I hate to be thought promiscuous,' she blurted out. As he opened his mouth to speak, her grey eyes flashing, she cried, 'Don't bother to deny it. That's why you walked away that morning without a word.'

'I did no such thing,' he denied flatly. He added, 'And *I* hate to be thought a swine.'

Brought up short, she gaped at him foolishly. 'What do you mean?'

'After the night we'd just spent together, only a complete and utter swine would have walked away without a word.'

As hope was reborn like a phoenix from the ashes, she began urgently, 'Then why—'

'Something unexpected happened. Look, I'll explain later. There's no time now, here's the welcoming committee arriving.'

The 'welcoming committee' consisted of a smart young man, who greeted them deferentially, and one of his minions who took Bethany's case and Joel's leather briefcase.

Joel's arm at her waist, her thoughts in a turmoil, she allowed herself to be escorted into the airport buildings without further protest.

But as she went through the checks and procedures, she realized that even if there *was* an explanation, it didn't necessarily follow that it would make any difference to what he believed. It certainly wouldn't alter what he'd said in the car a short time ago…

After all the formalities had been completed, they were welcomed aboard the gleaming executive jet by a middle-aged quietly spoken steward with a French accent whom Joel addressed as Henri.

While Bethany's belongings were stowed away and the door closed and secured, they took their seats and fastened their belts before the plane began to taxi down the runway.

Take-off was smooth and effortless and, after climbing steeply, they were soon above the cloud layer and into bright sunshine.

When they levelled out, Joel unfastened his seat belt and said politely, 'I'd like to have a word with the pilot, if you'll excuse me?'

'Of course.'

'Perhaps you'd care to take a look round? Oh, and in the meantime if there's anything you want, just ask Henri.'

As Joel went into the cockpit, the white-jacketed steward came from the galley and showed Bethany into an attractive lounge area.

She refused the champagne and caviare he offered but accepted a cup of coffee, which appeared as if by magic and proved to be excellent.

While she sipped, she looked around her. She had never travelled in a privately owned jet before and was bowled over by the opulence of her surroundings.

A cream cushioned couch and two armchairs, an inlaid coffee table between them, stood on a sumptuous carpet, while to the right was a video screen and music centre. Opposite, hung a beautiful Monet whose colours echoed the delicate blues and pinks and lilacs of the carpet.

The only utilitarian thing there was a small businesslike desk with a laptop computer and a black leather swivel chair.

Her coffee finished, she put her cup and saucer on the table and went to explore further.

At the far end of the cabin, next to a well-appointed shower room and toilet, was a small, but luxurious bedroom.

Looking at the bed, she frowned. Why did a businessman need a bed with black silk sheets that fairly breathed seduction, unless he regularly mixed business with pleasure?

Perhaps he did. Maybe she was just one of many who'd been only too willing to accompany him on his 'business' trips.

Though she knew from his sexual expertise that he was an experienced man with a powerful libido, he had a certain asceticism, and she knew—or *thought* she knew—that he was capable of exercising a remarkable degree of restraint and self-control.

Did that self-control, that apparent restraint, that touch of asceticism, serve to conceal the soul of a libertine?

It was a far from pleasant thought and she faced the undeniable fact that she'd been a fool to come. But she didn't *have* to sleep with him. She could always refuse.

Shaken to realize just what kind of man she might have fallen in love with, she made her way back to the lounge and sat down in one of the armchairs.

She had only been there a short time when the door opened and Joel appeared. He put his briefcase on the desk and, taking off his jacket, dropped it over the back of the swivel chair, saying cheerfully, 'Jack says it should be a good, smooth flight.'

Then, his eyes fixed on her face, he queried, 'What's wrong?'

'Nothing's wrong,' she denied swiftly.

'Something's upset you,' he said with certainty. 'What is it?'

'I was just wondering why you needed a bed,' she said in a rush.

He raised a well-marked brow. 'You mean apart from to sleep in?'

'Is that all you use it for?'

His eyes gleamed silver. 'It's all I've used it for up to press, though I must confess I was hoping this trip might be different.'

'I imagine every trip is *different*.' There was scorn in her voice.

He raised a brow. 'You think I regularly mix business and pleasure?'

'Don't you?'

'As a rule I keep business and pleasure strictly separate. *You* are the exception to that rule and, incidentally, the only woman I've ever brought aboard.'

His words held the ring of truth. And, thinking so little of her, why would he bother to lie?

'But would any man on his own choose to have black silk sheets?' She spoke the thought aloud.

'I've never asked for black silk sheets. I leave the details to Henri.'

Drily, he added, 'Perhaps he's trying to live up to the millionaire image? Or maybe his taste runs to the exotic? Either way, if black silk sheets bother you, I'll ask to have them replaced by white linen.'

'They don't bother me,' she said hurriedly. 'As I've absolutely no intention of—'

A knock at the door made her stop in mid-sentence and a moment later the soft-footed steward wheeled in a lunch trolley.

'Thank you, Henri,' Joel said briskly. 'We can serve ourselves.'

Turning to Bethany he asked, 'What would you like? Seafood? Chicken? Salad?'

'I'm not hungry.' It was the truth. She felt too churned up to eat.

'Did you have any breakfast?'

'No,' she admitted.

'Then, as I object to eating alone, I'd like you to join me.'

'I'm really not hungry,' she said tersely.

'You're plenty slim enough, and going without food this long can't be good for you.'

When she stayed stubbornly silent, he sighed. 'Well, I can't force you to eat…'

She was just feeling a sense of triumph when he went on blandly, 'But after looking forward to having someone to share things with, I'll have to think of some other activity we can indulge in.'

As, her heart picking up speed, she stared at him, he added, 'I'm reluctant to ask Henri to change the sheets before lunch, so it's just as well they won't bother you.'

Agitation brought her to her feet. 'You can't force me to go to bed with you either.'

'I wouldn't bet on that if I were you. Though *force* is hardly the right word…'

Rising in one lithe movement, he eased her backwards, leaning into her so that she was trapped between his body and the bulkhead. Then, one arm each side of her, he bent until his lips were almost brushing hers and added softly, 'Persuade is nearer the mark.'

She could smell the clean scent of his skin mingling with his spicy aftershave and, shivers running down her spine, she threatened, 'If you don't let me go I'll call for Henri.'

He laughed as if genuinely amused. 'Do you imagine that a man who is dissolute enough to have black silk sheets on his bed won't employ a steward who is conveniently deaf?'

'You said the sheets weren't your choice,' she said in a strangled voice.

'Did you believe me?'

Angry that he was laughing at her, she snapped, 'No, I didn't,' and tried to break free, but his arms were like steel bars.

He touched his lips to the side of her neck. 'Well, it happens to be the truth. Though, having agreed to spend the weekend with me, I would have thought you'd take silk sheets in your stride.'

'You make it sound as if I'm in the habit of spending weekends with men...'

He leant back and raised a quizzical brow. 'And you're not?'

'No, I'm not.'

'You mean I'm an exception?' He laughed.

'Yes.'

'So tell me why, having agreed to come with me, you now don't want to sleep with me.'

'Because you think I'm promiscuous,' she burst out.

He smiled languidly. 'But I've already said I don't think that.'

She shook her head. 'That isn't what you said. You simply denied that you'd walked out on me.'

'Which again is the truth, but I suppose you don't believe that either.'

Wanting to believe him, she said distractedly, 'You said you'd explain... I don't know what to believe until I've heard that explanation.'

'Then let's call a truce and over lunch I'll tell you exactly what happened.'

'Even if I believe you it won't make any difference. It won't alter the way you feel about me. It won't alter what you said in the car.'

Innocently, he asked, 'What did I say in the car?'

The cynical words seemed burnt into her brain. 'You said, "As you didn't know then that Michael and I were related, what was there to have stopped you?"'

He smiled to himself, amused that she could recollect what he had said, word for word. 'That was a question, not an accusation. Perhaps I expected you to answer something like, Because I'm not that kind of woman… I have a conscience… A code of morals…'

'If I had said any of those things, would you have believed me?'

'I might have, except for one thing…'

She knew quite well what that one thing was. She had agreed to spend the weekend with him, though she still hadn't given Michael a final answer.

Clearly, she said, 'If I'd had any intention of marrying Michael I would never have agreed to come away with you, whether you were related or not.'

He cocked his head to one side. 'So you haven't any intention of marrying him?'

'No, I haven't. I tried to tell him so at the time but he wouldn't take no for an answer.'

'If you hadn't any intention of marrying him, why didn't you admit it when I asked?'

'Because you didn't ask. You *told* me to say no. I thought you were too arrogant by half. You put my back up,' she said emphatically.

'I see.' Then, quick as a rattlesnake striking, 'Why did you turn Michael down?'

'Because I don't love him.'

'What's love got to do with it?'

She looked down shyly. 'As far as I'm concerned, everything. I would never marry a man I didn't love.'

Studying her through long thick lashes tipped with gold—lashes any woman might have envied—he began thoughtfully, 'Tell me something…'

Thrown by the way he was looking at her, she said uncertainly, 'What?'

'Why did you agree to come on this weekend jaunt?'

After a momentary hesitation, she answered as casually as possible, 'Because I wanted to be with you.' It was the truth, yet not the whole truth.

He straightened and, taking her hand, raised it to his lips and kissed the palm. 'That's a good enough answer. Suppose we take it from there and see where we get to?'

She half nodded.

Touching his lips to hers, he asked lightly, 'Now what would you like to eat? And don't tell me you're not hungry.'

'I wouldn't dare.'

He laughed. 'So what's it to be?'

'A little seafood and salad, please.'

When they both had a plate of fresh salmon, prawns and lobster and a glass of chilled white wine, she reminded him, 'You said you would explain.'

He raised his wineglass and took a sip before beginning. 'I woke quite early and it was barely light when I left to fetch my car. You were fast asleep and—'

She looked up at him with innocent grey eyes. 'Why didn't you wake me?'

'I had every intention of coming straight back, but when I got outside I found there was an emergency. The local mountain rescue team had been called out to an injured climber who'd fallen into a ravine the previous night when he was caught in the mist.

'In the early hours of the morning, when the mist started to lift, his companion managed to make it as far as Dundale and raise the alarm.

'The rescue team were desperately short-handed. Two of their men were down with flu and the caretaker, who sometimes goes out with them, was hardly able to move for rheumatism.

'As I know those fells like the back of my hand, and I've been out with the team before, I agreed to go with them.' He leant forward and brushed her cheek affectionately with the back of his hand.

'I would have stopped to explain, but there wasn't a second to lose. In those conditions any delay could have made the difference between life and death. I asked the caretaker to tell you what had happened, and say that if you could wait at the Dundale Inn I'd try to be there by lunch time.

'Presumably he didn't tell you?'

'No... I didn't see him.' If only she had spoken to the man before she'd left, it would have saved her so much pain.

'In the event,' Joel went on, 'the climber was badly injured and it took so long to bring him safely down that it was almost three o'clock when I finally got to Dundale.

'I asked for a Miss Seaton.' His smile crooked, he added, 'Needless to say, there was no Miss Seaton in the register, only a Mr and Mrs Feldon.'

So that was how he'd known.

'I presumed that was why you hadn't waited,' he added evenly.

As she half shook her head, he said, 'Tell me, if the caretaker *had* given you my message, would you have waited?'

'Yes,' she answered without hesitation. She would have waited even if it had meant catching a train back to London.

After a moment, he pursued, 'So are you satisfied that I wasn't rotten enough to just walk out on you?'

'Yes,' she said in a small voice. 'I'm sorry.'

They finished their lunch without speaking, each, it seemed, busy with their thoughts.

Henri had removed the trolley and served coffee before Joel broke the silence to ask reflectively, 'How long have you known Michael?'

'About three months.'

'How many times have you been to Lanervic Square?'

'That was the only time.'

'He hasn't taken you there before?'

'No.' Something about Joel's expression made her ask, 'Why should he?'

Then, putting her cup down with a rattle, 'You think we've been going there to spend the night?'

'It did cross my mind that as each of you are encumbered with a flatmate it would have been… shall we say… convenient.'

Tightly, she said, 'I've already told you that I've never slept with Michael.'

'Then if you weren't intending to spend the night with him, why did you go?'

'He wanted me to—' Seeing the wolfish look that had appeared on Joel's face, she broke off, her thoughts suddenly racing, a serious doubt in her mind.

For some reason, encountering his stepbrother at Lanervic Square had upset Michael almost as much as it had upset her. All the colour had drained from his face when Joel had asked him what he was doing there.

But surely if the house was his, he had every right to be there and take who he pleased? Unless it wasn't officially his and he shouldn't have been disposing of the contents until probate had been granted?

'You were saying?' Joel prompted smoothly.

Unwilling to mention the real reason for her visit and perhaps get Michael into trouble, she stuck with the story he'd told. 'He wanted me to see where he used to live.'

For an instant a hard, angry look darkened Joel's handsome face. Then a shutter came down and he said coolly, 'Yes, if I remember rightly, that's what he said at the time.'

Jumping in with both feet, she added, 'I understand the house is his now?'

'So it is...' Joel agreed.

She breathed a sigh of relief. So Michael *had* been speaking the truth. For a minute she had begun to doubt him, to wonder if he could have been lying.

'And he's very anxious to sell it,' Joel went on. 'But, because of the terms of the will, he can't do anything with it for the next two years... Apart from live in it, that is. And he doesn't want to do that.'

He paused, his eyes on her face, as though expecting some comment.

Carefully, she said, 'Yes, he told me that too.' She added, 'Two years seems a long time to wait.'

'Michael's always had a fondness for the good life—wine, women and a predilection for gambling—which makes him an easy prey for the more unscrupulous...'

Bethany heard the ring of steel in his voice as he went on, 'Our grandmother knew that he needed to be protected, so she gave me control until he's twenty-five, in the hope that he would get a bit of sense before then and not throw it all away.'

CHAPTER FIVE

AFTER a few seconds, when Bethany made no comment, Joel changed tack. 'So where did you and Michael meet?'

'He came into the shop early one evening,' she admitted unguardedly.

The sudden tightening of Joel's mouth convinced her she was on dangerous ground and she found herself wondering, as Michael wasn't supposed to sell the house until he was twenty-five—even after probate had been granted—did that go for the contents as well?

Maybe *that* was why, when she'd asked, 'How many pieces do you want to part with?' he'd said, 'One… Two at the most. Otherwise it might be—' Had he been going to say *obvious* and thought better of it?

'What did he come into the shop for?' Joel asked, his voice casual.

Worried now, she lied awkwardly, 'I imagine it was just to browse.'

'I wasn't aware that he was interested in antiques,' Joel observed mildly.

'I don't think he is,' she admitted.

'Then why go into an antiques shop to browse?'

'Sometimes people who know nothing about antiques will

come in to choose a piece of silver or porcelain as, say, a wedding gift,' she told him truthfully.

'I see. So what happened when he came in?'

'We… we got talking.' She began to feel a little frustrated.

'What did you talk about?'

Feeling as though she was being given the third degree, she prevaricated, 'I really don't remember.'

'Perhaps that was when he told you he'd inherited his grand-mother's house?'

'It might have been,' she admitted.

'But he didn't mention me?'

She shook her head. 'No. I didn't even know he had a step-brother until the other night.'

On a sudden impulse, she added, 'I gather you and he don't get on too well?'

'No, unfortunately not…'

She saw by the bleakness of Joel's expression that he cared about his young stepbrother and the poor relations between them.

'I've done my best to look after his interests but, as you can imagine, he bitterly resents the fact that I have control… Which makes things difficult, without an added complication.'

Painfully aware that *she* was the 'added complication' Bethany said carefully, 'Rather than make things any more dif-ficult, I could step out of both your lives, make certain I never saw either of you again…'

At that instant there was a knock at the door.

Frowning a little, Joel called, 'Come in.'

When the steward appeared, he said shortly, 'Yes, Henri, what is it?'

'Captain Ross sends his apologies, sir, but could he take another look at the chart you showed him earlier? Apparently he has a query.'

'I'll only be a minute,' Joel said to Bethany and, while the steward began to gather up the coffee cups, took a small flip chart from his briefcase and vanished into the forward cabin.

Henri had started to follow Joel, the loaded tray in his hands, when he caught the protruding corner of the briefcase and toppled it on to the floor, spilling its contents.

Murmuring an apology, he was about to put the tray back on the table when Bethany said, 'It's all right, Henri, I'll pick it up.'

'Thank you, miss.' A moment later the door slid to behind him.

Crouching, she righted the briefcase and began to gather together the various papers. As she did so, her fingers touched something metallic.

Her heart suddenly pounding, and feeling as though she had just been kicked in the solar plexus, Bethany found herself looking down at an intricate gold bracelet set with deep red stones.

Rooted to the spot, she was still staring at it when the door opened and Joel reappeared.

Following the direction of her gaze, he observed, 'Ah, you've found it.' He strode over and, taking her arm, helped her to her feet.

Feeling guilty for no reason, she explained uncomfortably, 'Your case got knocked off the desk and I was just…'

'Yes, Henri mentioned it,' he said evenly.

Picking up the bracelet, he took her hand and slipped it on to her wrist.

While he replaced the contents of the briefcase and fastened it, she stared at the bracelet. 'I thought I'd left it at The Dunbeck. I tried ringing the caretaker, but I couldn't get any answer.'

Then, lifting puzzled grey eyes to his face, 'I don't understand how it came to be in your briefcase.'

'I brought it along with the intention of returning it to you.'

'But where did you get it?' she questioned.

'You'd left it in the bathroom, so on an impulse I picked it up.' He shrugged.

'Why did you keep it?'

Just for a split second he looked disconcerted, before he said lightly, 'You could call it safeguarding my interests. If you didn't happen to wait for me at the Dundale Inn, at least I'd have an excuse to see you again.'

She felt a rush of gladness. He had wanted, *intended,* to see her again. Yet, even as warmth spread through her, part of her brain insisted that his explanation wasn't logical. Somewhere there was a flaw in it.

Before she could pin it down, he said, 'But, to get back to what we were saying before Henri came in. You had just offered to step out of both Michael's life and mine… Make certain you never saw either of us again. Would you be prepared to do that?'

She hesitated. The thought of never seeing Joel again made her feel as though she was mortally wounded. But if that was what he wanted now he'd had time to think about it and consider the possible repercussions…

Lifting her chin, she said quietly, 'Yes. If that's what you want.'

He pierced her with his gaze. 'It isn't.'

As she looked at him, hoping against hope that she'd heard right, he went on, 'I happen to want you in my bed, in my life. In fact I wouldn't be prepared to let you go, even for Michael's sake.'

Her heart swelled.

As though pushing away any lingering concern, Joel took her hand and, a glint in his eye, suggested softly, 'Speaking of bed, what if I ask Henri to change the sheets?'

Embarrassed, she begged. 'Oh, no… Please don't.'

'Does that mean you still don't want to go to bed with me?'

She shook her head. 'No, it means I've decided I like black silk sheets.'

Laughing, he said, 'I do love a woman who isn't afraid to change her mind. I'll just tell Henri that we're going to bed for a couple of hours and don't want to be disturbed.'

'Oh, but what will he think?' She turned away shyly.

'He won't think anything. And, if he does, he's French and a man of the world.'

Seeing she still looked uncomfortable, Joel said a shade mockingly, 'Don't worry, I'll make sure he doesn't class you as a lady of easy virtue.'

Refusing to rise to the bait, she stayed silent and watched as he slid aside the door and disappeared into the forward section.

He came back a minute or so later carrying a bottle of vintage champagne and a couple of glasses. With a lazy smile he said, 'Henri seemed to think champagne was fitting, and I didn't want to disappoint him.'

Having unwired the cork and eased it out with a satisfying pop, Joel filled the flutes with a foaming gush of wine. When the bubbles had subsided he handed her a glass and raised his own. 'To us.'

Then, finding it a sweet amusement to tease her, 'Here's to joining the Mile-High Club.'

'The Mile-High Club?' She looked puzzled.

'A mere handful of people who are able to make love more than a mile above the earth's surface.'

Feeling her colour rise, she said, 'Oh… I see…'

An innate shyness making her unable to meet his laughing eyes, she looked down at her glass and watched the bubbles rising in a golden shower to the surface before taking her first sip.

The wine was cool and crisp on her tongue, making her whole body tingle as it went down. Or was that simply excitement and anticipation?

As soon as their glasses were empty, he put them both on the table and, taking her hand, led her through to the bedroom.

He lowered the blinds, shutting out the brightness, before taking the pins from her hair and letting the dark, silky mass tumble round her shoulders. Then, burying his face in it, he breathed in its perfume while his hands traced her slender curves.

When he began to undress her it was slow and erotic, as he caressed and tasted each new piece of creamy flesh until she was totally naked and on fire for him.

Murmuring how lovely she was, how much he wanted her, he held her hips between his hands and leaned her gently back until she was on the bed. Then, his eyes heavy-lidded and sensual, he stroked his fingertips up and down the smooth satiny skin of her inner thighs.

Her breathing quickened as he explored further, his probing touch light, delicate, yet already producing the most exquisite sensations.

When he brought her right to the very brink and then drew back, it was all she could do to prevent herself from begging.

Her stomach was still tied in knots when he put his hands beneath her buttocks and, lifting her higher, bent his head. The flick of his tongue sent her up like a young supernova exploding into being.

As she plucked a star from the firmament of pleasure, he gently eased her head on to the pillow and settled her into a more comfortable position, before stepping away.

When she floated back to earth and opened her eyes, he was stripping off his own clothes. The black silk sheets felt cool and exotic against her heated flesh as she lay watching him.

With broad shoulders and lean hips and carrying not an ounce of spare weight, he had a superb male physique. Muscles rippled beneath a clear, lightly bronzed skin that gleamed like oiled silk, making her want to stroke it. His legs were straight, with a scattering of golden hair, the line of his spine long and elegant.

When he took off his dark silk boxer shorts, though she had thought herself more than satisfied, her stomach clenched in anticipation.

Glancing up and seeing her watching him, he smiled at her, a smile that was neither self-conscious nor vain. He looked assured, confident, like a man completely at ease with his own masculinity.

He was a passionate lover, yet he made love with a care and sensitivity that showed he put his partner's pleasure ahead of his own.

After—sated and content—she had slept for a while in his arms, he wakened her with a kiss and made love to her again, this time displaying an inventive ardour that had them rolling in an erotic tangle of limbs on the black silk sheets.

When she awoke for the second time, she was alone in the bed. A glance at her watch told her they must be approaching their destination.

Her clothes had been placed on a gold velvet boudoir chair and, gathering them up, she went through to the adjoining shower room.

It appeared that Joel had already showered. The clean, fresh scent of his shower gel still hung in the air and fine drops of water spangled the glass.

Swiftly she took her hair up into a knot and stepped under the flow of hot water.

When she was dried and dressed, her dark hair once more in a smooth coil, she glanced at her reflection in the mirror. A tinge of apricot colour lay along her high cheekbones and the smoke-grey eyes that looked back at her had a lit-from-within radiance.

Satisfied that she no longer looked like a ghost, and needed no help from cosmetics, she made her way back to the lounge.

There was no sign of Joel and she was wondering whether to go in search of him when there was a tap at the door and Henri came in carrying a tray set with delicate china.

She felt her face grow warm.

But, his eyes respectfully lowered, he informed her, 'Mr McAlister asked me to say that we will be landing in just over half an hour. He's with Captain Ross at the moment, but he'll be joining you shortly. In the meantime he thought you might like a cup of tea.'

'Thank you, I would.'

Putting the tray down, the steward enquired, 'Would madam prefer milk or lemon?'

'Milk, please.'

When he'd poured the pale amber liquid, he enquired solicitously, 'Would madam care for anything to eat?'

'Oh, no, thank you. The tea will do fine.'

He gave a half bow and, eyes still lowered, made his way out.

Feeling a little dazed, Bethany stared after him. Where earlier the steward had been merely polite, this time his manner had been positively deferential and she noted with surprise that he had changed her mode of address from miss to madam.

What on earth had Joel said to him? she wondered as she sat and sipped her tea. She was still wondering a few minutes later when the door opened and Joel came in.

Tilting her face proprietorially, he kissed her and said, 'You look quite glowing. Making love in the afternoon must suit you.'

Watching her colour rise, he added, 'In this day and age it's rare to see a woman blush so delightfully.'

Knowing that if she allowed it he could have her in a perpetual state of turmoil, she tried to ignore his teasing and, in an attempt to hide how much he could affect her, said as coolly as possible, 'I understand we'll be landing soon.'

He glanced at his watch. 'That's right. By the way, I take it you couldn't fault Henri's demeanour?'

She shook her head. 'In fact, he was so deferential I couldn't help but wonder what you'd said to him.'

'I made it clear that you were special, not just some casual girlfriend.' He smirked.

If only he meant it. Her voice a little uneven, she asked, 'Why did you tell him that?'

'You were afraid of being classed as 'easy' so it seemed to be the best way to ensure his respect…

'Incidentally, I spoke to my housekeeper a short time ago and, as we'll be sharing a room, I told her the same.' His tone was casual, but the hint of authority made her stomach flip.

Briskly, he added, 'Now, as we're due to land in a matter of minutes, I suggest we get belted up.'

The landing was a smooth one and in no time at all they had cleared the runway and were taxiing towards the airport buildings.

When all the formalities were over, with a great deal of pomp and circumstance, they were escorted out to a waiting limousine.

It was a bitterly cold afternoon but still bright and sunny, with a sky the pale, delicate blue of forget-me-nots, criss-crossed with the gauzy white ribbons of vapour trails.

Standing to attention by the sleek silver car, the chauffeur gave them a smart salute. 'Good afternoon, sir, madam, nice to have you back. I hope you had a good flight?'

'Very good, thank you, Tom. How's the traffic?'

'Much as usual, Mr McAlister. Could be worse. Shouldn't be too late getting home.'

'That's good.'

When Joel had fastened their seat belts and they were heading for Manhattan, Bethany remarked, 'You haven't told me where you live.'

'I live in an old brownstone on Mulberry Street, Lower Manhattan, a house I originally bought and had refurbished for my mother.'

'Oh…' She was surprised.

Picking up that surprise, he asked quizzically, 'What did you expect? Some glass and chromium penthouse overlooking Central Park?'

That was almost exactly what she had expected.

When she admitted it, he grinned and said, 'Don't look so sheepish. A lot of people who don't know me well make that mistake.

'And, as a matter of fact, I did have a Fifth Avenue penthouse for a while; it was only after my mother died that I moved into Mulberry Street.'

'And you like living there?'

'It suits me very well. When I first bought the brownstone it was in a poor state, but after it was refurbished it became a pleasant place to live…'

Then, on her wavelength as he often was, he observed drily, 'I see you're wondering why I didn't simply buy a house that didn't need refurbishing. And of course I could have done. But my mother wanted one that could be restored to its original character, so this place was ideal.

'There was a great deal of skilled work to do when I first bought it, and it took a dedicated team six months to turn it back into the beautiful house it had once been.'

Bethany smiled at him adoringly. 'So your mother was pleased with it?'

'Oh, yes, she loved it. Just before she died she told me that the two years she had lived there had been the happiest of her life…'

In spite of the heavy traffic it didn't seem long before Manhattan's skyscrapers came into view and, as always, Bethany was enthralled.

Watching her face, he asked, 'Glad to be back?'

Suddenly full up, she nodded. No matter what the future held, she was in New York with the man she loved. It was a wonderful thought.

By the time they reached Mulberry Street, a pleasant tree-lined street not far from Greenwich Village, the sun had gone down and lights were starting to twinkle in the blue dusk.

When they drew to a halt by the kerb, Joel helped Bethany out and, while the chauffeur dealt with the luggage, escorted her up the front stairs and into the lighted hallway.

The walls had been painted ivory, while the floor and stairs were carpeted in rich burgundy. The line of the staircase was elegant, the cherry wood banisters and newel posts polished to gleaming perfection.

As she glanced around her, a door opened and a neatly dressed middle-aged woman appeared.

Smiling at them both, she said, 'Welcome home. It's nice to see you back, Mr McAlister. I hope you had an enjoyable flight?'

'Most enjoyable,' Joel assured her, giving Bethany a wicked sideways glance that made her cheeks grow warm.

Then, taking her hand, he said, 'Bethany, darling, this is Mrs Brannigan, Tom's wife and a housekeeper *par excellence*.'

Clearly pleased by the compliment, Mrs Brannigan gave them both a beaming smile and said, 'It's nice to meet you, Miss Seaton.'

Though shaken by the *darling,* Bethany managed to smile back.

'Will you be wanting dinner?' the housekeeper pursued.

As Bethany hesitated, Joel answered, 'No thanks, Molly. I thought we'd eat out.'

'Then a cup of tea, perhaps?'

'That would fit the bill nicely.'

When the housekeeper had taken their coats and hung them in the hall cupboard, a hand at Bethany's waist, Joel suggested, 'While we're waiting, let me give you a quick tour of the place, so you feel at home…

'Molly and Tom have the ground floor,' he went on as they crossed the hall, 'and the kitchens are at the rear. This is the living room and, next to it, my office…'

The living room, a spacious, attractive room, was classically decorated in warm shades of red and cream, while his study was a restful mint-green.

As he showed her round, it was apparent that Joel's interior designer was an artist who liked clear, clean colours.

There were pocket doors with exquisitely etched birds and flowers, dark, gleaming woodwork and rich, jewel-bright colours: sapphire and jade, gold and garnet, purple and lapis lazuli.

It was as beautiful and vivid as a stained glass window and, though she had always tended to be conservative when it came to colour, Bethany was caught up by a wave of pleasure.

'What do you think?' he asked as they returned to the living room.

Turning shining eyes on him, she answered, 'It's absolutely wonderful.'

He smiled. 'I'm glad you like it.'

So far most of the furniture had been made up of carefully chosen antiques, but the suite was up-to-date and comfortable-looking, and the music centre and television were state-of-the-art.

As they sat down on the cushioned couch there was a tap at the door and the housekeeper came in with their tea.

'Could I have a word, Mr McAlister?'

'Of course, Molly. What is it?'

After a momentary hesitation, the housekeeper said, 'Miss Lampton rang again this morning to ask when you would be back.'

'Did you tell her?'

'Yes… I tried to put her off, but she was very insistent.' Molly's lips tightened with disapproval. 'I hope I did the right thing.'

He sat back. 'That's fine. Don't worry about it.'

Looking relieved, the housekeeper went, closing the door behind her.

Joel poured the tea and handed Bethany a cup before asking, 'How are you coping with the jet lag?'

'Fine. As a rule when I come to the States I try to stay awake until bedtime, and I find that usually works well.' She sipped her tea.

'Good. Fancy going to the Trocadero tonight?'

Bethany was well aware that the Fifth Avenue nightclub was *the* place to be seen, and she'd heard it said that if you weren't royalty, a top celebrity, or a multi-millionaire it was next to impossible to get a table.

She was shaken to realize afresh that the man she loved belonged in that bracket. It put him among the elite, and right out of her league.

Suddenly she wished passionately that he wasn't wealthy, but just an ordinary man. If he didn't have money, there might be some chance of *staying* in his life—working alongside him, buying a small house, having his children, building a future together…

'You're looking very serious.' Joel's voice broke into her thoughts. 'If the Trocadero isn't a good choice, we can—'

'Oh, it *is*,' she broke in. 'Except that I've nothing to wear.'

'What about the little black cocktail dress I saw you packing? That will—'

He broke off as the door opened and a tall, slender girl in her late teens or early twenties, wearing a mink coat and a soft matching hat, came in.

As he rose to his feet, she cried, 'Joel, darling! So you're back at last. You'll never know how I've missed you!'

Her accent was upper-class and an aura of wealth and breeding and privilege hung round her like a jewelled cloak.

Polished and sophisticated, trailing a cloud of French perfume, she crossed the room and, throwing her arms around his neck, stood on tiptoe to kiss him on the lips.

Sitting frozen, watching how she pressed herself against him, Bethany had no doubt at all that they were lovers.

After a moment or two, he reached up to unwind her arms.

'How are you, Tara?' he asked coolly. 'You're looking very well.'

That was an understatement, Bethany thought. A natural redhead, with an oval face, huge blue eyes fringed with long, dark lashes and a full passionate mouth painted a rich coral, the newcomer looked like a vivid oil painting.

Beside her, Bethany felt drab and colourless.

For the first time in her life, she found herself envying another woman. Not only because of her glowing looks, but because of her class and her secure place in Joel's world.

This was the sort of woman he would doubtless choose to marry.

Sounding a shade uncertain, Tara asked, 'Is Michael with you?'

Almost curtly, Joel answered, 'No.'

Looking relieved, she rushed on, 'Why on earth didn't you let me know you were coming? I'd have met you at the airport.

'Oh darling, it seems an age since I saw you. I'd started to think you were never coming back—'

Joel's quiet voice cut through the flow. 'I didn't hear the doorbell.'

She held up a fob with a key attached. 'I still have my key.'

He took it neatly from her fingers and dropped it into his pocket.

Pouting prettily, she coaxed, 'You're not still cross with me, are you?'

His voice was cool as her replied. 'Not at all.'

'Then why are you being so horrid? I told you at the time it didn't mean a thing. It was just a bit of fun. We happened to be at the same party and we got high. He asked me back here, and I—'

'Perhaps you should save the explanations for when we're alone?'

Bethany had got to her feet and was heading blindly for the door, when Joel stopped her in her tracks. 'Please don't go.' His voice cracked like a whip.

Tara looked at Bethany as if noticing her for the first time. Then, clearly dismissing her as being of little consequence, she turned back to Joel and, caressing his chin with one coral-tipped finger, coaxed, 'Why don't you take me to the Trocadero tonight and I'll—'

'I already have arrangements for tonight,' he broke in smoothly.

She pouted. 'Can't you alter them?'

'No.'

'Tomorrow, then… It's Lisa's party, and she told me you'd promised both her and her father you'd go. Brian was going to escort me, but I can easily put him off. If you pick me up at seven—'

'I'm afraid I can't do that.'

Obviously getting angry and frustrated, she demanded, 'Why not?'

'Because I'll be escorting my guest…'

As Tara's eyes swivelled in Bethany's direction, he added, 'Now, as you two ladies haven't met, allow me to introduce you…'

While Bethany stood numbly, he crossed the room to take her

hand and draw her forward. 'Darling, this is Tara Lampton…
Tara, Bethany Seaton.'

Guessing that the endearment was intended to make the other
woman jealous, or to bring her to heel, Bethany said through stiff
lips, 'How do you do?'

Tara gave her a look that, if looks could kill, would have
shrivelled her up and, without a word, turned on her heel and
stormed out.

A moment later the front door slammed.

His face expressionless, Joel drew Bethany back to the couch
and, sitting down by her side, observed, 'I'm sorry Tara was so
rude to you. She's always been something of a spoilt brat.'

Without meaning to, Bethany found herself saying accus-
ingly, 'You were trying to make her jealous.'

He lifted a level brow. 'Oh? What makes you think that?'

'You called me darling.'

'I called you darling earlier, if you remember, and I can assure
you that I wasn't trying to make my housekeeper jealous.'

Knowing he was laughing at her, Bethany bit her lip and said
nothing further.

'Now, where were we? Oh, yes, the Trocadero. If you're not
happy wearing the dress you brought I can phone Joshua
Dellon and get a selection of dresses sent round. I have an
account there and—'

'Oh, no!'

'There's no need to look quite so horrified. I've bought clothes
for women before now.'

I just bet you have, she thought. Aloud, she said stiffly, 'Thank
you, but I prefer to buy my own clothes and, as there's no way
I could afford any Joshua Dellon designs, I'll stick with what I've
got. That is if you still want to take me?'

He looked puzzled. 'Why shouldn't I still want to take you?'

'Your girlfriend wasn't happy about it.' Bethany found she could barely meet his gaze.

'My ex-girlfriend,' he corrected. 'It was over several weeks ago, before I went back to London.'

Recalling how possessive the redhead had been, Bethany said drily, *'She* didn't seem to think so.'

'Even if she doesn't want a man any longer, Tara can't bear to lose him.'

'I got the impression that she did want you. That she's still in love with you.'

Using a single finger to tilt her chin, he asked quizzically, 'Jealous?'

'Certainly not,' she denied emphatically.

'So *you're* not in love with me?'

Ambushed by the unexpected question, she gazed at him in silence.

'Well?' he pressed.

Somehow she gathered herself and asked, 'If I said I was, would you believe me?'

'Would you expect me to?'

'No,' she admitted.

His teeth gleamed as he smiled. 'So you're *not* in love with me?'

She took a deep breath. 'No.'

'Well, at least you're more honest than Tara, who swore she loved me madly. Whereas I suspect that all she really wanted was my money and the kind of lifestyle I can offer.'

Remembering the mink, and the air of wealth and breeding the girl had exuded, Bethany said, 'She appeared to already have those things.'

'She's always been privileged. Her father's an English baronet and comparatively wealthy, but last year, after his first wife died, he remarried.

'Tara and her stepmother don't get along too well. And, even if they did, as they both let money run through their fingers like water, it's doubtful if Sir William could afford to keep them both.

'So you see there's pressure on Tara to find a rich and doting husband and move out.' His silvery-green eyes gleaming, he added, 'She seemed to think I'd fit the bill…'

CHAPTER SIX

'But *you* don't.' Bethany held her breath.

'No, I don't,' Joel said flatly.

'You don't intend to marry?'

'Oh, yes, I have every intention of getting married. And before too long. But not to Tara. She's a beautiful woman, and I've no doubt that she would make a glamorous and stimulating wife. But unfortunately not a faithful one.'

Married to a man like Joel, Bethany thought, who in their right mind would want to stray? Aloud she ventured, 'And being faithful is important to you?'

'Yes.' His answer was uncompromising. 'With all this sexual freedom it may seem an old-fashioned concept, but when I marry I want a wife I can trust and respect. Not one I have to continually watch and wonder who else she's going to bed with…'

But would that cut both ways? Bethany wondered.

Displaying that unnerving ability to walk in and out of her mind, he said, 'I only need one woman in my life and when I'm satisfied that I've found the right one I have every intention of being faithful to her.'

If only she was that lucky woman.

But circumstances had already destroyed any faint chance she *might* have stood had things happened differently. All she was and ever would be to him was a fling, a short term affair while he looked for a woman he could trust and respect.

It wasn't what she'd wanted, what she had desperately hoped for. But it was what she'd let herself in for by jumping into bed with him whenever he lifted a finger, and by agreeing to spend these few days with him…

If she had held back, though she wasn't in his league, things *might* have been different. She *might* have gained his respect.

But it was too late now to make him see her in a different light… Or was it? Surely it had to be worth a try?

As she sat silently, feeling as if her heart was being squeezed by a giant fist, he stroked a finger down her cheek.

When she looked up at him, her face defenceless, vulnerable, he remarked, 'If we're going to the Trocadero, perhaps we ought to get moving. Time's getting on and you know what New York traffic's like…'

As they climbed the stairs together, with a sideways glance he suggested enticingly, 'However, we can make time if you'd care to share a shower?'

Her pulses leapt at the thought but, resolved not to commit herself any further until she'd had a chance to think, to decide on her policy, she shook her head.

He looked at her, assessment in his glance, and as though reading what was behind the refusal he made no attempt to persuade her.

Instead, he said, 'Oh, well, I suppose it wouldn't do any harm to save a bit of excitement for later.'

The master bedroom where her small amount of luggage now reposed, was a most attractive room. It had primrose walls, a cream carpet, a king-sized bed, walk-in wardrobes and twin bathrooms tiled in peach. Joel disappeared into the far one and, as she began to unpack her case, she heard the shower start to run.

Just for an instant she was sorely tempted to change her mind and follow him in, but then she found herself wondering how many times he and Tara had shared a shower.

It was a sobering thought, and one which served to stiffen her resolve.

She found fresh panties, her dress, her fun-fur jacket and the necessary accessories, before stowing away the rest of her belongings in the nearest wardrobe, which she was cheered to find was empty.

Then, leaving her bracelet and her pearl studs on the dressing table, she went into the luxuriously fitted bathroom, with its off-white carpet and mirrored walls.

Fifteen minutes later, showered, dried and perfumed, she made up with care and took her newly washed hair up into a fashionable chignon, before putting on her panties and returning to the bedroom.

There was no sign of Joel and no sound from the other bathroom.

Having rolled on silk stockings and slipped her slim feet into high-heeled strappy sandals, she donned her black cocktail dress, the material moulding itself lovingly to her curves as she zipped up the close-fitting bodice and adjusted the spaghetti shoulder straps.

That done, she gave herself a critical glance in the nearest mirror and decided that while she looked no better then all right, she would do.

There had been no time to think about her course of action, but for the evening at least, she decided firmly, she would leave all her worries behind her and simply enjoy the chance to be with Joel.

Leaving the earrings where they were, she slipped the bracelet back on her wrist, gathered up her evening bag and jacket and closed the bedroom door behind her.

As she made her way down the stairs, her earlier half-formed thought that there was some flaw in Joel's explanation of why he'd kept the bracelet returned to chafe her.

He had said something like, 'On an impulse…I picked it up'

That was straightforward and believable.

But then, when pressed, he had added, 'You could call it safe-guarding my interests. If you didn't happen to wait for me at the Dundale Inn, at least I'd have an excuse to see you again…'

That was the part that wasn't logical.

Earlier he had assured her that after fetching his car he'd meant to return, and that only joining the rescue party had stopped him.

At the time he had taken her bracelet, he could have had no idea that he might *need* an excuse to see her again.

So why had he taken it? Why had he lied to her?

As Bethany reached the living room she heard Joel's voice and hesitated. Had he another visitor? Or had Tara returned for a second try?

After a moment it became clear that he was talking on the phone.

'It's of the utmost importance…' he was saying. 'I need the document ready to be signed by tomorrow afternoon…' Then, 'Yes… Yes… Exactly as I've outlined…'

Unwilling to interrupt what was obviously an important business call, she waited.

'Well, at the moment, as far as money and power goes, I'm the best bet. And, however you look at it, the organ grinder has got to be a better proposition than the monkey…

'Yes, Paul, I know it must seem drastic to you, and I admit it's taking a big risk, but I can't see any other way. And I assure you that whether it works or not it has its compensations…

'Yes, yes… If there's any way I can *make* it work, I'm prepared to stick with it…

'I can't rule it out. That's why I want to be sure I can't be ripped off…'

As she waited for the call to end, Bethany became aware of the housekeeper approaching and, unwilling to be found hovering outside the door, turned the knob and walked in.

Joel was standing by the window, the phone in his hand, looking devastatingly handsome in well-cut evening clothes.

As she put her bag and jacket on the couch he acknowledged her presence with a little smile, before ending the call with a brisk, 'Thanks, then, Paul. See you tomorrow afternoon.'

Replacing the phone, he turned to Bethany and, taking both her hands in his, let his eyes travel from her shining head to her slender silk-clad legs. Suddenly uncertain, she asked, 'Will I do?'

'You look wonderful.'

Though she knew he was exaggerating, she could tell he was quite happy with her appearance.

His voice casual, he added, 'But you could do with a necklace and some earrings to complete the picture.'

'I'm afraid I only brought my pearl studs and they don't really go with the bracelet.' Then, awkwardly, 'Joel, about the bracelet…'

'What about the bracelet?' he asked evenly.

'You said you'd taken it so that if I didn't happen to wait at the Dundale Inn you'd have an excuse to see me again…'

'That's what I said,' he agreed evenly.

'But you must have taken it before you knew you might need an excuse.'

His white teeth gleamed in a grin. 'Of course you're right.' Then, curiously, 'What stopped you calling me a liar at the time?'

'I half knew there was a flaw, that your explanation wasn't logical, but I didn't have chance to think it through. Why did you say what you did?' She was hurt; she could feel him laughing at her again.

He smiled wryly. 'Because, at that point, I didn't want to tell you the truth and it was the best explanation I could come up with on the spur of the moment. A poor best, I admit. That's why I changed the subject so hurriedly…

'Now, about that necklace and earrings…'

Standing her ground, she pointed out, 'You still haven't told me why you lied.'

Without answering, he crossed to the far wall and opened a hinged picture to reveal a small safe.

Bethany watched him key in a number and a moment later the door swung open.

Reaching inside, he withdrew a blue leather jewel case and opened the lid. Taking out a necklace and a pair of long earrings, the intricate gold loops of each set with red stones, he told her, 'Because I wanted these to be a surprise.'

Her gaze going from the sparkling jewellery in his hand to the bracelet on her wrist, she said numbly, 'They look as if they match.'

'That's what I thought when I first saw the bracelet, only until then I'd understood that the stones in the earrings and necklace were rubies. When you told me the ones in the bracelet were garnets, I began to have doubts.

'I wanted to see the three pieces together before I said anything…'

Laying the items he was holding on the coffee table, he invited, 'Take a closer look.'

Filled with a kind of agitated excitement, her thoughts stampeding in all directions, she examined the pieces.

'What do you think?' he queried. 'Are they a set?'

'They appear to be.'

His face hard, he asked, 'How did you say you came by the bracelet?'

Completely thrown, wishing she could tell him the truth, but afraid of dropping Michael in it, she answered, 'Someone brought it into the shop.'

'Who?'

'Tony dealt with it.'

'But Feldon didn't want the bracelet so you bought it?'

'Yes.'

'And you don't remember anything about the seller?'

Hating to lie, even tacitly, she shook her head.

'Was it a man or a woman?'

'A man.'

'Feldon Antiques don't ask sellers for any proof of identity or ownership?' He raised a brow quizzically.

They always had when James Feldon had been alive, but she was convinced that Tony wasn't so scrupulous.

Carefully, she answered, 'It all depends.'

'On what?'

'On how valuable the item is. Or if we happen to know the seller.'

'In this case?'

'The bracelet alone wasn't really that valuable.'

'I see.'

After a moment the hardness disappeared from his face and he remarked, 'Well, now you have your set. Let's see how it looks on.'

As he picked up the necklace and moved behind her to clasp it round her neck, she began, 'But the necklace and the earrings aren't—'

'I want you to wear them.' Seeing she was about to argue, he said firmly, 'Wear them now to please me and we'll talk about it later.'

He touched his lips to the warmth of her nape, making her shiver. 'Tom will be outside with the car, and I don't know about you, but I'm getting hungry.'

Responding to his urging, she put on the glamorous drop earrings.

'Let me look at you.' Standing back a little, Joel gave her a critical appraisal. 'They provide the finishing touch. Now you look a million dollars.'

He smiled at her and, like magic, the tension lifted and her heart lightened.

As he helped her into her fun-fur jacket, she got a vivid mental picture of Tara swathed in mink.

As if picking up the thought, he asked, 'Would you like a mink?'

Shaking her head, she said, 'I've never liked real fur,' and caught his look of surprise.

'Most of the women I've met would kill to be dressed in mink.'

'And you approve of that sentiment?'

'Not at all,' he said coolly. 'I've always considered that real fur looks better on animals.'

He put on his own coat and a few seconds later they were descending the front stairs to the waiting limousine.

The night was cold and clear. The sidewalks gleamed and the air had a frosty sparkle to it. Street lamps shone through the skeletal trees and a three-quarter moon was riding high in the indigo sky.

It was a perfect night for romance, Bethany found herself thinking.

As though echoing that sentiment, when Joel reached across to fasten her seat belt he brushed her cheek softly with his lips.

Her heart suddenly felt too big for her chest.

As soon as they were settled into the sleek car, it pulled out to join the stream of traffic that was flowing along Mulberry Street.

Bethany had always found New York vibrant and exciting, especially at night, but with Joel by her side it acquired an extra special magic.

Watching her face in the shifting light and shadow, he said, 'You look as if you enjoy New York as much as I do.'

'It was love at first sight,' she admitted.

'And for me.'

Eager to know more about him, she said, 'Tell me what it's like to live here.'

As they headed Uptown, he talked about his love of New York, of the simple, everyday things that made up his life. Manhattan's canyon-like streets lined with skyscrapers, the parks and open spaces, the theatres and museums, the restaurants and cafés, the little delicatessens and the bookstores.

He told her all about the old-fashioned shop in Little Italy that smelt of cheeses and savoury sausages, of wine and pickles and herbs and spices; the restaurant in Chinatown that served steaming *dim sum* and pots of jasmine tea...

Spoken with less enthusiasm, it might have sounded mundane, ordinary, but what made it extraordinary was the warmth, the sheer enjoyment of life, that emanated from every word.

It provided an insight into the man himself and she listened, enthralled. This was someone not in the least materialistic, someone who, even had he been poor, would still have known how to get the best out of life...

'Here we are.' Joel's voice broke into her thoughts and a second or two later they were drawing up at the kerb.

From the outside, the Trocadero appeared simple and understated, a sheer expanse of black glass with only its name in discreet gold letters.

A black and gold awning stretched across the sidewalk to where a man in black and gold livery was waiting to open the door.

As soon as they were inside the elegant black and white foyer, a man in immaculate evening dress came forward to greet them.

'Good evening, Mr McAlister, madam.'

They were relieved of their coats and led through to an inner foyer, where a double archway led to a spectacular black and white dining area with a central dance floor.

The *maître d'* was about to show them to their table when a female voice cried, 'Joel, darling! What luck!'

With a sinking heart, Bethany turned to see Tara, looking striking in an emerald-green dress and matching stole, standing close by. She was accompanied by a narrow-faced, effeminate-looking young man and a well-dressed older couple.

Taking Joel's arm possessively, she smiled up at him. 'You will join us, won't you…? He must join us, mustn't he, Daddy?' she appealed to the older man.

'Please do,' he returned civilly.

'Thank you,' Joel began politely, 'but, as you can see, I'm with—'

'Of course your little friend can come too,' Tara broke in condescendingly.

Ignoring her, Joel turned to address the older man, who was looking downright uncomfortable. 'It's very kind of you to invite us, sir,' he said smoothly. 'But we had planned on a romantic tête à tête.'

Turning to Bethany, he went on, 'May I introduce Sir William Lampton… Sir William, my fiancée, Bethany Seaton.'

Though she knew that Joel was only paying Tara back, Bethany felt as though she'd been kicked in the chest. Somehow she managed to summon a smile and murmur, 'How do you do?'

'Miss Seaton, how nice to meet you.' Taking her proffered hand, Sir William added gallantly, 'If you will allow me to say so, you look delightful…

'May I introduce my wife, Eleanor…? And Tara's friend, Carl Spencer…'

When the polite murmurs had subsided, without so much as a glance in Tara's direction, Joel said, 'Well, if you'll excuse us, I hope you all have an enjoyable evening.'

He put a hand at Bethany's waist and they followed the *maître d'*—who had been hovering at a discreet distance—through the nearest archway and into the dining area where, on a central dais, a small orchestra was playing softly.

Most of the widely spaced tables were already occupied by a well-dressed clientele ranging from the quietly wealthy to the downright ostentatious.

Perfume wafted, jewels glittered and champagne corks popped, while soft-footed waiters moved about and conversation and laughter mingled.

Led by the *maître d'* and followed by two of his minions, they were shown to a table adjoining the dance floor, where a bottle of vintage champagne was waiting in an ice bucket.

As soon as they were seated they were handed white leather menus with gold tassels to peruse, while the wine waiter eased off the champagne cork with a satisfying pop and poured the sparkling wine.

When their order had been given and they were alone, lifting his glass, Joel smiled at Bethany over the rim and toasted, 'To the most beautiful woman in the room.'

Flustered by what she saw as an over-the-top compliment, she said, 'I'm afraid that, compared to some women, I'm nondescript.'

'If you mean Tara, then not in my opinion,' he disagreed. 'Tara is blatantly beautiful, but you have a quiet, haunting loveliness that gets under a man's skin, a luminous, lit-from-within quality that lifts you into a different class.'

'But Tara is—'

'Tara is wilful and unkind,' he said dispassionately.

'I just wish you wouldn't use *me* to pay her back,' Bethany said quietly.

'You think that's what I was doing?'

She looked down at her hands in her lap. 'Wasn't it?'

'No.'

'Oh, I see… You were trying to salvage my pride. I suppose I should feel grateful, but—'

His voice smooth as silk, he told her, 'As I was doing nothing of the kind, there's really no need to feel grateful.'

For a moment she just stared at him before asking, 'Then what made you lie to Sir William?'

He clicked his tongue reprovingly. 'Now, do I look like a man who would lie to a baronet?'

Determinedly ignoring his levity, she said flatly, 'You told him I was your fiancée.'

'I don't regard that as lying, merely jumping the gun a little.'

'Jumping the gun?' she echoed blankly. 'I don't understand.'

'It's quite simple. If we go to Tiffany's tomorrow morning you can choose a ring…'

Her heart beginning to do strange things, she echoed, 'A ring?'

'An engagement ring.' Reaching across the table, he put a finger under her jaw and made a pretence of lifting it. 'Isn't that what couples who are planning to get married usually do?'

Wondering if this was some cruel joke, she said unsteadily, 'But we're not planning to get married.'

'Don't you want to marry me? Or are you just vexed because I haven't proposed in the good old-fashioned way? If it's the latter, then I'll see about rectifying matters later.'

'It's not… I mean…'

'You don't want to be my wife?'

She did. Oh, she did.

Unsteadily, she said, 'This idea of getting married… It's so sudden… So spur of the moment.'

'Not at all. I've had it in mind almost since we met… I told Henri you were my fiancée and we were planning to get married in New York…'

That accounted for the champagne and the change in the steward's manner, Bethany realized dazedly.

'And Molly believes we are,' Joel went on. 'Otherwise she would never have approved of us sharing a room…

'Ah, this appears to be our first course arriving, so I suggest we leave any further discussion until tomorrow and simply enjoy the rest of the evening.'

When the avocado starter had been placed in front of them and the waiter had retired, Joel changed the subject smoothly by asking, 'When were you last in New York?'

'A couple of months ago,' she answered abstractedly.

For the remainder of what proved to be an excellent meal— although afterwards Bethany could not remember what she'd eaten—he kept the conversation light and general.

Allowing herself to be swept along by the tide, she gave up all attempts to think and followed his lead.

When, their coffee finished, he took her hand and led her on to the dance floor, she went into his arms like someone coming home.

He held her close, his cheek against her hair, while for the next hour or so they danced every dance and, for Bethany at least, the time passed in a haze of pleasure.

Even the occasional glimpse of a sparkling Tara dancing with a series of young men failed to douse that pleasure.

After a particularly slow smoochy number, her head on Joel's shoulder, her eyes closed, Bethany was half asleep when he queried, 'Tired?'

'A bit,' she mumbled.

'As it will be the early hours of the morning in London, I suspect that's an understatement, so I suggest we leave before the cabaret starts.'

As though admitting she was tired had compounded that tiredness, she collected her evening bag and sleepwalked her way back to the foyer, where their coats appeared as if by magic.

A supporting arm around her, Joel escorted her out to the waiting limousine and settled her in. By the time he slid in beside her and drew her close, she was fast asleep.

When they reached the brownstone, she surfaced long enough to cross the sidewalk and, Joel's arm about her waist, climb the stairs on legs that felt like indiarubber.

Once in the hallway, Joel slipped her coat from her shoulders before helping her up the stairs and into the bathroom.

Lowering her on to a stool, he asked, 'Think you can manage now?'

She nodded and with fumbling fingers she cleaned her teeth and unpinned her hair…

It was broad daylight when she opened her eyes. She was alone in her bed. Only it wasn't her bed and, though her surroundings were attractive, the room was a strange one.

Her mind a blank, for a moment or two she couldn't think where she was.

Then it all came rushing back. She was in New York. In Joel's house. In Joel's bed. Though without the slightest notion of how she'd got there.

She was naked—apart from the necklace, earrings and bracelet she still wore—but with no recollection of taking off her clothes.

The last thing she could vaguely remember was leaving the Trocadero with Joel's supporting arm around her.

A lethal combination of champagne and jet lag must have suddenly caught up with her.

Frowning, she made an effort to think back, but now the whole evening seemed unreal, the focus shifting, the boundaries blurred. Had Joel really talked about marriage? Or was that just wishful thinking? Something she'd dreamt up…?

She jumped as, without warning, the door opened and Joel strolled in carrying a tray of tea.

Smartly dressed, his corn-coloured hair smoothly brushed, his silvery-green eyes bright, he looked the picture of health and vitality.

Smiling at her, he observed, 'So you're awake at last. How do you feel?'

Knocked sideways by that smile, she pushed herself upright and said huskily, 'Fine, thank you.'

His appreciative gaze on her bare breasts, he murmured, 'That's good.'

Blushing, she pulled up the duvet and trapped it under her arms. 'I don't remember getting undressed or going to bed.'

He put the tray on the cabinet and sat down on the edge of the mattress to pour the tea before he told her, 'I undressed you and put you to bed. You were absolutely shattered. Out on your feet.'

'Oh…' She blushed even harder.

Straight faced, he asked, 'Would it make you feel any better if I told you I kept my eyes closed?'

In no mood to be made fun of, she said crossly, 'No, it wouldn't.'

'Well, in that case I may as well admit that I enjoyed the scenery enormously.'

Then, unrepentantly, 'There's no need to look so *bothered*. I have seen you naked before.'

That was true enough. But somehow the fact that she hadn't been *conscious* made a difference.

Watching her face, reading her discomfort, he frowned. 'Before you put me down as a voyeur or a violator, my interest was healthy and wholesome and, apart from lifting you into bed, I never laid a finger on you.'

An edge to his voice, he added, 'Believe me, I like my women wide awake and cooperative.'

Instantly contrite, and upset because she'd angered him, she whispered, 'I'm sorry. I didn't mean to suggest…' Her smoke-grey eyes filled with tears. Unwilling to let him see them, she bent her head.

Putting a finger beneath her chin, he lifted it.

She blinked and a single bright tear escaped and began to trickle down her cheek.

He cursed himself for his brutish behaviour. Leaning forward, he caught it on the tip of his tongue. 'Don't cry, my darling,' he said softly. 'It's my fault. I was being offensive.'

Almost to himself, he added, 'I tend to think of you as being tougher than you are.'

He kissed her lightly on the lips and, handing her a cup and saucer, ordered gently, 'Now drink your tea.'

Her heart once again full to overflowing, she began to sip.

Studying the faint flush of sleep still lying along her high cheekbones and the dark silky hair tumbling round her shoulders, he sighed.

At her enquiring glance, he told her, 'You look so beautifully tousled and sexy. If you're not out of that bed pretty soon I may well give way to the temptation to rejoin you.'

Uncombed and unwashed, feeling anything but desirable, she was cheered by his words.

Reaching out a hand, he set one of the earrings swinging. 'Far from being nondescript, you look as exotic as Cleopatra in those and the necklace.'

'Why didn't you take them off?'

His even white teeth gleamed in a smile. 'I've always fancied sleeping in the same bed as Cleopatra.'

'How do you come to have them?' she asked cautiously.

'They were my mother's.'

'Oh…' Michael had told her that the bracelet had been his grandmother's.

'My father gave them to her as a wedding gift.'

Her voice not quite steady, Bethany asked, 'Was there a bracelet too?'

'There was originally,' Joel answered. 'The last time I saw my mother wear the set was after my father and his second wife had been killed in a road accident. She wore it when she came over to London for the funeral.'

Seeing Bethany's puzzled frown, he explained, 'My mother left my father and the family home and went back to the States when I was three years old.'

'So you were brought up in the States.'

He shook his head. 'She didn't take me. My mother had never wanted children and after my birth she suffered from depression. We saw virtually nothing of each other until I was grown up.'

There was a bleakness in his voice that—thinking of her own happy childhood—almost brought tears to Bethany's eyes. 'Oh, I'm sorry…' she whispered.

'Which goes to prove you have a kind heart,' he said derisively. 'But there's really no need to feel sorry for me. My grandmother was very fond of me and looked after me extremely well until I was seven.

'It was then my father met and married a young widow with a one-year-old baby…'

'Michael?'

'That's right.'

'So you had a real mother at last.' She smiled up at him with wide innocent eyes. Joel leant forward and tucked a stray tendril behind her ear.

'Unfortunately not. My stepmother didn't like me. I can't say I blame her. I was an awkward brat who fiercely resented her taking over my father's life.

'Finally she got fed up and told him either I went or she did…'

Her eyes on his face, Bethany waited.

After a moment he said bleakly, 'There was no contest. Despite my grandmother's objections—she thought I was too young—my father decided to send me away to boarding school.'

Sorry for the child who must have felt rejected by both of his parents, she put her hand on his.

For an instant he looked startled. Then he took her hand and gave it a squeeze. 'As I just said, you have a kind heart.'

This time there was no derision in the words.

CHAPTER SEVEN

AFTER a short pause, feeling the need to know, Bethany asked, 'So you went to boarding school?'

'For a few months, but I was so unhappy that I ran away. Needless to say, I was soon tracked down and taken home.' His laugh was cold.

'My father was furious and made arrangements to send me back. But this time my grandmother put her foot down and refused to let me go. Instead she suggested that my aunt and her husband, who had no children of their own, might have me for a while.

'They said they'd be happy to give it a try. Looking back, I don't think any of them really expected me to settle so far away from London…'

'Your aunt… did she live in Cumbria?'

'Got it in one. She and her husband have a farm in the Dundale Valley that's been in her husband's family for generations.'

Bethany urged him to continue. 'And you liked it there?'

'Loved it. Even when I was finally sent away to boarding school I regarded the farm as home and always went back there during the holidays. I still visit them regularly.'

So that explained his connection with the Lakes, and his knowledge of the fells…

Glancing at his watch, he said, 'I suggest we get moving. It's almost eleven and we've a busy day ahead.'

'Doing what?' she asked.

His voice casual, he told her, 'Visiting my solicitor, lunching in China Town—that is if you like Chinese food…?'

'I've never tried it,' she answered shyly.

'In that case you must certainly try it.' Then, with no change in tone, 'After lunch we'll go and choose a ring and if we're getting married tomorrow, as I'd planned—'

Bethany was shocked. 'But we can't possibly get married to-morrow.'

'Of course we can. All we have to do is go to the nearest city clerk and apply for a marriage licence, which we then sign in his presence. That's all there is to it.'

Not sure whether she was on her head or her heels, she said, 'Surely there's more to it than that?'

'Not in New York State. After a waiting period of twenty-four hours, the wedding can take place. All we need is someone in authority to actually perform the marriage ceremony.'

Though it was all her dreams and wishes realized and gift-wrapped, with a sudden, unreasonable feeling of panic she remembered the old warning, *Be careful what you wish for, it may come true.*

Watching her face, he said carefully, 'Of course there's one very important thing that still needs to be done.'

He took her hand and, raising it to his lips, dropped a kiss in the palm. 'Will you marry me?'

Her heart leapt wildly in her breast and for an instant she was tempted to say yes, to snatch at the happiness he seemed to be offering. But common sense stopped her.

Her throat desert dry, she said huskily, 'I don't understand why you want to marry me.'

His raffish smile melted her heart. 'Then you underrate your feminine charms.'

It was, in a way, a flattering answer. But as he was a man who, not only because of his wealth and position but because of his looks and charisma, could have his pick of beautiful women, it wasn't one she was prepared to accept at face value and she said so.

His eyes glinting between long, thick lashes, he said, 'In that case I'll put it even more simply. It's you I want in my bed.'

With a mixture of pain and pleasure and regret, she pointed out, 'I'm already there. You don't have to marry me.'

'I *want* to marry you.'

She still didn't believe him…couldn't let herself believe him. 'Why? Though my parents are decent people, I'm not from a wealthy background or—'

'As I've no intention of asking for a dowry—' he grinned '—I don't need anyone from a wealthy background.'

Her voice sounded meek as she continued. 'I don't really belong in your world—'

'Let me be the judge of that.' He lifted her chin so her gaze met his.

Trying to keep a level head despite the passion in his eyes, she said hesitantly, 'You don't really know me. I could be spiteful, mean-spirited, bad-tempered, awful to live with—'

'I don't believe you're any of those things,' he broke in calmly. 'And, as for not knowing you, when you're my wife, I'll get to know you.'

'But if you discover then that you've made a mistake, that you really don't like me, it will be too late. If we waited a while, got to know each other first…'

Joel frowned. After what he'd seen as a token hesitation the previous night, he had fully expected her to agree without further ado and this resistance surprised him.

Levelly, he said, 'I don't want to wait. Believe me, I'm not only used to making snap decisions, I'm used to those decisions being right.'

She sighed. 'But in business it's not such a big risk. If it happens to be the wrong decision it should be possible to rectify it. Marriage isn't like that…'

He raised an eyebrow. 'If you look at—'

'I know what you're going to say. That one in three couples get divorced, and that's one of the reasons I think it would be better to wait. It doesn't make sense to rush into it.'

Attacking from a different angle, he said, 'I take it you don't find me repulsive or you wouldn't be where you are now.'

'Of course I don't find you repulsive.'

He raised his eyebrow questioningly. 'Then what do I need to say to persuade you?'

All he needed to say was, I love you, but she could hardly tell him that.

Instead, she said, 'You're not in love with me.'

'*You're* not in love with me,' he countered. 'But that doesn't mean our marriage won't work.

'As far as marrying for love goes, I've known more than one marriage fail when the couple have been madly in love and then discovered that love alone isn't enough.

'The main thing is, I believe we're compatible in a lot of ways. We're on the same wavelength, the chemistry between us is fantastic…'

Leaning forward, he took her face between his palms. 'Let's give it a try.'

She wavered, *wanting* to, but held back by the knowledge that he didn't love her. Though if she agreed to marry him there was a chance he might come to care for her. While if she refused she could well have lost her one and only opportunity.

'Is the answer yes?' he pressed.

Knowing she couldn't turn down this prospect of happiness, she nodded, and heard his sigh of relief before his mouth covered hers.

As he kissed her, his hands moved across her shoulders and slid beneath the duvet until they reached the swell of her breasts.

When he had stroked and teased the nipples into firmness, his mouth left hers to pleasure first one and then the other, while his hand travelled over her flat stomach to the silky warmth of her inner thighs.

She was just abandoning herself to the pleasure, when he drew away and said reluctantly, 'We ought to be moving. We haven't much time. After we're married we'll be able to forget about everything else and concentrate exclusively on each other.' He grinned raffishly.

Hearing *after we're married* spoken so casually served to make the notion more real, and for the first time she was almost able to believe it.

Rising to his feet, suddenly businesslike, he said, 'While you shower and dress I've a couple of phone calls to make, then we can get started.'

For a little while after he'd gone she sat quite still, staring after him. It was only four days since they'd met, and so much had happened so quickly that she was starting to feel like a piece of tumbleweed caught and bowled along by the wind.

When she had taken off the jewellery and put it safely in the top drawer of the bedside cabinet, she cleaned her teeth and showered.

Then, dressed in a fine wool dress the colour of lilac and suede boots, she made her way downstairs to find Joel waiting in the hall.

Smiling at her, he said, 'I've had a word with a friend of mine, the Reverend John Daintree. He'll be happy to marry us at the Church of the Holy Shepherd at two o'clock tomorrow afternoon.'

'Oh…' She stopped abruptly and stood silently.

He looked at her steadily. 'Do you have a problem with that?'

'No… No. Only for some reason I'd expected a civil ceremony.'

His voice cool, he asked, 'Does that mean you would prefer one?'

'Not at all. I'd much prefer to get married in a church. It's just…' She bit her lower lip.

'Just what?' He pressed her to continue.

'I've always thought that a church wedding seems more *binding* somehow.'

'And you don't want that?'

'I wasn't totally sure *you* did.' She spoke the half-formed thought.

'I can assure you that, having decided on a wife, if at all possible I intend to stay married.'

Vastly relieved, she gave him a radiant smile.

'If you smile at me like that I'll forget all my good intentions and take you back to bed.'

'You said we hadn't much time,' she reminded him.

'Mmm…So I did. I'll just have to settle for a kiss then, won't I?'

She waited.

His hands on her hips, he lifted her on to her toes. 'Now *you* can kiss *me*.'

Just looking at his mouth made her heart beat faster and butterflies dance in her stomach.

Putting her hands on his shoulders, she touched her lips to that beautiful mouth and felt her heart start to thump against her chest bone.

He slanted his head, his lips parted, and he deepened the kiss until every nerve in her body came to life and her stomach clenched.

Fully aware of his effect on her, a very male smile of satisfaction curved his mouth before he said, 'We'd better get started or we'll never get everything done.'

As they reached the front door, a phone started to ring. When Bethany glanced at him, he shook his head decidedly. 'We'll leave it for Molly or the answering machine to pick up.'

The limousine was waiting by the kerb, with Tom standing by to open the door. He greeted them cheerfully. 'Morning, sir, madam… Lovely day, isn't it? Let's hope it stays like this. Where to first?'

As Bethany hadn't eaten any breakfast they went first to China Town for an early lunch at Joel's favourite restaurant, a small, simple place where the locals ate.

The *dim sum* he ordered were brought in a selection of bamboo steamers. They looked to Bethany like small white dumplings.

'What do you think?' he queried, when he'd watched her sample a couple. 'If you really don't like them, I'll ask for something else.'

She beamed at him. 'Oh, I do. They're delicious.'

'Then that's another thing we agree on.'

Lunch over, their next port of call was to the office of the city clerk where they duly applied for, and signed, a marriage licence.

From there he surprised her by taking her to Tiffany's to buy a ring. She was wondering why he'd chosen to take her to the famous Fifth Avenue store, rather than a quieter, more private venue, when she recalled their conversation that very first night.

As though reading her thoughts, he grinned and said, 'In view of what you told me, I thought you might find Tiffany's romantic.'

The moment they entered the jewellery department, Bethany was very conscious of the overt interest that Joel, with his tough good looks, his powerful physique and his well-tailored clothes, aroused.

While they looked at a wonderful selection of engagement rings, though Bethany herself received a few envious glances, she was well aware that the attention of most of the females there was firmly focused on him.

He obviously knew it too.

His little smile ironic and with a kind of quizzical self-mockery, he deliberately set out to play the part of an attentive fiancé.

When, between them, they had narrowed the choice of rings down to two—a wonderful glowing ruby and a magnificent diamond solitaire—she tried them both on again. And again. Before, dazzled and dazed, she was forced to admit, 'I really can't decide.'

Joel took the solitaire and, slipping it back on her finger, lifted her hand to admire it. Then, turning to the elegantly turned out sales lady, he told her casually, 'We'll take them both.'

Obviously unsure that she'd heard him correctly, she asked, 'Did you say both, sir?'

Coming to life, Bethany began in an agitated whisper, 'Oh, but I don't—'

'Both,' Joel broke in firmly. Then, to Bethany, 'The diamond for your engagement ring and the ruby to go with your set.'

'Please, Joel,' she begged desperately, 'I really don't need—'

He leaned down and kissed her lightly, stopping the protest. 'Call it your wedding present.'

Smothering a romantic sigh, the sales lady asked, 'Will there be anything else?'

'We'll need a wedding ring.'

Bethany felt a little pang of disappointment. She had been hoping against hope that he would say *two* wedding rings.

A selection of plain and chased rings in varying widths was produced and, after trying a couple on along with the solitaire, she chose a plain one, narrow and dainty.

As the sales lady began to assemble them ready to pack, Joel said, 'Just the wedding ring and the ruby, if you please. My fiancée will wear the diamond.'

A few minutes later, Bethany walked out of the store with Joel's hand at her waist and his ring on her finger. Her joy was slightly shadowed by regret that she hadn't been brave enough to suggest that he too had a ring.

'Where to now, sir?' the chauffeur asked as he held open the car door.

'Paul Rosco's office, please, Tom,' Joel answered.

When they reached the glass and concrete tower block that housed Joel's solicitor, thinking that he might prefer privacy, Bethany suggested that she could wait in the car.

'Not at all. I need you to be there.'

Puzzled, she asked, 'Why?'

As they crossed the marble-floored foyer and took the high-speed lift up to the sixty-fifth floor, he told her, 'Paul is drawing up a marriage contract for us both to sign.'

It sounded so cold-blooded that a chill ran down her spine. 'A marriage contract?'

Perhaps he heard the dismay in her voice because he said reassuringly, 'I assure you, it's quite usual these days.'

When she continued to look unhappy, he added with the merest touch of impatience, 'I know it's practical rather than romantic, but a contract protects both our interests. It sets out clearly where each of us would stand if, by any chance, our marriage failed…'

Bethany fought back her tears; it all seemed so businesslike and unfeeling. When they reached the solicitor's offices, a smart young woman sitting at a computer in the outer office glanced up with a friendly smile that included them both. 'If you'd like to go on through, Mr McAlister, Mr Rosco is expecting you.'

Bethany had presumed that Paul Rosco's office would be all glass and chrome and sharp angles, but it was unexpectedly comfortable and welcoming with a thick pile carpet, a doe-coloured leather couch and a couple of deep armchairs.

A vase of fresh flowers stood on a side table and on a nearby bookcase there were several family photographs in silver frames.

Tall and dark, ruggedly good-looking, Paul Rosco came forward to greet them and the two men shook hands with real warmth.

An arm at Bethany's waist, Joel said, 'May I introduce my solicitor and good friend, Paul Rosco…? Paul, this is Bethany Seaton, my fiancée…'

'I'm very pleased to meet you.' Though the solicitor greeted her courteously, his expression was guarded, his blue eyes distinctly wary, as he shook her proffered hand.

'Won't you sit down?'

Feeling ill at ease, Bethany sat down on the soft leather couch.

'All set?' Joel queried, taking a seat by her side.

'All set,' Paul Rosco confirmed, producing a sheaf of legal-looking documents. 'I've laid it out exactly as you asked. All you have to do is each read through the contracts and agree to the contents before signing them.'

In silence she took the double page document she was handed.

Watching her face and noting that she wasn't happy, Paul Rosco began, 'I'm sure you'll find the suggested divorce settlement quite generous—'

'If you don't agree on the amount of support I've outlined,' Joel butted in, 'I'm quite willing to discuss it further.'

Wishing once again that he was a poor man and none of this was necessary, she said flatly, 'I don't want a divorce settlement. I don't need you to support me. If our marriage should break up, I'm quite capable of earning my own living.'

'It's not quite that simple,' Paul Rosco said carefully. 'For both your sakes you have to know exactly where you stand. If you haven't agreed on a settlement and the marriage does break up it could make things extremely difficult. Especially if there was any acrimony.'

She understood that he meant that Joel was a very wealthy man and, with no agreement, she could take him to court and try to fleece him. And, while she could vehemently deny that she would do any such thing, she knew that no one in their right senses would simply take her word. But a contract suggested that the man she loved didn't trust her. She felt belittled, humiliated.

Though why should he trust her? He didn't really know her any more than she knew him. She *might* be the kind of woman who would try to take a man for everything he had.

'And of course there's the question of children,' Paul went on blandly. 'If you were intending to have a family…'

Things had happened so quickly that she hadn't thought that far ahead, let alone discussed it with Joel. Now, chilled by uncertainty, she glanced at him, her grey eyes revealing how troubled she was.

He took her hand and squeezed it gently, a gesture that warmed her and made the situation seem more endurable. 'You do want children, don't you?'

'Yes,' she said in a small voice, and was rewarded with a smile that lifted her spirits even more.

'Then it would be wise to cover all eventualities, so I suggest that before you worry your head any more, you read the document.

'I've asked Paul to keep the whole thing simple and straight-forward, so it shouldn't take long to go through it.'

Realizing that if she wanted to marry Joel she had no choice, she began to read.

As the solicitor had said, the suggested divorce settlement was generous indeed, as were all the other maintenance commitments.

Telling herself that if the worst came to the worst and their marriage ended before they had a family, she could refuse Joel's money and simply walk away, she agreed to sign.

'Are you happy with it?' Joel pressed.

She nodded.

'Sure?' he asked quizzically. 'You look as if you're about to sign your own death warrant.'

'Quite sure.' Now the ordeal was over, she couldn't wait to put her signature to the document and have the whole thing over and done with.

'If you're both ready to sign, I'll ask Roz to come in and act as witness.' The solicitor touched a button and a moment later the girl from the outer office came hurrying in.

'So when is the wedding taking place?' Paul asked when both copies had been duly signed and witnessed.

'Two o'clock tomorrow afternoon at the Church of the Holy Shepherd. I was hoping you could spare the time to act as my best man.'

After the briefest of hesitations, Paul agreed. 'If you're sure that's what you want, I'll make time.'

The acceptance was courteous rather than enthusiastic, and Bethany felt sure he disapproved of such haste.

His manner, while scrupulously polite, hadn't really warmed towards her and, anxious to leave, she gathered up her bag, holding it against her chest like a bulletproof vest.

Apparently guessing how she felt, Joel declined Paul's offer of refreshments on the grounds that they still had things to do.

When they got outside the sun had gone down and it was clear and bitterly cold. Dusk and a myriad lights had magically combined to make a blue-velvet, jewel-encrusted evening cloak for the town to wear.

Bethany had presumed that Joel's statement that they still had things to do had simply been an excuse to get away. But when they were settled in the warmth and luxury of the limousine, he gave the chauffeur a strange address she didn't quite catch.

Unable to think of anything he had listed that morning that still needed to be done, she queried, 'Where are we going?'

'To buy you a wedding dress and a trousseau.' As her lips parted, he said, 'Don't argue. Tomorrow you'll be my wife…'

Tomorrow you'll be my wife… She was filled with a quiet happiness that dispelled the last of her lingering agitation, as he added firmly, 'And it's a husband's privilege to buy his wife's clothes.'

In the changing light she caught sight of a clock on the façade of a building that showed it was almost five o'clock. 'Isn't it a bit late to go shopping?' she ventured.

'Not to Joshua Dellon's. We're somewhat later than I'd hoped to be, but they're expecting us. I made all the arrangements this morning.'

When they drew up outside the famous fashion house, with its simple, yet stunning window displays, Bethany felt a stir of excitement.

She had always loved the flair and quiet elegance of Dellon's designs, but had never visualized herself in a position where she could afford to buy his exclusive creations.

As they crossed the sidewalk and approached the heavy smoked-glass door, it was opened by a stylishly dressed older woman with silver-blonde hair, who had obviously been watching out for them.

'Good evening.' She smiled at them both, adding, 'It's nice to see you, Mr McAlister.'

'It's good to see you, Berenice. I'm sorry we're a little late.'

She brushed aside his apology. 'That's quite all right. The traffic gets worse.'

'This is Miss Seaton, my fiancée.'

'Miss Seaton…' Berenice acknowledged the introduction gracefully.

Then, having passed her expert eye assessingly over Bethany, she turned to Joel and said, 'Miss Seaton has a beautifully proportioned figure and the size you suggested should fit perfectly.

'If there are any slight alterations needed I'll see that they're dealt with straight away. Now if you'll come through to the salon, everything's ready for you.'

The salon was palatial with rich carpets and sparkling chandeliers, rose-coloured velvet chairs and couches and polished woodwork..

There wasn't an article of clothing in sight.

A pair of chairs had been placed ready, and when Bethany was seated Joel sat down by her side. Though he appeared to be perfectly at ease, she thought how powerfully masculine he looked in such a very feminine setting.

As soon as they were seated, Berenice lifted a hand and at the given signal the dress show began.

For the next fifteen minutes a series of models paraded up and down, showing off coats and suits, day dresses and evening dresses, nightwear and lingerie.

While Devlin had been uninterested in what she wore, it soon became apparent to Bethany that Joel knew exactly what would suit her and how he wanted her to look.

From time to time, after an assessing glance in her direction, he'd nod, and Berenice would make a note in a small gold book with a gold pen.

In almost every case it was what Bethany would have chosen

for herself. The only thing she quibbled about was an evening
dress with a fur wrap that he selected. And then not because of
the dress itself, which was beautiful, but because it was clearly
extremely expensive—even by Dellon's standards—and she felt
he was spending quite enough.

'Of course you must have an evening dress,' Joel overrode her
objection. 'And don't worry about the wrap,' he added. 'It may
look like silver fox but it's not real fur, just dead teddy.'

'But I really don't need—' She protested.

'Oh, but you do. Tonight we're going to a very select twenty-first birthday party,' he went on ironically. 'A senator's
daughter, no less… And I'd like to show you off.'

'Oh…' She wasn't at all sure she liked the idea of being
'shown off'. But, aware that if Joel was determined to take her
to the party, she couldn't let him down by going in her inexpen-
sive off-the-peg cocktail dress, she agreed meekly, 'Very well,'
and the show went on.

The wedding gowns came last, glorious creations that would
have made any bride look her best.

Joel sat back, one ankle crossed negligently over the other,
and watched in silence while satin and lace, net and tulle swished
and rustled past.

When the parade ended, Berenice gave him an enquiring
glance.

'Can we see the first one again?'

'Of course.'

She snapped her fingers and the tall, slender, dark-haired
model who had come on first, reappeared. The dress she was
wearing was an ankle-length ivory sheath in wild silk, the way
it was cut and the sheer beauty of the material making it look
almost ethereal. With it was a short veil, fine as a spider's web,
that was held in place by a simple coronet.

Glancing at Bethany, Joel asked, 'Do you like it?'

It was the one she would have chosen for herself and, pleasure and excitement making her sound breathless, she said, 'I love it.'

'Then we'll take it if it fits.'

As Berenice made a note in the gold book, a young woman brought in a still-smoking bottle of champagne and two crystal flutes.

After they had sipped the cool, sparkling wine and discussed shoe size and accessories, Berenice led Bethany away to try on the dress.

It fitted to perfection and she caught her breath as she saw herself in the long mirror, delighted that she would look beautiful for Joel.

Berenice nodded her approval. 'As that fits so well, everything else will,' she announced with certainty.

When they got back to a waiting Joel, she informed him, 'The evening dress and accessories are being packed and everything else will be delivered first thing in the morning.'

Just as she finished speaking, an elegant black box with the name Joshua Dellon in gold script, was carried in and handed over.

They thanked Berenice and, looking well pleased, she escorted them to the door and bade them a courteous, 'Goodnight.'

The limousine appeared as if by magic and, as soon as they were settled in, Tom started for home.

It had been a day full to overflowing and Bethany felt like pinching herself to prove that she wasn't dreaming. Instead she looked at the magnificent diamond on her finger that picked up every stray gleam of light and thought how lucky she was.

But, even as the thought crossed her mind, she knew that, had she the chance, she would give up the ring and everything she owned in exchange for Joel's love.

Glancing sideways at him, she saw the gleam of his eyes and realized he was watching her.

'Penny for them,' he offered.

'I was just thinking how lucky I am.'

His mouth seemed to tighten and, feeling as if she was in a lift that was dropping too fast, she wondered what she'd said to annoy him. But a split second later that tautness was gone and she knew it must have been a trick of the light.

Taking her hand, he raised it to his lips. 'Not at all. I'm the lucky one to win you for a wife…'

Though she was thrilled by his words, she was wondering for the umpteenth time why, when he didn't love her, he was so set on marrying her, when he added, 'You could have chosen to marry Michael.'

The mention of Michael, and the thought of hurting him, cast a shadow over her happiness. 'I really must talk to him and tell him the truth.' Guiltily, she added, 'I've treated him very badly.'

'I agree that we need to talk to him, but I suggest that we leave it until after we're married. Better to present him with a *fait accompli*. That way, instead of arguing, he'll be forced to accept the situation.'

But would he accept it? Or would it cause trouble between the two men? Unconsciously she sighed.

Joel put an arm around her and drew her close. When his lips sought and found hers, she wondered briefly if he was kissing her to take her mind off Michael.

Then he deepened the kiss and she could think of nothing but him. The best of companions, the sweetest of lovers, the man she adored and hoped to spend the rest of her life with.

CHAPTER EIGHT

WHEN THEY ARRIVED at Mulberry Street, Joel gathered up Dellon's black and gold box and helped Bethany out. Who said you could never see stars in New York? she thought as, held securely in the crook of his arm, leaning a little against him, she looked up at the star-spangled sky.

'Will you be wanting me again tonight, sir?' the chauffeur asked.

Joel shook his head. 'No, you've had a full day. Put the car away and take the evening off. We'll get a taxi.'

'Thank you, sir,' Tom said gratefully. 'Goodnight, sir. Goodnight, madam.'

As Joel opened the front door, the housekeeper came into the hall. 'Oh, Mr McAlister, young Mr Michael's been trying to get through to you all afternoon. He asked me to ask you to ring him as soon as you got back. He says it's absolutely essential that he speaks to you.'

'Thank you, Molly,' Joel said easily. 'I'll take care of it.'

'Will you be wanting a meal tonight?'

'No, we'll be going out. You and Tom can relax.'

She smiled her thanks and left them alone.

With his arm around Bethany's waist, Joel shepherded her towards the stairs.

When they reached their bedroom, feeling anything but easy, she began, 'Perhaps I'd better talk to Michael after all—'

'We're due at the party in less than an hour,' Joel pointed out evenly, as he put the black and gold box on the bed. 'There's no time tonight to make explanations or listen to what will no doubt be long, impassioned appeals.'

'I expect you're right.' Not looking forward to talking to Michael, Bethany was cravenly pleased to put it off.

Determinedly changing the subject, Joel said, 'Red stones won't go with your dress so I thought you might care to wear these.' As he spoke he crossed to a bow-fronted chest and, unlocking one of the top drawers, took out a small case and handed it to her. She opened the lid to find a pair of earrings, each made up of a single long strand of diamonds that sparkled and glittered in the light.

'They're lovely,' she breathed.

'I'm glad you like them.'

Before she could even thank him, he added, 'Now I've a couple of things to do and some emails to read before I shower, so I'll leave you to get on.'

He made no mention of showering together, as he had done the previous night, and she didn't know whether to be pleased or sorry.

But, considering they hadn't a great deal of time, it was perhaps as well, she told herself sternly as she put the case on the bed and began to unpack her new finery.

Lifting the dress carefully from its cocoon of fine black tissue paper, she found herself thinking that she had never before owned anything so lovely.

It was midnight-blue and made of shimmering silk chiffon, with a daringly-cut bodice and a skirt that swooped from just below knee-length at the front to a long, graceful fish-tail at the back.

Packed with it were a matching bra and briefs, sheer silk

stockings, evening sandals in her size, a small purse with a silver wrist chain and the soft, man-made fur wrap.

Leaving them all laid out on the bed, she took off her ring and went to shower.

She emerged some twenty minutes later, powdered and perfumed and lightly made-up, her long dark hair taken up into a smooth, elegant chignon that showed the pure line of her throat and jaw.

There was no sign of Joel.

Taking off her dressing gown, she put on the delicate under-wear and the sheer silk stockings and shoes, before replacing her ring and fastening the earrings to her neat lobes.

Then, feeling a kind of awe, she slipped into the dress. Like gossamer against her skin, it settled into place, clinging lovingly to her slender curves. The bodice was a little lower-cut than she usually wore and she hoped there wasn't too much cleavage showing as, holding her breath, she looked in the long mirror.

She was still gazing speechlessly at the beautiful stranger who stood gazing back at her, when Joel appeared behind her, looking devastatingly handsome in an immaculate evening suit.

He was freshly shaven and his thick corn-coloured hair was making efforts to curl a little against his well-shaped head.

His hands lightly on her shoulders, he turned her round and, holding her at arm's length, studied her in silence.

After what seemed an age, he said huskily, 'You look enchant-ing. Every man there will envy me and I'll be madly jealous of every man who dares to look at you.'

A catch in her voice, she pointed out, 'You said you wanted to show me off.'

'Now I'm not so sure. I don't want a lot of strange men feasting their eyes on you. I'm beginning to see why some cultures prefer to keep their women veiled.' His eyes fixed on her mouth, he asked, 'Will it do irreparable damage to your lip-gloss if I kiss you?'

By way of answer, she lifted her face like a flower to the sun.

He kissed her lightly, but with a sweet thoroughness that brought a faint flush to her cheeks and enough warmth to the rest of her body to make her wish they weren't going out.

When he reluctantly lifted his head, she opened her eyes and saw by the expression on his face that he was wishing much the same.

'Do we have to go?' she asked impulsively.

'I'm afraid so. I promised Lisa.'

Bethany's heart sank. It had been Lisa's party that Tara had asked Joel to take her to, although she already had an escort.

'Tara will be going.' She spoke the thought aloud.

'Does that bother you?'

Lifting her chin, she lied, 'Not really.'

Not taken in for a moment, he said, 'Don't worry, with so many people present, we might never even set eyes on her…'

I do hope so, Bethany thought, and it was almost like a prayer.

'And I'll be there with you. Though I must admit I'd much sooner be here alone with you.'

Sighing, he added, 'However, I'll console myself with the thought that if we so desire we can spend our entire honeymoon in bed.'

'Are we having a honeymoon?'

'I thought a few days in the Catskills. I've a cabin there.' A shadow crossed his face as he added, 'Then there's something I have to take care of. Though, hopefully, when everything's finally resolved, we can have another honeymoon anywhere you fancy.

'Now, about ready? The taxi should be here.'

When she had dropped one or two things into her evening purse, he put the fur wrap around her shoulders and escorted her down the stairs to the waiting taxi.

The party was being held at the Cardinal, Joel told her as they headed Uptown. Rated as one of the oldest of New York's top hotels, it was also one of the smallest. Yet it was almost an institution, with all the cachet to make it select and sought after.

He went on to say that with money no object—the Senator came from a very wealthy and privileged background—the entire hotel had been taken over for the party and the many distinguished guests who were staying the night.

Wondering afresh if she would fit into his world and starting to feel newly anxious at the prospect of the coming evening, Bethany found herself praying that she wouldn't let Joel down.

Watching her face in the changing light, he asked, 'You're not nervous, are you?'

'A bit,' she admitted.

He squeezed her hand. 'There's no need to be, I assure you. You speak well and look great and, unlike some of the empty-headed socialites I know, you're intelligent and articulate.'

Somewhat cheered by his praise, she made an effort to stop worrying about the coming evening, though the possibility of running into Tara still lingered like a shadowy threat at the back of her mind.

They found the traffic was heavy and by the time their taxi drew on to the hotel's forecourt, the proceedings appeared to be well under way.

Inside the sumptuous foyer, Bethany was handed a cloakroom ticket and her wrap was whisked away. Then one of the many circulating waiters offered them a choice of champagne or freshly squeezed orange juice and a wonderful selection of tiny canapés.

They both refused the canapés, but Bethany accepted a glass of orange juice and Joel a glass of champagne. 'Ready for the fray?' he asked.

'As ready as I'll ever be,' she admitted wryly, and they made their way inside.

The party spread over three rooms—a long, elegant salon, a spacious supper room where a magnificent buffet was laid out and the chandelier-hung ballroom, where a small orchestra was playing softly.

Distinguished-looking men and beautifully dressed, bejewelled women were gathered in little groups laughing and talking.

The atmosphere was redolent of wealth and breeding and, though she was well aware that she didn't belong in that class, dressed as she was, Joel's arm at her waist and his words of praise still echoing in her head, she suddenly felt almost confident.

Their hostess, her father by her side, was waiting to greet them. It was immediately obvious that Senator Harvey, a tall, heavily built, balding man, liked the limelight, while his daughter didn't.

She was a pretty fair-haired girl, shy and mild-mannered who, though she was extremely well-dressed, seemed to be eclipsed by her august parent, if not by the occasion itself.

Her face lit up at the sight of Joel and Bethany found herself wondering if Lisa wasn't more than a little in love with him.

Holding out her hand, she told him breathlessly, 'When Tara said you were still in England, I'd begun to think you'd forgotten your promise.'

Taking the proffered hand, he raised it to his lips. 'Not at all. I wouldn't have missed your party for worlds.'

She flushed with pleasure.

'May I introduce my fiancée, Bethany Seaton...'

Some of the pleasure faded.

'Bethany, this is Lisa Harvey.'

Feeling sorry for the girl, Bethany murmured a pleasant greeting, which was returned.

Then, with a great deal more grace than Tara had shown, Lisa managed to smile and say, 'I'm so pleased you could come.'

Indicating the man by her side, she added, 'I'd like you to meet my father…'

Taking Bethany's hand, he said, 'It's nice to meet you, my dear.' He added gallantly, 'You look absolutely delightful.'

'Thank you,' she said demurely.

Still holding her hand, he asked, 'Dare I hope that later you'll dance with me?'

Knowing it was expected of her, she agreed. 'I'd love to.'

He glanced at Joel. 'Then all I need is your fiancé's permission.'

'You have it,' Joel said at once, 'so long as I can dance with your charming daughter.'

Looking looked both delighted and flustered, Lisa said breathlessly, 'Of course. Though I don't dance very well.'

Her father gave her a swift, irritated look that spoke volumes and made her soft mouth tighten.

Feeling sorry for the girl once more, Bethany said swiftly, 'I don't dance very well either, but I didn't have the courage to admit it, so I was going to let your father find out for himself.'

Some of the tension left Lisa's fair, wholesome, girl-next-door face and she smiled.

'Having danced with each of you ladies—' Joel entered the conversation '—I'm fully aware that you're both being far too modest.'

'Though it's not really the occasion for business,' the Senator remarked to Joel, 'I'd like a private word with you later, if Bethany—may I call you Bethany?—doesn't mind sparing you for ten minutes or so?'

'I certainly don't mind,' she agreed pleasantly and, in order to cover her initial slight hesitation, smiled at him.

'My dear,' he said, 'if you smile at me like that, you'll make me your slave for life.'

Greatly daring, she said, 'I think it would take more than a smile to enslave a man like you.'

Chuckling at her reply, he gave Joel a hearty slap on the shoulder. 'Joel, you old son of a gun, you're a very lucky man.'

Joel's dark gaze remaining on his fiancée, he smiled. 'Don't I know it.'

After some further conversation, when some late arrivals came they moved away to 'circulate and enjoy the party' as instructed.

For a while they drifted from group to group sipping their drinks, while Bethany was introduced to quite a number of Joel's personal friends as well as some of his business acquaintances.

To her very great relief there was no sign of Tara, and everyone she met was most pleasant and friendly. But when one young man, after goggling at her, tried to turn the conversation into personal channels, Joel put a masterful arm around her and whisked her off to the dance floor.

As they went into a slow dance, his cheek against her hair, he muttered, 'If that young oaf hadn't taken his eyes off you when he did, it would have been pistols at dawn.'

Feeling secretly a little thrilled by his proprietary manner, she half shook her head. 'He might have been young and a bit wet behind the ears, but there was no harm in him.'

'You have a kind heart,' Joel told her. 'I noticed it earlier when you lied to Lisa about not being a good dancer.'

'I know it sounds silly,' Bethany said a shade apologetically, 'but I felt sorry for her.'

'It's not silly. On the surface, Lisa has everything, but in reality she's just a poor little rich girl. She spends most of her time trying to please her father and failing. He's been trying to turn her into a society butterfly so she can marry a real go-getter.

'But, in my opinion, she would be a great deal happier married to a man who would appreciate her just as she is.'

As they finished their dance the Senator came up, his daughter on his arm, to claim his dance.

The next number was a quickstep and, seeing Lisa's anxious look, Joel suggested casually, 'As I've been out of town for a while, shall we have a drink before we dance and catch up on the latest gossip?'

She nodded gratefully.

Though a shade on the heavy side and without Joel's masculine grace, the Senator proved to be a good, if slightly flamboyant, dancer.

They had circled the floor before he remarked with just a suggestion of relief, 'My dear, you underrate yourself. You're a very good dancer.'

'Why, thank you,' she said demurely. Then so he wouldn't realize she'd lied, 'But I find it all depends on my partner. You're so easy to follow.'

Obviously pleased by her reply, he said, 'Judging by your accent, you're from England?'

'Yes. I live in London.'

'Lisa spent a year at St Elphins, which was reputed to be one of the best finishing schools in England. But, unfortunately, it didn't give her much in the way of social graces…'

Having a beautiful partner who was also a good dancer and listener suited the Senator very well and, as he seemed loath to give her up, they danced several dances.

Then the band began to play a modern waltz and Joel and Lisa joined them on the floor. Thanks to Joel's care, Lisa made a good showing and, happy to see it, Bethany remarked, 'Your daughter dances well.'

'Lisa's never been able to sell herself. She always comes over as shy and awkward.'

'I think you underrate her,' Bethany said firmly.

As soon as the waltz came to an end, though it was obvious that Lisa—flushed with success—would have liked to have stayed on the floor, Senator Harvey commandeered Joel.

'I'd like to have that word now, Joel, my boy, if the ladies will excuse us?'

Knowing there was nothing else for it, both women murmured assent and, the Senator's arm around Joel's shoulders, the men walked away.

Seeing that Lisa looked suddenly lost, Bethany suggested, 'I thought I might take this chance to slip off to the Ladies' Room and check my make-up.'

'I'll go with you,' the other girl responded with undisguised eagerness.

As they made their way back to the foyer, in a burst of confidence she said, 'Knowing he'd be busy at least part of the time, Daddy press-ganged Martin into being my escort, but I've hardly caught a glimpse of him so far.'

Then, with a flash of spirit, 'And I've no intention of going looking for him. Would you?'

'No, I wouldn't,' Bethany said. 'There must be nicer, more attentive men around.'

'David would have been happy to have escorted me,' Lisa went on, her blue eyes wistful, 'but he's only a junior partner in a struggling law firm and Daddy doesn't think he's good enough for me.'

Remembering what Joel had said, Bethany remarked quietly, 'Shouldn't it depend on what *you* think?'

Lisa gave her a thoughtful glance. 'Yes, it should, shouldn't it?

'We're not in love, or anything like that,' she added after a moment, 'but he does seem to like me, and he doesn't make me nervous like some of Daddy's friends do.'

The Ladies' Room was frankly luxurious. It was decorated

in rose and old gold and had soft lighting and a deep pile ivory carpet. Opposite a long dressing-table with gilt mirrors and vel-vet-covered stools, were several cushioned chairs and couches. Through an archway, Bethany glimpsed a row of gleaming wash-basins with gold-plated taps.

There were three beautifully dressed, sophisticated-looking women already there, chatting together in a little clique.

Ignoring Bethany, they gave the Senator's daughter smiles that held a combination of respect and envy and murmured how much they were enjoying the party.

After a moment or two, Lisa went through to wash her hands, while the women remained where they were. Conscious of their covert glances, Bethany took a seat on one of the stools and made a pretence of fixing her make-up.

Their conversation became *sotto voce* and, feeling a lot less confident without Joel's support, she was wondering uneasily if they were discussing her, when the door opened and through the mirror she saw Tara, resplendent in gold lamé, walk in.

'Well, well, well, look who's here!' she exclaimed. 'Joel's little friend. Where is he, by the way? Don't tell me he's abandoned you?'

Turning to face her, Bethany said evenly, 'He's talking to Senator Harvey.'

Eyeing Bethany's dress, Tara remarked, 'That looks like a Dellon... I presume Joel's taken you shopping. Payment for services rendered, no doubt.'

Her speech was slightly slurred and, judging by the glitter in her eyes and the flush lying along her cheekbones, she had drunk rather more champagne than was good for her.

Bethany bit her inner lip and said nothing.

'And diamond earrings too!' Tara went on shrilly. Then, with added venom, 'You must think you're on to a good thing—'

Bethany, very aware of the other women who were now staring openly, gathered up her bag and headed for the door.

Tara barred her way. 'But don't make any mistake about it, Joel's only using you to get his own back on me. A week or two at the most and you'll be out on your ear—'

Catching sight of Bethany's ring, she abruptly stopped speaking and simply gaped.

Then, rallying somewhat, 'You may be wearing a ring, but don't imagine for a moment that he seriously intends to tie himself to a little nobody like you. When it comes to actually applying for a marriage licence you'll find—'

'As a matter of fact we applied for a licence today,' Bethany said clearly, 'and we're getting married tomorrow afternoon.'

Her face twisted with rage, Tara hissed, 'Joel must be mad to marry a scheming little bitch he's only known a few days and who's been having it off with his stepbrother.

'Oh, yes, I know all about you and Michael. He got a nasty shock when I happened to mention your name. Until then he had no idea that you'd dumped him to go to New York with Joel…'

So Michael knew she was here…

'But then he should have had the sense to know that women like you always plump for the highest bidder…

'Well, if Joel is fool enough to marry you, don't think you've got it made. You'll never be accepted in good society, and it won't be pleasant to find yourself ostracised…'

Lisa, who had been standing silently in the background, moved forward and, slipping an arm through Bethany's, said, 'Come on, Bethany, we'd better be getting back.' As she brushed past Tara, adding, 'Lord Peter will be wondering where we've got to,' Bethany caught a glimpse of the other women's faces, all aghast.

When they reached the door, Lisa said in a stage whisper, 'I only hope you didn't take any notice of poor Tara. A combination of jealousy and too much champagne must have made her tongue run away with her.'

As soon as they were out of earshot, Bethany, her legs feeling oddly shaky, said, 'I can't thank you enough. You were great.'

Lisa giggled. 'I was rather good, wasn't I? To be honest, I surprised myself.' Then, more seriously, 'Don't let Tara upset you. She can be a cat at times, but she's usually sorry afterwards.'

Doubting that, Bethany said nothing.

'Now, just in case they keep an eye on us,' Lisa continued almost gaily, 'let's go and talk to Peter.'

Thinking of Michael and trying to push the guilt she felt to the back of her mind, Bethany asked, 'Is this Peter really a lord?'

'Oh, yes, though he doesn't use his title. His elder brother is the Duke of Dunway.'

Bethany giggled. 'I thought you might have made him up.'

'I'm afraid I'm not that resourceful. I met him when I was at finishing school in England. I was friends with his sister, Sarah.'

'Does he live in New York?'

Lisa shook her head. 'He lives on the family estate in Surrey, but he came over specially for my birthday…'

Bethany wondered how, when Lisa had such good friends amongst the aristocracy, the Senator could belittle his daughter's social graces.

After Bethany had been introduced to Lord Peter, a tall, fair, innocuous-looking young man with a nice smile and a cut-glass accent, he said, 'So you're English too?'

'Yes.' She smiled politely.

'Whereabouts do you live?'

Bethany took another orange juice from a passing waiter, and replied. 'London.'

'Are you London born and bred?'

She shook her head. 'I was born in Youldon.'

'Ah,' he sighed. 'Not far from the ancestral home. It's a real pain, nowadays, for seven months of the year it draws crowds of visitors, while the family live in what used to be the stables.'

'The old order changeth,' Bethany quoted.

'Too true,' he agreed. 'These days it's money that impresses people. Not blue blood or titles.'

With a glance at Lisa, Bethany murmured, 'Oh, I don't know.'

When Lisa, who seemed to sparkle in his company, admitted that she had used his title to impress, he threw back his head and laughed.

He was still laughing when Joel appeared out of the crowd and, putting an arm around Bethany's waist, said, 'I was starting to wonder where you'd got to.'

Introductions over, they stood chatting for a few minutes before going through to the supper room to eat, listen to the toasts and watch Lisa—her father by her side—cut the cake.

When Peter excused himself and moved away to have a word with someone he knew, Bethany said to Joel in an agitated whisper, 'I *should* have talked to Michael. He knows I'm in New York with you.'

His grip on her waist tightened. 'Are you sure?'

'Quite sure.' She nodded anxiously.

Joel's beautiful mouth tightened perceptibly. 'How does he know?'

'Apparently Tara mentioned my name to him.'

'I might have expected it,' he said grimly. 'I know they talk to each other on a regular basis.' Then, sharply, 'What else has she been saying to you?'

Bethany gave him a quick edited version of what had happened in the Ladies' Room.

Frowning, he said, 'Try not to let her spitefulness bother you. And don't fret about Michael. Though I would have much preferred to break the news myself, he had to know some time.'

'But I—'

Putting a finger to her lips to stop the words, he said, 'Don't worry. We'll talk to him tomorrow.'

Feeling bad about it, she pleaded, 'Couldn't we talk to him now?'

'I think not. For one thing, it'll be the middle of the night in London.'

Of course he was right. But how could he take the whole thing so *calmly*? she wondered.

The rest of the evening would have been enjoyable if the guilt she felt towards Michael hadn't hovered like a dark shadow at the back of her mind. As it was, she was pleased when, in the early hours of the morning, the party began to break up.

As they went to thank Lisa and her father and say their fare-wells, she asked Bethany in a whisper, 'Are you really getting married tomorrow…?'

'We are indeed,' Joel answered.

Looking uncomfortable, Lisa went on, 'Only Tara said you'd only known each other a few days…'

'It was love at first sight,' Joel told her. 'On my part, at least…'

If only that were true, Bethany thought wistfully. If it had been, despite all the problems caused by her association with Michael, she would have counted herself as one of the happiest girls in the world.

'So I'm afraid I rather swept Bethany off her feet,' Joel added with a smile.

'How romantic.' Lisa sighed deeply. 'I've always loved wed-dings.'

Acting on an impulse, Bethany began, 'Are you by any chance…?'

Suddenly remembering that the other girl might have a crush on Joel, and uncertain whether or not she was doing the right thing, she paused, wishing she'd kept her mouth shut.

Then, glancing at Joel, she caught his little nod of encouragement and, her heart lifting that they were so close that he often knew what she was thinking, she began again. 'Are you by any chance free tomorrow?'

'I am until early evening,' Lisa said. 'Then David is taking me to a special charity ball game. Why do you ask?'

A shade diffidently, Bethany explained. 'As I have no friends in New York, I was wondering if you might like to…'

As she hesitated, Lisa asked excitedly, 'Help you get ready? Of course I will.'

'We were thinking of a little more than that,' Joel put in. 'We were hoping you'd be a bridesmaid.'

'A bridesmaid…?' Lisa breathed. Then, colouring with pleasure, 'I'd love to.'

'It's only a quiet affair,' Bethany added.

'I'm sure it'll be wonderful.'

Smiling at her glowing face, Joel went on, 'You'll need a dress and all the trimmings, so can you be ready to go shopping by nine o'clock… say nine-thirty at the latest?'

At Lisa's eager nod, he went on. 'In that case I'll pick you up from home.'

Realizing too late that they had virtually ignored Lisa's father, Bethany made an effort to retrieve the situation. Turning to him with a brilliant smile, she said, 'I do hope you'll be able to come…'

'I'd certainly like to, my dear,' the Senator said. 'The only trouble is that I have to be at the airport by four-thirty.'

'That would be fine. The ceremony is at two o'clock at the Church of the Holy Shepherd,' Joel told him.

He smiled warmly at the couple. 'Then I'd love to attend.'

'Again we were thinking of something more than that,' Joel said. Then, in answer to the Senator's questioning glance, 'Though it's extremely short notice, we were rather hoping you would give the bride away.'

All at once Bethany's stomach knotted, as though his words were stones he'd hit her with.

'I'd be delighted, my boy,' Senator Harvey said heartily. 'Fill me in on the details tomorrow morning when you pick Lisa up.'

'I'll do that,' Joel responded.

As soon as he and Bethany had reiterated their thanks and said their goodnights, they made their way into the foyer, where she handed her cloakroom ticket to a hovering attendant.

'You look upset,' Joel said the moment they were alone. 'What's wrong?'

When, unable to speak for the lump in her throat, she stayed silent, he pressed, 'Do you have a problem with Lisa's father giving you away? If you do I'll—'

She shook her head. 'No, it's not that…'

'Then what is it?'

Her voice just a thread of sound, she said, 'I suddenly realized I'm getting married tomorrow and my mother and father don't even know.'

'And you're close to your parents?'

She nodded. 'Very.'

A frown drew Joel's well-marked brows together. 'Of course it's entirely my fault for rushing you so.'

His frown deepening, he added, 'Unfortunately, the jet's on this side of the pond, so it would mean them catching an ordinary flight, which would—'

She half shook her head. 'They wouldn't come anyway. Dad has a heart condition that makes him unable to fly, and Mum wouldn't come without him. It's just that I should have phoned them…'

Glancing at his watch, Joel said, 'Well, if you want to get them out of bed…?'

She shook her head. 'No, no… I'll talk to them in the morning.'

Feeling happier now, she smiled at him.

In return he squeezed her hand.

At that moment the attendant reappeared with Bethany's wrap and handed it to Joel, who put it around her shoulders.

Then, a hand at her waist, he escorted her through the handsome doors and out into the cold night air. The party, with its highs and lows, was over.

CHAPTER NINE

OUTSIDE the air seemed curiously still and a few flakes of snow were starting to drift down. After the warmth of the hotel it felt bitter and Bethany shivered as, amidst the departing bustle, Joel hurried her towards the waiting cab.

Just as they reached it there was a little flurry of footsteps, then Tara was by his side, clutching his arm. 'Joel, wait... I *have* to talk to you...'

Shaking off her hand, he opened the cab door and said to Bethany, 'Get in out of the cold.'

She obeyed and, as he closed the door behind her, he asked Tara coldly, 'What is it?'

Unwilling to be a spectator at what she felt sure would be an unpleasant little scene, Bethany turned her head away but she could still hear what was being said.

'Please, Joel,' Tara begged, 'tell me you have no intention of getting married tomorrow.'

'I have every intention of getting married tomorrow.'

He turned away to open the cab door but, catching his arm once more, she rushed on, 'I would have thought someone like you would find it too degrading to share a woman with another man... Especially his own stepbrother...'

'As a matter of fact I do, that's why I ended *our* relationship.'

'And that's what all this is about, isn't it?' Tara cried shrilly. 'If you hadn't caught Michael and me together and got angry, none of this would have happened. I believe you're just trying to get your own back and punish us both.'

He laughed coldly. 'If I was, could you blame me?'

'I don't know why you can't forget the whole thing. I told you it was just a one off, nothing serious. It would never have happened if we hadn't both been stoned out of our minds…'

'It's you I love, which is more than *she* does. Surely you can see she's just a common little slut who's on the make…'

'Watch your tongue,' Joel warned curtly.

'Well, she *is* a slut,' Tara insisted. 'Michael told me how she tried her wiles on him first and managed to get him to propose to her. But then, as soon as she realized you were a better bet, she dumped him and turned her attention to you…' Tara turned to stare at Bethany.

'Oh, she's clever, there's no doubt about it. Somehow she's managed to get Lisa eating out of her hand…'

Then, with a kind of helpless fury, 'When I asked Lisa why she'd stuck up for the scheming little bitch, she said, "I like her, she's been kind to me". *Kind*…'

Joel smiled grimly. 'Kindness is an attractive quality; you should try it some time.'

Tara was furious. 'How can you say—'

But Joel continued before she had a choice to finish. 'Bethany has a warm, spontaneous kindness that comes from a generous spirit, something you would know little about, Tara.'

Leaving Tara standing there, he got into the cab and gave the driver the Mulberry Street address.

As they turned to follow the trickle of cars and taxis, their dipped headlights like searching antennae, Bethany caught a glimpse of the other woman standing there dejectedly and felt sorry for her.

In a moment or two they had left the forecourt and joined the traffic still flowing through the streets of a city that never slept.

As they started to make their way downtown, Bethany tried to sort out her jumbled thoughts and feelings. Two things were uppermost in her mind. It was *Michael* that Tara had slept with, and when the girl had accused Joel of marrying *her* to punish them both he hadn't denied it.

His eyes on her face, Joel ordered quietly, 'Go on, spit it out.'

She took a deep breath. 'Why are you marrying me?'

'You've already asked me that question.'

'I asked you, but you didn't really give me an answer.'

Categorically, he said, 'I'm not marrying you to get my own back on Tara and Michael, if that's what you're thinking.'

'Oh…' She experienced such a rush of relief that momentarily she felt dizzy.

'I hope you believe me?'

'Yes, I do.' There had been a ring of truth in his voice that had left her in no doubt.

'Good.' He drew her to him and gave her a squeeze. 'I should hate it if Tara's venom poisoned your mind.'

The snow was coming faster now, small, feathery flakes that swirled and danced as they drifted down, gold and silver, caught in the headlights of the oncoming cars.

Sighing, she remarked, 'I love snow.'

'Though common sense insists that in town it's just a nuisance, so do I,' Joel admitted.

There was silence for a minute or so, then, harking back, he asked carefully, 'Apart from Tara, was the evening as bad as you'd feared?'

Bethany shook her head. 'No, everyone was very nice to me. Especially Lisa.'

'Lisa's a sweet kid. But not half as sweet as you.'

Warmed by his words, she nestled against him. It seemed he was starting to *like* her. Perhaps, given time, he might come to love her.

The future would have looked bright if only she had never met Michael… If only he hadn't wanted to marry her…

After a moment, with his usual acumen, Joel said, 'But there's still something bothering you?'

'It's Michael… I'm concerned about causing trouble between you,' she admitted.

His tone hard, uncompromising, Joel said, 'He'll be angry, I dare say. But he's unlikely to be heartbroken. And, knowing him, I'm pretty sure he'll soon bounce back.'

She bit her bottom lip and in a worried voice said, 'I just wish I'd told him straight away.'

'As it's much too late for regrets on that score, I suggest you stop worrying about it.' Gently, he added, 'Everything will work out fine, I'm sure.'

Cheered by his confidence, she made an effort to put the problem out of her mind.

After a while, finding the swish of the windscreen wipers soporific, she stifled a yawn.

'Tired?' Joel queried.

'A little.'

He drew her closer and, snuggled against him, she was almost asleep by the time they stopped outside the brownstone in Mulberry Street.

With an effort she roused herself and, climbing out, stood watching the softly falling snow caught in the golden halo of the street lamp like motes swimming in the beam of a spotlight.

It was a magical sight.

As soon as Joel had paid and tipped the driver, he turned to join her.

He was about to hurry her inside, when something about her stillness made him pause and look at her more closely. Then, as if under a spell, he remained stock still gazing down at her.

Her eyes were wide, her lips slightly parted and, framed by the soft, pale fur of her wrap, her lovely face looked luminous. Snowflakes spangled her dark hair and, as he watched, entranced, a couple settled on her long lashes, making her blink.

He hadn't intended to make love to her tonight, hadn't meant to touch her, but now he sighed softly and, as if there was no help for it, bent his head to kiss her.

Taken by surprise, it was a second before she responded, then she went into his arms gladly.

At first his lips felt cold, then he deepened the kiss and warmth spread through her until she glowed from head to toe.

Standing there in the falling snow, with Joel's arms wrapped around her and his mouth claiming hers, the rest of the world ceased to exist.

When, finally, he lifted his head and his voice husky, said, 'Let's get you indoors before you freeze,' in a kind of daze she allowed herself to be shepherded inside and up the stairs.

Once in their room, Joel lifted her wrap from her shoulders, gave it a shake and draped it over a chair. Then, when she straightened after removing her evening sandals, he produced a small towel he'd brought from the bathroom and handed it to her.

While she patted her hair dry he took off his jacket and tie, his movements measured and precise, and as she unfastened her earrings and put them on the dressing table he came round behind her and, bending his head, dropped a kiss on her nape.

Feeling the little shiver of pleasure that ran through her, he turned her into his arms and lifted her chin.

Looking up into his silvery eyes she saw they were dark and smoky with desire.

'You said earlier you were tired?'

Her heart picking up speed and new heat starting to spread through her, she answered, 'I am, a little.'

'But not too tired, I hope?'

'No,' she breathed, and reached up to wipe away a snowflake that had melted on his blond hair and was trickling down his cheek.

He turned his head to kiss her slim fingers before his mouth found hers. This time it was a light, controlled kiss that coaxed and teased and, for the moment at least, kept passion at bay.

Then his face intent, full of purpose, he began to undress her. Before the last wisp of underwear had been disposed of, a pool of liquid heat had formed in the pit of her stomach and she was quivering with desire and anticipation.

But, when she was naked, instead of stripping off his own clothes, he just discarded his shoes and socks and waited.

As she stood looking at him, his smile slightly mocking, he said, 'Fair's fair. Now you undress me.'

Though her fingers fumbled a little at their unaccustomed task, she undid the buttons of his silk shirt and, when he gave her no help, reached up to slip it off.

His chest and shoulders were broad and smoothly muscled with clear, healthy skin. Over his breastbone was a light scattering of golden hair which tapered to a vee and disappeared into the waistband of his trousers.

He looked eminently touchable and, longing to do just that, she reached out a cautious hand.

'Go ahead,' he invited. 'Touch me. I don't bite.'

Stroking her fingertips through the fine mat of curly hair, and fascinated by its silkiness, she leaned forward to rub her cheek against it.

Standing perfectly still, he made a low sound in his throat, as though urging her on.

Giving full rein to her impulse to touch and taste and know him, she turned her head and brushed her lips across his smoothly muscled expanse of chest until they reached a small, firm nipple. Then, her eyes closed and using the tip of her tongue, she explored its shape and size, its slightly rough, leathery texture.

His skin, fresh and clean and still carrying the faint scent of his shower gel, tasted slightly salty and, enjoying the novel sensation, she sucked and tugged a little, before biting delicately.

Feeling the tremor that ran through him, she felt a sense of power that she could give him at least some of the pleasure he had given her.

While her tongue and lips travelled on, learning the masculine secrets of flesh and muscle and bone, her hands slid down to the waistband of his trousers.

Bolder now, her fingers found and released the clip before sliding down the zip and easing the fine material over his lean hips. After a moment, his dark silk boxer shorts followed.

Stepping out of them, he pushed both garments aside with his foot and stood before her totally naked.

For a moment she simply stared at him, fascinated by his beauty, his sheer maleness.

'Go on,' he urged softly. 'Touch me; you know you want to.'

Reminding herself that this wasn't just a sexual encounter, that tomorrow he would be her husband, she let her hand follow the vee of hair downward, and heard the breath hiss through his teeth as her fingers found and caressed his firm flesh.

She was both excited and pleased by the knowledge that for the first time in her life she was making the running, making him feel the male equivalent of all the things he had made her feel.

Her triumph was short-lived.

With an inarticulate murmur, he caught her wrist and held her hand away from him. 'As things are, my love, your touch, though inexperienced, is too potent. It might be wise to take things more slowly.'

Conscious only that he'd called her *my love,* she made no protest when he lifted her on to the bed and proceeded to demonstrate precisely what he meant by slowly.

It wasn't until he'd almost driven her out of her mind that he answered her pleas and proceeded to give her the satisfaction she craved, before taking his own.

When she surfaced next morning she was alone in the big bed. Half asleep and half awake, she glanced blearily at her watch to find it was going up the hill for twelve o'clock.

Jolted into wakefulness by the realization that she was due to be married in a little over two hours, she sat bolt upright just as there was a tap at the door. Pulling up the duvet, she called, 'Come in.'

Molly appeared with a tray of coffee and scrambled eggs. 'Mr McAlister said if you weren't moving by eleven-thirty I was to bring this up.'

'Thank you,' Bethany said confusedly. 'I'm sorry to have given you all this trouble.'

'Why, bless you, it's no trouble. I've had all morning. I told Mr McAlister I would have plenty of time to do a small wedding buffet, but he said not to worry, all the arrangements are made and he's hired a firm of caterers.'

A note of excitement creeping into her voice, she went on, 'He asked Tom and me to come to the wedding and act as witnesses… That is if you haven't any objections?'

'Of course I haven't,' Bethany answered without hesitation. 'It'll be nice to have someone we know rather than a couple of strangers.'

Mrs Brannigan beamed.

Setting the tray carefully across Bethany's knees, she crossed the room to open the curtains, remarking as she did, 'I'm pleased to say it's a beautiful day. There's a light covering of fresh snow, but the sky's blue and the sun's shining. It's just perfect for a winter wedding.

'The flowers have arrived, so when you've had a bite to eat and showered I'll get Tom to bring them up along with the boxes and packages Dellon's delivered earlier.'

Then, in a burst of confidence, 'If I may say so, I'm pleased Mr McAlister's marrying a nice young lady like you. He's a fine man who deserves a good wife.'

'Have you been with him long?' Bethany asked, between sips of coffee.

'I was his mother's housekeeper until she died and I've been with him since. In all those months I've never known him to raise his voice or get in a temper, even though at times young Mr Michael must have tried his patience sorely—'

Molly pulled herself up short and, obviously afraid she'd let her tongue run away with her, murmured hurriedly, 'Well, I'd better be getting along.'

At the door she paused to say, 'I understand that Miss Harvey's going to be your bridesmaid, but if you need any help before the young lady gets here, just let me know.'

'Thanks, I will.'

Though she was too excited to be hungry, Bethany ate the scrambled eggs, which were light and fluffy, before going to clean her teeth and shower.

When she returned to the bedroom wrapped in a towelling robe, her hair still slightly damp, a pile of black and gold packages and a florist's cellophane box were waiting.

The box contained a bridal bouquet of pale yellow rosebuds and fragrant stephanotis and a matching bridesmaid's posy.

She had just finished admiring them when there was a tap at the door and a voice called, 'Hi, it's me.'

Bethany opened the door to find Lisa, slightly dishevelled and flushed with excitement, hovering outside clutching a handbag and several of the now familiar black and gold boxes.

Catching the top one, which had started to slip, Bethany invited, 'Come on in. Did you manage to get all you needed?'

Dropping her bag and packages on the nearest chair, Lisa said happily, 'Oh, yes. Joel drove me to Dellon's and they took care of everything.'

'That's great.'

All at once, wanting very much to see Joel, needing the reassurance of his presence, Bethany asked, 'Did he come back with you?'

'Yes, he's downstairs. He said to tell you he'll see you in church.'

'Oh…' A little deflated, Bethany wondered if he was merely busy or following the tradition of the groom not seeing the bride prior to the wedding.

Lisa sighed. 'Isn't it romantic being swept off your feet like that? You must feel so excited.'

'I feel rather like Alice in Wonderland. Nothing's quite real—' Breaking off, Bethany added with a shaky smile, 'I'll be a married woman in less than two hours and I still haven't told my parents. I intended to ring them first thing this morning, but I'm afraid I overslept.'

Seeing the shadow that fell across her face, Lisa suggested practically, 'Well, I know there isn't much time, but if I get on and unpack everything, couldn't you tell them now?'

While the younger girl emptied the boxes and laid everything out neatly on the bed, Bethany tapped in the international code and the familiar Notting Hill number of her parents' home.

It rang three or four times, then she heard the click as the receiver was lifted.

'Hello?' It was her father's voice.

'Dad, it's me…'

'Well, hello, love.'

'I've some news for you and Mum…'

'You can tell me, but I'm afraid your mother's not here. She's staying at her sister's for a few days.'

With a guilty feeling of relief—her mother was an inveterate talker—Bethany quickly and concisely told her father the bare facts.

He listened without interrupting.

When she finished he said seriously, 'It all seems very sudden, but you've always been a sensible girl, so I presume you know what you're doing… I take it you love him?'

'Yes, I love him,' she said steadily.

'Then you have my blessing. When you get back, I'd like to meet my new son-in-law.'

'Of course. I think you'll like him. Will you explain to Mum, and tell her I'm sorry to spring it on you both like this?'

'I'll do that. All our love…'

Bethany replaced the receiver, then, obeying an impulse, picked it up again and tapped in Michael's number. If she could just talk to him briefly and tell him she was sorry, it would take a weight off her mind.

But he didn't seem to be answering and she gave it up for the time being.

Lisa glanced across to smile at her. 'What a beautiful wedding dress… And Joel was quite right, the bridesmaid's dress will go perfectly.

'By the way, he said the cars will be arriving about one-thirty, so we haven't a lot of time.'

'Oh, Lord,' Bethany muttered, 'and I've still got to pack some things to take away.'

'If you find a case and get out everything you need I'll pack while you do your hair and make-up.'

'Thanks,' Bethany said gratefully, producing a case and starting to pile stuff on a chair. 'I don't know what I would have done without you.'

Looking pleased, Lisa began to pack swiftly and efficiently, while Bethany made-up lightly and brushed and coiled her hair.

'Where are you going on honeymoon?' Lisa asked as, her packing finished, she helped Bethany into her dress. 'Or is it a secret?'

'We're having a few days in the Catskills. Joel's driving us up after the wedding.'

'Sounds great,' Lisa remarked enthusiastically.

Having fastened the tiny covered buttons that ran down the back of the dress, she said, 'It fits like a dream…' Then, hastily, 'Oh, I mustn't forget…'

From her bag she took a small blue velvet case. 'Joel asked me to say he'd like you to wear these. They belonged to his grandmother.'

The case contained a double string of perfectly graded lustrous pearls and a pair of beautiful pearl-drop earrings.

'He said he meant to give them to you last night, but somehow he got distracted.'

When, blushing and misty-eyed, Bethany had donned the necklace and earrings, Lisa set her coronet in place and arranged the short filmy veil.

Stepping back to admire her handiwork, she exclaimed, 'Wow! You look sensational. Joel will be bowled over.'

While Bethany slipped into her shoes and took the flowers out of their cellophane wrapping, Lisa quickly did her own hair and face and put on her pretty apricot silk bridesmaid's dress, a matching headband and a silver necklace.

'What a pretty necklace,' Bethany remarked.

Lisa looked delighted. 'Yes, isn't it? Joel insisted on buying it for me as a bridesmaid's thank you present.'

Then, reaching for her bag, from a piece of tissue paper she produced a dainty garter embroidered with blue butterflies and asked, a shade diffidently, 'By the way, I wondered if you'd like to borrow this?

'You know the old wedding rhyme,' she went on. "Something old, something new, something borrowed and something blue"…? Well, you have something old and something new and I thought…' Looking a little flustered, she broke off.

Swallowing the lump in her throat, Bethany said warmly, 'What a lovely idea. I'd be delighted to borrow it.' Lifting her silken skirts, she slipped the garter on and settled it above her right knee.

There was a tap at the door and Molly, attired in her best hat, a flower pinned to her jacket, appeared to announce that the caterers were here and both the bridesmaid's car and the bridal car were waiting.

Picking up her posy, Lisa said, 'I should go first, shouldn't I?' Then, suddenly nervous, needing reassurance, 'Will I do?'

'You look lovely,' Bethany said sincerely.

Lisa beamed. 'It *is* a pretty dress, isn't it? David's picking me up after the wedding. I hope he gets here in time to see it.'

As the younger girl, flushed with pride and excitement, hurried away, Molly added cheerfully, 'And Senator Harvey's just arrived. He's waiting in the hall.'

'Perhaps you'll tell him I'll be down in just a minute? Then, if you and Tom want to get off…'

When Molly had gone, Bethany swapped her engagement ring to her right hand, gathered up her bouquet and took a last look in the mirror before making her way down the stairs.

Having stood and watched her descend, the Senator, smartly dressed in a grey pinstripe suit and with a cream carnation in his buttonhole, said, 'My dear, you look absolutely radiant.'

'Thank you.' She smiled at him. 'I must say you look very smart yourself.'

He preened a little before asking, 'All ready?'

'All ready.'

'Then we mustn't keep the groom waiting.' He offered her his arm.

It was another clear, cold day with sunshine gilding the skeletal trees and ricocheting from the windscreens of passing cars as they drove to the Church of the Holy Shepherd.

The lovely old building, with its elegant spires and intricate stonework, was sandwiched between two skyscrapers. It should have looked incongruous, but somehow it didn't. Its air of timeless beauty, of *belonging*, contrived to make its glass and concrete neighbours look like modern upstarts.

As the Senator helped Bethany from the car, a photographer appeared and began to take pictures, backing into the church in front of them.

Inside it was serene and dim, despite the bright shafts of light slanting through the stained glass windows and the lighted candles. The scent of flowers hung on the still air and in the background an organ was playing softly.

Joel, wearing a well-cut grey suit, a cream carnation in his buttonhole and looking like every woman's dream of a handsome bridegroom, was waiting by the chancel steps, Paul Rosco beside him.

Apart from Molly and Tom, the rows of polished pews were empty.

Lisa was standing at the back of the church with the Reverend

John Daintree who, after greeting them, went to take his place in front of the altar.

The organist changed to Bach and, as Bethany walked up the aisle on the Senator's arm, Joel turned to smile at her.

Since leaving Mulberry Street nothing had seemed quite real and, feeling as though she was dreaming the whole thing, she handed her bouquet to Lisa and moved to stand by her bridegroom's side.

When, after a second or two, the organ music faded into silence, the Reverend John Daintree cleared his throat and began the service. 'Dearly beloved...'

Afterwards, though the dreamlike state still persisted, Bethany retained a clear, jewel-bright memory of the ceremony. The firmness of Joel's responses; his serious expression as he slipped the gold wedding band on to her finger; the joy as they were pronounced man and wife; the feeling of coming home as he turned back her veil and kissed her.

But her most treasured memory was her surprise when the best man produced not one ring but two and her gladness as she slid the heavy gold signet ring on to Joel's finger.

When the wedding certificate had been signed and witnessed, there were handshakes and kisses all round. Then more photographs were taken before the Senator left for La Guardia, Paul returned to his office and the Reverend John Daintree began to get ready for his next engagement.

Once outside, the bride and groom were showered with rice before they and the remainder of the wedding party returned in convoy to Mulberry Street.

When they arrived they found a young man with fair curly hair and a thin intelligent face waiting on the front stairs. 'Sorry, I'm afraid I'm early,' David remarked apologetically when Lisa had introduced them. 'I'll take a walk and come back in half an hour or so.'

'You'll do no such thing,' Joel said firmly. 'We need you to even up the numbers.'

'Please do come in and have something to eat and a glass of champagne,' Bethany added persuasively.

'Well, if you're sure?'

She smiled at him. 'Quite sure.'

As he escorted Lisa up the steps, Bethany heard him say, 'You look beautiful,' and was pleased to note that the younger girl went pink with pleasure.

In the event she wasn't the only one. As they reached the door, Bethany was swept, blushing and laughing, into Joel's arms and carried over the threshold.

'I believe in keeping up old traditions,' he told a grinning David.

'I must say I approve,' that young man said. 'So long as the bride is as slim as Bethany and Lisa,' he said with a grin.

In the dining room the caterers had set out a small but excellent buffet with fresh flowers, a beautifully decorated wedding cake and some perfectly chilled champagne.

Joel insisted that Molly and Tom joined them, which they did as soon as Tom had brought the car round to the door and loaded the luggage into the boot.

After the party of six had done justice to the meal, Bethany, Joel's arm round her waist, his hand over hers, cut the cake.

Then, when their glasses had been refilled, David, standing in for the best man, proved to be unexpectedly eloquent as he proposed a toast to the bride and groom.

The toast over, he announced that Lisa and he ought to be moving, while Molly and Tom, who both declared they were woozy, slipped off quietly.

Because he was driving later Joel had drunk very little, but after two glasses of the vintage champagne Bethany too had started to feel pleasantly floaty and light-headed.

Having given the caterers permission to clear away, Joel took David through to the living room, where he looked at the evening paper while the other three went upstairs to change.

When the two girls returned carrying their outdoor things, they saw that Joel, who had used the spare room to change into smart casuals, was in his study apparently reading his emails.

Seeing them pass his partly open door, he abandoned what he was doing and returned to the living-room to see Lisa and David off.

'If it's okay with you,' Lisa said, as the two men shook hands and the women exchanged warm hugs, 'I'll call and collect the rest of my things when you get back from your honeymoon.'

'Of course,' Bethany told her.

'And you must see the photographs,' Joel said. He added, 'Then perhaps we could make up a foursome for dinner and dancing?'

Looking as if she'd been given a present, Lisa cried, 'Oh, that would be great,' and got David's nod of approval.

When the pair had been waved off, Joel, appearing happy and relaxed, as though any underlying tension with regard to the wedding had drained away, gathered Bethany close. 'Alone at last,' he said deeply. 'Do you realize, woman, that you've been my wife for almost two hours and I still haven't kissed you properly?'

Lifting her face to his, she suggested, 'I'm sure you could remedy that.'

'I fully intend to. In fact, had we changed together, I would have done rather more than simply kiss you. But, unfortunately, the presence of a bridesmaid, no matter how sweet, is inhibiting.'

Looking at him from beneath long lashes, she asked, 'How soon do we have to start?'

'We can start whenever we want to.'

'In that case,' she began demurely, 'as Lisa's no longer here…'

He laughed and, his silvery-green eyes gleaming, said, 'What a s-sensible woman you are.'

She pretended to be disappointed. 'I thought you were going to say sexy.'

'Oh, you're that too.' Then, punctuating the words with soft baby kisses, 'Not to mention sensuous and seductive and sensational… Can you think of any other suitable words beginning with an s…?'

Enjoying this lighter side he was showing, she suggested, 'Spellbinding…'

'Undoubtedly the best yet.' With a little growl, he swept her up in his arms. 'Come on then, my little witch, let's go somewhere more private and make mad, passionate love…'

Gladness and joy bubbling inside her, and knowing she'd never been so happy in her life, she put her arms round his neck and gave herself up to the promise of delight.

They were halfway to the door when it was thrown open abruptly and Michael, looking flushed and dishevelled, burst into the room.

Joel froze and after a second or two put Bethany down and steadied her until she had found her balance. Then, looking at the newcomer, his face set and grim, he asked quietly, 'What the devil are you doing here?'

CHAPTER TEN

IGNORING his stepmother and looking at Bethany, Michael said hoarsely, 'Tara seemed to think you and Joel were planning to get married, and I came to warn you not to be taken in by—'

Catching sight of her left hand where her new wedding ring gleamed, he broke off and muttered an angry oath. Then, after a moment, 'But it seems I'm too late. Who said money talks?'

'I didn't marry Joel for his money.'

'Well, as you've only known him five minutes, it must have been love at first sight,' he sneered.

Bethany raised her chin in a gesture of defiance. 'As a matter of fact, it was.'

For a moment he stared at her, then he said bitterly, 'Do you know, I'm almost inclined to believe you. You said you couldn't marry me because you didn't love me, now you look like a woman in love, the epitome of a happy bride—'

'Michael, I'm sorry,' Bethany broke in. 'I should have told you straight away how things were. I know I've treated you badly and I—'

Brushing her apology aside, he went on, 'But you won't look quite so happy when I tell you exactly why the swine married you.'

Lifting her chin, she said, 'I already know about Tara and you, and I don't believe—'

'Tara has nothing to do with this. What has *everything* to do with it is that when I marry I become independent. My own master. As soon as probate is granted I can sell the blasted house and raise some cash.'

'But I thought—'

'The terms of Grandmother's will state that I can sell the house either when I'm twenty-five or when I "settle down and marry". Big brother didn't want that. It takes away his power. He was determined to stop you marrying me…'

There was some truth in that last statement, as Bethany well knew. She could still hear the ring of steel in Joel's voice as he'd told her, "Well, get this into your pretty little head, there's no way I'll allow you to marry him".

When she had asked him why, he'd answered, "Perhaps I'm jealous. Perhaps I want you for myself".

She had wanted desperately to believe that, and had *almost* succeeded in doing so. But maybe she had been wrong? Maybe he had had other reasons?

'And the only way he could be *sure* you wouldn't,' Michael went on, 'was to marry you himself.'

After a moment's thought, she said firmly, 'That's utter rubbish. I'd already told him I had no intention of marrying you.'

Michael smirked. 'It seems he didn't believe you.'

'Even if he didn't, no man in his right senses would tie himself to a woman he didn't want just to stop her marrying his stepbrother.

'In any case, if you were set on getting married, how could he stop you?'

'He bought Glenda off,' Michael said resentfully.

'If she was willing to be bought off, she couldn't have loved you,' Bethany pointed out quietly. 'And there must be plenty of nice women who would jump at the chance to marry you.'

Michael laughed at her innocence. 'Sam, the girl I'm bunking down with, would marry me like a shot if I asked her, but—'

He stopped short, looking a bit sheepish. Then, with a shrug, muttered, 'Oh, what the hell! I know I told you I was flatsharing with a friend, but when you wouldn't come across... Well, a man has needs and—'

'It really doesn't matter,' Bethany said. She added crisply, 'So why don't you go ahead and ask her?'

He sighed. 'I considered that a few months ago, but I realized she was a mercenary bitch who would take me for everything I had if we split up.

'Then, after I met you, no one else would do. *You* were the one I wanted. As soon as Big Brother realized that, he stepped in...'

As Bethany began to shake her head, Michael went on angrily, 'He's prepared to go to any lengths to keep control of my life, even to marrying a woman he believes is a liar and a thief—'

'That's quite enough.' Joel's words were softly spoken but they fell like a whiplash.

Though he looked scared, Michael faced up to his stepbrother. '*I* know you're wrong about that, but don't try to tell me it isn't what *you* believe. I *know* what you were out to prove, about the trap you set for her. That loopy old woman let the cat out of the bag.' Michael carried on regardless of the warning look in his stepbrother's eyes.

'I happened to be at your flat picking up some of my clothes when she phoned. She thought she was talking to you. You'll no doubt be surprised to know that she's "found" the things she assured you had been stolen—'

He stopped speaking abruptly and backed away as Joel took a step towards him.

'Don't worry,' Joel said grimly. 'I've no intention of laying a finger on you. However, it's high time you stopped and listened to some straight speaking.

'You're blaming me for trying to control your life but all I've done is try to protect you, to keep you out of trouble, as I promised our Grandmother.'

'Damn it all, I don't want your help…' Michael began to bluster.

'You may not want it, but you certainly *need* it. You're nothing but a young fool who, at the rate you're going, will end up penniless and in real trouble…'

Upset and agitated, needing a chance to think, Bethany turned on her heel and fled into Joel's study.

Her legs feeling oddly shaky, barely able to support her, she sank down on the black leather swivel chair by his desk.

Michael's words, 'He's prepared to go to any lengths to keep control of my life, even to marrying a woman he believes is a liar and a thief…' seemed branded on her mind.

And Joel had said, 'All I've done is try to protect you, to keep you out of trouble…' Which was virtually admitting it.

The feeling of warmth and trust that exchanging rings had brought shrivelled and died and a kind of bewildered anger took its place.

Joel might believe she'd lied, but what possible justification had he for believing she was a thief?

What was it Michael had said? 'I know what you were out to prove, about the trap you set for her. That loopy old woman let the cat out of the bag…'

But that didn't make any sense… Unless…

Recalling the evening she and Joel had met, the night they had spent together at Dunscar, his questions, his marked interest in her job, light began to dawn.

'The loopy old woman' had to be Mrs Deramack, and the 'trap' he had set must have been connected to her visit to Bosthwaite to look at the antiques.

He must have planted something there, something small and

valuable, that a dishonest person, thinking they were dealing with a confused old woman, could easily have slipped into a pocket or a handbag.

But to have set up a trap of any kind he must have known about her visit in advance.

Which raised the question—how much else had he known about her? Obviously about her job and presumably about her relationship—innocent as it was—with Michael.

So did that mean he knew Michael had been selling things to Feldon Antiques?

If he did that would account for his interest in the bracelet she had been wearing. He'd obviously recognized it as belonging to his mother's set.

Guessing she'd bought it from Michael and believing that the stones were rubies, had he assumed that she'd cheated his step-brother and paid a lot less for it than it was worth?

Or—her stomach tightened as an even worse thought struck her—had he suspected her of stealing it?

If he had, and he'd known of—or possibly even *arranged?*—her visit to the Lake District to see Mrs Deramack, their meeting that night hadn't been a chance one.

Or perhaps in a way it had?

Maybe he hadn't actually *intended* them to meet. Maybe he had simply been tailing her that day. She recalled how a similar Range Rover to the one he'd been driving had followed her on her outward journey. If it hadn't been for the flat tyre and the fog, he might have just followed her back to the Dundale Inn. But, as circumstances had thrown them together and altered his plans, he had turned the meeting to his advantage. Had used the opportunity to check her out and try to confirm her guilt.

A hollow feeling in the pit of her stomach, she recalled the jammed zip in her handbag and the way her phone had been replaced in the wrong pocket.

He must have searched through her bag in the belief that his plan had worked, that she'd stolen whatever it was he'd planted, because Mrs Deramack had told him so.

'You'll no doubt be surprised to know that she's "found" the things she assured you had been stolen…'

Bethany bit her lip. Still at least he now knew she was innocent on that score. But what if Michael hadn't admitted selling the vase and other things to Feldon Antiques? What if Joel thought *she* had contrived to steal them?

Oh, surely not?

Yet it made a terrible kind of sense.

Suppose he'd believed her to be an unscrupulous liar and a thief and had been afraid she might marry a besotted Michael and take him for everything he had, what would have been the best way to deal with it?

One sure way to protect his stepbrother would be to marry her himself.

But, being no fool, he had first taken steps to protect himself. That was why he had insisted on a marriage contract.

For the first time she realized the full significance of the phone call she had overheard and, with excellent verbal recall, played it through in her mind.

'It's of the utmost importance…' Joel had said. 'I need the document ready to be signed by tomorrow afternoon…'

Then, 'Yes… Yes… Exactly as I've outlined…'

Paul Rosco must have said something like, *But will she forget your stepbrother and marry you?*

And Joel had responded, 'Well, at the moment, as far as money and power goes, I'm the best bet. And, however you look at it, the organ grinder has got to be a better proposition than the monkey…

'Yes, Paul, I know it must seem drastic to you, and I admit it's taking a big risk, but I can't see any other way. And I assure you that whether it works or not it has its compensations…

'Yes, yes… If there's any way I can *make* it work, I'm prepared to stick with it…'

And what would Paul Rosco have said? Something like, *But suppose she tries to take you for a ride?*

And Joel had answered, 'I can't rule it out. That's why I want to be sure I can't be ripped off…'

For the first time she understood why the solicitor had been so cool and guarded with her. He had known why Joel was marrying her in such haste and, regarding her as a scheming little bitch, disapproved of the whole thing…

Trying to blink back tears of anger and humiliation, Bethany bent her head, feeling wretched, sick and hollow inside.

At that instant the door opened and Joel strode in. With a glance at her stricken face, he said, 'I'm sorry you had to find out like this.'

As she opened her mouth to speak, he added, 'I can see how upset you are, but we'll have plenty of time to clear the air when we get to the cabin.' Briskly, he added, 'There's snow forecast for later tonight, so it's time we got going…'

She fought the urge to laugh hysterically. Did he seriously think she was going to meekly go on honeymoon with him as if nothing was wrong?

But instinctively she knew that he would brook no alteration to his plans and it would be difficult, not to say impossible, to fight him.

But somehow she *had* to get away.

Gathering up the papers from his desk, he put them in his briefcase and said, 'Michael's staying here tonight, so while you collect your coat and bag I'll just have a quick word with Molly.'

Bethany felt her heart leap. It was the chance she needed.

To run in that way would mean leaving all her belongings and she had no dollars, but she could give the driver English money and use her credit card to get a flight back to London.

To her great relief there was no sign of Michael and as soon as Joel had gone in search of the housekeeper she hastily pulled on her coat and gathered up her shoulder bag.

A moment later she had let herself out of the front door and was hurrying down the steps. Joel's sleek saloon was standing by the kerb and she wished fleetingly that she had the keys.

There were no taxis in sight and, her coat flapping open, she set off down the lamplit street at a trot. She had almost reached the end when she heard her name called and, glancing back, saw Joel in pursuit.

Running now, she turned the corner and started along Mulberry Square. She had only gone a short distance when she saw a yellow cab coming towards her and waved frantically.

The driver did a U-turn and a few seconds later he was drawing up beside her. Pulling open the door, she scrambled in and said breathlessly, 'JFK please, as fast as you can.'

Sinking back in her seat, she fastened her safety belt and sighed with relief.

They had left Mulberry Square behind them and were halfway along Brand Street when they were held up by a red light.

Suddenly the door was yanked open, her seat belt was unfastened and a moment later she was half hauled, half lifted, out on to the sidewalk.

'Leave me alone. Let me go…' She struggled to free herself.

The cab driver turned to see what was happening and, lowering his window began, 'Hey there, what's going on?'

As passers-by looked in their direction, Joel pulled her into his arms and kissed her, stifling her attempts to protest.

Then, holding her firmly with one arm, he thrust a handful of dollar bills at the driver and said, 'Sorry about this. We've only been married a few hours and this is our first quarrel—'

Making a fresh attempt to pull free, Bethany cried, 'This wasn't just a quarrel and you know it. Now let me go, I'm leaving…'

In a long-suffering voice, Joel said, 'Women do make mountains out of molehills…'

'Don't I know it! Well, best of luck, pal!'

'Please, driver, don't listen to him. I want to—' But Bethany's plea fell on deaf ears as the lights changed and the cab moved forward.

Despite her protests she was hustled to where Joel's car, its door still standing open, was holding up the stream of evening traffic.

Fairly bundling her inside, he clicked the seat belt into place and slammed the door.

As he went round to the driver's side, she fumbled for the door handle, but the door wouldn't open. Gritting her teeth, she realized he must have put some kind of child-lock into place.

A moment later they were underway, the traffic began to flow again and the little incident was over and done with.

Taking a deep breath, she said as steadily as possible, 'If you think you can make me go on honeymoon with you as if nothing has happened, you're quite wrong. I'm leaving you.'

'Perhaps when we've had a chance to talk you'll change your mind.'

'There's nothing you could say or do that will make me change my mind, so if you'll please stop the car and let me get out, I'll take a taxi to the airport.'

He showed no sign of obeying and, glancing at his handsome profile, noting the set of his jaw, she knew she was wasting her breath.

Having achieved what he'd set out to achieve, and thinking so badly of her, why couldn't he just let her go? she wondered bleakly. But, even as her mind formed the question, she knew the answer.

No doubt against his will, and in spite of his better judgement, he still wanted her physically.

Well, he might still want her, but no matter how much she loved him, her pride wouldn't let her go on with this mockery of a honeymoon.

Knowing, however, that further protests would be of no avail, she sat in resentful silence while they made their way out of the city.

True to the forecast, it had started to snow and, despite the traffic, the road was soon covered, the tracks of the cars ahead making continuous black patterns against the white.

For a while Bethany watched the swirling flakes before, physically weary and emotionally exhausted, she drifted into sleep.

Fingers stroking her cheek awakened her. Lifting her head, she opened heavy eyes to find they had stopped in a small snowy clearing surrounded by trees.

In front of them was a one-storey clapboard house with a wooden veranda running round it. The long square-paned windows were lit and a lantern in the open porch spilled a pool of yellow light.

Still half asleep, she stumbled a little as Joel helped her out and he put an arm around her as they climbed the wooden steps and crossed the porch to the white-painted door.

It was unlocked and the trail of fresh footprints in the snow between the car and the house showed that he had taken their luggage inside before waking her.

The big living room, with its rustic furniture, was warm and welcoming, though the fire in the stove had died to a red glow.

His arm still encircling her, he asked, 'Would you like anything to eat or drink?'

Longing only to drift back into sleep, she shook her head.

'Then straight to bed, I think.'

'I won't sleep with you.'

Silkily, he asked, 'Have you considered that you may have no choice in the matter? You're my wife.'

Pushing his arm away, she said, 'I'm not your *wife* and I've no intention of ever being your wife. Knowing what you think of me—'

'But you *don't* know what I think of you.'

Swaying a little, she insisted thickly, 'I don't want to sleep with you, and if you force me to I'll never forgive you.'

He sighed. 'Very well. Until things are sorted out, I'll use the other room.'

The bedroom he led her to was as warm and comfortable as the living room had been and the double bed looked soft and cosy.

Her small case had been placed on a blanket chest and, like a zombie, neither thinking nor feeling, she found her toilet things and cleaned her teeth in the *en-suite* bathroom.

She returned to the bedroom to find her nightdress and dressing-gown had been laid out on the bed and the duvet turned back.

There was no sign of Joel.

When she had taken off her clothes and donned her nightie she climbed into bed, turned out the light and slept as soon as her head touched the pillow.

She awoke to the appetizing aroma of freshly brewed coffee and bacon frying. Climbing out of bed, she drew aside the heavy folkweave curtains and looked through the window at a winter wonderland.

Hemlock and pine, their green arms weighed down with snow,

stood at the edge of the clearing. On the opposite slopes she could see a scattering of houses and, in the far distance, snow-covered mountains.

It was a beautiful, secluded place, perfect for a romantic honeymoon, if only things had been other than they were.

But after almost believing that her dreams had come true and she had everything she had ever wanted in life—even a chance to win Joel's love—she had ended up with nothing.

Less than nothing, as he thought so badly of her.

Feeling empty and desolate, she went through to the bathroom to clean her teeth and shower, before dressing in fine wool trousers and a cream sweater.

Though she dreaded the thought of having to confront him, the sooner she could convince him that she had no intention of going through with this marriage, the better. Then, hopefully, he would take her back to New York City.

As she brushed her hair she glanced in the mirror. A vulnerable-looking woman with bleak, disillusioned, cloudy-grey eyes, too big for her pale face, stared back at her.

She turned away abruptly and, leaving her long dark hair loose about her shoulders, her head held high, made her way to the kitchen to face Joel.

The sophisticated city man who owned a jet plane, wore silk shirts and hand-tailored suits, was gone. Dressed in jeans and a dark blue shirt open at the throat, he was standing by the stove, turning sizzling bacon in a pan.

'Excellent timing,' he greeted her cheerfully. 'I'm just about ready to dish up.'

'I'm not hungry. I need to talk to you.'

He looked at her squarely. 'We'll talk as soon as we've eaten.'

A glance at his face told her she would get nowhere unless she did things his way, so she allowed herself to be seated at the table.

The big kitchen was warm and homely, with a black wood-stove and natural pine furniture. On the table was a pitcher of freshly squeezed orange juice and two glasses, a crusty sour-dough loaf, butter, blueberry jam and a jug of cream.

He helped her to orange juice before filling two plates with crispy bacon and fluffy scrambled eggs. Then, sitting down opposite, he waited for her to begin her breakfast.

Feeling anything but hungry, she picked up her knife and fork.

After a moment he followed suit and, his eyes on her face, observed, 'With your hair loose like that and no make-up you look about seventeen.'

She made no comment and he relapsed into silence.

When their plates were empty and the coffee was finished, he led the way over to where two cushioned chairs were drawn up in front of the glowing stove.

As soon as they were both seated he began without preamble. 'Some months ago I discovered that a very valuable antique bowl appeared to be missing from my grandmother's house. Michael, the only person apart from myself who had a key to Lanervic Square, denied all knowledge of it.

'When, over the next few weeks, other smaller items started to disappear at regular intervals, I hired a private detective.

'He found that Michael had a girlfriend who was a buyer for Feldon Antiques and—'

'And, suspecting me of stealing them, you arranged for me to visit Mrs Deramack and set a trap...'

A wry twist to his mouth, Joel admitted, 'Though I'm not proud of it, at the time it seemed the best way to obtain some proof. So I asked her to phone Feldon Antiques and say she had some pieces of silver and porcelain for sale.

'When I was sure you were going, I planted two valuable silver vinaigrettes amongst a jumble of worthless stuff in the parlour.

'I was keeping an eye on you and after you'd left I phoned Alice and she told me the vinaigrettes were missing. I believed her, having failed to realize just how senile the old lady has become—'

'Then you saw me wearing the bracelet and jumped to the conclusion that I'd stolen that too,' Bethany said bitterly.

He shook his head. 'The set had been in my mother's wall safe in what used to be her bedroom, but was now Michael's when he came over to New York. So he was the only person who could possibly have taken it.

'I presumed you'd bought it from him—'

'And you took it, believing I'd paid him for garnets when they were actually rubies—'

'I took it to a jeweller to get to the truth. When he confirmed that they were garnets I was delighted.'

She shook her head, denying his statement. 'You believed I was a thief and a liar—'

'I *suspected* you might be. And when I questioned you and you wouldn't tell me the truth…

'I realize now you were just trying to protect Michael, but then I—'

She cut him off. 'You thought I was an unscrupulous bitch who had battened on to him and, knowing you could deal with me better, you married me to protect him.'

'I kept trying to tell myself that was why I was doing it,' Joel admitted, 'but in the end I married you because I wanted you to be my wife—'

'I don't believe you,' she broke in furiously. 'I overheard your conversation with Paul Rosco. I know exactly what you thought of me, why you insisted on a marriage contract.

'Well, I've no intention of staying with you, but don't worry, the only thing I want from you is my freedom. I've still got a job so I'll be—'

'That's just it, you haven't.' He cut in authoritatively. 'I've already made it clear to your boss that you won't be going back.'

'How dare you?' she choked. 'You've no right to make decisions for me. Whether or not I go back to Feldon's is none of your business.'

His voice remained calm as he replied. 'You're my wife, which makes it my business. And there's no way I'll allow you to go back there.'

'If you think for one minute—' Bethany was furious.

'Stansfield, the detective I hired, found that the police are interested in Feldon. They suspect him of dealing in stolen property, and it should be only a matter of time before they catch him.'

Though she herself had had doubts about the scrupulousness of Tony's business methods, she had never thought that he might be seriously crooked.

'I don't believe it,' she said without conviction.

Joel passed her a couple of sheets of paper. 'After I'd got changed yesterday I checked my emails and found this waiting. I suggest you read it.'

The email read:

After further and more extensive enquiries, I can find no proof that Miss Seaton is anything other than honest. While she is still officially Feldon's buyer, since Tony Feldon took over the business on his father's death he has made himself responsible for all the pricing and buying.

His father, James Feldon, whom Miss Seaton worked for for almost four years, had an excellent reputation for fair and honest dealing.

However, it appears that his son is under police scrutiny. They suspect him of dealing in stolen property, which apparently he sells on to wealthy private collectors who don't ask questions.

With regard to the missing bowl, I've managed to take a look through the register that Feldon keeps. There is no record of any such bowl being either bought or sold.

That being the case, it will be extremely difficult, not to say impossible, to prove anything against Feldon, unless your stepbrother will admit to selling him the vase.

Following the line of enquiry you advised, I found that some three months ago your stepbrother paid over a very considerable sum in gambling debts. Which strongly indicates that he *did* sell the bowl. Though what he appears to have received for it suggests that it hadn't been properly identified as Ming...

Going cold, Bethany admitted, 'I saw the bowl...'

His silvery-green eyes narrowing, Joel asked, 'What did you think?'

Through stiff lips, she said, 'I thought it was Ming, but Tony said he'd taken it to an expert on Chinese porcelain who had identified it as Qing. Which, of course, made it worth a lot less.'

'I see,' Joel said quietly.

After a moment she returned her attention to the email, which continued:

Since then your stepbrother has run up new, and considerable, gambling debts. However, he has no more money left and he is using your name to obtain credit.

I don't hold out much hope of getting any further with my enquiries and, as you are adamant that you don't want to involve the police, I'll wait to hear from you...

As Bethany looked up, Joel said grimly, 'Feldon Antiques appears to have made a killing on the bowl but, of course, having stolen it himself, Michael wasn't in a position to argue.'

'Perhaps he shouldn't have sold it until after probate has been granted, but how can you call it *stealing* when it belonged to him?' she objected.

'It didn't belong to him,' Joel said flatly, 'nor did the other things he sold. The house itself is his, but the contents were be-queathed to my aunt and uncle who intend to auction them and retire on the proceeds.'

Stricken, she admitted, 'Tony wasn't interested in the smaller items. I bought those for my collection, along with the bracelet.'

'Well, don't worry about it. Even though, when I talked to Michael yesterday, he finally admitted taking the bowl and other things, I can't imagine they will want to press charges. Especially if I make up the shortfall.

'Which I've agreed to do, as well as pay off his current gambling debts, but only on condition that he takes the post I've offered him in Los Angeles, sorts out his gambling problem and keeps to the straight and narrow.'

There was silence for a little while, then Joel asked quietly, 'Do you feel any happier now you know the truth?'

Still icy cold and resentful inside, she demanded, 'Why should I feel any happier? The truth is, you married me believing me to be a thief and a liar. Married me to save Michael…'

He took her hand and looked into her eyes. 'The truth is I wanted you and was jealous of Michael from the word go. I shouldn't have seduced you that night, but I couldn't help myself.

'I tried to fight it, but after a couple of days of knowing you I no longer cared what you might or might not have done. I was so madly in love with you I would always have married you and done my best to make it work.' She tried to remain impassive to his dazzling smile but her heart leapt at his words.

Joel continued. 'If Michael hadn't burst in when he did I'd intended to tell you everything when we got back from honeymoon, and ask your forgiveness.' Joel reached up and tenderly stroked her face with the back of his hand. 'I just hope you can understand why I acted as I did. But I didn't know you then. Finding that you're blameless, as lovely and innocent inside as you are out, is the best gift I've ever received.'

His words and his obvious sincerity warmed her like a blazing fire on a bleak winter's day, thawing the ice and dissipating any lingering resentment.

'From the moment I set eyes on you, I was lost,' he went on quietly. 'In some strange way I felt as if you were already under my skin, in my heart, in my bloodstream. Part of me. I felt as if I'd known and loved you for years.

'When you said you wouldn't marry a man you didn't love, and then you told Michael it had been love at first sight, I began to hope that a miracle had happened and that you felt the same way about me…'

Bethany rose to her feet a shade unsteadily and saw the look of despair on his face when he thought she was leaving.

He caught her hand. 'Please don't go. I know you must feel angry and bitter but—'

She stooped and her kiss stopped his words.

With a sound almost like a groan, his arms went around her and he pulled her on to his knee.

It was a little while before they surfaced, then he said huskily, 'Tell me I'm not dreaming this. Tell me you do feel the same way about me.'

'I do. I've loved you since I was seventeen. After a holiday in Scotland my parents and I were staying one night in Dundale, and we went to a village concert—'

He laughed as he thought back to his youth. 'Now I remember,' he said wonderingly. 'You were the loveliest thing I'd ever seen…' He kissed her deeply. 'I dreamt about you for months, and bitterly regretted not taking the chance to talk to you, but my then girlfriend had been with me. But I remembered that night for years…'

He kissed her passionately, then observed, 'Fate works in mysterious ways. Once you were just a beautiful face that haunted me, now you're my wife…'

'Well, not quite,' she said demurely and, getting off his knee, took his hand. 'But I'm sure we could remedy that.'

Laughing, he rose to his feet and swept her up in his arms. 'We could indeed, my love.'

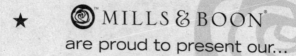

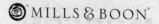

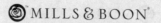

1009/26/MB235

From No. 1 *New York Times* bestselling author Nora Roberts

Nightshade available 2nd January 2010
When a teenager gets caught up in making sadistic violent films, Colt Nightshade and Lieutenant Althea Grayson must find her before she winds up dead...

Night Smoke available 5th February 2010
When Natalie Fletcher's office is set ablaze, she must find out who wants her ruined – before someone is killed...

Night Shield available 5th March 2010
When a revengeful robber leaves blood-stained words on Detective Allison Fletcher's walls, she knows her cop's shield won't be enough to protect her...

**Passion. Power. Suspense.
It's time to fall under the spell of Nora Roberts.**

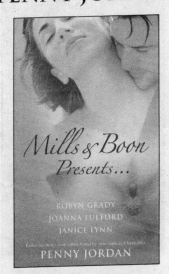

His innocent mistress

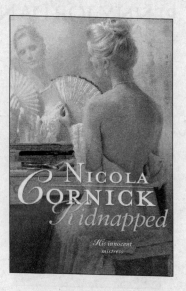

Orphaned and vulnerable, Catriona is doing
her best to resist the skilful seduction of the
scandalous heir to the Earl of Strathconan.
Then her newly discovered inheritance
places them both in terrible danger.

First kidnapped, then shipwrecked with only
this fascinating rake as company, her
adventure has just begun…

Available 18th September 2009

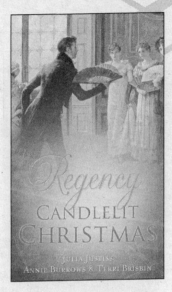

Indulge yourself...

With over forty stories to choose from, this fabulous collection has something for everyone.

Including fresh new stories from bestselling authors Joanna Trollope, Maureen Lee, Adele Parks, and Katie Flynn, *Loves Me, Loves Me Not* is a true celebration of the very best in romantic fiction!

Available 18th September 2009

www.mirabooks.co.uk